NIGHT OF LOVE AND DEATH

Sonji had personally selected the other kisaeng girls, telling
them only that their fee would be 500 American dollars for
the evening's work and that the guests of honor would be
President Park and his lifelong comrade, Commander of
the KCIA Kyu. Sonji had been with President Park on two
previous occasions. But tonight would be a new experience.
She would be secretly betraying him. A deadly deception
was taking place within the planned web of violence. She
had to participate in the killing . . .

THE CIRCLE
The bestselling new superthriller from
STEVE SHAGAN
author of *The Formula*

Bantam Books by Steve Shagan

THE CIRCLE
THE FORMULA
SAVE THE TIGER

THE CIRCLE

Steve Shagan

BANTAM BOOKS
TORONTO • NEW YORK • LONDON • SYDNEY • AUCKLAND

THE CIRCLE
*A Bantam/Perigord Book/published in association with
William Morrow and Company, Inc.*

*PRINTING HISTORY
Morrow/Perigord edition published May 1982
A selection of Literary Guild of America, October 1982
Bantam/Perigord edition/April 1985*

ISBN 0-553-17160-7

Printed and bound in Great Britain by Hunt Barnard Printing Ltd.

O   0 9 8 7 6 5 4 3 2 1

FOR
Betty . . .

The end of the fight is a tombstone
    white with the name of the late deceased,
and the epitaph drear: "A Fool lies here
    who tried to hustle the East."

—RUDYARD KIPLING, *The Naulahka*, 1892

The author wishes to express his gratitude to the Bonnie Rothbart Research Associates—and to Beverly Dvorett for her time and patience.

AUTHOR'S NOTE

In keeping with certain recent international events the author has reworked the opening passage in this novel to keep this edition current.

Seoul, Republic
of Korea
October 26, 1979

The first harbingers of the brutal Korean winter had arrived. A chilly Siberian wind dispelled the warmth of the late October sun. A line of glistening snow draped itself across the tops of the mountains ringing the city, and a cold silver glint rippled over the surface of the Han River. The life of Seoul's eight million people circulated in the few square miles of valley between the mountains and the river.

A curving bedlam of concave skyscrapers slammed against each other, fighting for the meager space. Serpentine expressways choked with traffic snaked their way through the confused jungle of steel and glass.

The exhaust of 600,000 cars and 10,000 buses rose like a cyan plume, obscuring the tops of buildings. It was as if Picasso had cubed a futuristic city on a smoky blue canvas.

In the midst of the jarring Western architecture a cluster of graceful pagodas huddled in a small park, like frightened relics of another age. The once-peaceful valley of the Yi dynasty, the place of wind, water and earth, the ancient walled city of eight gates, was dying of progress.

Seoul was no longer a city. It had become the nation—a nation under permanent siege. Twenty-five miles to the north the DMZ truce line, laced with minefields, trenches, tank traps and coils of barbed wire, bisected the Korean peninsula, separating the armies of North and South. The one million men facing each other across its 150-mile length were the same people sharing the same life habits, separated for nearly forty years by alien political systems imposed upon them by the Soviet Union and the United States.

* * *

It was 4:30 P.M. in Seoul, and the millions of office workers, factory hands and government employées were plotting the daily chore of returning to their homes and apartments.

The arc of the October sun dropped as the cacophony of Seoul's rush hour rose. The closing times of offices and factories were staggered to relieve the monstrous traffic jams, but the relief was slight. Along the motorways and boulevards, huge red signs extolled the virtue of patience.

The cold wind stirred the flag of the republic flying over the modern government buildings, its very design in conflict with the buildings it graced. The red and navy blue circle with its black yin and yang bars represented the essential unity of all being: past and present, good and evil, male and female, life and death—all harmoniously contained within the perfection of the circle.

Soon Yi Sonji maneuvered her Italian-designed, Korean-made Pony car through the erratic traffic flowing along the sixteen-lane Sejong Avenue. Sonji was twenty-eight, and Buddha had blessed her with classic Oriental beauty. She had those perfect features used by American advertising agencies to sell the delights of flying on Asian airlines.

Sonji stopped for a light, rolled down her window, and the chilly breeze invaded the car, playing with the tips of her long, silky jet black hair. She took a final drag of her American cigarette, then, in violation of all rules, tossed it out onto the boulevard.

She quickly rolled the window back up, shuddering slightly at the cold. Sonji detested winter and hoped they would assign her to a warm place like Bangkok. Well, the events of this evening would decide many things. She slipped the clutch gently as the light went from red to green. The sleek compact car rolled past the huge helmeted statue of Admiral Yi. The admiral had earned his marble position of honor by destroying two Japanese invasion fleets in the year 1592, employing ironclad warships almost three centuries before the *Monitor* and *Merrimac* clashed off the Virginia coast. Sonji took no notice of the great bronze statue but stared instead at the passing ginkgo trees, taking pleasure in the fact that bright yellow leaves still clung to their branches—a sign that perhaps winter was not yet ready to descend on the city.

The traffic picked up speed, streaming past the National Museum with its blue-tiled five-story pagoda. Sonji steered carefully, avoiding other Ponys that flitted from lane to lane. The boulevard curved around the foot of Pugak Mountain past the presidential complex. She shivered reflexively, thinking of the presidential mansion and the Blue House, the place of the president. The Iron Man. Park. The man they would murder this night.

Sonji had personally selected the other kisaeng girls, telling them only that their fee would be 500 American dollars for the evening's work and that the guests of honor would be President Park and his lifelong comrade, Commander of the KCIA Kyu. Sonji had been with President Park on two previous occasions. He had been fast and easy, but tonight she must be careful to keep him interested, aroused but nothing more. She had performed many tasks for the KCIA in many places. The best time had been in America when she was a cultural attaché with the South Korean Embassy. Her assignments were relatively simple: the seduction of certain American congressmen and occasionally transporting illicit funds from the Reverend Rhee to Kimsan. Her three years of duty had been pleasant until the fall—the Koreagate scandal.

But tonight would be a new experience. She had never knowingly been part of bloodletting, and while she was following Commander Kyu's orders, she would be secretly betraying him. A deadly deception was taking place within the planned web of violence. She had to participate in the killing. Kyu's orders had to be obeyed, but the deception was by choice. She was gambling on an intricate power play. Her own life and the life of her father hung in the balance.

Soon Yi Sonji was an imperial Kisaeng, recruited by the KCIA at age fourteen. Her mother had died shortly after Sonji's birth. She was raised by her father, a distinguished writer and professor of philosophy at Pusan National University whose libertarian views won the admiration and respect of the students and faculty alike. He was arrested for "inspiring" the bloody student uprising in the spring of 1967. The riots had been ruthlessly crushed by General

Chung and his elite paratroopers of the Garrison Command. Sonji was taken into custody by agents of the KCIA.

After weeks of isolation and relentless grilling about her father's activities, she caught the eye of KCIA Chief Kyu. She was, at fourteen, a fully developed, breathtaking beauty. Kyu's proposal was simple: In return for Sonji's services her father's life would be spared. She was placed in an Angel Cloud house and began a three-year program of indoctrination into the vast and secret sensual techniques prescribed in the *Tao* and Tantra. She learned how to marshal all the senses to convey erotica: mind, sight, sound, taste and smell. She mastered the art of looking, of staring into others' eyes and taking them all the way to passion. She could satisfy the primal sexual urges of men and women by use of body, mouth, hands and any of the sixty-four positions of the *Sutra*, holding man or woman in a constant state of sexual arousal. Adept in the use of perfume, incense and the sweet odors of rose, jasmine and marijuana, she possessed the skills to reduce man or woman to a state of total helplessness—a place of sensual nirvana.

Sonji was endowed with the strongest power in life, but it could be used only to service others. She would always be a performer, never a participant. The state dictated the actions of her life, and her record of service was above reproach.

Her only lapse had been with Kimsan in those years in Washington. She was taken with the dashing Korean playboy whose charm and wealth had influenced half the American Congress. Sonji disobeyed orders and protected Kimsan when the Koreagate scandal broke. This emotional action was not tolerated, and Sonji had been severely reprimanded. A kisaeng of imperial class was not permitted to fall in love. Later she was forgiven, and the scandal vanished along with Kimsan. But she wondered about recent rumors circulating in Seoul that her former lover was involved in the Golden Triangle heroin traffic.

She switched on the radio and swung the Pony into busy Chong-Ro Street. Donna Summer's "Last Dance" flooded the car and struck a nostalgic nerve. Sonji missed America. It was vibrant and remarkably free; one did not see the squads of green-fatigued, black-helmeted riot police and Garrison Command parachute troops constantly patrolling the cities.

She drove slowly down the crowded street, hoping to find a parking space, but she knew at this hour it would be unlikely. She checked her watch—there was no time to cruise up and down the busy section. Sonji parked the Pony in a forbidden red zone, switched off the ignition, set the hand brake and took a gold compact out of her Fendi bag. She carefully checked the hint of rouge on her high cheekbones and the perfect curve of a pale-toned lipstick on her full mouth.

A traffic policeman tapped his club against the window. Sonji got out of the car and produced her green and white KCIA identity card. The policeman's hard black eyes flashed from the photo on the card to her face. He returned the card and silently moved on.

She wore French jeans, a cashmere jacket, and gleaming leather boots. The sidewalk vendors offered her roasted chestnuts, Korean dolls, smoked eels, dancers' masks and a variety of aphrodisiacs. Two black American soldiers of the 2nd Division smiled at her, and a cluster of Japanese businessmen muttered undecipherable entreaties, struggling with the Korean dialect. Sonji ignored them all. She was working now, concentrating. Each passing minute brought the treacherous events of the evening inexorably closer.

The smoke-filled café was crowded and noisy; an old Beatles tune blared out of overhead speakers. Exotic aromas filled the heated air: tobacco, sweat, perfume and the pungent odor of thin strips of meat marinating in garlic, being grilled over charcoal burners. Businessmen sat around low tables, spearing the meat and washing it down with hot rice wine. Students from the University of Seoul crowded the length of the bar, rubbing shoulders with office workers and a sprinkling of American fighter pilots. They drank beer and munched on dried squid and bean cakes. The businessmen glanced up from their food as Sonji worked her way to the bar. She squeezed between two young girls and a middle-aged couple. The girls stared at Sonji and whispered to each other. They mistook her for a famous Korean movie star.

Sonji ordered a Coca-Cola. The bartender poured the dark effervescent liquid and nodded surreptitiously. He was a KCIA informant and had passed a silent signal. Sonji flirted long distance with an American fighter pilot, sipped some Coke, waited a few moments, then circled away from the bar and headed toward the rear. She reached the ladies' room, glanced back down the corridor, saw no one following and went directly to a heavy fire door, opened it and stepped outside.

Sonji stood in a small garden surrounded by a high wall. A wooden staircase attached to the back of the café led up to a second floor. Three soldiers of the Garrison Command carrying M-16 automatic rifles loitered at the foot of the stairs. One of them, a tough-looking youth with captain's bars on his camouflage jacket, nodded at her. She walked toward the soldiers, passed them silently and quickly climbed the staircase. She knocked twice on the bamboo door.

General Yi Chung, dressed in a black karate robe, smiled nervously as he ushered her into the apartment. The living room was wide and sparsely furnished. Sliding shoji screens led off to other rooms. The general's small flat features and slit eyes were in sharp contrast with his massive six-foot frame. He stared at her silently; a tic in his right cheek convulsed.

"A moment," Sonji said softly, and went to the sliding screen that led to the bedroom. She glanced back at the general for an instant. It was a look that conveyed seduction and conspiracy.

The general soaked up the scent of her perfume, already feeling a tightening in his testicles. Sonji was his one weakness, but he relaxed in the knowledge that his control of her father insured his control of her. He lit a cigarette and slowly paced the room.

He commanded the elite 12,000-man capital Garrison Brigade. His troops had crushed the bloody student uprising in May by employing a vicious mixture of tear gas and anti-personnel grenades. Chung's slogan was well known: *The Army is everything.* He disliked President Park and despised the KCIA commander Kyu. They had subverted the power of the Army. But tonight all that would change. Chung prayed for success. He offered his soul to Buddha in return for a chance to rule, for enough time to purify the nation, to reunite the two Koreas and to eradicate the rising Christian influence. The people would be made to realize that opposition was futile. Military dictatorship was Buddha's will. There was a reason that the Korean language did not contain the word "freedom."

Sonji lay on the low bed, staring up at her own naked image in the mirrored ceiling. Her shaved body was covered with oil of jasmine. The general sat down on the edge of the bed. His hand trembled slightly as he touched her thigh.

"I would like some marijuana," she said.

He took a machine-rolled marijuana cigarette out of the large pocket of his robe, lit it quickly, inhaled and handed it to her. The sounds of the café below floated up through the floor and they could clearly hear Streisand singing "Evergreen."

Sonji inhaled deeply, holding the sweet smoke down in her lungs. She felt an instant rush of release, as if a tight clasp had been removed from her brain. She took another hit and passed it back to the general. "It's quite strong."

"A present from the Golden Triangle." He took another drag and smiled. "From Kimsan."

Sonji betrayed only a passing interest at the mention of her former lover's name. She kept the tone of her voice matter-of-fact. "How is Kimsan?"

"Well. He is at the moment in Italy. His organizational skills provide income for many people in government. We are beginning to take our rightful share of opium proceeds from the Thais." He passed the joint back to her.

"I would like a drink," she said.

The general rose, went over to a portable bar and poured some scotch into two glasses. He handed one to her, and they clicked glasses. "Tonight," he toasted.

"Tonight," she replied.

He sat down on the edge of the bed. "Remember, you have only to follow my instructions."

Sonji was feeling heady now. "What of my father?"

"You must speak to him," Chung said. "If I gain his release, you must convince him to refrain from public speeches. His political views inflame the students."

"That is not possible."

"On the contrary, Daughter. Buddha teaches that all things are possible. It's contained in the mandala."

There was no margin for argument. The general truly believed in the infinite wisdom of Buddha. It was incredible to Sonji that a military man could be influenced by any theology more sophisticated than the operation of a tank. She stared up at the mirror, and her own nakedness aroused her. The rose-colored nipples on her full breasts grew hard. She suspected the marijuana had been laced with ginseng root, the perfect aphrodisiac. "What of me?" she asked. "What will you do with me?"

"You will be assigned to our embassy in Washington. You will be my eyes and ears."

"I'm frightened of Kyu."

"So are we all, Daughter."

"What if Kyu is aware of our deception?"

"In that unlikely event, we all will be killed." Chung placed his drink down. "But I don't believe that will happen. Do you know who the greatest general is?"

Sonji shook her head.

"The spider." He smiled. "Because he weaves his web and waits. I have waited twenty-five years for this night. And Buddha teaches that patience is a bitter cup that only the strong can drink. You must trust me, Daughter."

She stared at him for a moment, then took a sip of scotch and seductively asked, "What do you wish?"

"Vishnu," he replied.

Her large oval eyes penetrated the small black slits of his eyes. She slowly sucked the last of the marijuana and carefully crushed out the stub. Holding the sweet smoke in her lungs, she bent over Chung and slipped open his robe.

The general looked up at the ceiling mirror and watched her head descend between his thighs. Sonji finally exhaled, and the blue marijuana smoke floated over his genitals. The warm moisture of her mouth and slow, delicate probing of her tongue sent a ball of heat spreading up from his testicles to his belly. All thoughts of deception, intrigue and murder vanished under the maddening skills of the kisaeng girl. She was taking him to the sensual place of the goddess Vishnu.

But the dark beauty kneeling over him had other ideas. The strong marijuana activated a pool of seething anger that lurked just below the surface of her consciousness. His swollen male organ became a sudden symbol of her own subjugation. She felt a rush of power, purpose and total concentration. The task of bringing the general to orgasm became a conscious act of vengeance. She was going to transport him to a place of excruciating pain and in the process reduce him to a trembling mound of pleading flesh.

She slowed her circular movements and cupped his full sac in her hands, squeezing gently. He moaned loudly as her mouth continued to tease him. His thighs trembled and his stomach convulsed. He pleaded with her to grant him release. But Sonji did not hear him. Her mouth moved from place to place. She was like a vicious architect of erotica practicing her talents with a controlled frenzy. She looked up and saw his sweat-covered face grimacing in anguish. But she would not grant him release until he crossed into that place of pain.

The second most powerful man in South Korea peered out the wall of glass. His office was on the eighteenth floor of the Nam-San Building. The Domestic Division of the KCIA contained three critical bureaus: the Second Bureau of Propaganda and Censorship; the Fifth Bureau of Surveillance and Espionage; and the Sixth Bureau of Sabotage and Assassination—the bureau that would be operative tonight.

Commander Kyu stared through the haze and smoke of the city, his soft black eyes barely able to discern the Imun-Dong Building which contained the First, Third, Seventh, Eighth and Ninth bureaus of Foreign Operations. Kyu had omitted the Fourth Bureau. The number 4 was considered bad luck in Korean superstition. Kyu moved to his desk, the sinewy muscles in his arms rippling against the tight-fitting suit. Commander Kyu practiced the art of karate for two hours every day. He was alert and fit; neither his face nor his body betrayed his sixty-three years.

He sat behind the huge teak desk, opened the top drawer and took out a nine-shot blue-steel Beretta automatic. The Italian gun was small but highly effective at close range. Its .25-caliber hollow-head slug would enter a man's body and explode internally, and its fail-safe operation was unparalleled.

He tucked the automatic into a holster strapped to his right calf, leaned forward in the leather chair and held his arm straight out. His hand was steady. Once again he ran over the checklist for tonight's action. The kisaeng girl, Sonji, was professional and totally reliable. Her loyalty was assured because he held her father's life in his hands. She would perform precisely as instructed.

The chef for tonight's dinner had been chosen by Sonji, each dish selected with great care—all preferences of President Park—and the scotch was Bell's, his favorite drink. The signals had been gone over countless times, among himself, Sonji and his bodyguards.

During the months of meticulous planning only one action he had taken made him uneasy. After weeks of agonizing he had decided to inform General Chung of the plot. It was risky, but the general's participation was critical to the ultimate success of the plan, and Kyu's secret data on Chung indicated the risk was worth taking. The general had an unquenchable thirst for power, matched only by his disdain for President Park. Besides, Chung had everything to gain if the plot succeeded. When Kyu had promised to promote him to Chief of Staff, the general had been instantly receptive. He had assured Kyu that immediately following the assassination all communications systems would be seized, all highways, key bridges and military installations taken. Martial law would be enforced until the aftershocks of the assassination had been absorbed by the people.

Kyu lit a cigarette, inhaled deeply and thought he had made the correct decision. Six weeks had passed since he enlisted Chung's cooperation. If the general had intended to betray him, he would have acted long ago. Kyu would eventually have to eliminate the general, but for the moment he required Chung's connivance and participation.

Commander Kyu rose from the desk and walked to the huge glass window. He could not shake off a nagging fear that something would go wrong. The lingering doubts became pervasive. What of the Americans? The men in the Glass Room? He mistrusted Dr. Belgrave. Still, Washington had no choice but to go along. No, it was all in order.

He stared down at the street below. People were standing at attention, facing the presidential compound. It was 6:15 P.M., and the national anthem was being played from loudspeakers attached to trees and light poles. Kyu thought of the Iron Man in the Blue House—the president for the last sixteen years—and despite himself, he felt a touch of compassion for Park. They were lifelong friends, closer than brothers, fellow graduates of the Japanese Manchurian Academy, the only Koreans selected by the Japanese conquerors to attend the Imperial Military Academy in Tokyo.

After the war, when Korea was divided by the Soviets and Americans, Kyu and Park returned to the South. They collected around them old comrades and planned the coup that brought Park to power in 1961. With the advice and assistance of the CIA they formed the Korean Central Intelligence Agency: a vast, venal and highly effective network of 300,000 operatives. The KCIA used informers, spies and killers to infiltrate and manipulate every sector of Korean life. It was largely through Kyu's efforts that Park had ruled with absolute power for eighteen years. But the Iron Man had forgotten his old comrade of the Manchurian Academy. He had forgotten how to deal with dissidents. He had made entreaties to Kim Il Sung, ignoring the leader of North Korea's avowed dedication to destroy the South. Park could no longer be trusted with the nation's destiny. Action was required. History would record the assassination not as an act of treachery, but as one of supreme patriotism.

Kyu glanced at his watch; in two hours he would pass through the presidential gates and enter the Blue House. He suddenly felt a cold circle in the pit of his stomach and took deep breaths of air and exhaled. He repeated the exercise for five minutes. The rush of oxygen seemed to restore his courage, and the cold steel of the Italian automatic against his calf was reassuring. President Park was many things, but he was not bulletproof.

On the fourth floor of the Blue House in the failing light of dusk, the Man of Iron stood alone at the window, looking down at the Garden of Four Seasons. Two Huey helicopters sat on their pads, their crews on twenty-four-hour alert.

In the anteroom just outside his spacious office, five handpicked bodyguards were on duty. Each man an expert in the highest order of karate, each a sharpshooter, each had sworn to surrender his life to protect Park. The presidential compound was patrolled by a detachment of security police. In 1968 thirty-one North Korean guerrillas had charged down the slope of Pugak Mountain, tossing grenades and firing their Soviet-made AK-47's. They were only a thousand yards from the Blue House before the security force cut them down. Their orders were clear: "Kill Park!" He remembered the gunfire. He had stood at this very window, unafraid. Now he wished they had succeeded. He would have died the death of a martyr, the burden of state gone forever. He was, of late, consumed by fatigue and melancholy. But there was no one to take his place.

He opened the French windows, permitting the cold night air to hit his face. It felt refreshing and relieved the burning sensation in his reddish brown eyes. He sniffed the air, welcoming its Siberian bite. He loved the winters. The snow would fall and drape itself across the dirty city like a mantle of white purity. The bitter winter winds chased away the summer smells of decay and pollution. He sighed and thought he must bear the responsibility of ecological ruin. He had inherited a primitive state and hurled it 400 years ahead in a single decade. The gross national product for 1979 would exceed $50 billion. Steel, ships and automobiles bearing the imprint "Made in the Republic of Korea" circulated in the major world markets.

He carried the nation's aspirations alone, working twenty hours a day. He had outmaneuvered his external enemies and eradicated domestic opposition. Heeding the advice of his close friend J. Edgar Hoover, he had bargained brilliantly with the Pentagon, dispatching 50,000 troops to aid the beleaguered Americans in Vietnam, and in return extracted billions in military hardware. The tentacles of his power were long and diverse. Every Korean consulate and embassy abroad was a branch of the KCIA. And at home all members of the National Assembly were under permanent surveillance, along with the faculties of schools and universities. It was an iron country run by an iron man.

Park took another deep breath of the frigid air and reflected that liberty and freedom of expression had no place in the Korean philosophy. Duty, family and absolute loyalty to the dynasty were the historic traditions. He had restored the integrity of the Korean people, but at a terrible personal price. His wife had been killed at his side by an assassin's bullet. His daughters no longer spoke to him. His dreams were populated by ghosts. Many people despised him. Many wished him dead. And the problems were endless. The monster of progress stalked the nation. Seoul was the fifteenth largest city in the world, but its streets were a choking hell. Inflation was close to thirty percent; the people lacked proper housing; there were bloody student uprisings, corruption in high places, Christian influences and a continuous exodus of skilled workers: 100,000 to Saudi Arabia, 300,000 to Japan. Farmers were leaving their land, seeking nonexistent jobs in the capital. And dangling over the nation, like the sword of Damocles—the constant threat from the North.

Park slipped a cigarette into a pearl holder and took out a gold lighter given to him by his murdered wife. He rubbed its smooth surface, then lit the cigarette. He walked slowly back to his desk, sank into the huge Louis XV chair, leaned back and thought somehow he must arrange a meeting with Kim Il Sung. Unification must be achieved. It would be his greatest triumph. They were, after all, the same people. Together they would manipulate East and West to their own advantage and perhaps achieve an alliance with China and Japan. It was the Buddha's prophecy that his children would rise to the pinnacle of world power. The practice of Christianity would be forbidden. The people would return to the ancient traditions. The glorious epoch of the Yi dynasty would be restored.

The buzzer on the intercom phone sounded. Park leaned forward and lifted the receiver. His chief bodyguard, San Ki, advised him that Commander Kyu's limousine had just passed through the main gate. Park rose and walked back to the window. He looked forward to this evening with his old comrade Kyu. As always he would enjoy the food, the scotch and the kisaeng girls, in particular the one called Sonji.

As he turned to go, he heard a familiar tinkling sound from below that bathed him in a glow of happiness. The sound was unmistakable. His eldest daughter was playing a Chopin interlude. She had not touched the piano in years. It was a good omen—a sign of the mandala. Buddha was present. The nation would return to his safekeeping, to the place where there is no beginning, no end, only the infinite perfection of the circle.

The president went to his desk and pressed a button. The huge oak doors opened, and his five black-suited bodyguards entered.

They would surround him while he walked the fifty yards to the small pagoda where the party was to take place.

●

A red moon rose up out of the Yellow Sea, painting crimson swirls across the breaking waves. Soldiers of the White Horse Division patrolled the beach with specially trained guard dogs. Swift PT boats of the South Korean Navy crisscrossed up and down the shoreline. In bunkers behind sloping sand dunes, technicians operated sophisticated electronic gear capable of detecting the body heat of seaborne infiltrators. In the hills above Seoul, giant webbed radar screens revolved slowly, their scanning signals radiating north toward the DMZ. At secret sites, missile domes opened and nuclear-tipped nose cones protruded, rising majestically on elevated launch pads, their ominous phallic shapes like cubist paintings of twentieth-century man's final erection.

Ten miles off the coast of Seoul the American aircraft carriers *Coral Sea* and *Kitty Hawk* steamed into the wind, their flight decks crammed with F-14 fighter bombers. Twenty miles high, flying at the edge of outer space, the SR-71 spy plane circled over the Korean peninsula, its infrared cameras photographing the positions of North and South. The American Air Force commands at Osan, Taegu and Kunsan were on full alert. On Okinawa the Strategic Air Command's B-52's were rolled out of their concrete hangars, fueled, serviced and manned. They stood poised on the long runways like great silver birds of prey. Twenty-seven miles due east of the big island of Hawaii the nuclear submarine *Kingfish* surfaced silently, in position to recover the photo canisters of the SR-71. The massive sophisticated array of military hardware was poised to carry out its objective—the murder of one human being.

In Seoul the silence of the nightly curfew was disturbed by a column of armored personnel carriers transporting 300 paratroopers of the elite Garrison Command. The column rumbled down blacked-out Sejong Avenue toward the presidential compound. The handpicked force was under the command of General Chung.

The general turned his collar up against the night wind and checked the luminous dials of his digital watch. By now the party in the presidential compound was well under way. He hoped Sonji would not lose her courage. His own life was now in the balance. She had put him through a hell of sexual hatred that afternoon, but he understood her anger and admired her strength. He thought it an ironic turn of events that the entire plot and counterplot revolved on the unique talents of the beautiful kisaeng girl.

It was 11:24 P.M., October 26, 1979, and all the pawns set in motion were now in place.

The president of the republic and the commander of the nation's intelligence agency were seated on floor cushions,

facing each other across a low mahogany table. The walls
of the spacious living room were decorated with pornographic woodcuts dating back to the Yi dynasty. Soft, traditional Japanese music floated out of hidden speakers,
and cones of red light from ceiling spots created pools of
crimson. The reflected light painted the faces of Park and
Kyu the color of blood.

The old comrades of the Manchurian Academy had already consumed fish cakes, oyster broth and pork
dumplings. They chatted amiably and smoked strong, thin
cigars while waiting for the next course being prepared by
a pretty kisaeng girl. The red-robed girl turned the shrimp
slowly on skewers. She then poured scotch for the
president and yakju rice wine for the commander. Kyu relit his cigar and mentioned a certain professor of philosophy at Seoul University whose activities were to be
terminated. But Park's attention had drifted. He mumbled
something to himself and smiled curiously. The commander asked Park why he smiled, but the president did
not respond. The Gioconda smile on the Iron Man's face
made Kyu uneasy, and he wondered if Park was alert to
the plot.

Kyu sipped the strong wine and dismissed the thought.
Park would never have permitted his chief bodyguard,
San Ki, to go into the bedroom with Sonji and the other
kisaeng girls. Still, the smile was ominous. Kyu attempted
once again to engage Park in conversation, but the Iron
Man had fallen silent, the smile his only response.

Kyu was sweating profusely and spit a command at the
kisaeng girl, who immediately brought him a cold face
towel. He tried to calm himself. He had to control his
nerves. He could not act until Sonji came out of the bedroom. Her reappearance would confirm that she and the
other kisaeng girls had murdered Park's chief bodyguard.

The other four presidential bodyguards were in the
kitchen, gorging themselves on garlic beef and kimchi
cabbage, served by another red-robed kisaeng. The men
swilled the strong rice wine and rolled dice to determine
who would be next to enjoy the sexual circus taking place
in the bedroom. The youngest of the four bodyguards did
not share the euphoria of his colleagues. He kept thinking
that there were only four of them in the kitchen. The

number 4 was bad luck. He felt again the bulky German-made Mauser automatic in his shoulder holster. But somehow its hefty presence brought no reassurance against the unlucky number.

In the long, dimly lit corridor outside the living room Commander Kyu's five bodyguards stood silently, chain-smoking nervously. They openly carried Ingram MAC-10 nine-millimeter parabellum automatics, fitted with silencers, capable of firing a clip of fifty bullets in three seconds without noise or recoil. It was customary for Park's bodyguards and Kyu's bodyguards to be present but separated when the two leaders met. Nevertheless, the men were tense. There was nothing customary about tonight's assignment. They flicked their eyes toward the shoji screen at the end of the corridor. They could not act until the girl Sonji gave them the signal.

Outside the presidential compound General Chung's armored column lumbered to a halt at the main gate. The police security watch commander and the general exchanged salutes. Chung produced an order signed by the Chief of Staff permitting the Garrison Command to enter the compound and conduct one of its periodic security exercises. The watch commander examined the order and handed it back.

There was nothing unusual about the operation; it was conducted with unannounced frequency. The policeman walked quickly to a wall box, opened it and pressed a coded combination of buttons. The massive iron gates swung open slowly.

The floor of the low-ceilinged bedroom was dominated by a silk-covered mattress. Chief presidential bodyguard San Ki lay naked on his back. His head was cradled in the lap of a kisaeng girl who massaged his temples. Another kisaeng girl knelt between his thighs, her busy mouth coaxing him to climax. The sweet odors of jasmine and marijuana clung to their bodies. They were illuminated by the dancing light of huge incense candles. Sonji, dressed in a white silk kimono emblazoned with green dragons, watched intently as the bodyguard neared his orgasm. A low moan escaped the lips of the muscular bodyguard. Sonji noticed his eyes close and the muscles in his stomach begin to convulse. She knelt down alongside the girl massaging the man's temples and removed a pearl-handled straight razor from the deep pockets of her robe. Sonji opened it, exposing the glistening five-inch blade. She then slipped the razor into the robe sleeve of the girl who massaged the bodyguard's temples. The eyes of the sucking girl flicked up at Sonji, who nodded. The girl increased her tempo. San Ki moaned loudly, his body arched and he ejaculated into the girl's mouth. The kisaeng at his head quickly pressed the blade of the razor under his left ear, dug it in and pulled the blade across his throat, severing his jugular. The dark blood spurted out as the girl drained the last of the dying man's semen.

The girl whose lap cradled San Ki's head placed a towel against the gaping wound. The other girl rose and stood alongside Sonji and watched the bodyguard bleed silently to death. It was a ceremonial death. Painless, as prescribed in the manifesto of *Hevajra Tantra*.

Sonji entered the living room and caught Commander Kyu's eye. She nodded and went to President Park, knelt and whispered the details of San Ki's ecstasy, omitting the fact of his slaughter. Park nodded and smiled but said nothing. Sonji looked over at Kyu.

"Go to the kitchen, Daughter," the commander said, forcing a smile. "Select the next candidate for the delights of Vishnu."

Sonji rose, crossed the room, slid the shoji screen open and entered the kitchen. She informed the four presidential bodyguards that their chief, San Ki, was washing and asked who would be next. Three of them turned to the youngest. The wiry youth fixed his murderous black eyes on Sonji, and for a split second she thought he knew. She felt her pulse quicken and moved quickly to the young man. Placing her hand against his crotch, she turned to the others and commented about the size of the young man's sexual weapon. The three bodyguards laughed. Sonji said she would be back for the young man in a moment.

She went out into the corridor and walked down its dim length for fifty feet before Kyu's bodyguards saw her.

She nodded at their leader and stood aside as they clicked the safeties off their MAC-10 parabellum automatics.

In the kitchen Park's four remaining bodyguards were chewing on pieces of smoked duck between drafts of yakju wine. They anxiously awaited Sonji's return. One of them stated that the only kisaeng for him would be Sonji and went on to describe in brutal detail what he would do with her. The others, absorbed with his vivid imagery, failed to notice the shoji screen slide open. Kyu's bodyguards opened fire on entry. The hissing sound of 250 nine-millimeter hollow-head slugs tearing into the four men was barely audible. The force of the fusillade lifted their bodies into the air, pieces of smoked duck still clinging to their mouths, their eyes wide with surprise as vital parts of their bodies were blown away. A crimson spume sprayed off the ceiling. Their bodies spun slowly in the air. It was as if the dying men were not allowed to fall but were kept dancing hideously on a steady stream of bullets.

President Park had his glass raised just as Kyu's bodyguards entered the room. Park did not have to notice the bloodstains on their black suits to know what had taken place in the kitchen. He tossed down his scotch and smiled across at Kyu, who had the Italian automatic clutched in both hands, arms extended, pointed a foot from Park's face. Kyu pulled the trigger, and President Park's face exploded. Kyu was on his feet. His black crescent eyes blazed as he pumped six more slugs into the fallen leader. He then calmly fired into the heart of the kisaeng girl who had serviced him. She fell over the charcoal brazier, and her robe began to smoke. One of the men kicked her body aside. Kyu motioned to the bedroom. Two bodyguards went inside and dragged the cowering kisaeng girls into the living room. They forced them into kneeling positions and fired three bullets into the back of their skulls. The girls fell over like broken Korean dolls.

The men stood stock-still, sweat-covered, adrenaline pumping. The smell of blood mixing with the fragrance of sweet jasmine filled their lungs as they panted for breath.

Their eyes were fierce, primeval, like a pride of blood-smeared lions after the kill.

The momentary silence was shattered as twenty-five paratroopers of the Garrison Command burst into the living room from three sides. Kyu and his men understood their predicament at once—they were experts in the fine art of betrayal.

Soon Yi Sonji raced down the last of the spiral steps and hurled herself out the front door. The cold air hit her face like a splash of ice water. She blinked against the spotlights of the armored cars surrounding the entrance and gasped for breath in the frigid night air. She slowly discerned the buglike shapes of the armored vehicles and the clouds of vaporized breath rising from hundreds of helmeted shadows. She saw a tall, powerful figure coming toward her. It was General Chung, accompanied by a captain.

The General's firm hands gripped Sonji's shoulders, and he looked into her eyes; but his words were addressed to the captain. "Take Soon Yi Sonji home. See that she is provided with sufficient security. I hold you responsible for her safety." The captain nodded and saluted. Chung pulled Sonji close to him and whispered, "I will not forget what you did for me this night. You rode the tiger, Daughter." He went quickly past her into the Angel Cloud house.

Kyu's men had already been led out of the room. The KCIA commander stood in the midst of the carnage, his hands manacled behind his back. He stared unafraid at General Chung and spoke with defiance. "You may have deceived me, but the Americans will not tolerate your deception. Promises were made by the men in the Glass Room."

"You can take those promises to your grave," Chung replied. The tone of his voice was flat and deadly. "There's only one promise—the promise of Buddha. He has placed the destiny of the nation in my hands." The general motioned to an officer, who quickly hustled the KCIA commander out.

Chung lit a cigarette and stared at the riddled corpse of the fallen president, reflecting that there was no hatred as profound as one born out of the debris of long friendship.

The President of the United States had been jogging on the White House grounds when news of the assassination reached him. The crisis team was immediately summoned to the Oval Office: Presidential Adviser Dr. Eric Belgrave, Director of Defense Intelligence Charles Gruenwald, and Director of CIA Covert Operations Robert Burgess. The men were seated in orange damask chairs in a semicircle in front of the heavy mahogany desk. Wood crackled and spit against the flames in the white marble fireplace. It was 5:40 P.M. eastern daylight time. A weary President again studied the Xerox copy of the cable he had sent to Leonid I. Brezhnev, chairman of the Presidium of the Supreme Soviet USSR, the Kremlin, Moscow:

DEAR MR. CHAIRMAN: IN VIEW OF THE TRAGIC EVENTS IN THE REPUBLIC OF KOREA, I BESEECH YOU TO USE YOUR GOOD OFFICES WITH PREMIER KIM IL SUNG OF THE DEMOCRATIC KOREAN PEOPLE'S REPUBLIC NOT TO UNDERTAKE ANY OVERT MILITARY ACTION AGAINST THE SOUTH. I AM DUTY BOUND TO REMIND YOU, SIR, THE UNITED STATES HAS A MUTUAL DEFENSE TREATY WITH THE REPUBLIC OF KOREA, AND SHOULD THAT NATION'S SECURITY BE VIOLATED, WE WOULD HAVE NO CHOICE BUT TO COME TO ITS DEFENSE WITH ALL OUR VIGOR AND MIGHT. OUR FORCES IN THAT AREA WILL REMAIN IN A STRICTLY DEFENSIVE POSTURE UNTIL THE POLITICAL SITUATION IN THE REPUBLIC OF KOREA STABILIZES. I ASSURE YOU THAT THE UNITED STATES AND ITS ALLY THE REPUBLIC OF KOREA CONTINUE TO RESPECT THE 1953 ARMISTICE LINE. YOUR UNDERSTANDING AND COOPERATION IN THIS MATTER ARE GREATLY APPRECIATED. I LOOK FORWARD TO YOUR RESPONSE, AND TO OUR FORTHCOMING MEETING IN THE HAGUE.

The President leaned back and rubbed his hand over his eyes, then turned to his chief adviser. "It's five hours, Eric—still no response."

Belgrave brushed the sides of his silver hair and calmly replied, "We have been advised that Chairman Brezhnev is not in Moscow. He is spending the weekend at his dacha on the Baltic. We should be receiving his answer momentarily."

Gruenwald then addressed the President. "In any case, we have detected absolutely no indications of unusual military activity in the North. We must assume that your cable has achieved its purpose."

The President rose and walked to the French windows overlooking the Rose Garden. The lights of the White House glowed softly through the misty night rain falling on the city. He was deeply disturbed by the assassination of Park. The events of the last ten hours as relayed to him defied logic. After a long moment he turned back to the men in the room. "Let's review these events once more."

The three men exchanged wary looks as the President continued. "Sometime shortly before midnight Commander of the KCIA Kyu assassinated President Park. Kyu and his bodyguards were then taken into custody by a general named Chung, who has assumed control of the government."

Burgess replied, "That is correct. The assassination occurred at a party in a pagodalike building in the presidential compound."

"In other words, President Park was set up by his lifelong friend Kyu, who was himself crossed up by this General Chung."

"That is essentially our conclusion."

"Then it would seem to me," the President said, "a logical assumption that General Chung had prior knowledge of the scheme to murder Park—in essence, he used Kyu as an assassin."

"Not necessarily," Defense Intelligence Chief Gruenwald cut in. "Chung commands the Garrison Brigade. They routinely conduct periodic security checks within the compound."

Dr. Belgrave admired Gruenwald's calm response. In truth, none of them fully understood how Kyu's plot had gone awry. And not knowing was unforgivable. General Chung had pulled the rug out from under them. Their only recourse now was to put the matter to bed and hope they could conceal their own involvement in Park's murder from the President.

The Oval Office fell silent. The rain increased in tempo, beating against the windows. After a long moment the President turned to Burgess. "I must tell you, Robert, that considering our special relationship with the KCIA, I find it inconceivable that your agency had no prior intelligence of the plot to kill Park."

Burgess flicked his eyes at Dr. Belgrave before responding. "Mr. President, during the eighteen years of Park's rule we've received numerous reports of palace coups and plots against his life. Discontent at high and low levels of Korean society is historic."

"Discontent is one thing. Assassination by the chief of the KCIA is another." The President's face reddened. "I want to be certain that our own skirts are clean." He had thrown down the gauntlet, and only one man was qualified to pick it up.

Belgrave's voice contained the proper amount of indignation. "We are not responsible for political assassinations in a foreign country."

The President walked slowly back behind his desk. He placed his hands on the high-backed chair and spoke directly to the thin, gaunt adviser. "I'm suspicious of the fact that our armed forces and photo satellites were on full alert at the precise hour of assassination. And if I'm suspicious, the press will be accusatory. All of us will be placed under an inexplicable cloud of suspicion."

"Suspicion of what?" Burgess innocently asked.

"Collusion," the President snapped.

"But, sir, our armed forces conduct frequent alert exercises in South Korea."

"Another case of fortunate coincidence," the President responded sarcastically.

Belgrave's eyes flicked at Burgess, and the specialist in covert operations deferred to him. Belgrave chose his words carefully. "Fortunate perhaps, Mr. President, but coincidental certainly."

"Well, Eric, perhaps I'm confusing coincidence with

faulty intelligence. I can't perceive of Kyu's murdering Park and seconds later being apprehended by an obscure general, all of this taking place without a trace of prior intelligence information." He shifted his attention to Burgess. "We possess the most sophisticated intelligence techniques. You have assured me of that, Robert, on countless occasions."

Belgrave broke in before Burgess could respond. "Mr. President, there is no intelligence device capable of reading the human mind. The very philosophy and thought process of the Asian culture are obscure, murky and defy prediction." He calmly filled the bowl of his pipe and continued. "They operate out of an exotic Buddhist theology. It could well be that Kyu woke up with a directive from Buddha to eliminate his old colleague Park."

The President wondered if Buddha had also directed the American military alert. "All right, gentlemen, I can see no constructive purpose in reviewing the events of last night." He paused, then directed his question to Charles Gruenwald. "What do we know about General Chung?"

The defense intelligence chief answered reflexively, relieved that the interrogation was over. "Chung is an honor graduate of the Korean Military Academy. Attended paratroop training at Fort Bragg, again graduating with honors. He commanded the Korean Tiger Division in Vietnam and served with distinction. He's an avowed anti-Communist and a dedicated patriot."

"What's his religion?"

"Buddhist."

The buzzer sounded on the President's console. He pressed a button and lifted the receiver. "Yes, Mary? . . . Bring it in, please." He hung up and said, "The cable reply from Brezhnev."

A trim, pretty brunette entered the Oval Office, went quickly to the President and handed him the cable.

"Thank you, Mary." He read the reply aloud: "Dear Mr. President: In response to your cable, we view the violent acts in the puppet regime of the so-called Republic of Korea as symptomatic of a nation tormented by colonial oppression. It is inevitable that this despotic oligarchy will fall of its own corruption and repression. I can assure you, Mr. President, that neither the USSR nor its ally the Democratic People's Republic has any aggressive designs on the suffering people of the South. We do, however, continue to support social justice for victims of capitalistic anarchy. I, too, look forward to our January meeting in The Hague. Most respectfully, Leonid Ilyich Brezhnev."

Belgrave smiled. "We've come out of this unscathed."

"Perhaps," the President replied. "All right, gentlemen, keep me informed."

Alone in his office the President studied the cable again. He then rose and walked to the rain-streaked window. He was certain his advisers had given him only a portion of the truth. He thought of Jack Kennedy standing at this same window on November 2, 1963, after hearing the news of the Diem assassination, and wondered if he had been told the truth of those killings. But Kennedy himself was running out of time; he would be assassinated three weeks later.

The President shook his head. Perhaps he was doing his advisers a disservice. The possibility did exist that the events in Korea were coincidental. Presidential murder was by no means exclusive to Asian governments. Assassination had become part of the American electoral process. It was the last precinct to report.

The black limousine glided through the rain-swept capital streets. In the spacious rear seat Belgrave and Gruenwald conversed in low, conspiratorial tones. Burgess had the car phone cradled to his ear. A cigarette dangled from between his lips, and pieces of fallen ash dotted his topcoat. His flat gray eyes widened with interest at something being said to him over the phone.

Belgrave was annoyed at his close proximity to Gruenwald. The defense intelligence chief's breath was sour, as if he had just sipped a glass of warm urine. The Doctor wondered how the man's wife tolerated his foul breath. But Belgrave's confidential file on Gruenwald indicated the last connubial activity he and his wife had shared was the taking of a blood test.

Belgrave nodded at Gruenwald's last words, then said, "There's no question about it, Charles. General Chung had prior knowledge of Kyu's plot. The President was right on target: Chung used Kyu as a hit man to serve his own purpose."

"The question is, how the hell did Chung find out?"

"It might have been Kyu himself," Belgrave mused. "He may have enlisted Chung's participation."

"I doubt it, Eric. Kyu was a fanatic about secrecy. He was a man who trusted no one."

"Perhaps . . . but it's still a possibility. In any case our primary concern now is that Kyu doesn't expose us all at a public trial."

"That's not likely," Burgess said as he hung up the car phone. "Kyu and his five bodyguards were executed at 6:05 A.M. Seoul time."

BOOK ONE

Washington, D.C.
April 1981

Chapter One

The deputy attorney general of the United States, Phil Ricker, sucked the vodka-flavored ice and perused the "Weekend Events" section of the Washington *Post*.

The Japanese cherry trees had blossomed ten days late, but their serpentine blaze of pink and red circled the Tidal Basin attracting thousands of tourists, marching bands, Shriners on horseback and assorted bureaucrats. Along with the annual spectacle of the blooming cherry trees, the nation's capital offered a feast of cultural attractions.

At the Kennedy Center for Performing Arts, De Burgos conducted the National Symphony Orchestra, and Elizabeth Taylor graced the Eisenhower Theater in a revival of *The Little Foxes*. Mikhail Baryshnikov danced *La Sonnambula* at the Opera House. And the National Gallery of Art featured an exhibit of the brilliant French Impressionist Camille Pissarro.

Phil turned to the movie side of the paper. Last year's Oscar-winning picture was advertised alongside a pornographic film featuring Marilyn Chambers, aptly titled *Insatiable*. He dropped the *Post*, rubbed his eyes, got to his feet and thought about going upstairs, but instead walked over to the soft leather couch, stretched out and placed the heavy Sunday edition of the New York *Times* on an end table.

Phil raised the glass of melting ice cubes up to the light thrown by a stained glass Tiffany lamp and watched the rays refract into small angular pieces of colored light. He wished he had not gone up to New York Friday night on still another failed attempt at reconciliation with Audrey. He marveled at his own refusal to recognize there was that moment in human relationships when a woman with whom you've shared your soul can look over the rim of a martini and say, "I simply don't feel *anything* for you."

They talked, ate pasta and drank a good Bardolino at Orsini's; they even made love. But it was all ritual, a paean to the past. There was a polite kiss good-bye followed by the long dull train ride back to Washington. Now he had to get through the remnants of Sunday evening alone, and Sunday had never been his favorite day. As far back as Phil could remember, Sunday was a day to get past. Sunday was a day for funerals, weddings and watching dull football games on television. Sundays were all about failed Saturday nights and guilty feelings over lack of preparation for Monday court appearances.

Phil glanced over at the three brown cardboard file boxes containing Xerox copies of critical case data on the Reverend Rhee and his Universal Order of Buddha. He'd have been better served staying home, studying those files. But the emotional tug for his former wife had taken precedence. And he was too old to change. He had always been seduced by lost causes.

He picked up the first section of the *Times*. The news was a surreal collage of carefully orchestrated madness designed by nonelected international power brokers playing their eternal game of East-West confrontation. NATO's naval forces were conducting war games off the coast of Norway. A Soviet submarine made of titanium cruised beneath the coastal waters of Maine; the speed and depth of the submerged Soviet vessel shocked the military experts at the Pentagon. Two Israeli children had been killed in the northern Galilee by a PLO rocket.

The newly elected President had pardoned two FBI men convicted of illegal wiretaps and break-ins.

Phil dropped the paper and got to his feet. He paced the room, thinking the presidential pardon of the FBI men would once again unleash the zealots in the intelligence community. And those same clandestine operatives could directly affect the outcome of his own case against the Korean Reverend Rhee. He now had sufficient proof to expose Rhee as a KCIA agent masquerading behind an evangelical cover. Once that information became public knowledge, it would have international ramifications.

South Korea was an ally, and Phil knew the president

of that Asian nation, former General Yi Chung. They had met in South Vietnam in 1967. Chung would protest to the State Department if Rhee were on the griddle. Phil's boss would be pressured to halt the investigation in the name of national security. Well, he would cross that bridge when he came to it. So far the attorney general, Arthur Browning, had backed him all the way.

Phil went up to the second-floor study of the three-story Georgetown house. He paid $1,200 a month for the 200-year-old red clapboard town house, but he loved the neighborhood. It was steeped in early American history and was only minutes from the Justice Department. A straight run on Massachusetts Avenue. His neighbors were Kissinger, Harriman, two senators and a group of five Georgetown University students who shared a house next door. The historic section was safe and comfortable.

The study was a spacious, high-beamed room with comfortable leather furniture and Navajo throw rugs over scored wooden floors. Two framed posters decorated the redwood walls. One was a movie poster of Steve McQueen from a film called Le Mans. The other framed poster was a blurred stop-action shot of Mario Andretti hitting the finish line at Jarama.

Phil poured a Stolichnaya over fresh ice and let the drink chill while he put on an old Beatles album. Since John Lennon's murder he had begun to play their early recordings. The legendary voices sang "She's Got a Ticket to Ride."

Phil picked up his drink and was suddenly startled by his own reflected image in the large oval mirror behind the bar.

It was the face of a stranger. The regular features still made familiar sense, although the definition of his high cheekbones was less pronounced and permanent dark circles rimmed his soft brown eyes. The stranger seemed to be growing out of that part of his face that had been rebuilt by an army surgeon at the Nha Trang Field Hospital in the summer of 1967. It was at the height of the war, when McNamara maintained the war was not only winnable but cost-effective.

He was then Captain Ricker, attached to the Military Intelligence Group, First Field Force, at Nha Trang, part

of the same headquarters group shared by the South
Korean Tiger Division, commanded by General Yi Chung.

The day he was wounded Phil was questioning a Vietnamese woman in a ruined village that had been razed by
a battalion of Chung's Koreans. Fifty-seven villagers had
been killed, burned or wounded. He was standing in the
shade of a lean-to, talking to the old woman through an
ARVN interpreter, when a nine-millimeter bullet whistled
out of the brush, glanced off a retaining post and lodged
in his jaw. The ensuing months of structural surgery,
drainage tubes and opening and closing of stitches had
left a permanent bluish scar that ran from his chin up to
the corner of his mouth. The scar threw the focus of attention to the right side of his face and of late the line of
the scar seemed to be traveling. The growing tentacle was
barely visible, but he knew it was moving. He sipped the
fine Russian vodka and brushed his wavy brown hair,
which showed increasing evidence of silver flecks. At
forty-one his six-foot frame was still trim, but daily exercise was required to keep a persistent roll off his waist.

He walked up to the big bay window and looked out at
the darkened street. The strong vodka gave his lagging
spirits a lift. All in all, he hadn't done badly. The big
break had come in 1969, when he won his first major case
for the U.S. attorney's office in New York. He had gained
a flash of national attention by successfully prosecuting
the godfather Don Carlo Carelli. After a long, bitter trial
he had succeeded in obtaining Carelli's deportation to his
native Palermo—the same year he and Audrey were di-
vorced.

Audrey had left New York for Paris to pursue a career
in fashion design, and Phil had gone to Washington to
join the Justice Department. While his legal knowledge
was no better than ordinary, his investigatory skills were
remarkable. A former attorney general had once complimented him: "You would have made a top-drawer cop.
You have all the proper instincts." But he never wanted
anything but law. He was one of the very few U.S. attorneys to survive changes of political administrations. Phil
had broken the Koreagate scandal in '77; but a deal had
been struck in the name of "national security," and the
handsome Korean playboy Kimsan had been permitted to

testify under limited legal ground rules. Kimsan owned half the United States Congress, and even the eminent jurist Leon Jaworski could do nothing with the case. Kimsan disappeared. But his coconspirator, the Korean beauty Soon Yi Sonji, had surfaced once again. She was now attached to the Cultural Affairs Section of the South Korean Embassy. She was in evidence at all Korean social functions in the capital.

The Beatles sang "Michelle," and Phil thought about Sonji. She had a dazzling smile and perfect features, a long spill of fine jet black hair, and her expressive eyes were incredible. He had questioned her during the Koreagate scandal, but she remained stoic, silent and loyal to Kimsan. Phil sipped the vodka and smiled, wondering how anyone could blame some congressman from Eagle's Asshole, Montana, for surrendering his public trust to her Oriental charms. He decided to see Sonji. She would certainly have a line on the Reverend Rhee—they all were KCIA operatives. Maybe, for old times' sake, she would give him a piece of information. Hell, a piece of anything from that lady would be interesting.

He drained the last of the vodka and, feeling a little heady, went over to the red phone and punched a combination of buttons. The number belonged to a pretty California girl who worked for the gun lobby.

"Hello?" Her voice sounded like someone sobbing in another room.

"Hi, Gloria."

"Oh—it's you. . . ."

"Yeah. I just got off the Metroliner and thought—"

"Forget it, Phil," she interrupted. "You decide to go see wifey and expect me to be on call."

"Sweetheart, I'm alone. The captain of your fan club. Alone, Gloria. On both knees, begging you to get your marvelous ass over here."

"I'm with someone."

"Who?"

"My boss," she whispered. "He's in the bedroom, stoned out of his head."

"I certainly hope his gun is loaded."

"Fuck off, Phil."

The line clicked dead. He went back to the big window

and lit a cigarillo. Just as he started to shake the match
out, his hand froze. Someone in a parked car across the
street was watching him through a pair of binoculars. He
snapped the match out and moved quickly to the wall
switch, killing the lights. He then sidled up to the edge of
the bay window; if the binoculars were equipped with infrared sensors, they could see in pitch-darkness. He carefully parted the drape. The car was gone.

His boss had warned him the Reverend Rhee's disciples
were dangerous. Browning had asked him if he wanted
the protection of federal marshals until the case was concluded, but Phil had refused. The security was tanta-
mount to being a prisoner.

For an instant he wondered if the car had actually been
there. The street was dark, and the car 200 feet away.
Had it been an illusion? The car, the man, the binoculars?
Was it an hallucination induced by growing paranoia? Or
was it the vodka mixed with fatigue, and the lost weekend, and the spreading line of scar, and the two frustrat-
ing years of pursuing the Reverend Rhee? Or was it the
shadowy gray-faced spooks who belonged to initials like
CIA, DIA, NSA, SDI, FBI? Or was it his pervasive
doubts that justice could no longer be rendered under a
system that had surrendered its integrity to the intelligence community?

He snapped the lights back on and picked up his suede
jacket. He would walk to Wisconsin Avenue and M Street
and have a drink at Harvey's. The four-block walk would
determine whether he was under surveillance.

Phil enjoyed the ambiance of Harvey's Café. On Sunday nights one could find intelligence chiefs, senators and
foreign diplomats mingling with Georgetown University
students. But he would have to be careful and go easy on
the booze. The bartender at Harvey's was a CIA informer.

Washington was like that. It was a city of informers
floating in a sea of Russian vodka.

Phil sat on the high stool at the long mahogany bar,
munching pretzel sticks and sipping a foul-tasting red

house wine. The walk to Harvey's had been uneventful, and he was certain no one had followed him.

In the mirror behind the bar Phil recognized Robert Burgess. The gray-faced CIA covert operations chief had a cigarette in his mouth. His companion was a stubby, crew-cut man with a bulbous nose. In an adjacent booth Senator Percy dined with an elegantly dressed Saudi diplomat. The remaining booths were taken by jeaned college students from Georgetown University and a smattering of neighborhood people.

Framed prints of the English hunt hung on the oak-paneled walls, and small colorful ceramics of jockeys were spotted at odd places and lit by stained-glass lamps. The waiters were young men working their way through college. They scurried across the tiled floor, carrying trays of fried clams and pitchers of beer. Bruce Springsteen on tape, sang a number from his hit album *The River*. Phil thought if Harvey's were dropped into one of those cobblestoned alleys behind the Dorchester Hotel in London, it would fit in perfectly with the old English pubs. He took another sip of wine and wondered if there was a national conspiracy among restaurant owners to serve house wine that tasted like Lavoris.

"A refill?" The heavyset bartender had a red face topped by red hair, but people who knew him called him Whitey.

"Not this mouthwash," Phil answered. "Let me have some Stolichnaya on the rocks."

The man looked at him curiously but managed to smile. "Coming up, Comrade."

The bartender reported the drinking habits and conversations of his star clients to the CIA. It was somehow ironically correct that Burgess was in the booth across the room. Phil lit a cigarillo and thought of the deepening rift between the Justice Department and the anonymous spooks in the intelligence community. It was as if they were in the service of different governments.

The bartender placed the drink down, and Phil watched the thick veins of vodka curl slowly around the ice cubes.

The man sitting next to him tapped his shoulder.

"Would you mind—if I—that is, we—borrowed the pretzels?"

"Help yourself," Phil said. He studied the faces of the couple seated next to him. The man sported a perfectly trimmed dark vandyke beard laced with gray. His features were sharp and ferretlike. His companion appeared to be twenty years younger. She was a big, handsome, rawboned blonde with high Slavic cheekbones, large gray eyes and a full mouth. Her thrusting breasts pressed tightly against her T-shirt. She had the look of those broad-hipped pioneer women who battled Indians, hard winters, cattle barons and died of boredom at ninety-three, sitting on a porch, chewing tobacco and squinting against the sun coming up over the twentieth century.

The ferretlike man stared at his wineglass while the big blonde shelled him with names like Dickens, Conrad, Faulkner and Hemingway.

The bartender came up to Phil. "How goes things in Justice?"

"You know what they say, Whitey." Phil sighed. "The wheels of justice grind slowly."

"Well, for whatever it's worth, I hope you nail that phony Korean preacher."

Phil wanted to be rid of the man and asked, "Isn't that CIA Director Robert Burgess over there in that booth?"

"How would I know?" Whitey replied, and abruptly walked to the far end of the bar.

The husky voice of the pioneer girl picked up some volume. She had turned full face to her small companion. "Goddammit, Harold! It's three weeks and you haven't read it."

The man stroked his beard and put his left hand on her big shoulder. "Be calm, Kate. I have read your novel. Twice." His hand fell from her shoulder, and he managed a sip of wine before continuing. "I find the work—well, obvious."

Phil had the picture. The girl was a student at Georgetown. She had written a novel, and the bearded man was her English lit professor.

"Just what the hell do you mean by 'obvious'?" she demanded.

"The Russians," he said meekly. "I repeatedly asked.

you to study the Russians—to steep yourself in Tolstoy, Dostoevsky, Gorky and Chekhov."

Phil smiled. The pioneer girl's gray eyes were full of Indians coming up over the ridge, and she was going for the Winchester. She slid off the barstool and towered over the little man. She moved her face to within inches of the professor's and in a calm fury said, "Fuck Tolstoy, fuck Dostoevsky, fuck Gorky, fuck Chekhov." Her voice rose. "And fuck you, Harold!" She picked up the wineglass, poured the remnants over his head, then turned and strode out of the room like a linebacker ejected from the game.

Phil handed the professor a napkin. "Thank you," he said, wiping the red liquid from his face. "I was merely trying to be honest with her. There's no point in false praise, don't you agree?"

Phil tossed down the last of the vodka. "I don't know anything about teaching, but I know a little about women. And if I were alone on a Sunday night with a girl who looked like that, I would have liked her novel." Phil called to the bartender, "Put this on my tab, Whitey."

He started for the door but then, acting on impulse, cut across the room to CIA Director Burgess. "You slumming tonight, Robert?" Phil asked.

"Hello, Counselor." Burgess smiled through his cigarette and indicated his companion. "Tony Sorenson, my public affairs director. Tony, this is Phil Ricker, deputy attorney general."

The man with the bulbous nose stood up and shook hands. "Pleased to meet you."

Phil noticed the man's shoes. You could usually spot a CIA man by his shoes. They wore heavy shoes, laced, surrounded by ribbed soles. They almost never wore loafers.

"Looks like the President's taken the wraps off," Phil said.

Burgess smiled. "We have high hopes the present administration will restore the agency to its full capacity."

"I'll bet you do. See you around, gents."

"Good luck with the Rhee case," Burgess added.

"Thanks. Remember, guys, the walls have ears."

Outside Harvey's at Wisconsin and M Street a teenaged

girl wearing a serape sat on the sidewalk, playing an old Dylan tune on her guitar. Phil thought she was like a ghost out of the sixties.

The night air was balmy, and he enjoyed the short walk back to Dumbarton Street. But a nagging feeling that an invisible trap was closing around him would not let go. Why was Burgess in Harvey's? Why had he referred to the Rhee case? *Why the hell did I go over to him?* Phil asked himself. But he knew the answers: heavy drinking induced by old scars, old frustrations and long-lost relationships, along with the persistent fear of being manipulated by a system he no longer understood. He reached the front door of his house, but before inserting the key, he reflexively looked up and down the street. The parked cars were uninhabited.

He entered the living room, flicked the lights on, walked over to his desk and wrote a name on the reminder pad: Soon Yi Sonji. He slipped off his jacket and glanced at the far corner of the room. The three brown cardboard case files on the Reverend Rhee were gone.

Chapter Two

The Watergate complex squatted on the banks of the Potomac River like a grotesque concrete toad. Its lights were the fixed, unblinking eyes of the primeval monster. The dark gaps between floors were filled by illuminated cement spikes, as if the creature's mouth had opened to reveal hideous stone teeth. The soul of its design oozed a pervasive sinister feeling. It was like an architectural prophecy anticipating the evil act that would forever mark it as a place of treachery.

Soon Yi Sonji stood on the open terrace of a tenth-floor apartment. It was a warm night with no moon and a red sky that promised rain. She wore a classic black Dior dress, and brilliant diamonds sparkled at her earlobes. Ivory bracelets circled her wrists, and the heavy-sweet scent of expensive French perfume clung to her body.

Her large curving black eyes stared out at the distant amber glow of the presidential monuments. She admired the variety of their design: the tall, clean marble needle of Washington; the domed Ionic columns of Jefferson; the Roman temple of Lincoln . . . She wondered why Americans erected statues exclusively to dead leaders. In her own country there were huge figures of President Chung scattered throughout Seoul. Perhaps America was still too young to shrug off its past.

The sliding glass door of the bedroom terrace was open, and Sonji could hear the shower running in the bathroom. The name of the girl in the shower was Joyce Raymond. KCIA agents had selected her after weeks of computerized research. She worked for the gambling industry's Washington lobby. She was twenty-eight, blond, pretty and lesbian.

The intelligence operatives had focused on individuals

41

whose occupations and background coalesced with American underworld operations in Nevada. KCIA agents knew the Las Vegas casinos were controlled by Nick Carelli, the West Coast Mafia boss President Chung had ordered Sonji to contact. Sonji did not know Chung's motive for ordering the contact, only that once the connection to Carelli had been achieved, she would receive further orders.

Joyce Raymond's name had spun out of the IBM computer in the Korean Embassy. There had been several other candidates, but it was decided that Sonji would be perfectly positioned with this girl—Joyce Raymond had all the proper connections, and her sexual proclivities would insure her silence.

Several weeks ago a meeting between Sonji and the pretty lobbyist had been arranged, ostensibly to discuss the possibility of Miss Raymond's clients supplying the gaming apparatus for Seoul's casinos.

The luncheon had taken place in the floral gardens of the Korean Embassy. Joyce Raymond's wine was laced with pulverized marijuana, and Sonji employed all her wiles on the unsuspecting American girl. It had been easy and almost pleasurable. Joyce possessed fine aristocratic features set off by intelligent green eyes. Her blond hair parted in the center, and two soft waves of gold framed her oval face. As the luncheon progressed, Joyce grew light-headed. She returned Sonji's knowing looks and casually brushed her fingers across her hand. The imperial kisaeng chose her moment with the calculated perfection of a great artist in full command of her craft. She conveyed an unmistakable image of the selfless Oriental goddess seduced by the blond American huntress.

As they sipped creamy Amarettos, Sonji turned the conversation to Eastern culture. She spoke of *Ramayana* Scriptures wherein the natural narcissism of woman is exalted and the attraction between women considered normal.

The following Friday they had gone to see a foreign film and afterward dined at an elegant French restaurant. The stunning Oriental girl and the classic Western blonde drew admiring male glances. But the two women were oblivious to the attention. By the time they finished their chocolate mousse Sonji made it apparent that she was Joyce's for the asking.

Sonji had driven carefully through the sudden spring rain and parked at Joyce's Watergate apartment building. She cupped the girl's face in her hands and began the maddeningly slow oral connection prescribed by Vishnu. She moved her lips across Joyce's mouth while her tongue traced the soft curve of the girl's lips. She felt Joyce's body yielding and slipped her hand beneath the girl's skirt to caress her firm thighs. Joyce's arms went around the imperial kisaeng's neck, and she crushed her lips against Sonji's, locking them in a furious embrace.

She kissed the girl in a carefully orchestrated rising crescendo while her hand stroked the girl's trembling thighs, but at the height of their fiery connection Sonji pulled her mouth away. She stared into Joyce's green eyes for a long moment, then placed her lips against the girl's ear. She whispered things that Joyce had never before heard. They were the ritual pornographic words contained in the Sapphist texts of Siddha Saraha. Sonji permitted the girl to unbutton her blouse and fondle her full breasts. But when the blond head bent toward her nipple, Sonji moved gently away, whispering, "Not here. Not now."

Joyce had pleaded with her to spend the night, but Sonji declined, promising another time. As Joyce started out of the car, Sonji touched her sleeve and gave her a final look—the same seductive, conspiratorial look she had thrown at Chung the afternoon of Park's murder.

Sonji quickly put the car in gear and sped away from the curb. She glanced in the rear-view mirror and saw Joyce standing motionless in the rain, watching the disappearing red taillights.

The pretty blond girl had phoned daily, and Sonji had tantalized her mercilessly before finally agreeing to spend this night with her.

The sound of the shower stopped abruptly, and after a long moment the bathroom door opened. Joyce came out, slipped off the body towel and crawled across the black silk sheets of the king-size bed.

Sonji walked to the bedside and stared down at the naked girl. Her eyes roamed Joyce's body from the erect pink nipples to the flat stomach and slim hips, the tuft of

blond hair and the long, pretty legs. A small spill of light
came out of the partially opened bathroom door.

Joyce slipped her arm around Sonji's waist and pressed
her cheek against Sonji's pelvis. Feeling the girl's arm
tremble, Sonji thrust herself into the girl's embrace. Joyce
kissed her through the dress and murmured, "Please . . .
please."

Sonji stroked the blond head and said, "Make the call."

Joyce leaned back against the pillow; her pretty mouth
pouted. "Why?"

"It's a favor."

Joyce tossed her blond hair. "I don't understand why
you want to meet him."

"I have business with Nick Carelli."

"What kind of business?"

Sonji sat on the edge of the bed, letting her left hand
rest on Joyce's thigh while she traced the curve of the
girl's cheekbone with her right forefinger. "It's state
business," she said.

"Nicky is not someone you play games with," Joyce replied.

"Please call him."

"Now?"

"It's only seven o'clock in Los Angeles."

Joyce stared at Sonji for a brief moment and noticed
something dangerous in the black oval eyes.

Sonji's hand moved to the mound of blond hair. "Do
this favor for me, Joyce."

Joyce stared at her for a long moment. "What do I say
to him?"

"The truth. A girl friend of yours with the Korean Embassy has a business proposition for him and would like to
meet with him."

Joyce rose and strode across the room. Sonji marveled
at the perfection of the girl's long legs. They were firm
and beautifully shaped, tapering down into race horse
ankles. She thought it might even be interesting to make
love to this American girl, but she would have to take
care; she did not want Joyce to become addicted to her.

Joyce came back with a small notebook. She thumbed
through the pages until she found the correct number,

then sat down on the edge of the bed and lifted the receiver.

Sonji leaned over and kissed her gently. "I'll never forget this favor." Buddha himself would have believed her.

The blond girl carefully and quickly punched a series of eleven buttons. Sonji rose and began to undress.

"Hello?" Joyce's voice grew husky as she watched Sonji's skirt fall. She cleared her throat and said, "Nicky, this is Joyce Raymond. . . ."

Chapter Three

The silver doors opened onto the fifth floor of the Justice Building, and Phil came out of the elevator, feeling the weight of fatigue pulling at his legs. He walked slowly past huge New Deal murals depicting downtrodden factory workers looking through the spokes of colossal gear wheels toward a distant sunrise. He thought the paintings would have made more political sense on any wall in the Kremlin. He turned left and stopped briefly to admire two naked young girls. The white marble sculptures had similar faces; it was their disparate attitudes that fascinated him. One of the girls had her right arm raised in the classic Bolshevik clenched fist, while her twin sister's arms were raised to throw a discus. It was as if the artist had believed human history began in ancient Greece and ended with the Russian Revolution. Phil had never understood their relationship to American justice.

He continued down the long marble corridor toward the attorney general's office. The blue walls were lit by Art Deco globes and featured a violently colored painting of Ramsey Clark. The Hall of Justice was strangely quiet, as if crime had vanished from the American scene.

Arthur Browning, the attorney general of the United States, sat in a high-backed leather chair. The size of his office was diminished by the hexagon shape of the concave blue walls. Behind him, flanking his desk, were the flags of the United States and his home state flag of Texas. Browning was on the phone and motioned to Phil to be seated.

The attorney general was a small, morose man with sandy hair, soft black eyes, a square nose and a puckish mouth. He reminded Phil of Truman Capote with a baritone voice. There was a small wooden sign on Browning's desk that read THE PLACE OF JUSTICE IS A HALLOWED PLACE.

Phil sank down into the soft red leather and stared up at the high oval ceiling. He had not slept at all the previous night. After discovering the theft of the Rhee case files, he had phoned the Metropolitan Police.

A pair of overweight, cigar-chewing detectives had shown up an hour later. After poking around for a while, they suggested that someone who knew him intimately, someone who possessed the key to the front door had done the job. Their thesis carried the unmistakable accusation that Phil had been betrayed by a girl friend.

He had replied that his maid was the only one other than himself who had a key, and she was above suspicion. She had been with him for five years. The detectives stated the maid would have to be questioned despite his trust. Phil then related the incident of the parked car and the man with binoculars. The detectives duly noted the time and place of the alleged surveillance and promised to check if any of his neighbors had seen the car or witnessed the clandestine break-in. It was close to 4:00 A.M. before the cynical pair departed in a cloud of cigar smoke.

Arthur Browning hung up, rose and peered out the window, across to the Smithsonian Museum of Natural History. The momentary silence was underscored by sounds of heavy traffic floating up from Constitution Avenue.

After a long moment Browning turned to him. "You can't say I didn't warn you. I offered you protection."

"Look, Arthur, the last time I carried a gun was in Vietnam. It didn't help then. It won't help now. I don't want federal marshals dogging my life."

"It's up to you, Phil. But remember, the Reverend Rhee controls the minds of two hundred thousand people. In the past, when his interests have been threatened, his followers have resorted to violence."

"Maybe so, but I've prosecuted Mafia overlords and never carried a gun—and never had bodyguards. Besides, this break-in was a professional job."

Browning scratched his right shoulder. "Why did you take those files home?"

"To study them. Hell, in two weeks I go before a grand jury."

"Wasn't very bright—taking those files home."

"Come on, Arthur, they were Xerox copies. If the right person wanted the files, he'd have taken the originals out of my office. It's happened before."

"Why did you go to New York?"

Phil sighed. "A mixture of romanticism and stupidity."

Browning chewed on his lower lip and said, "Why didn't they break in Saturday when you were out of town?"

"Saturday would've been chancy. The maid was in all day cleaning."

"What time did she leave?"

"Probably 6:00 P.M."

"They could have hit the place after she left."

"How did they know I wouldn't be coming home? Professionals break in only when they're certain of their intended victim's whereabouts." Phil rose. "They waited for me to come home Sunday, saw me go up to Harvey's and made their move."

Phil studied a Renoir painting on the wall. It was original, on loan to the attorney general from the National Gallery of Art.

"What do you think?" Browning asked.

"They were spooks. Spooks out of the CIA, NSA or DIA."

"What makes you so sure?"

"My key witness establishes Rhee as a KCIA operative, and they work in concert with the CIA. Someone high up in the intelligence community wants to know what we have on Rhee."

"You've been on this case for two years," Browning said. "Why would they hit us now?"

"Because it's a published fact that I'm going before a grand jury in two weeks. The case is a reality. Up to now it was just another investigation."

"How much damage has been done?" Browning asked.

"They now have the name, address, occupation and testimony of our key witness."

"Mrs. Hwan?"

Phil nodded. "Rhee's former mistress and executive secretary. He fired her after Park's murder in '79."

The attorney general walked back to his big chair and leaned on its top. "Who uncovered this witness?"

"Sid Greene."

"He's been effective, hasn't he?"

"Sid's been great."

"You see, the FBI is not our enemy," Browning said. "And I don't share your paranoia about our other security agencies."

"It's a bad analogy, Arthur. I handpicked Sid. He's a fellow graduate of NYU Law. He's young, ambitious and recognizes the Rhee case can further his career."

"Assuming you're right," Browning conjectured, "assuming someone high up on the intelligence ladder knows who your key witness is—and assuming that someone pays Mrs. Hwan a visit and convinces her not to go before the grand jury—where's your case?"

"I've got to drop the KCIA charge and focus on Rhee's tax evasions. But if Mrs. Hwan stands up, I can nail the bastard as an unregistered agent of a foreign power."

"I wish you hadn't taken those files home." Browning sighed.

"For chrissake, Arthur—"

Browning sat down and forced a smile. "I'm sorry."

The attorney general rocked back and forth for a moment. "I've been meaning to ask: Is there anything in your files concerning Gemstone?"

"No, I've always believed that missing Hoover file is American mythology. No one's ever seen it." Phil paused. "Why do you ask?"

"Just curious," Browning replied. "Well, go ahead as scheduled. And if there's anything I can do, let me know."

Phil entered his fourth-floor office. An attractive black girl sat at a desk, typing in a smooth staccato rhythm. She looked up at him and smiled. "You look awful."

"You look great, Martha. Any calls?"

"Joe Barnes at the *Post*. And Gloria Robbins from the gun lobby. Sid Greene's inside."

Sid Greene sat in a leather chair in front of Phil's desk. He was almost handsome, and his unlined face made it difficult to believe he was thirty-eight. He had been with the FBI for eight years and fully expected that one day he would head the bureau.

Phil greeted his liaison man and tossed his jacket on the sofa, sat down at his desk, loosened his tie and lit a cigarillo. "I see you copied our stolen files."

"As soon as I got your call, I came in and started." Sid paused. "You think we're out of business?"

"If they get to Mrs. Hwan, we're screwed," Phil replied. "Two years down the drain."

"We can still make a hell of a case for tax evasion."

"So he pays the fine," Phil said, "but he continues his KCIA activities."

"What about Soon Yi Sonji?" Sid asked.

"Not a chance. She wouldn't cooperate during Koreagate. She protected Kimsan down the line. Why would she give me anything on Rhee? They all play for the same team." Phil did not want Sid to know that he fully intended to call on the Asian beauty. It was a personal card to play. A long shot. "Sid, I'd like you to sweep my phones. Here and at home."

"No problem. We ought to get new double-bolt locks on your doors."

Phil nodded, but his thoughts had suddenly drifted to Arthur Browning—and the word "Gemstone." He wondered why Browning had mentioned it.

"What is it?" Sid Greene asked.

"Nothing. Let's get some lunch. Then we'll tackle these files."

"Where do you want to go?"

"Maison Blanche."

"Food's not up to the prices."

"Yeah," Phil said, "but on a good day you can see Kissinger, Art Buchwald and half the CIA."

They went into the outer office.

"Lunch, Martha."

"Where?"

"Maison Blanche."

"You white folks sure live good."

"Don't leave till we get back."

"Yassuh—den after Ahz gwane to iron Gloria Steinem's panteez—"

"Christ," Sidney muttered.

"Christ was just another misguided leftist honky," Martha replied with a smile.

Chapter Four

The three men in the Glass Room deep below the CIA headquarters building were discussing ways and means of convincing the President to approve a proposed $8 billion sale of sophisticated military hardware to Saudi Arabia. Dr. Belgrave smoked his pipe and listened attentively to the report of Defense Intelligence Chief Gruenwald.

Belgrave's role had expanded with the election of the new President. He was now chairman of the National Security Council, governing a sixty-five-member group of specialists in academics, science, the military and intelligence. The council members concentrated their efforts on long-range planning and evaluation of geopolitical policy for the nation. They constituted the highest decision-making body in the executive section of government. Belgrave had chosen his people carefully, selecting men and women whose technical arrogance transcended their morality. He would analyze the opinions of the council, then take his conclusions to the President.

He waited patiently as Gruenwald concluded his remarks. "The Zionist lobby will of course oppose the sale, but they can be handled."

CIA Covert Operations Director Burgess nodded. "I agree. Without America there is no Israel."

"Gentlemen, Israel is not the problem," Belgrave advised. "The problem is Congress. They are not convinced the Saudis require these weapons. We must invent an external threat."

"Eric, every one of those congressmen has constituents who drive cars," Burgess stated. "If we refuse the Saudis arms, they'll cut their oil exports."

Belgrave shook his head. "My people on the council tell

me the national mood is one of revulsion at the spectacle of this nation paying blackmail to a gang of oily sheikhs. We must invent an external threat."

The Doctor tamped his pipe and proceeded to refill the bowl. There was a moment of silence, filled by the groan of the air conditioner.

Burgess lit a fresh cigarette and said, "South Yemen."

"Not bad," Belgrave said. "But too small."

Gruenwald cleared his throat. "South Yemen has a mutual defense treaty with that lunatic in Libya."

"It's possible." Belgrave nodded. "With Libya as an ally, South Yemen becomes a valid threat to Saudi security."

"Sometimes"—Gruenwald sighed—"I wish we could simply let Israel take out that Libyan madman."

"My dear Gruenwald," Belgrave said, "if that occurred, to whom would the Soviets sell their munitions? You cannot obliterate a huge marketplace for our Soviet colleagues and still preserve harmony. The balance of peace resides in the profitability of terror, and that marketplace must be shared."

A red light blinked on the phone console at Belgrave's side. He lifted the receiver and said, "Send him in."

Matt Crowley was Dr. Belgrave's longtime aide, a former CIA man whose principal achievements included designing the method of torture used on VC suspects during the Vietnam War; the recruiting of Cuban exiles for dirty tricks and enlisting the services of Mafia dons Giancana and Roselli in the scheme to assassinate Castro. On orders from Belgrave he periodically conducted clandestine tapping and surveillance of senators and congressmen.

Crowley was a much decorated hero of the Korean War. But the brutal treatment he had received at the hands of his Chinese captors left him with a lingering hatred of all Orientals. Dr. Belgrave had personally seen him through the long, painful period of rehabilitation, and Crowley's dedication to the Doctor bordered on worship. He believed Eric Belgrave represented the last hope for a renewal of American ideals, spirit and supremacy.

The door slid open, and a tall, wiry man with regular features and cold black eyes entered the glass chamber.

Crowley went to the far end of the long table, taking

care not to sit next to Gruenwald, whose foul breath was legend in the intelligence community. Crowley began his report in a clipped stacatto fashion.

"The only significant fact contained in the Rhee files relates to a Korean woman—a naturalized American citizen named Soo Hwan. She was employed by the Reverend Rhee as his executive secretary. The Reverend also maintained an apartment in Los Angeles for sexual liaisons with this woman. She served him in both capacities for five years. Upon Park's assassination Rhee fired her and terminated their personal relationship. Her testimony, as contained in Philip Ricker's files, indicates she can provide corroboration of Rhee's KCIA activities—and that his two principal bodyguards are full colonels in the KCIA."

Belgrave smiled benignly and said, "Thank you, Matt. Was there anything in those files alluding to Gemstone?"

"No, sir."

"You're certain of that?"

"Yes, sir. Our team acquired the files at twelve forty-six A.M. last night and spent the following six hours sifting the documents. Mrs. Hwan is the only damning factor in those files."

"What is your recommendation?" Burgess asked.

"I would like approval to pay Mrs. Hwan a visit. Not a terminal visit—rather one of friendly persuasion."

"When?" Belgrave asked.

"Immediately. I would also recommend that we deal forcibly with the deputy attorney general."

"I doubt that's necessary," Burgess offered. "The data on Ricker indicates he is an alcoholic. As a matter of fact, he approached me last night in Harvey's. The man could barely stand up; he had some altercation at the bar, spilled wine over a customer's head."

Gruenwald said, "Well then, it seems to me we can embarrass Ricker right out of Justice by leaking his drinking problem to the press."

"It's up to you gentlemen," Crowley said coolly. "But I strongly suggest we cause Mr. Ricker some physical pain."

There was a moment of silence, and then Belgrave spoke. "Matt, pay Mrs. Hwan a social call, and if you can find a propitious moment, you might remind Mr. Ricker that he is mortal."

"Thank you, sir."

The big glass door slid open, permitting Crowley to leave.

Burgess cleared his throat and said, "Forgive me, Eric, but there is a detectable shift in Crowley's demeanor of late. I have certain reports that—"

"I'm not interested in your reports." Belgrave cut him off. "Matt Crowley is the best operative I've ever known."

Gruenwald softly said, "I don't think Robert is questioning Crowley's professionalism, but rather the thin edge."

"Gentlemen," Belgrave said emphatically, "I want to put this discussion to bed. Matt Crowley has visited hell. He has been tortured by experts. And he *never*—I repeat—*never* cracked. He is a man who would give his life for this nation without a moment's hesitation. There is no one I trust more than Matt Crowley." There was a pause, and neither man responded. The austere chairman of the National Security Council then said, "Now let us address the problem at hand."

The three wise men in the translucent chamber began again the tedious task of inventing an external threat to the kingdom of Saudi Arabia.

Chapter Five

Phil pushed the tachometer up to 3,000 rpm, causing the night wind to whistle through the window curtains. The '55 red Porsche speedster was equipped with a new Targa turbo engine and fifteen-inch Pirelli tires. The souped-up classic car was his major indulgence. He had purchased a scarred shell from a Georgetown student and spent thousands of dollars restoring it.

He found a personal truth in the ultimate contest of man versus speed. A unique liberation of the spirit occurred in those complex split-second decisions when skill, courage and death battled for control. It was an exhilarating theology which carried only one commandment: Thou shalt make no mistake.

He was cruising through the Virginia countryside a few miles north of the huge CIA complex at Langley. He wondered if Burgess's spooks had stolen his case files. The clean entry had all the earmarks of a CIA operation. Still, he could not rule out the NSA, the DIA or even the FBI. He believed Sid Greene was on the level, but in Washington ambition dictated allegiance.

Phil swung the red sports car off 124 at the McLean exit ramp and picked up Brookhaven Drive. The road wound its way through thickly wooded rolling hills. White Colonial homes loomed up out of the dark forest like pale ghosts. He thought of the great armies that had clashed in these forests a century ago and the young men in blue and gray who had spilled their blood across the hallowed ground. But time had a way of turning battlefields into "choice real estate."

The high beams lit up a sign that read MENLO ROAD. He geared down, turned left and began searching for number 683. The homes were smaller and clustered together on poorly lit streets.

Mrs. Hwan opened the door of the dilapidated white-shingled two-story house. She was a small, attractive woman with troubled eyes.

He followed her into the shabbily furnished living room. Old lamps on tall iron stands with cracked shades stood like defeated soldiers amid the ruins of crumbling furniture. Mrs. Hwan indicated a green velvet sofa, and Phil heard its springs protest against his weight. There was a moment of silence as she nervously brushed imaginary lint from her blouse. She rubbed her wrists and went over to the window. The worn-out lace curtains moved slightly as the night wind stole through cracks in the pane.

She spoke with calm resignation. "My husband is now in Korea; my family is in Seoul. I support them with money. They have been denied work."

"That situation has been true all along," Phil said. "You nevertheless testified without reservation. What happened to change that?"

She turned from the window. "Two men came to see me at the university."

"When?"

"This afternoon. Perhaps three o'clock."

"Where?"

"In my office. Only one spoke. He said if I wanted to see my husband again, I must not appear before the grand jury. I must not testify against the Reverend Rhee."

"Were these men Korean or American?"

"The one who spoke was Korean."

"Did you know him?" Phil asked gently.

Tears welled up in her eyes. "The man is one of Rhee's bodyguards. His name is Colonel Kim Yee."

"What about the American?"

"I never saw him before. He was tall with cruel eyes—dead eyes. He never spoke."

"If I showed you some photographs, do you think you could identify him?"

She shook her head. "I don't want to see pictures. And

I will not identify anyone." Tears suddenly coursed down her cheeks.

Phil rose and went to her. "What is it?"

She stared at him for a moment, then pulled up the right sleeve of her blouse.

"Christ . . ." he murmured.

There were five circular festering wounds on her arm, forming a line of almost perfect scarlet circles with oozing yellow blisters at their core.

"The American held my arms," she explained. "He stuffed a cloth in my mouth to silence my screams while Colonel Yee pressed his cigarette into my arm."

Phil had seen those burn scars in Vietnam on the arms, chest and genitalia of VC prisoners.

Mrs. Hwan rolled down her sleeve and brushed the tears from her eyes. "What I don't understand is how they got my name."

"That's my fault. Some case files containing your testimony were stolen from my home last night."

She nodded slightly, but her eyes were clouded with suspicion.

"Do you think I betrayed you?" he asked.

"No." She rubbed her wrists again. "But the fact is they know who I am. Where I live and where I work."

"I can assure your protection, Mrs. Hwan."

"You can assure me?" she said with undisguised sarcasm. "You cannot protect your own President. How can you protect me?" She started toward the front door.

"I have your sworn testimony," Phil said.

"I will say it was false, taken under duress."

"I can have you subpoenaed."

"Do as you wish. You must leave now. Please."

"I've spent two years on this case. I'm not going to let it die."

She opened the front door and looked sadly into his eyes. "I'm sorry, but I cannot endanger the lives of innocent people."

"You think they would actually go after your family in Seoul?"

"Colonel Kim Yee made that quite clear."

"Colonel Yee doesn't speak for the Korean government."

"The burn marks are on my arm, Mr. Ricker."

Chapter Six

The red Porsche roared through the Virginia hills, its powerful engine turning 5,200 rpm pushing the speedometer needle up to 110 miles an hour. Phil drove with a controlled frenzy, trying to excise his anger and frustration by flirting with death. He double-clutched, geared down around the curves, then floored the gas pedal and geared up on the straightaways. The small car came perilously close to being airborne as it traversed the dips and hollows of the country road. He was soaked by a cold sweat and had the heater turned full up. All his thoughts were concentrated on the road and the green lights of the instrument panel. The sensitivity of touch, gear selection and dead reckoning of curves were reflexive. The high whine of the engine was his own primal scream against a night shadowed by demons.

Phil had only a vague recollection of slowing down upon entering the city. He parked illegally at Twenty-third and Constitution, got out of the car, lit a cigarillo and stared off at the luminous columns of the Lincoln Memorial. The monument had officially closed at midnight.

He started across the grassy Mall, passed the huge Reflecting Pool and climbed the worn marble steps of the monument. The white marble face of the murdered President gazed down at him. Lincoln's eyes radiated understanding and absolution for the misdeeds of mankind. Phil stared at the forgiving eyes for a long time.

He then crossed to the south wall and studied the Gettysburg Address engraved in the Indiana limestone. His eyes lingered on the last phrase: ". . . and that government of the people, by the people, for the people, shall not perish from the earth."

Phil descended the steps and crossed the damp grass to the Reflecting Pool. The turn-of-the-century lamps bordering the Mall glowed softly in the muggy night, and the air carried the salty aroma of the Potomac River. He stood at the shallow edge of the huge rectangular pool. The tall pristine obelisk of the nearby Washington Monument shimmered across the dark surface of the water.

A slight southern wind rose and blew across the Mall. *Then a face appeared in the water*. The face reflected no features, yet it possessed the contours of a human head. *Another similar shape appeared to the right of the reflected obelisk*.

Phil spun around and saw two men, one large and muscular, the other small and wiry, their faces covered by ski masks.

The big man's fist crashed into Phil's right cheekbone, splitting the skin and dropping him to his knees. The small man kicked him in the jaw, and he fell, the back of his head hitting the edge of the pool.

As the small man came forward, Phil brought his right knee up, raised his back and slammed his foot into the man's groin. The man screamed and dropped to his knees. The big man kicked Phil in the ribs and sat on his chest. He brought his fists down in a high arc, first the right, then the left, slamming into either side of Phil's face in measured cadence.

Blood poured from Phil's cheeks and seeped down into his neck. With a desperate animal instinct, he thrust his thumbs into the eye slits of the face mask. Using all the remaining strength in his arms, hands and fingers, Phil increased the pressure against the softness of the man's eyes. The big man clutched at Phil's hands but could not budge them. He shouted to his partner, who crawled over, raised a flat palm and brought its hard edge down into Phil's windpipe, cutting off his oxygen. Phil's thumbs fell away from the big man's eyes.

Phil saw an array of colors and felt himself floating through the air and splashing into the pool.

The men were waist-deep in the water, standing on either side of him. They grabbed his head and thrust him under. Four gloved hands held him down.

Phil's eyes were wide open under the dark water. He could see the torsos of the men. His lungs ached as he tried to force his head up against the pressure of the four hands. The remaining air in his lungs was expiring. The thought that they meant to kill him struck with a numbing terror. He opened his mouth and gagged as the water rushed in. Then suddenly and brutally his head was yanked up. He gasped desperately for air.

The men held him as if he were a fish on a hook whose gills opened and closed searching for oxygen. Once again they thrust his head under the fetid water. They were torturing him—and he had taken in very little air. He let his body go limp, offering no resistance as if accepting death.

Above the surface the men noticed Phil's suddenly slack body. The big man nodded at his partner, and they pulled Phil's head up out of the water.

The top of Phil's head was just under the big man's chin. Phil sucked some air and bent his legs against the floor of the pool for leverage. And in one final effort fueled by adrenaline, he thrust his body up, propelling his skull into the big man's chin.

He heard the scream and crunching sound of bone and teeth breaking apart. The big man fell back, face up in the pool. A geyser of dark blood shot out of the ski mask's mouth hole.

Phil waded toward the far side of the pool.

The small man went over to his bloody partner and began moving him toward the near edge of the pool.

Phil thought he heard the sound of a police whistle. He reached the far side and leaned against the marble edge. Gasping for air, he wiped the blood from his eyes and saw the two men running across the Mall toward Constitution Avenue. He pressed his hands against the edge of the pool and hoisted himself up. He lay prone against the cool marble, pumping air into his lungs. He saw two park policemen with drawn guns running after the fleeing assailants. He tried to sit up, but as he raised himself, an excruciating pain knifed across his chest. He knew the source of the pain; the big man's kick had broken a rib. Phil assumed a sitting position and felt a sudden drowsiness begin to invade various parts of his body. He seemed to be involuntarily falling asleep.

Sid Greene knelt down and wiped the blood from Phil's face.

"I . . . It was . . ." Phil mumbled, "impulse. I wanted to see the words . . . Lincoln's words."

"Take it easy," Sid said.

Phil could feel his circulation returning and raised his face.

"Christ," Sid whispered.

Phil's cheeks were cut and oozing blood. His eyes were swollen and reduced to slits. His lips were puffed and raw, and the right side of his face was purple.

Phil heard the distant wail of a siren and murmured, "Not too pretty, huh?"

"I've seen worse," Sid said, trying to manage a smile.

"Where did you come from?" Phil asked.

"I tailed you to McLean. But you lost me in the hills. You drove like Mario Andretti. I picked you up again when you crossed the Memorial Bridge."

"How did you manage that?"

"I had a radio transmitter placed under the fender of your car. Someone's got to look after you. I was homed in on you all the way. Did you get a look at those guys?"

Phil shook his head. "I didn't have to. I know who they were."

"Without seeing them?"

"They were spooks."

"From what agency?"

"Don't know." Phil sighed. "Got a cigarette?"

Sid lit one and handed it to him. Phil inhaled deeply, then suddenly shivered. Sid put his jacket around Phil's shoulders. The whoop and wail of the siren were very close.

"Paramedics," Sid said. "Be here in a few seconds."

Two middle-aged overweight park policemen carrying walkie-talkies came puffing up to Sid.

"We missed them. They had a guy waiting in a black

GTO and took off. We radioed Metro." The cop then glanced at Phil. "Is he okay?"

"He's fine," Sid replied.

"Christ!" the cop exclaimed. "He looks like a fucking tomato."

Phil's head again fell to his chest. He dropped the cigarette; the smoke had made him nauseous. His body trembled in the aftershocks of the assault. He felt a warm blanket drape across his shoulders. A pair of white sleeves followed by a very young male face came into focus.

"We've got you, Mr. Ricker. Just relax. You'll be in a warm bed in less than five minutes."

Phil looked up at Sidney. "I'm going to crack this fucking thing."

"Sure you will." Sid smiled.

Chapter Seven

At six o'clock in the evening the Polo Lounge in the Beverly Hills Hotel is like the club car on a crack European express train hurtling through the night with its cargo of the bad and the beautiful. There is a narcissistic din and throb to the L-shaped room that makes a case for anonymity. The sharp odors of tobacco, sweat and expensive perfume are like an aromatic silhouette of expectancy and hopelessness. Waiters in green uniforms carrying trays of drinks and bowls of guacamole move in and out of narrow lanes between the booths and tables. Stolen glances are exchanged; whispered requests are placed in waiters' ears; clandestine drinks are sent to old lovers. There is a feeling to the room of encapsulation, of being locked in an atmosphere where night is eternal.

Soon Yi Sonji was seated in a rear booth. She wore a white Basile Italian suit and a blue silk blouse. Her long black hair spilled casually over her shoulders as if it had just happened that way. She toyed with her tall gin and tonic and flirted with an Italian movie star who advertised his fame behind huge sunglasses.

She was nervous about seeing Nick Carelli. She had no idea why President Chung had ordered her to effect the underworld connection. It was not possible to perceive his motives. Chung listened only to Buddha and operated out of an exotic theory called the samsara: a force created by the mind, setting in motion a single circle of energy spreading into a vast infinite flow of concentric circles washing away all opposition. She knew Chung despised Dr. Eric Belgrave, but this mission did not seem to involve the chairman of the National Security Council.

Sonji checked her watch; fifteen minutes had passed since she entered the room. A waiter appeared and whispered, "The man in the dark glasses in that booth asked if you would join him."

She shook her head. "I'm expecting someone."

The waiter hurried off. She smiled at the Italian movie star and thought about the news story of Phil Ricker's mugging at the Lincoln Memorial. She knew the men who committed the assault were not muggers. They were professionals working for the CIA. Sonji toyed with her drink, and her thoughts drifted to another news story: There had been a major student uprising in Pusan. She hoped her father had not been involved. She stared intently into her drink as if the answer lurked in the sweating ice cubes.

"We're ready, miss." The gruff voice came out of sandpapered vocal cords. She looked up at a stocky middle-aged man with flat features, wearing a shiny blue suit. "Don't worry about the bill. Let's go."

A sea of eyes pursued the exquisite Korean girl as she followed the stocky man out the side entrance. They walked along the red brick pathway surrounded by palms, banyan trees, fuchsia-colored bougainvillaea and sinister-looking tropical foliage. The path wound its way through low single-story pink bungalows. Mexican maids pushed carts laden with pink towels, pink sheets and pink pillowcases. The stocky man walking beside Sonji seemed to be tense and from time to time glanced back over his shoulder.

They reached a bungalow where two young men dressed in quiet sports clothes lounged on the porch. Both wore dark sunglasses. They neither spoke, smiled nor acknowledged Sonji in any way. One of them opened the door of the bungalow and disappeared inside. The late May sun hit her face, and she moved under the portico. She felt a sudden apprehension, and beads of sweat oozed out of her armpits and rolled down her rib cage. It seemed an eternity before the sunglassed man came out of the room and nodded to her.

The suite was spacious, pink-walled and could have been furnished by the directorate of the Spanish Inquisition. The furniture was dark, heavy and foreboding. A rattan wet bar seemed to have been secreted into the room by someone out of another century.

Nick Carelli sat behind a black mahogany desk, holding a phone that came out of an attaché case. He wore beige linen slacks and a white silk shirt open at the neck. He glanced at her, cupped the receiver and said, "Fix yourself a drink and pour me a scotch on the rocks."

Sonji studied him as she fixed the drinks. He was better looking than the sunglassed movie star in the Polo Lounge. He was tall and built like an athlete, with thick, dark, wavy hair and fine, sensitive features. His eyes were large, warm and very blue. She thought his good looks and kind eyes did not fit his violent world.

She brought him the scotch, then walked across the room and sat down in a deep leather chair.

Nick Carelli had the receiver cradled between shoulder and ear. "You through?" he said into the phone. There was a slight pause before he continued. "Listen, Victor, Chicago isn't L.A. Chicago isn't New York. *Chicago is Pittsburgh.*"

He leaned forward, swallowed some scotch, and his words picked up speed. "Vegas is a gift. A present from me to him. I'll call Leo Meyers and take this thing to the council." Nick listened for a minute; then a trace of menace crept into his voice. "You tell that *stronzo* I'll send his cut to the fucking morgue! Vegas is my thing. Everyone gets a slice, but it's my thing. That's it. I got company here. *Ciao*, Victor." He placed the receiver on its cradle and closed the attaché case.

Sonji noticed his hands. There was a wafer-thin gold watch on his left wrist and a simple gold wedding band on the second finger of his left hand.

"That's an unusual phone," she said.

"It's a direct transmission by satellite." He got to his feet and smiled. "Someone would have a tough time bugging a satellite."

He studied her face for a moment. "I think I'm gonna call you Suzie."

"Whatever pleases you."

"So you're a friend of Joyce Raymond. . . ."

"Yes."

"I hear she's a dyke."

"A what?"

"A lesbian." He smiled. "But she swings both ways.

Joyce has some key congressmen sniffing her snatch. And that's just great. Vegas needs all the friends it can get." Nick sipped the scotch and said, "What can I do for you, Suzie?"

"Does the name Reverend Rhee mean anything to you?"

Nicky shrugged. "He's an overweight chink telling kids he's Buddha or Buddha's agent. What else should I know?"

She chose her words carefully. "The Reverend Rhee has amassed a fortune in America. His disciples send him two million dollars a week in cash. He owns hotels, oil wells, television stations and one million acres in Northern California. He collected over half a million dollars at an outdoor rally in April here in Los Angeles."

Nick paced the room for a moment.

She thought he moved with a desperate grace, like a tiger in captivity. She knew he was in his early forties, but he appeared to be much younger.

Nick stopped pacing, drank some more scotch and turned to her.

"What has all that got to do with me?" he asked.

"The president of Korea inherited Rhee from the former regime. President Chung wants him—well, let's say bothered. You control the underworld interests in California—" She paused and stared into his eyes. "You have our approval to share in the profits of Reverend Rhee's business."

Carelli nodded, moved to the desk, took a cigarette out of a silver box, lit it and asked, "Isn't Rhee under investigation by the feds?"

"Yes, but we believe the Justice Department has no case."

"Maybe, but the guy running that case, Phil Ricker, is a stubborn son of a bitch. He had my father deported to Palermo years ago. I know Ricker. He'll never let go."

"Mr. Ricker cannot prove anything. Certain agencies of the United States government are protecting the Reverend."

Nick fell silent. Sonji felt a growing tension and wondered if she had said the wrong thing. The silence was underscored by a 747 whining down over Beverly Hills, homing in on its southeast landing pattern to LAX. Nick paced for a moment, then put down his drink, came over and sat on the arm of her chair.

"What's that perfume?" He smiled.

"Joy. Does it please you?"

"Yeah, it's sweet like you." The smile vanished, and his voice was suddenly dangerous. "Don't fuck around with me, Suzie."

Sonji had never seen warm eyes go so cold so fast. She tried not to betray any fear. She sipped the gin and calmly said, "I have no wish to deceive you."

He grasped the back of her neck and pulled her face close to his. "Then you must be stupid."

"I don't understand," she said innocently.

Nick's dead blue eyes came slowly alive, and he released the pressure on her neck. "If you don't understand, it means you're stupid. And I like you again." He moved away from her, crossed to the desk and picked up his drink. He tossed down some scotch, then turned to her. "We never, *never* cross the feds. Sometimes we work for them, but we never touch their action. If this fucking chink, Reverend Rhee, is being protected by government agencies, how do I muscle him?"

She felt tiny beads of sweat forming on her upper lip. "He will no longer enjoy protection," she said shakily.

"You just told me Ricker's case is in the toilet," he snapped. "And that certain government agencies are protecting Rhee."

"Those agencies are in business with .us." She paused and brushed her finger across the beads of perspiration on her upper lip. "We are officially removing our protection. Our president holds Rhee in contempt."

"Why?"

"It's quite simple. The Reverend Rhee does not transfer his wealth to my government. He sends his money to a private Swiss account." She was careful not to mention Rhee's KCIA activities.

"Why doesn't your president have Rhee hit?"

"It's politically unsound for Koreans to be killing other Koreans in the United States."

"Let me get this straight. You work for the KCIA, right?"

"You know that," she admitted. "Your men took my credentials before I entered the Lounge."

"You'll get them back." He smiled.

She felt a sense of relief and asked, "Can you freshen this for me?"

"Help yourself. I'm not a fucking bartender."

She rose, and he watched her as she crossed over to the wet bar. He waited until she had fixed her drink, then moved to the opposite side of the bar.

"Let's run this down, Suzie." The tone of his voice was friendly. "You're KCIA. You can't hit Rhee—and you want him bothered. You come to me because his headquarters are in my state, right?"

"Yes."

He touched the curve of her high cheekbone. "So if I muscle Rhee, no one in government's gonna get angry. I mean that chink prick is a mark, right?"

"What do you mean by a mark?"

"A score, a setup."

"Yes," Sonji replied as she came around and faced him. "The Reverend Rhee is your mark."

"How do you suggest I become his partner?"

"He has a temple in the desert just outside Palm Springs. The temple is Rhee's collection center for Southern California."

She swallowed some gin and felt her courage returning. "There is an office on the second floor of that temple. Three people work there. They count and store the money—a quarter of a million dollars every week." She chanced a small smile. "A visit to that temple would be a good beginning."

"Why?"

"To make him aware that he has a new partner."

"Let me tell you something, Suzie. About ten years ago we killed ten black pimps in Harlem. And then said to the head nigger, 'Now that we have your attention, sir.'"

"We cannot approve that kind of violence."

Nick stared at her for a moment and then asked, "Do you play tennis?"

"No."

"Do you play?"

"Sometimes."

He walked up to her and put his hands on her shoulders. "If my wife wasn't very pregnant, I'd ask you to play with me; but I'm superstitious, and Catholic, and I never play when my wife's carrying a kid." His hands fell from her shoulders. "All right, Suzie, you let me kick this thing around." He walked her to the door and placed her back against it. His voice was ice-cold. "If you've given me a bad connection, I'll cut your heart out."

"I understand."

Nick was surprised at the courage in her large oval eyes. He touched her cheek affectionately. "Suppose I asked you to stay?"

"I would stay."

Nick smiled and opened the door. "Take care, Suzie."

She gave him a final look that graphically described what he was missing.

Chapter Eight

The dining room in the National Press Building is located on the thirteenth floor. Phil guessed the number of the floor had been chosen by design as an indication to the citizens that superstition played no part in journalism.

He walked past oak walls lined with bronzed reproductions of front-page headlines spanning the century. The banner stories read: YANKS ARE OVER THERE. GUERNICA DESTROYED BY BOMBS. MUNICH PEACE PACT. FDR LANDSLIDE. A-BOMB DROPPED ON HIROSHIMA. The headlines traveled the full length of the L-shaped walls.

Phil entered the high-ceilinged dining room with its curiously feminine gold damask walls and sherbet-colored curtains. A huge, badly crafted painting of pioneers crossing the prairie gave the place a Disneyland ambiance. There was nothing in its decor that related to journalism. The room was crowded and noisy.

Phil always marveled at its popularity. He knew it had nothing to do with the quality of the food. It was a place for lobbyists and politicians on the make and journalists who laced their contacts with expensive scotch while trying to crack a story.

He asked the headwaiter for Joe Barnes. The tuxedoed man eyed the bruises on Phil's face suspiciously.

"Something wrong?"

"No, sir. This way, please."

Joe Barnes was a bald, red-faced man whose prodigious eating and drinking had placed thirty extra pounds on his small frame. But he was a top-drawer journalist, a Pulitzer prizewinner and a man with informers in every critical agency of government.

Barnes looked up from his martini and shook Phil's hand. "Good to see you."

71

"Sorry I'm late."

"No problem. What are you drinking?"

"I'm off the sauce, Joe."

"Too bad."

"Not by choice," Phil said. "I'm still on antibiotics, and they don't mix with booze."

"They banged you up pretty good."

"A dislocated vertebra, ruptured blood vessels in my left eye, broken hand and two fractured ribs." Phil smiled. "Nothing serious."

"Did you do any damage?" Barnes asked.

"I think there's a guy walking around this town with a broken jaw and three thousand dollars' worth of new bridgework."

Barnes swallowed his olive. "Dentists have a way of turning muggings into Cadillacs."

"This was no mugging, Joe."

"Want to order?"

"Sure."

"You know what you want?"

"The usual."

Barnes signaled the waiter. "A tuna salad and iced coffee for Mr. Ricker, and I'll have a shrimp cocktail. Then give me the club sandwich with lots of mayonnaise, french fries and another martini."

The waiter hurried off, and Phil lit a cigarillo.

Barnes drained the last of his drink. "I hear you lost a key witness in the Rhee case."

Phil nodded but offered nothing more. One had to be careful with Barnes. He was a friend but a journalist first. The waiter placed a fresh martini in front of Barnes. He raised the glass and sipped some off the top, then picked up the toothpick with the speared olive.

"Phil," he said, biting into the green olive, "can you tell me why the witness was blown?"

"Off the record?"

"Off the record," Barnes agreed.

Phil proceeded to relate the circumstances surrounding Mrs. Hwan's refusal to testify. Barnes sipped his drink and listened attentively.

The waiter placed their food, and Barnes immediately speared the shrimp, dipped it into red sauce and chewed it carefully with obvious relish. "Who do you think put the arm on Mrs. Hwan?"

"You tell me, Joe."

"Spooks." The word oozed out between fleshy pieces of shrimp. "Someone high up is wired to the Reverend Rhee."

"You mean someone in the intelligence community?"

"Right," Barnes replied as he shoved the shrimp bowl aside and smeared a glob of mayonnaise across the club sandwich.

Phil watched him attack the sandwich and said, "If you consider the FBI, CIA, DIA and NSA, Rhee could be connected to any one of two dozen well-placed spooks."

"Not necessarily," Barnes murmured.

Phil waited for the obese, red-faced man to continue. But Barnes was absorbed with his gin, bread and mayonnaise.

"What do you mean?" Phil prodded.

Flakes of chicken and bits of bacon clung to Barnes's greasy lips as he replied. "I received a call while you were in the hospital. The caller stated you were an alcoholic and had an altercation in Harvey's and on the following evening, while inebriated, parked illegally and wandered into the Lincoln Memorial, where you were assaulted by muggers." He belched softly. "My informant stated your blood analysis upon entry to the hospital indicated a high level of alcohol."

Phil's brain began to race and compute. The Harvey's Café incident was crucial. Had the bartender reported the English lit professor's wine dunking as an act perpetrated by Phil? Or had CIA Director Burgess sitting across the room noticed the wine pouring and assumed Phil had been involved? Or had the bartender and Burgess twisted the incident to suit their purposes? The hospital blood analysis was pure fabrication.

Phil drank the last of his coffee, lit a fresh cigarillo and leaned toward Barnes. "Joe, let me tell you what actually happened in Harvey's."

"Shoot," Barnes said as he gnawed at a handful of french fries.

Phil told him the story in detail down to the pioneer girl's vivid rejection of the great Russian writers and her pouring the wine over the professor's head.

He also told him that the CIA director was present and related his brief exchange with Burgess. He then recounted the events of the following night: his visit to Mrs. Hwan; the wild drive through the Virginia hills, culminating in the fight at the Reflecting Pool.

"Why did you go to the memorial at that hour?"

"I don't know. It was an impulse. I suppose I wanted some affirmation that the system still operates for the people."

Barnes pushed the plate away and lit a stubby cigar. "Only a goddamn fool would enter that Mall after midnight."

"I said it was an impulse—a reflex. Who called you about my drinking?"

"You know better than to ask me to reveal a source. Suffice to say it was someone in the agency."

Barnes spit a shred of tobacco onto the green carpet. "When you take on a man with Rhee's power, a man who controls the minds of two hundred thousand people, a man who you know is a KCIA operative, how can you assume there will be no resistance?"

"I expected resistance, but not agency break-ins, not torture of a key witness. And not personal assaults."

"Come on, Phil." Barnes waved his cigar. "Once Mrs. Hwan indicated Rhee was KCIA, you knew he was wired to our intelligence community."

Phil shook his head. "There are thousands of foreign agents operating in this city, but you can't assume they're connected to our intelligence community."

"Want some cheap advice?"

"That's why I suffered through the tuna salad."

The waiter came over and inquired about dessert. Barnes ordered espresso and a chocolate éclair. Phil ordered coffee. Barnes permitted the waiter to leave, then said, "Drop the case. Turn everything you have over to me—Rhee's tax reports; Mrs. Hwan's recorded testimony; the works. I'll see that it's published and expose the son of a bitch to public scrutiny. But cut off your investigation."

"You actually think they'd take me out?"

"Look, Phil, a few summers ago, not five blocks from here, they blew up the former Chilean ambassador, days before he was to testify about ITT's activities in Chile."

The coffee and éclair arrived. Barnes bit into the pastry and washed it down with the dark espresso. "A few summers ago a journalist friend of mine was blown to bits in Phoenix. You recall the case?"

"It's still going on."

"But not with him. He's dead. He stepped on a dozen toes in the state of Arizona. Now two weeks ago some spooks leaned on you—put you in the hospital. You're goddamn lucky they didn't break your jaw and open that old wound. You're lucky they only leaned on you. Next time—" Barnes shrugged.

"So I go back to white-collar crime," Phil said, "or illegal immigration, or whatever the spook community allows me to pursue."

"Something like that."

"Christ, Joe, if I had knuckled under in the past I would never have deported Carlo Carelli. I would not have cracked Koreagate."

"Where did Koreagate go?"

"Nowhere. But it did get public view."

"And?"

"Nothing."

"I rest my case."

Phil sipped his lukewarm coffee. "I'm not alone, Joe. Sid Greene of the FBI is spearheading the investigation."

"I still rest my case. It's a city of thieves, of intrigue, of treachery and insane ambition. Everyone wants to be Caesar. Look, you see that handsome lady over there?"

Barnes indicated an attractive blonde who was having lunch with a notorious gossip columnist.

He leaned forward and in a hushed voice said, "She blew a couple dozen congressmen. Videotaped them down to the last groan. And why? She wanted material for a book. It's a goddamn fucking asylum, and you're dealing with giants. Rhee was Park's man. He's now Chung's man. Korea is our ace ally in Asia. He's wired to the top."

"Maybe, but I'm not certain about President Chung's position on Rhee. Chung despises everything and everyone connected to the Park administration."

"Then why is Rhee still operating?" Barnes asked. "Those guys will put a hit or snatch on anyone. Like they did with Kimsan. What happened to him?"

"True enough, but I have this feeling that Chung perceives some ultimate personal gain in permitting Rhee's activities."

"What kind of gain?"

"I wish to Christ I knew." Phil called for a check, but Barnes grabbed his hand.

"The lunch is on me." He signed the check with a flourish and heaved himself up from the chair. As they filed out, Barnes said, "Can you imagine taping blow jobs for book material?"

They walked out of the National Press Building into the brilliant spring sunshine.

"Can I give you a lift?" Barnes asked.

"No, I'll walk." Phil paused. "Joe, if you were me, where would you look for Rhee's intelligence contact?"

"If I were you, I'd drop the case. But to answer your question"—they moved aside as a gaggle of Japanese tourists flooded by—"I would focus on what it is that Rhee could possibly have on the intelligence establishment. What is it that enables him to enjoy their protection? What piece of intrigue, sabotage or treachery could have brought him into collusion with someone at the controls?"

"It's got to be related to U.S.-Korean affairs," Phil said.

"I would say so," Barnes agreed. "Well, good luck, kiddo. And remember my offer. I'll run anything you give me."

"Thanks, Joe."

"Take care, Phil."

The bulky Pulitzer prizewinning journalist hailed a taxi and with great effort managed to climb inside. Phil started up Pennsylvania Avenue. He did not notice a tall man with cold black eyes watching him from the doorway of the dilapidated Willard Hotel.

Chapter Nine

They were gathered in the rear office of the small Colonial church in Middleburg, Virginia. The village sat in a shallow valley surrounded by rolling green hills and was one of several exclusive suburbs ringing the nation's capital.

The eight men seated around the long table represented the national leadership of the Moral Crusade. And with the sole exception of the Reverend Rhee all of them were Caucasian. The subject of their meeting dealt with their continuing efforts to censor the literature used in the nation's public schools. They had just ruled against Faulkner's *Sanctuary* as a glorification of violence, lawlessness and prostitution. Their objection to Fitzgerald's *Tender Is the Night* was being summarized as an "insidious sanction of alcoholism, adultery and incest." Their nominal leader, the Reverend Casper Farley, was about to call for a vote when Clay Sherman, minister from the state of Kentucky, raised his hand.

"Yes, Clay?"

"Ah have to object to the word 'incest.'"

"Why is that?" Farley asked.

"Well, where Ah come from, in the hill country of Kentucky, incest is regarded as more or less traditional."

A pall of silence fell over the room. The men looked to Farley, who finally said, "Clay here has a point. There are times when we must defer to regional customs. This sort of flexibility is required by any ecumenical organization."

"So moved," said the Reverend Rhee.

"Moved and accepted," Farley replied. "Now let's turn our attention to Hemingway's *The Sun Also Rises*."

The minister from Louisiana, who was also a Grand Dragon in the Ku Klux Klan, said, "Ah juss don't know

why Lady Brett keeps on sayin', 'I require a bath.' Is she
allud'n' to some female perversion performed in the tub?"

"Like what?" Farley inquired.

"Well, everyone knows young girls masturbate under
the faucets."

"You miss the point, Tom," Farley said. "The whole
premise of this novel is salacious. A man without testicles,
in love with a promiscuous woman—what do they do together?"

The pastor from Christ's Drive-In Church in Glendale,
California, said, "As far as I can tell, they don't do anything."

"That's exactly my point," Farley replied. "What would
any of us do if we had no balls and loved a woman with
round heels?"

The Grand Dragon from Louisiana drawled, "Ah guess
we'd have to eat pussy."

"Precisely," Farley agreed. "This piece of trash cleverly
sanctions the practice of cunnilingus."

"What exactly is cunnilingus?" asked the Kentuckian
Clay Sherman.

"It means eatin' pussy," the Grand Dragon explained.

"I can tell you, gentlemen," the Reverend Rhee said,
"this novel is already forbidden to my disciples."

"Well then," Farley said, "I think we're all agreed in
banning this title. Can I see a show of hands?"

The vote was unanimous.

"Good," Farley said. "Now let's move on to this leftist
glorification of the Spanish Civil War."

"What's that, Casper?" asked a reverend from Florida
who had just opened his eyes.

For Whom the Bell Tolls," Farley replied.

The men shifted the pile of books, looking for the Hemingway classic. A young boy wearing a black and white
smock entered the office and went over to the Reverend
Rhee. The boy leaned down and whispered in the Reverend's ear. The pudgy Korean rose and said, "Excuse me
for a moment, gentlemen."

Rhee walked up the aisle of the empty church toward
the entrance where his two black-suited bodyguards

waited. The larger of the two men, Colonel Kim Yee, met him halfway.

"Forgive me, sir."

"What is it?"

"Sir, our temple in the California desert was struck last night."

Rhee's small black eyes narrowed. "What do you mean?"

"Three men entered the counting room and severely beat our workers, forcing them to open the safe."

"How much was taken?"

"Close to three hundred thousand dollars."

"I trust the police were not called."

"No, sir."

"Can our disciples identify these thieves?"

"It is not necessary, sir," Colonel Yee replied. "The assailants left a message. They said you have a new partner in California. His name is Nick Carelli."

Chapter Ten

Dr. Belgrave's sprawling English Tudor estate draped itself across a hill rise in the exclusive suburb of Kenwood,
Maryland. The grounds were floodlit and patrolled by security guards and trained killer Dobermans.

The attorney general's limousine was parked alongside
Belgrave's dark green Bentley. Lights blazed from all
eighteen rooms of the mansion. The Doctor did not practice energy conservation.

Arthur Browning stood in the great high-ceilinged
study, admiring an Impressionist painting by Sisley. He
sipped a fine Napolean brandy and smoked a Cuban
cigar. He marveled at the extraordinary beauty of the
painting and wondered how the artist had managed to
catch the snow scene in such exquisite light. Browning
was alone, waiting for Belgrave, who had excused himself
to take a private phone call. The attorney general had
been apprehensive about requesting the meeting but after
much soul-searching decided the risk was worth taking.
He would somehow have to make his point without antag-
onizing Belgrave.

Browning turned as he heard the walnut doors open.
The Doctor's tall, thin frame and thick silver hair belied
his seventy-one years. His bright blue eyes were alert and
confident. He wore a red velvet smoking jacket and carried a snifter of brandy. He indicated two easy chairs and
smiled. "Sit down, Arthur. I'm sorry about the phone call.
It was the President."

The men sat facing each other. "Now, what disturbs
you, my friend?" Belgrave asked.

Browning examined the soft red glow at the tip of his
cigar. "You know, Eric, I have made a public statement

about the immediate need to restrict the Freedom of Information Act."

"Duly noted and much appreciated, Arthur." Belgrave waited patiently for the small, antiseptic man to summon his courage and address the issue at hand.

The attorney general glanced up at the cream-colored ceiling, then knocked an ash off his cigar, cleared his throat and said, "I am aware of the intricacies of the Rhee case, and I respect all that is at stake—but the brutality used against Phil Ricker is something I cannot tolerate."

Belgrave nodded and gently asked, "That incident occurred two weeks ago. Why do you come to me with it now?"

"You were in Moscow for ten days, and I was reluctant to disturb you on your return."

"That was thoughtful of you, Arthur," Belgrave replied with amused annoyance. He swirled the gold-colored brandy in the large snifter.

Browning spoke nervously. "But I believe the assault on Phil Ricker was ill-conceived and counterproductive. It will tend only to fortify his obsession with this case."

"I have no interest in Ricker's psychological problems. And I despise the Reverend Rhee," Belgrave replied. "But I have to protect him. These are matters that affect the stability of our intelligence community. And that means national security."

"You're saying the end justifies the means."

"Since when has it been otherwise?" Belgrave got to his feet and paced the Oriental carpet for a moment. "Let me tell you something, Arthur. By acquiring those files, we have neutralized Ricker's key witness. We also determined there was nothing in the files that related to Gemstone. In one clean surgical stroke we protected the national security."

With the mention of Gemstone, the attorney general perceived an opportunity to shift gears, to continue the debate without focusing on the Rhee case. "Why would you assume Gemstone has any connection to Ricker's investigation?" he asked.

Belgrave swallowed some brandy, and his voice lost its scolding tone. "After Hoover's death there were persistent rumors that Gemstone had found its way into the hands of

the late Korean President Park. Rhee was Park's man in
America. The Gemstone file reportedly contains data on
the collusion of our intelligence apparatus with the underworld. It also indicts prominent bankers, industrialists and
internationalists. I could not assume that Ricker hadn't
stumbled upon Gemstone."

Browning puffed nervously on his cigar and laced his
voice with innocence. "Eric, for nine years, since Hoover's
death, we've all heard of this mythical Gemstone. Yet no
one's ever seen it."

"I've seen a portion of it."

The admission startled Browning. "Under what circumstances?" he asked.

"Hoover himself sent me a copy of a section. That
pansy son of a bitch used a portion of Gemstone to silence
me. He had a detailed transcript of a meeting I conducted
with the then godfather Don Carlo Carelli." Belgrave
paused, lit his pipe and then continued. "Mind you, the
meeting was undertaken in the national interest." He removed the pipe and used it as a pointer. "And nothing
takes precedence when the security of this nation is in
peril. And that dictum holds true for your zealous colleague Philip Ricker."

"For God's sake, Eric, I'm on your side. I always have
been."

"I'd like to believe that, Arthur."

"You have no reason not to. I just pointed out that violence is counterproductive."

Belgrave walked up to the diminutive, pale man. His
voice was cold. "I'm telling you to find a way to remove
Ricker from this case."

"That may not be possible," Browning said.

Belgrave's cheeks were magenta-colored, and his blue
eyes shone brightly. "You had better find a way. This
Rhee business has gone far enough. My energies cannot
be expended on irrelevant issues. Do you realize where
this nation stands at this moment in history? At the brink!
Pakistan has the H-bomb; it is presently manufacturing
nuclear warheads for Libya and Iraq. The last hope for
mankind's survival resides in an American-Soviet alliance.
Together we must pulverize those countries and thereby
insure the continuance of life on this planet. No one un-

derstands; no one wishes to understand. And you, Arthur, of all people, should not create problems for me. We still have the Yellow Peril in Asia to deal with!"

"You mean China?" Browning asked quietly.

"I mean Chung! Our intelligence operatives in Tokyo informed us that he has visions of reviving the old Japanese Greater Asia Co-Prosperity Sphere, an industrial colossus combining Japan, a unified Korea and the People's Republic of China. It was the same obsession that afflicted Park."

He paused. "You must always remember, Arthur, I alone stand between that malignant Asian despot and the preservation of American industrial supremacy."

Belgrave sipped his brandy and said, "I never wanted to carry this cross. I would have preferred life on the Vermont farm my father left me." He turned to Browning. The Doctor's bright blue eyes were misty, and his voice mellowed. "My wife was killed flying to see me. I was at a NATO conference at the time. The weather was foul. I warned her not to come—"

"I remember, Eric," Browning said softly.

"The curious thing is her death only confirmed the importance of my work," Belgrave continued. "I know that's difficult to understand, but it's true. Then, when my son was taken from me, when Roger fell in Vietnam, I realized a divine light was testing me, demanding sacrifice of me. I knew then it was my destiny to bear the cross of mankind's survival. I have paid a terrible price. But no man can argue with divine Providence."

For the first time Browning believed the Doctor was clinically insane. But you could not indict a man for geopolitical theories or bizarre religious beliefs. Nevertheless, it was chillingly clear to the attorney general that Dr. Belgrave's messianic fervor represented a distinct threat to the security of the nation.

"I didn't mean to upset you, Eric," Browning said warily. "I'm sorry if I did. I'll do my best to get Phil Ricker off the Rhee case." He paused. "You have my word."

Belgrave put his bony hand on Browning's shoulder. "I'm not asking for Ricker's removal with extreme prejudice. Only his removal. Do we understand each other?"

"Yes, Eric. We certainly do."

*   *   *

On the drive back to Washington, Browning kept turning over the same riddle: What act of treachery had
locked Belgrave and Rhee into their unholy alliance? But
the answer was unfathomable. The attorney general
turned his thoughts to Gemstone. The Doctor's admission
that Hoover had used a portion of its contents against him
confirmed Gemstone's existence. The missing Hoover file
was no myth. It was the key to Belgrave's demise. It was
the scepter of power.

Chapter Eleven

Phil paced the second-floor den and scratched at the elastic brace binding his rib cage. The skin beneath the brace was irritated, producing a maddening itch. The pain at the base of his neck had subsided, but in moments of tension it would snake down through his shoulders and lower back.

He walked slowly up to the bay window overlooking the street. Old-fashioned lamps illuminated the pink magnolia trees. The parked cars were deserted, and there were no suspicious pedestrians. Perhaps the surveillance had been called off, although that afternoon he'd noticed a tall, muscular man loitering in the street just outside the Justice Building.

The phones in Phil's house and office were "swept" daily, and the front and rear doors to his Georgetown house were equipped with new double-bolt locks. He no longer used his Porsche. The thought of turning on the ignition and risking an explosion was too nerve-racking.

Greene picked him up each morning in a different car taken from the FBI motor pool. Phil still refused the protection of federal marshals and would not carry a gun. He could not accommodate the idea that as the deputy attorney general of the United States he had to arm himself against agencies of his own government.

Phil went over to the wet bar and mixed a weak vodka and tonic. He had taken an ampicillin six hours ago and thought he could chance a small amount of alcohol. The stay in the hospital was still a blur, but he remembered the call from his ex-wife. He had assured Audrey it wasn't necessary for her to come down to Washington—he had survived the mugging without suffering major injury. The gun lobby girl Gloria Robbins had brought him a book,

and he was surprised at the quality of her selection. It
was a thick volume of Irwin Shaw's short stories, and he
had thoroughly enjoyed the collection. Sid Greene had
visited him daily and assured him that the tax evasion
phase of the Rhee case was continuing, although the
grand jury date had been postponed. Arthur Browning
had appeared once and, after the amenities, rigorously
questioned Phil about his motive for visiting the Lincoln
Memorial. The story released to the press had cloaked the
incident in the guise of an ordinary mugging.

Only one TV newscaster had raised the question of why
the deputy attorney general visited the memorial after
midnight. But the incident had disappeared from the
news, replaced by the story of the handsome blonde who
taped her sexual bouts with a wide variety of prominent
congressmen.

Phil walked up to the corkboard attached to the den
wall and examined the card graph.

He had designed the graph with names and events beginning with Koreagate in 1977. But a nagging doubt
about the chronology disturbed him. Something was missing. He scrutinized the index cards carefully.

He had set the events down on a yellow legal pad.
Each event raised its own questions, and the answers
defied logical connection.

1. Koreagate: *Deal effected to limit Kimsan's testimony
   —negotiated by CIA-KCIA.*

2. Kimsan: *Last seen in London summer of 1978—reported to be Korean conduit of heroin traffic moving
   from Asia to Italy. Unconfirmed.*

3. Soon Yi Sonji: *Worked Koreagate bribing of congressmen with Tongsun. Refused to testify. Recalled to
   Seoul in summer of '79. Surfaces again in January
   1981. Currently attached to Cultural Affairs Section,
   Korean Embassy.*

4. Reverend Rhee: *Arrived U.S. 1975. Naturalized
   1977 by special congressional act. KCIA operative.
   Formed the Universal Order of Buddha. Vast hold-
   ings, 200,000 disciples. Tax-free foundation funds
   used illegally to support politicians favorable to
   Korea. Unaccounted-for income. Does it go to Chung
   in Seoul? Two bodyguards reported to be colonels in*

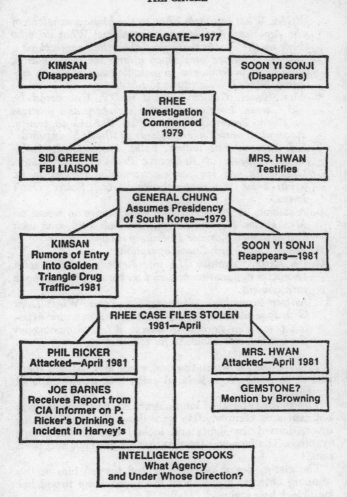

KOREAGATE—1977

KIMSAN (Disappears)

SOON YI SONJI (Disappears)

RHEE Investigation Commenced 1979

SID GREENE FBI LIAISON

MRS. HWAN Testifies

GENERAL CHUNG Assumes Presidency of South Korea—1979

KIMSAN Rumors of Entry into Golden Triangle Drug Traffic—1981

SOON YI SONJI Reappears—1981

RHEE CASE FILES STOLEN 1981—April

PHIL RICKER Attacked—April 1981

MRS. HWAN Attacked—April 1981

JOE BARNES Receives Report from CIA Informer on P. Ricker's Drinking & Incident in Harvey's

GEMSTONE? Mention by Browning

INTELLIGENCE SPOOKS What Agency and Under Whose Direction?

KCIA. *What connects Rhee to the highest echelons of the American intelligence community? What does he have on the spooks that affords him their protection?*

5. Chung: *Assumes presidency after Park assassination. Had to be instrumental in assigning Sonji to D.C. embassy. What is his attitude to Rhee?*

6. Mrs. Hwan: *Comes forward in '79. Uncovered by Sid Greene. Former executive secretary and mistress to Rhee. Tortured in April '81. Refuses to testify. Recognizes one of her assailants as Rhee's bodyguard.*

7. Sid Greene: *FBI liaison. Solid. Professional. Ambitious. Appears at Reflecting Pool night of attack. Claims he had my car electronically bugged so he could track my whereabouts. True? False? Don't know.*

8. Assailants at Pool: *Possibly same men who assaulted Mrs. Hwan. Big one American? Small wiry, man with karate moves. Korean? Definitely spooks.*

9. Stolen Case Files: *Spook operation.*

10. Joe Barnes: *Admits CIA informer phoned him with character defamation material on me confirming spook involvement.*

11. Arthur Browning: *Mentions Gemstone. Why? Does Gemstone file exist? If so, what does it contain? Missing piece that perhaps connects all? Is Browning on the level? Don't know. So far seems straight.*

Phil slumped down in the desk chair and thought there had to be some single isolated event that would tie it all together.

The sudden sound of loud chimes startled him. He was not expecting company. He went down the stairs into the foyer, doused the lights and looked through the door's eyepiece. The face was familiar, but its presence surprised him.

The sweet, heavy perfume drifted toward him as the stunning Oriental girl entered the foyer. Sonji tossed her long black hair and said, "Hello, Phil."

They faced each other in the darkened hallway.

"Are you going to ask me in?"

"Why didn't you call?"

"I don't trust phones."

"Were you followed?"

"I don't think so."

He snapped on the hall light, and Sonji noticed the residual bruise marks on his face. She followed him upstairs, thinking how much he had aged in the four years since Koreagate.

She draped her coat over the back of a chair and sat on the arm of a white sofa.

"What would you like?" he asked.

"A brandy, please."

"Soda?"

"Straight."

He freshened his own drink and poured a Hennessy for her. He wondered about the motive for her visit, but there was no point in questioning a gift horse. He handed the drink to her and raised his glass. "Cheers."

She glanced at the card graph on the wall.

"Trying to put the pieces together," he explained.

She examined the chronology of the cards for a moment, then said, "I have personnel files in my handbag that prove the Reverend Rhee's bodyguards are colonels in the KCIA."

"That won't restore my case against Rhee."

"Perhaps you can release these documents to the press."

"I'm not interested in embarrassing Rhee. I want him in prison."

She turned again to the diagrammed cards.

Phil studied her profile: the high, perfect cheekbones and the full curve of her lips. He wondered about the true motives for her visit.

"I've been ordered to help you," she said.

"By whom?"

"President Chung."

"Why?"

"I don't ask questions. I follow orders."

"How is that big bastard?"

"He is well."

"I read about the student riots."

"President Chung is expert in dealing with students."

"Yeah, I'll bet he is," Phil said caustically. "I remember a village in the central highlands of Vietnam. Chung's men found a warm kettle. It was the wrong time of day for that kettle to be warm. They suspected an old woman had cooked rice for the VC. They blew her head off—and burned the village. Hell of a man, Chung."

"He is a strong man," she replied, turning her attention back to the card graph. There was a long moment before she said, "There is a card missing."

Phil walked over and stood beside her.

She pointed to the center cards of "Koreagate—'77" and "Rhee Investigation Commenced 1979." "Between these cards the most crucial event is missing."

"What's that?"

"The murder of President Park."

There was a moment of silence as Phil stared at the card graph. Sonji glared at him as if she had given him new life and he were unappreciative. She walked to the bar and poured another brandy.

"What makes that event critical?"

"Do you remember the circumstances surrounding the assassination?" she asked.

"I think so. Park was hit by the chief of Korean Central Intelligence—Kyu."

"Commander Kyu," she corrected him.

"Right—so what?"

"The CIA formed, organized and administered the KCIA—it still does. Killing the president of Korea could not have been undertaken without prior knowledge and consent of the CIA."

Phil tossed that around for a moment then asked, "When was Park killed?"

"The night of October twenty-sixth, 1979," she replied.

"Which means a meeting had to have taken place in Washington long before with all our security agencies present."

Sonji nodded. "That meeting took place July fifth, 1979, in the Glass Room beneath the CIA building. If the killing of Park had misfired or led to civil war in the South, the North Koreans might have moved against us—and your country would have been at war."

"I remember the press reports," Phil said. "All our forces were on full alert that night."

"As were ours."

"Meaning the execution of Park was planned and approved by someone at the top of our intelligence pyramid."

Her oval eyes were enormous, and a blue cloud of smoke hovered over her head.

"But how does this tie into the Reverend Rhee?" Phil asked.

"The Reverend was then a KCIA courier. He was at the meeting with your security people when they planned the assassination."

"How does Chung know that?"

"Commander Kyu confessed that information while undergoing torture."

Phil paced for a moment, then said, "A meeting like that would involve the CIA, DIA, NSA and State Intelligence, the directors of Southeast Asia, Soviet and Eastern Europe, and probably the chairman of the National Security Council. Rhee may be blackmailing any one of six different agencies."

"Or all of them," she added.

Phil poured fresh vodka over ice. He no longer worried about mixing the alcohol with ampicillin. He was exhilarated by the information and the presence of the dazzling Oriental girl. He stared at her for a moment. "There's still a missing piece."

"Yes?"

"Commander Kyu was obviously approved by our security people to replace Park. Why was he arrested, tortured and executed? What went wrong? How did Chung take over?"

"I helped him," she said.

Phil stared at her in disbelief. "You set Kyu up?"

"And Park."

"For Chung?"

"Yes."

"Why? What was in it for you?"

"Nothing. I follow orders."

"That sounds familiar," he said sarcastically.

"I had no choice," she replied.

"Can you tell me how Park was killed?"

"It was a bloody night. A night of horror. I do not wish to speak of it."

He looked at her and thought of the incredible treachery and violence she had witnessed and wondered how she managed to retain her surface serenity. "I guess there's not a chance in hell you would go before a grand jury."

"How can you ask me that?" she replied incredulously.

"Easy." Phil walked up to her. "How long can you serve a man who holds your country in an iron grip? It's your generation who will do the dying in the next war. For chrissake, Sonji, there must be something inside you that's still alive."

"I feel nothing. I am nothing. I would sleep with you if ordered or kill you if ordered. I would take my own life if ordered."

He wondered what nightmarish history had reduced her to this robotlike state.

Sonji studied his bruised irregular features. She had always considered him interesting since Koreagate days. He wasn't pretty like Nick Carelli, but there was something special about a man who placed his life in jeopardy for no personal gain.

She removed two files from her tote bag. "Here are the KCIA histories of Rhee's bodyguards. Use them as you wish."

"Sonji, is there anything in KCIA files that refers to Gemstone?"

"I've never seen that word."

"Has Chung ever mentioned Gemstone?"

"Not to me."

"Is there anything I should know about my boss, Arthur Browning?"

"No."

"What about Sid Greene?"

"I know nothing of those men."

He placed his hands on her shoulders. "I appreciate your help."

She smiled the kind of smile that masked some terrible secret. She kissed his cheek, turned and left.

Phil heard the front door open and close. He walked to the window and watched her enter the small Mustang and pull away from the curb. He waited, checking to see if she was followed, but there was no visible surveillance.

Phil crossed to the desk, sat down and made out a five

by seven index card that read: "Park Assassinated October 26, 1979." He then marked another card: "Intelligence Chiefs July 1979." Under that heading he jotted down a series of names:

CIA—Burgess (still in charge).

DIA—Gruenwald (still in charge).

NSA—Smithfield (deceased).

Presidential Adviser—Dr. Eric Belgrave
(now chairman National Security Council).

Director Intelligence, East Asia and Pacific—?

Director Intelligence, Soviet Union and Eastern Europe—?

Director National Reconnaissance Office—?

He would have to get the last three names from FBI records. But one of those names had directed the theft of his files, authorized the torture of Mrs. Hwan and dispatched the two men who had assaulted him at the Reflecting Pool.

The conspiratorial meeting of July 5, 1979, had to require the presence of Robert Burgess, CIA director of Covert Operations. It would make sense to start with Burgess. He was present that night at Harvey's Café. Joe Barnes said a CIA informer had reported Phil's drinking habits. Yes, Burgess was the first step.

Phil placed the pen down and rubbed his hand wearily across his eyes. He picked up his drink and had barely tasted the cold vodka when the incredible irony of his situation struck him. His actions were being directed by the man in the Blue House, 12,000 miles away, President Yi Chung.

The angry ring of the phone jarred his thoughts. It was Sid Greene. "Did I wake you?"

"No."

"One hour ago Mrs. Hwan was found floating faceup in Chesapeake Bay."

Phil felt a severe line of pain shoot from his neck down

his spinal column. His pulse raced, and a red flush appeared on his cheeks.

"You there?" Sid asked.

"Yeah, I'm here."

"Medical examiner's preliminary report indicates she was killed elsewhere and dumped in the bay."

"Killed how?"

"A thirty-eight slug behind her left ear. We'll have a complete report by noon."

"Who's on it?"

"Metro squad."

"Pick me up early, Sid. I want to go down to the morgue."

"Okay."

The line clicked off. And Phil remembered Mrs. Hwan's words: "You can't protect your own President."

Chapter Twelve

The South Korean Embassy is on the eastern curve of Sheridan Circle and Massachusetts Avenue. The three-story undistinguished gray-cement structure is in perfect harmony with the character of the nation it represents: squat, tough and ominous.

Three men were gathered in the first-floor study. The Reverend Rhee stood in front of a massive marble fireplace. Dr. Eric Belgrave faced him across the room. And in the shadow of the alcove, Matt Crowley watched the men in silence. Above them, high up on the wall in a gold frame, was a huge black-and-white photograph of President Chung.

The Reverend had just concluded his remarks.

"You're certain the name was Carelli?" Belgrave asked.

The fat, sweating face nodded. "Nick Carelli."

"All right, I will look into the matter."

Rhee moved with surprising agility. He came up to Belgrave, his waxy skin flushed. "Looking into the matter is not enough. I've had two of my churches violated and six of my disciples badly beaten. I will not abide any delays in the resolution of this matter."

Belgrave's blue eyes smoldered with anger, but his voice remained calm and matter-of-fact. "My dear Reverend, you must be aware by now that I have colossal contempt for you. I might even go so far as to say I am appalled just being in the same room with you. You are the most despicable of all men. You trade on the ignorance, fear and superstition of our youth. You wear the mantle of Buddha while you milk the funds of the poor and the desperate. You pollute the spirit of this nation. And I find it unbearable that I am obliged to protect your interests. However, the security of the nation dictates my actions. Therefore, I will accede to your request. But never—never give me ultimatums. Do you understand?"

Matt Crowley silently observed the fat man's reaction.

"You do not impress me," Rhee replied. "You will perform this task for me because of what I know. None of us are required to admire one another, only to protect our mutual interests. And at this moment my interests are being invaded by the American underworld. You control them, and you do business with them. I want this man Carelli stopped. And your 'looking into the matter' is insufficient. I can force you to take immediate steps, and you know very well what I mean."

Belgrave examined the bowl of his pipe. "You're quite right, Reverend." He looked at the watery brown eyes in the round flat face. "But let me remind you—there is a classic method of dealing with blackmail."

"Don't threaten me, Doctor. There is a document in proper hands. And should I meet with a violent end, that document will be made public. I refer to the meeting in the Glass Room, July fifth, 1979."

"I did not threaten you, sir," Belgrave replied. "I merely reminded you there are limits beyond which I will not go. Now rest assured, Reverend, the matter will be handled forthwith."

"I appreciate that, Doctor."

"Is there anything else?"

"Yes," Rhee said. "I think it would be in all our interests to have Ricker removed from his investigation of my activities."

"But, my dear man," Belgrave replied, "his only witness, the late Mrs. Hwan, is no longer a factor. And without that lady, Mr. Ricker has no case."

The fat man looked directly at the security chief. "There are matters above and beyond my KCIA involvement, matters that would interest the IRS."

"Yes." Belgrave sighed. "Well, I have obtained assurance from the attorney general that Ricker will shortly be reassigned."

"Thank you, Doctor."

The bronze statue of General Sheridan in the center of the circle gazed sternly down at Crowley and Belgrave as they entered the chauffeured limousine. The official car glided past the gold lions fronting the Embassy of Kenya and proceeded down Massachusetts Avenue.

In the rear seat, Belgrave whispered, "Matt . . ."

"Yes, sir?"

"Get the name of the Reverend Rhee's attorney."

"To what purpose?"

"If the good Reverend has any documented proof of my involvement in Park's assassination, he would undoubtedly have placed it in the hands of his attorney."

"Yes, sir, but—" Crowley stopped.

"But what?" Dr. Belgrave asked.

"Wouldn't that document be in a vault?"

The Doctor shook his head. "Vaults are automatically sealed upon the death of their owners. There is extensive legal red tape before they are released. No, the Reverend would want those documents in safe hands—wise hands."

Crowley nodded, cracked his knuckles and asked, "What about the Carelli situation?"

"I will arrange a meeting with Victor Maldonado."

"That's dangerous," Crowley advised.

"Ah, Matt, you're a man amongst men. Your concern for me is the bright light in my life. The meeting will be out of the country."

Chapter Thirteen

The president of the Republic of Korea, the former General Yi Chung, stared out the open windows, contemplating the Garden of Four Seasons. The evergreens of winter, the water lilies of summer and the persimmons of fall were barren of color. It was the season of azaleas. The president watched the aged gardener in his traditional black robe and stovepipe hat gently troweling the earth. Chung thought he must remember to ask the old man to plant something that would bloom all year round, negating the unlucky number four. Chung drew hard on the American cigarette and hated himself for it; he was consuming more than three packs a day. And in the two years of his presidency severe lines had etched their way across his flat, pugilistic face. He tossed the cigarette out the window and instantly craved another.

He turned from the window and glanced at a framed photograph on the far wall. It was a picture of himself and the newly elected American President taken in the Oval Office. He had been the first foreign leader to visit the President despite the vociferous objections of Dr. Eric Belgrave, who had once again survived a change in administrations. The Doctor's current title was chairman of the National Security Council. His liver-spotted hands were once again on the levers of power.

President Chung leaned back in the big leather chair and stared up at the tiger heads carved into the high oval ceiling. The destruction of Belgrave was a challenge he relished. His removal was a patriotic necessity. The Doctor embraced the view that Korea be maintained in a dependent posture: armed, warlike, Spartan, pro-American, but primitive. KCIA reports from the Korean Embassy in Washington indicated Belgrave had argued that American auto, steel and electronics industries could not tolerate another Japan in the Far East. Well, Chung mused, the Doctor was in for a surprise.

He leaned forward, picked another cigarette out of the burnished gold case, lit it and watched the blue smoke drift out toward the open windows. Yes, Belgrave was marked, along with the Reverend Rhee. Chung had taken subtle, surreptitious measures against the Christian movement in Korea, while permitting the obese Reverend Rhee to continue his evangelical activities in America. The spider crawling through Chung's brain spun the delicate strands that would trap Belgrave and Rhee in the same web. And Soon Yi Sonji operating out of the Korean Embassy in Washington was the spider's messenger. She had achieved contact with Nick Carelli, the California underworld figure. She had given Phil Ricker the key piece to the Belgrave-Rhee connection. The first strands of the lacy web were in place.

The buzzer on his huge desk sounded. Chung pressed a button releasing the lock on the great oak doors. His executive secretary, Kim Won, entered the presidential office. Won was the same officer who had escorted Sonji home the night of Park's murder. He was slight of build but wiry, and his curving black eyes were bright and alert. He walked quickly up to Chung and placed a small tape recorder on the glass top of the desk.

"Sit down, Captain." The President still referred to Won by his former military title. Chung had replaced Park's old palace security force with his own trusted comrades of the Tiger Division. Some 6,000 civil servants of Park's regime had been fired, and 2,000 members of Kyu's former KCIA staff languished in military prisons. In his two years in office Chung had sifted leftists, intellectuals and Christian libertarians from their posts at all major universities. But despite those measures, there had been student riots at Seoul's major universities.

Chung suppressed the uprisings with characteristic brutality. He could not understand what it was the students wanted. Freedom and progress were mutually exclusive. He had secretly begun to sympathize with the positions taken by former President Park. The nation had to be kept on course; and democracy was as grave a threat to stability as was the external threat of communism.

Won waited patiently for the president to speak. He knew that of late Chung fell into sudden periods of meditation.

The president crushed his cigarette out and came slowly around the desk. He placed his big hand on the secretary's shoulder. "So this is the tape that has taken twenty-six months to uncover."

"Yes, sir. It is apparent from the tape that Edgar Hoover was the only American official Park trusted and respected."

"We knew from Park's file," Chung replied. "Hoover made six state visits to Seoul at Park's invitation." His hand fell from Won's shoulder. He lit an unfiltered American cigarette and glanced at a bronze plaque on the wall. The inscription testified to General Chung's valor during his service in Vietnam. It was signed by Lyndon B. Johnson.

"Mr. President, what led you to believe this tape would be hidden in Park's tomb?" Won asked.

"It was the voice of Buddha," Chung replied.

Won shifted nervously in his chair. He knew Park's tomb was the last logical place to look for the tape. The young man did not believe in Buddhism or any other theology, and he regarded the president's mysticism as a danger to the nation.

"When was this recording made?" Chung inquired.

"On May fifteenth, 1971—one year before Hoover died. Shall I play it?"

The president ignored his aide's question: "Where was this recorded?"

"In this office."

"Did Hoover know he was being taped?"

"I doubt it, sir."

"Why?"

"History tells us otherwise. The recording bug was planted in Park's office by agents of the CIA in 1967." Won continued, "The American ambassador, Porter, admitted that fact. But the Americans did not know Park was aware of the tap and had carefully edited the tapes for his own purposes."

"How do you come by this information?"

"It is contained in Park's secret papers."

"Play the tape, Captain."

Won pressed the red button activating the tape, and they fell silent, waiting to hear the voices of the murdered Korean president and the former director of the American Federal Bureau of Investigation.

Hoover's hoarse, reedy voice was the first to be heard. *In my long tenure as chief of the Federal Bureau of Investigation, I compiled extensive intelligence data on government officials, elected and appointed. I also gathered reports on internationalists, civil servants, industrialists, journalists, educators and the military.*

Park's response was innocence laced with Oriental humility. *But, sir, all this surely could not be contained in Gemstone.*

Hoover chuckled. *No, my dear friend. Gemstone is a composite of critical data principally exposing the collusion of the American overworld with the American underworld, dating back to 1934.*

What names would one find in Gemstone?

Quite a variety, Mr. President.

It would be helpful to me, dear friend, to acquire those names.

Yes, Hoover responded softly. *I'm certain it would be.*

Park did not press the point, and there was a pause, punctuated by the squeaking sound of a chair rocking back and forth. Chung believed it to be Park's chair, the one still in use behind the presidential desk. The periodic squeaks stopped, and Park's voice humbly inquired, *Excellency, are you able to tell me if Gemstone in any way implicates Dr. Eric Belgrave?*

Hoover's response was immediate. *The data on Dr. Belgrave contained in the Gemstone file would prove fatal to his career. As a matter of fact, on occasion I used a portion of its contents.* The sound of liquid being poured into a glass rose from the tape, and Hoover's voice seemed to smile. *This is truly excellent wine, Mr. President. It has a marvelous bite.*

Park spoke, but for the first time the Oriental humility was missing. *The wine is made in the vineyards of Chunchon. You see, my friend, we are not so primitive, contrary to the stated beliefs of certain American political figures.*

You mean people like Eric Belgrave? Hoover asked.

Precisely, Park replied. *This Gemstone file fascinates me, Excellency. What do you intend to do with it?*

Hoover coughed twice. *That file has permitted me to govern the actions of a wide variety of individuals in the American power structure. For thirty years, sir, I have guarded the American store. Upon my death Gemstone will be destroyed with the rest of my files.* There was a pause as Hoover audibly swallowed some more yakju wine. *You see, Mr. President, there is no one I trust. No one I can pass the torch of power to.*

We are not in dissimilar positions, Park replied. *That is why I bear the heavy burden of this office.* The iron could now be heard in Park's voice. *I stand alone against leftist students. I stand alone against labor dissidents. I stand alone against the Communist hordes massed at our very gates.* There was a pause, and in subdued fashion Park said, *But without firm American support . . .* His voice trailed off.

Chung admired the slain president's tactic. Hoover was famous for his rigid authoritarian views. The two men were political clones. Park was weaving a perfect web around the American, and the strong yakju wine was part of that web. Hoover's alcoholic excesses were well known to the KCIA.

The sound of pouring liquid once again emanated from the tape. Seconds later Hoover spoke. His voice was god-like. *Mr. President, rest assured that as long as I am alive the Korean people will have total American support.* There was a pause, followed by Park's response.

But we all face our eternal reward, and the Belgraves walk among us. He and others wish us to remain primitive dependents of American charity, while our brave soldiers guard the very frontier of American interests in Asia. Yet we are denied sophisticated weapons systems. We beg for monetary grants. We undertake a Spartan existence while our soldiers fight alongside your men in Vietnam. We, Excellency, come to your side at a time of peril, yet we are denied the true relationship of an honored ally.

There was a long beat of silence as if a portion of the tape had been erased.

A beam of sunlight streamed through the open windows, producing a perfect cone of light on the Oriental rug. Chung recognized the brilliant circle as a good omen. He crushed his cigarette out in the cavity of a jade elephant ashtray.

Hoover's voice came on suddenly. *There is truth and wisdom in what you say, Mr. President. You have my word that upon my death the Gemstone file will be placed in your hands.*

The sound of Park's rising from his chair was unmistakable. *How would this be achieved?*

You must designate a courier you trust.

I have such a man, Park replied.

Then it is done.

The gratitude of the Korean people is yours eternally, Excellency.

On the contrary, Mr. President. The gratitude is mine. I can go to my grave with the knowledge that my lifelong political beliefs will be preserved in your hands.

Iron hands, Excellency—iron hands. Park's voice fairly oozed. *Come now, we will lunch. I have arranged certain amusements in your honor.*

Won pressed the stop button on the small Japanese recorder and got to his feet. "Mr. President, the KCIA files covering 1971 and 1972 clearly indicate that Kimsan was the Gemstone courier."

"We do not require files to arrive at that conclusion," Chung replied. "Gemstone was the sole factor for Kimsan's survival. It was the reason Park protected him through Koreagate and, in all probability, the motive for taking Kimsan from London in '78 and placing him in the drug traffic of the Golden Triangle."

"It is fortunate we did not eliminate him."

The president's crafty black eyes narrowed. "Why?"

"So long as Kimsan possessed that file his life was secure," Won stated. "He never passed the Gemstone file to Park." The presidential secretary beamed, proud of his analytical response.

A small red warning light flickered way back in Chung's consciousness. Won would have to be reckoned with. It would be prudent to place the ambitious young man under surveillance. The president spoke softly. "Your thesis is correct, Captain. But Kimsan is not alive by virtue of good fortune. I perceived a value to his continued good health."

There was an unmistakable reprimand in Chung's statement that was not lost on his executive secretary. He eyed Won with a cold, brutal stare but affected a small smile. "This day is a gift from Buddha—let us walk in his holy sunshine."

●

They strolled through the manicured presidential grounds, passing the three-story pagoda where Park had been assassinated. The former Angel Cloud house was now a temple. A large gold statue of Buddha guarded the entrance. Buddha's palm was raised in eternal peace.

The president and his aide were followed at a distance by five soldiers of the Tiger Division. Black-helmeted parachutists manned watchtowers commanding a view of the Blue House and beyond to the slopes of Pugak Mountain. Two Huey helicopters beat the air 800 feet above the compound. But the heavy security did not diminish the serenity of the Garden of Four Seasons. Chung walked up to the Buddha and stared at him silently for a moment. Won watched the muscular president meditate and felt drops of sweat leaking from his armpits. He was tense and disappointed that Chung had not praised him for discovering the Hoover tape.

The president turned from Buddha and resumed walking. "Tell me, Captain, do the men of the security force pray?"

"Twice daily, Mr. President."

Chung stopped to stare at a blue jay perched on the branch of a pine tree. He spoke to Won, but his eyes remained fixed on the blue jay. The color blue on a winged creature was a good omen. "I understand they killed Mrs. Hwan."

"Yes, sir."

Chung nodded and with satisfaction said, "Killing Mrs.

Hwan was unnecessary. Dr. Belgrave is beginning to make faulty decisions."

The wings of the blue jay beat suddenly, and the bird flashed through the brilliant sunshine. The president resumed his measured pace, following the winding path through the gardens.

A half mile up ahead a jeep with four security soldiers came out of a thick stand of pines. Chung checked his watch; the mobile patrol was precisely on schedule.

"Sir," Won asked, "why did you not have Sonji inform Ricker that it is Dr. Belgrave who supports Rhee?"

"I want Ricker to sow suspicion among all three American intelligence chiefs. The same web can hold many flies." Chung paused. "Did you see the blue jay, Captain?"

Won was startled by the question and found himself speechless.

"I asked if you had seen the blue jay."

"No, sir. I saw no blue jay."

"A pity."

The president turned and squeezed Won's narrow shoulder. "Never assume any action I undertake on behalf of the nation is merely good fortune."

Beads of sweat oozed out of Won's forehead and ran down his face.

"Do you understand me, Captain?"

"Yes, sir."

"Good." The president's menacing black eyes softened. "Freshen yourself, Captain. We meet in fifteen minutes in my private dining room."

Chung started back toward the converted temple. The circle of sunlight on the rug and the blue jay were Buddha's messengers. It was a divine moment. The spider would sleep while he prayed.

Chapter Fourteen

Yellow flashes of lightning flickered against a leaden sky and rolling thunder cracked ominously over the Virginia hills. It was as if a great artillery duel were raging at the gates of the nation's capital. Only the rhythmic snap of windshield wipers against sheets of summer rain dispelled the warlike illusion.

Sid Greene drove the black Mustang carefully along the rain-swept highway. The digital clock on the dashboard read 11:08 A.M. They had been driving for fifteen minutes and had not exchanged a word. Sid stole a quick glance at Phil and decided to break the silence.

"Get off the cross. She was marked." Sid's voice was soothing. "No one could have saved her."

Phil nodded but did not respond. He had tried to obliterate the image of Mrs. Hwan's violated flesh, but her accusatory eyes penetrated his consciousness. They were like two black pearls staring out of a frozen milky substance, condemning him for failing to protect her.

Phil had not seen a murdered human being since Vietnam, and the torn body of Mrs. Hwan reminded him of fallen comrades in a war everyone had been in a rush to forget. The bullet behind her ear had shattered the right side of her face. Her fists were clenched, and the betrayed look in her frozen eyes demanded vengeance.

She had been shot six hours before her body floated to the surface of Chesapeake Bay. The contents of her home had been torn apart—drawers, closets, boxes in total disarray—and the coroner's report indicated she had been raped and sodomized. Phil knew the rape and break-in were a brutal cover to disguise a professional assassination.

He had given the district attorney the complete history

of Mrs. Hwan's involvement in the Rhee case and his own hypothesis that the same men who visited Mrs. Hwan, burned her arm and threatened her family had killed her. They were in all probability the same men who had assaulted him at the Reflecting Pool, the same spooks operating at the direction of the CIA or DIA or NSA who had stolen his case files. The district attorney had promised a thorough investigation, but in the ensuing three weeks not a single suspect had been taken into custody.

Phil crushed out his cigarillo and said, "I just wish to Christ I understood their motive for killing Mrs. Hwan."

"The same motive for sticking cigarettes in her arm," Sid replied. "They were nervous about her nailing Rhee as a foreign agent."

"That doesn't hold up. They knew she wouldn't testify"

"How?"

"When we were forced to postpone our grand jury appearance, any goddamn fool would've known our key witness had been compromised."

An angry horn of a speeding car blared at them. Phil said, "They killed her because someone at the top was nervous about Mrs. Hwan's having second thoughts; that she might have summoned the courage to come forward despite the torture, despite the threats to her family."

They turned off the rain-slick highway at Langley and followed the unmarked asphalt road toward the CIA headquarters.

"I don't know," Sid offered, "it might have been coincidence. It may have been a couple of common street killers."

"Not a chance," Phil snapped. "You were right the first time. She was marked by one of those bastards: Burgess, Gruenwald or Belgrave. They were in the Glass Room with Rhee when the approval to kill Park was given. Rhee is blackmailing them." Phil paused. "It's one of those three—or all of them."

"Well, if you're right, the field may be wider. It could be any intelligence desk in State or even the Assassination Bureau in Defense Control."

"Or the FBI."

"Let's not get paranoid." Sid smiled.

The road had narrowed and curved sharply through a pine forest. Phil lit another cigarillo. "What do you think of the Reverend Rhee's temples in California getting knocked over?"

"Beats me." Sid shrugged. "Maybe that's a question for Sonji."

"Why?"

"No reason. Just a thought."

Phil glanced at the handsome FBI man and knew the reference to Sonji was not without reason. But he did not pursue the matter.

They slowed down at the sentry post. The security man stepped out into the rain, and Sid rolled the window down. "Sid Greene and Phil Ricker to see Robert Burgess." The guard went back into the glass cubicle and checked a list on a clipboard. He then dialed a number, spoke briefly, hung up and nodded at Sid.

"Right up the road. You'll be met at the main entrance."

The huge black wire mesh gates swung open.

Phil noticed miniature TV cameras attached to high trees on either side of the road. He knew there were hidden infrared night-seeing devices along with electronic trip alarms strategically placed throughout the forest.

They followed the winding road up to the circular entrance of the huge seven-story headquarters complex. The massive square building was faced with blocks of marble and cement studded by a maze of small oblong windows. An oddly modern gull-like wing of marble waved over the entrance in curious counterpoint to the otherwise sterile architecture of the building.

They walked along the marble corridor, escorted by two armed security guards. The walls were decorated with abstract paintings selected by the CIA Fine Arts Committee. Phil thought the paintings reflected the spook mentality: The images were so obscure they defied understanding. A tired potted palm stood near the elevator doors like a misplaced prop out of an old Graham Greene novel.

The office was oak-paneled with windows on one side facing the pine forest. A single photograph hung on the wall behind Burgess's spotless desk. It was a blowup of canvas-covered Soviet missiles hidden in the Cuban jungle. The photograph represented one of the agency's major espionage coups that precipitated the Cuban missile crisis. The fact that the missiles had gone undetected for months had not been advertised.

Burgess's shirtfront bore traces of ashes from the ever-present cigarette dangling from his lips. "Sit down, gentlemen." His flat gray eyes were almost merry.

Sid Greene sat in a chair facing the desk. Phil remained standing.

"Well," the head of Covert Operations said, "to what do I owe the honor?"

His geniality and accommodating tone triggered a flash of anger that lodged in Phil's throat. "Let's cut the bullshit, okay?"

Burgess's eyes lost their merriment. He placed the cigarette in a white enamel ashtray and leaned forward. "I'd be careful about my tone of voice if I were you. You're in my office, at my invitation. Now just keep a civil tongue in your head."

Phil's hands trembled, and he fought against the surging anger, trying desperately to maintain his composure. "A month ago, on a Sunday night, my case files on the Reverend Rhee were stolen from my home. Clean. A pure clandestine CIA operation. My key witness was tortured. I was worked over. And finally, that same witness was brutally murdered, removed with extreme prejudice, as you fellows say."

"Is that so?"

Phil felt the rush and icy kick of adrenaline, but he contained his anger. "I know you bastards had a meeting in the Glass Room in the basement of this building, July fifth, 1979. The purpose of that meeting was to discuss the means and timing of killing President Park."

Behind Phil's back, Sid motioned with his hands for Burgess to remain calm. Burgess took the cue and soothingly said, "Look, Counselor, I know you've been pursuing the Rhee case for two years. I've also tracked cases which have fallen apart. I understand frustration. I sympathize with you. But your actions are indefensible." He paused.

"Now, I'm a reasonable man. I'm willing to turn the other cheek. You wanted help, I said to come over. But I will not tolerate accusations and street-corner tactics."

"Listen to me, you hypocritical son of a bitch!" Phil exclaimed. "I've been subjected to street violence! I've got the hospital bills to prove it."

"Well, muggings do take place in this city," Burgess replied softly. "And to my knowledge you've never given a satisfactory answer as to what you were doing in the Mall area after midnight. Besides, the night you came over to my table in Harvey's you were three sheets to the wind. Hardly the mode of behavior for the deputy attorney general of the United States."

"Let's skip my drinking habits for a minute."

"Whatever you say, Counselor."

"Do you deny that you and Defense Intelligence Chief Gruenwald and Security Council Chief Belgrave met in the Glass Room in the summer of '79 with the Reverend Rhee and others to approve the murder of Korean President Park?"

"Categorically. There is no Glass Room. There was no such meeting."

"Do you also deny that Rhee is using that meeting to blackmail you and your colleagues?"

"I've never met the Reverend Rhee."

"Do you deny that Rhee forced the theft of my files and the killing of my witness?"

Burgess did not respond, and Phil continued. "Do you deny that the Reverend Rhee is or was a KCIA operative?"

The director of covert operations took a deep drag on his cigarette. "If you can prove any of these allegations, due process of law is certainly available to you." He then leaned forward. "Gentlemen, this meeting is over."

"This meeting may be over, but not this case," Phil replied. "I'll nail Rhee, and I'll nail you bastards along with him."

"You do that, Counselor."

Phil reached the door, turned back and calmly said, "By the way, I also happen to know why your plot went sour."

A trace of concern dulled Burgess's gray eyes. "What plot?"

"The plot to kill Park. You and your colleagues blew it."

"Did we?" Burgess's tone remained nonchalant.

"You planned to turn Korea over to the chief of the KCIA, Commander Kyu, but you wound up with General Chung." Phil smiled. "Christ, I'd give a year's salary to have seen your faces that morning. You still don't know what went wrong, do you?"

"I said the meeting is over."

"I'm willing to make a deal with you," Phil said. "Tell me who's calling the signals, and I'll let you off the hook."

"You would be well served to drop this entire matter," Burgess replied. "Remember, Counselor, bad facts make for bad law."

Phil placed his hands on Burgess's desk and leaned toward the chief of clandestine operations. "If anyone has expertise in the use of bad facts, it's you. You're a master of disinformation. You push the panic buttons and send kids off to die in bullshit wars. You murder leaders of foreign countries. You hire Mafia hit men. You torture freedom and violate the Constitution, all in the name of national security. But let me tell you, I'm not going to abandon this case." Phil lowered his voice. "And if I'm bothered again, I'm coming right for you. Pass that word up the line. I hope we understand each other."

"Perfectly," Burgess replied.

Burgess smoked in silence for fifteen minutes, then pulled a glass phone out of the desk drawer and dialed a secure number belonging to Charles Gruenwald, director of Defense Intelligence. Burgess carefully related the facts of his meeting with Phil Ricker.

"You may be unduly alarmed," Gruenwald replied. "Ricker is speculating."

"Up to a point," Burgess said. "He claims to know why Kyu was nailed and how Chung assumed control."

"But *we* don't know that. How the hell would he?"

"Ricker has obviously reached someone high up in the

Korean power structure. I tell you, Charles, it's a dicey situation. We ought to speak to the Doctor."

"All right." Gruenwald sighed. "I'll try to contact him."

"Where is he?"

"Acapulco."

Chapter Fifteen

The sun slowly bled to death over the Pacific. Thick fingers of crimson and indigo rose from the horizon line, clutching the cobalt sky as if trying to prevent night from coming on. The view from the pink villa encompassed the panoramic irony of Acapulco: Forlorn huts clung to scruffy green hills that sloped down to tall, elegant hotels surrounding a gleaming turquoise bay. Poverty and opulence flourished side by side in the tropical paradise.

Two men were seated alongside the private pool in the big villa high above the Las Brisas Hotel. Their bodyguards were in the living room watching a bullfight being telecast from Mexico City.

Victor Maldonado wore a blue cotton robe over a Gucci bathing suit. He was stretched out on a lounge, sipping a tequila and tonic and chewing a long cigar. Maldonado was thin, bony and hairy. His eyes were coal black and peered out of a scarred face that looked like a used razor blade. His pitted skin was the residue of an untreated acne infection, a lifelong reminder of his impoverished Sicilian youth. Maldonado had assumed the title of *capo di tutti capi* after the deportation of Don Carlo Carelli. He had risen to the top post in organized crime by employing one simple dictate: Anything that worked was right. He possessed natural organizational skills and a predatory sense of when and how to employ his brutal gifts.

Maldonado's use of an ice pick had made him a legend before he reached the tender age of twenty. During the halcyon days of Murder Incorporated the back alleys of the Brownsville section of Brooklyn were littered with his victims. But age, power and responsibility had tempered the more violent aspects of his nature.

He glanced at Leo Meyers, sitting under the shade of a

113

gaily colored umbrella. Maldonado disliked the old man for three reasons: He was a Jew; he was a financial wizard; and he was a man who enjoyed the respect of the entire organization. In point of fact, Leo Meyers had been the reigning Jewish Pope of the Mafia for half a century. Leo and his lifelong friend Don Carlo Carelli had co-founded organized crime in America. Together they had emerged from the Italian-Jewish ghetto of the Lower East Side and whipped a loosely knit group of immigrants into the most powerful secret organization in the Western world. It was Carelli's control of the Sicilians and Meyers's fiscal genius that had converted illicit mob funds into legitimate commercial enterprises. The annual gross income of organized crime in the United States exceeded $50 billion. Leo Meyers not only directed the investment of that capital but dictated the various territorial shares of its colossal revenue. The power and respect Leo enjoyed from his Sicilian colleagues resided in one indisputable fact: He had made them all millionaires. No major business discussions, no killings, no territorial disputes were decided without the old man's advice and consent.

Leo Meyers sipped his Tecate beer and shifted his weight in the chair. He was seventy-three years old, but age had not brought with it those cruel lines that attached themselves to the eyes and mouth. His aesthetic features were remarkably unlined. Only his thinning gray hair and frail body and the use of a cane indicated a life that spanned seven decades.

Leo Meyers neither liked nor disliked Maldonado. He thought nothing of him. Like all dictators, Victor Maldonado was a transient. Leo had seen them all come and go: Maranzano, Capone, Luciano, Costello, Lepke, Adonis, Genovese, Gambino. The only one he truly respected was Don Carlo Carelli. Leo still made annual pilgrimages to Palermo to visit his old friend. Theirs was a unique relationship that transcended business. They were like brothers. Leo vividly remembered a particular conversation out of his youth. Carelli's Italian sidekick had criticized his friendship with Leo Meyers. "How could you be friends with that kike?" he asked. And Carlo had replied, "We need Leo. He's smart." The Italian boy then said, "But he killed Christ." And Carlo had growled, "Well, maybe Christ had it coming."

Leo smiled at the memory, gripped his cane, got to his feet and moved to the iron railing that circled the poolside terrace. He studied the panorama of Acapulco and marveled at the irony of Mexican citizens living in grinding poverty while carefree tourists played on their beaches. It reminded Leo of Havana in the thirties. You could sip a cold daiquiri at the Floridita Bar and rub shoulders with Howard Hughes, Gary Cooper, Hemingway and slumming tourists. And not fifty feet from the restaurant twelve-year-old girls were selling themselves to anyone with fifty cents.

In those days Leo Meyers had the Cuban dictator Batista in his pocket. The mob controlled the Havana casinos and ran illegal booze from Cuba to the Florida Keys. But Leo knew time was running out, that "a man on a white horse" was Cuba's inevitable destiny. Castro was born out of the poverty of the Cuban people. And those same conditions now existed in Mexico. Leo shook his head at the stupidity of the American power structure, expending billions of dollars in the jungles of Asia when at its very border Mexico was about to explode. But Leo had long ago written off American geopolitical strategy as an amateurish operation.

Leo Meyers currently controlled the flood of dollars pouring into Miami from South American cocaine smuggling. He created a baffling array of multinational offshore corporations laundering thirty million in cash every week. The dollars were funneled through Bahamian banks to dummy corporations in Panama, then recycled to secret accounts in Liechtenstein and Switzerland.

The old man watched the red sun rush into the Pacific as if it were late for Hawaii. The trip from Miami had tired him. He enjoyed the simplicity of his life: the fishing, the business, and his wife of fifty years. He glanced at his watch. It was 7:10 P.M. He resented Dr. Belgrave's tardiness. Leo Meyers regarded the chairman of the National Security Council as the classic example of genius crossed with insanity, of brilliance corrupted by power. His word meant nothing; his allegiance, even less. But this modern-day Machiavelli had the ear of the President of

116 STEVE SHAGAN

the United States, and there were certain benefits in keeping a line open with the government. Business was business.

Leo turned from the view in time to see a pretty blond girl wearing a scanty bikini bring Victor Maldonado a fresh drink. Maldonado took the drink and gruffly said, "Go to the bedroom and stay there."

"Sure, Victor." The blonde smiled.

Maldonado glanced at the old man. "Beautiful, eh, Leo?"

"Yes. She's very pretty."

"Want a drink?"

"No."

"What's bothering you, Leo?"

"I dislike meetings with these bastards."

"Well, they got a legitimate beef this time. Besides, you can't refuse a meeting with Uncle Sam."

"Did you speak to our associates?"

Maldonado nodded. "I told them we were meeting with Belgrave. They said it's up to us."

The old man glanced at his watch again. "The son of a bitch is twenty minutes late."

"Relax." Maldonado smiled. "I got some high-class young pussy coming down from L.A. tonight. Might be good for you."

The old man's gray eyes became hard as granite. "I've always been the best judge of what's good for me."

Maldonado chewed nervously on his cigar. He had to be careful. Besides the respect Leo enjoyed, he employed some of the best hit men in the business: Cuban exiles. Leo took care of them, and they worshiped the old man.

"I meant no disrespect," Maldonado offered.

"I know that. And there's nothing wrong with young girls. But I never asked anyone to provide a woman for me. Never."

There was a sudden rustling from inside the villa, and Maldonado's bodyguard came out onto the terrace with Dr. Eric Belgrave and Matt Crowley. Victor rose, and the men shook hands.

"How about a drink?" Maldonado asked.

"Not for me," Belgrave replied.

"Straight tequila," Crowley grunted.

Maldonado nodded to his bodyguard. The men were seated, all but Leo Meyers, who remained standing at the rail, leaning heavily on his cane.

"Sit down, Leo," Maldonado said.

"My ass is tired from sitting."

"An affliction that comes with age." Belgrave smiled. "I see your bodyguards enjoy the bullfights. Wonderful spectacle. Man against beast."

"You can sell anything to the dark side of human nature," Leo replied.

"You don't approve of bullfighting, Mr. Meyers?"

"No. It reminds me of the old days in Havana. People would pay five hundred dollars to see a mule screw a twelve-year-old girl."

The night lights came on, and a pall of silence fell over the terrace. The bodyguard brought Crowley his tequila.

"Have you gentlemen heard the news?" Dr. Belgrave asked. "The Israeli Air Force destroyed the Iraqi nuclear facility in Baghdad."

"Is that good for America or bad for America?" Maldonado inquired.

"There is no America," Belgrave replied. "There is only universal economic intercourse."

Crowley suddenly glared at the Doctor, his black eyes glittering dangerously. He was shocked by the Doctor's words: "There is no America."

Belgrave cleared his throat and stated, "The Israelis have gone too far this time."

"I am going to be buried in Jerusalem," Leo Meyers said matter-of-factly. "I will leave my fortune to the state of Israel."

Maldonado smiled. "I hope that day never comes, Leo."

"My sentiments exactly," Belgrave agreed. "Now, gentlemen, for the business at hand."

"I think I will sit down now." The old man moved to the edge of a chaise lounge, lowered himself carefully and said, "We're both about the same age, Doctor, but you've worn the years much better than I have."

"Thank you, Leo," Belgrave replied. The old Jew with the hard gray eyes was beginning to make the Doctor edgy. "Well, gentlemen, let me start in chronological order. Two years ago a matter of national security arose

which required my approval to remove a foreign leader."
Belgrave's voice assumed his usual tone of authority. "The
target was the then president of South Korea. Unfortunately the Reverend Rhee participated in that plot. He
has since resorted to blackmail, forcing me and my associates to protect him."

"Protect him from what?" Maldonado inquired.

"The deputy attorney general has Rhee under investigation. We've had to take certain actions to thwart that investigation. But there is another more recent threat to
Rhee that is in your province: Nick Carelli."

Victor Maldonado relit his cigar and blew a cloud of
smoke into the tropical night. "I'm sorry about this thing,
Doctor. I don't know why Nicky's been muscling the Reverend Rhee. I asked for this meeting because I wanted to
tell you this face-to-face. We never cross your action. But
hell, the president of General Motors doesn't know what
all his employees are doing."

"I understand perfectly," Belgrave agreed, "but I need
action and quickly."

"You have my word."

"Good." The Doctor rose and turned to Maldonado. "In
return for this favor I will see to it that those teamster
files are returned to you."

Leo Meyers glanced at Belgrave and asked, "Why don't
you have this Reverend Rhee hit? There's no other way to
deal with blackmail."

"There are complications, Mr. Meyers," Belgrave replied, then turned to Maldonado. "We may require some
additional help at a later date."

"You know where I am," Maldonado replied.

"Tell me, Doctor," Leo Meyers asked, "what is the
man's name in the Justice Department?"

"I don't understand your question."

"The man in charge of the Rhee investigation."

"Phil Ricker."

"He's the same fellow who years ago had Don Carlo
deported. He is a man who refuses money, a man who
cannot be bought. You'll have trouble with him."

"You're quite right," Belgrave agreed. "By the way,
would you gentlemen happen to know the present whereabouts of the missing Korean playboy Kimsan?"

"He's operating out of Palermo," Maldonado said. "Don Carlo and Kimsan run heroin from Sicily to Amsterdam."

Belgrave nodded. "You will act on Nick Carelli?"

"You can sleep on it, Doctor," Maldonado replied.

The air-conditioned limousine hugged the winding road down through the pink villas toward the Costera Miguel Alemán. Matt Crowley kept running over the Doctor's words "There is no America." He wondered if the master he served so well for so long could be an internationalist, a secret member of the Trilateral Commission? The serpent of suspicion uncoiled and moved restlessly in his brain.

The Doctor whispered, "Matt, you must get to Rhee's attorney."

"I've got a line on him."

"See him, Matt."

●

Leo Meyers stared at the gaily lit tour boat gliding gracefully through the tranquil bay of Acapulco. After a moment he sighed heavily and said, "I want to speak with Nicky."

"Leo . . . Leo," Maldonado whined. "I like the boy, too. And you know my respect for his father. But Nicky is way out of line. Besides the Rhee business, Nicky's a showboat. He plays tennis with movie stars. His name is in the columns. He shaves his Vegas cut to me and to the Gaspari family in Chicago. He goes his own way. He reminds me of the Bug."

"Let the dead rest, Victor. Without Ben Siegel there would be no Vegas."

"Well, you know what I mean. The Bug went his own way. Nicky's just like him. He has to be hit, Leo."

"Nicky's wife is pregnant. She carries the only seed of Don Carlo."

"We're not gonna hit his wife."

"I'm talking about timing. Out of respect to Don Carlo."

"My hands are tied, Leo. You know the rules. You made them. When Uncle Sam talks, we listen."

The old man turned away from the view and signaled to his bodyguard. A tough-looking Cuban came out onto the terrace and handed Leo his jacket.

"*Gracias, Luis.*"

"*Por nada, señor.*"

Leo slipped the jacket over his narrow shoulders. His gray eyes were reflective. "I don't trust Belgrave. He'd cross any line. Hit anyone. Betray anyone. He moved us to hit Jimmy Hoffa. And because of him, Roselli and Giancana were killed. Belgrave gave President Johnson bad information, and fifty-eight thousand boys died in the jungle. He's worried about that Hoover file Gemstone. Nicky is just the first problem."

The old man's litany was making Maldonado nervous, but he could take no action without Leo's approval. "What do you suggest we do?" he asked.

"I'm going to the airport now," Leo said. "I will be in Miami tomorrow. I'll have Nicky come to see me." The old man's voice took on the unmistakable tone of an order. "I expect no action until after I meet with him. I want your hand on this, Victor."

Maldonado gripped the old man's hand. "You have my word, Leo."

Chapter Sixteen

Phil peered out his window at the line of children across the street waiting to enter the Smithsonian Museum of Natural History.

The door opened, and a troubled Sid Greene entered. "Browning's not available. He's in a meeting with Senator Westlake. The anti-abortion bill."

"Terrific." Phil sighed.

Sid went behind Phil's desk and slumped into the high-backed leather chair. "You worry me, Phil. You were way out of line with Burgess."

"You're absolutely right," Phil replied.

"There are times when I think you're going over the edge."

"I know exactly what I'm doing, Sid. I had to play all my cards with Burgess."

"Why?"

"Because in actual fact I have no cards. So I sprayed a lot of anger and innuendo at the son of a bitch, hoping to turn up a card. I've got to create an atmosphere of distrust among Burgess, Gruenwald and Belgrave. Maybe someone will crack."

Sid lit a cigarette. "Do you really know why the Park assassination went wrong? Do you actually know how Chung knocked off Kyu and took over the country?"

"Yes."

"Can you prove it?"

"Not without the testimony of someone who was an accessory before and after the fact of Park's murder."

"That someone wouldn't be Sonji?"

"Ask Martha to bring us a couple of drinks," Phil said.

Sid pressed the intercom button. "Martha?"

"That's me."

"One vodka on the rocks for the counselor and a double scotch and water for me."

Sid released the button and walked up to the card graph.

"It's interesting," Sid said, "the way Sonji moves in and out of this chronology."

The door opened, and Martha appeared, carrying the drinks. She handed Phil the vodka and Sid the scotch.

"Martha," Phil said, "leave word with Browning's secretary. I want to see him."

"Okay." She swung her hips seductively as she left.

The door closed, and Sid said, "Would it surprise you to know that Sonji had a sexual liaison with a girl named Joyce Raymond?"

"Nothing Sonji did would surprise me."

"The Raymond girl is a lobbyist for the gaming industry."

"I still don't get the significance."

"Shortly after establishing a relationship with Joyce Raymond, Sonji met with Nick Carelli in Los Angeles. Carelli controls the casino operations in Vegas."

Phil nodded. "I had his father deported ten years ago. I remember Nicky from the trial."

Phil lit a cigarillo and studied Sid Greene for a moment. "How did you come by this information?"

"I've had Sonji tailed for months," Sid replied.

"And you're suggesting that Joyce Raymond arranged the meeting between Sonji and Nick Carelli."

"Absolutely. And by the way, Joyce Raymond is a dyke."

"Interesting," Phil murmured.

"Why the hell would Sonji want a mob contact?" Sid asked.

"Sonji doesn't want anything," Phil said. "Sonji's a soldier, a messenger for Chung. The question is why the president of Korea wanted a connection to the Mafia capo of California."

Phil's question hung in the air like a missing piece in a complex jigsaw puzzle. They sipped their drinks in silence. Phil then rose and went back to the card graph and examined it slowly.

Two of the fresh entries were both murders: the assas-

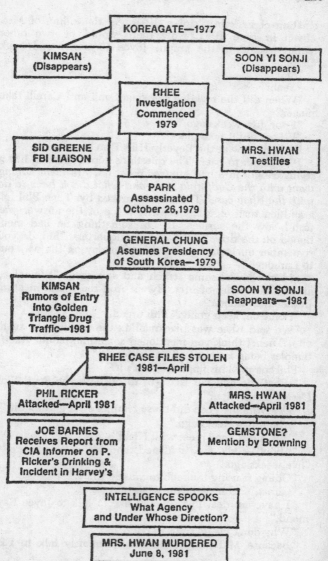

KOREAGATE—1977

KIMSAN
(Disappears)

SOON YI SONJI
(Disappears)

RHEE
Investigation
Commenced
1979

SID GREENE
FBI LIAISON

MRS. HWAN
Testifies

PARK
Assassinated
October 26, 1979

GENERAL CHUNG
Assumes Presidency
of South Korea—1979

KIMSAN
Rumors of Entry
Into Golden
Triangle Drug
Traffic—1981

SOON YI SONJI
Reappears—1981

RHEE CASE FILES STOLEN
1981—April

PHIL RICKER
Attacked—April 1981

MRS. HWAN
Attacked—April 1981

JOE BARNES
Receives Report from
CIA Informer on P.
Ricker's Drinking &
Incident in Harvey's

GEMSTONE?
Mention by Browning

INTELLIGENCE SPOOKS
What Agency
and Under Whose Direction?

MRS. HWAN MURDERED
June 8, 1981

sination of Park in October 1979 and the killing of Mrs.
Hwan in June 1981. Now there would be two other
names to add to the graph: Joyce Raymond and Nick
Carelli.

"Sid?"

"Yeah?"

"When did the meeting between Sonji and Carelli take
place?"

"Four, five weeks ago."

"Where did it take place?"

"A bungalow at the Beverly Hills Hotel."

Phil began to pace. The questions kept repeating like a
stylus caught in a bad groove. *What did President Chung
want with the California mob, and what did it have to do
with the Rhee case?* The minutes ticked by. Then Phil felt
a sudden rush of excitement. A piece of the answer was
just below the surface. It was something he had mentioned on the drive to the CIA headquarters. "Sid, do you
remember our conversation the other day on the way out
to Langley?"

Sid swallowed some scotch and shrugged. "We talked
about the murder of Mrs. Hwan. And the secret meeting
in the Glass Room."

"Come on, keep going," Phil urged.

"We said Rhee was blackmailing the intelligence agencies. Then I think you mentioned something about Rhee's
temples being knocked off in California."

Phil snapped his fingers. "That's it."

"What the hell has that got to do with the Sonji-Nick
Carelli connection?"

"Everything. When did those temples start getting hit?"

"About five weeks ago."

"When did Sonji meet with Nick?"

"About"—Sid's eyes widened, and his voice wavered—
"five weeks ago."

"Chung is using the mob to muscle Rhee."

"Christ," Sid hissed, "for what purpose?"

"I have an idea. But I would like to talk to Joyce Raymond."

"Why don't we go right to Nick?"

"Because Mafia capos do not voluntarily talk to FBI

and Justice Department employees. Get us an appointment with Joyce Raymond. But don't frighten her."

"Right," Sid replied, and started for the door.

"Sid?"

The handsome FBI man stopped and turned.

"You're full of surprises," Phil said.

"What do you mean?"

"You appear magically at the Reflecting Pool after I was beaten, claiming you placed a bug on my fender."

"Absolutely true. I was trying to keep you in sight. Trying to keep you alive."

"Then I find out you've been tailing Sonji for months."

"Part of the job. You're an attorney. I'm an investigator. You're getting paranoid, my friend."

"In this business, paranoia keeps you alive," Phil replied.

Chapter Seventeen

Joyce Raymond wore a white silk pantsuit that clung to her classic curves like a layer of cold cream. Phil was startled by her beauty. Her hair shone like spun gold, framing her oval face, and her sea green eyes were alive and intelligent. There was nothing in her movements or attitudes that betrayed homosexuality. Even the decor of the living room was totally feminine: pink walls and ruffled drapes and peach-colored country French chairs mixed with large twin Belgian linen sofas. The only clue to any Sapphist tendencies was the paintings. They were cubistic images of naked girls in a variety of erotic poses. But their extreme surreal rendering diluted the lesbian connotation.

Joyce Raymond came around the wet bar and handed Sid Greene a scotch on the rocks. She then sat on the beige sofa opposite the two men.

"Miss Raymond," Sid Greene said, "I want you to know that this interview is absolutely unofficial. Nothing you tell us will ever be used against you."

"I just wonder"—she smiled—"what I've done to deserve this visit."

"Nothing illegal, I can assure you."

"Well, that's comforting." She crossed her legs and swung her right leg up and down.

Sid sipped some scotch and said, "Miss Raymond, it's our understanding that you're employed as a lobbyist for the gaming industry."

"That's right."

"It would then be logical to assume you have strong connections with casino operations in Las Vegas."

"Are you asking me or telling me?"

"I'm asking you," Sid replied.

She swirled the ice cubes in her Coca-Cola. "Well, we sell a lot of our equipment to Vegas. But I have no contact with casino management."

"Miss Raymond, do you know a man named Nick Carelli?"

Her leg stopped swinging, and she reached for a cigarette. "I know of him. That is to say, I've heard of him."

"But no personal connection?"

"No," she said, lighting the cigarette. Her lips made a perfect circle around the word "no." She glanced at Phil and thought there was an edgy quality beneath his soft brown eyes, a trace of menace. She recalled reading something about his having been mugged on the Mall. "You have to understand." She turned to Sid Greene. "My job is to contact congressmen and senators, people who can influence legislation favorable to our industry. I don't actually deal with customers."

"Would you say Nick Carelli is a major customer?" Sid asked.

"I don't think that's a state secret."

The distant wail of an ambulance floated through the open terrace door.

"Miss Raymond." Phil spoke for the first time. "Do you know a Korean girl named Soon Yi Sonji?"

The glitter went out of her sea green eyes. "Should I?"

"You tell me."

Joyce took a long drag on the cigarette. "Sonji is an acquaintance."

"Not a friend?"

"I said she was an acquaintance."

Sid Greene took out a small note pad and said, "During the past six weeks Sonji spent ten nights here in your apartment."

A sudden breeze drifted in from the terrace and grabbed the smoke of her cigarette. "You're not being very nice."

"This is not a very nice case," Phil replied. "I've been beaten. My witness was tortured and brutally murdered. For your own safety, Miss Raymond, I urge you to tell us the truth."

She crushed the cigarette out. "Are you suggesting that I'm in jeopardy?"

"It's a possibility. I can't answer with any authority until I know more about your relationship with Sonji."

Joyce rose and moved to the terrace doors. She looked out over the twinkling lights of the capital. There was a moment of silence underscored by the distant city traffic. She then turned to Phil. "Sonji and I are lovers." And with a trace of sadness added, "That's not illegal, is it?"

"Not yet," Phil said. "Miss Raymond, did you arrange a meeting for Sonji with Nick Carelli?"

"You know the answer." She sighed. "It's obvious you've had my telephone tapped. I think I'd better phone my lawyer."

"You have every right to have your lawyer present," Phil advised, "but if we continue this interview under subpoena, everything is on the record. Your employers will be aware of the situation. I would like to avoid that."

Tears welled up in her eyes, and her voice trembled. "I've already betrayed the confidence of someone who's innocent. Someone who trusts me."

"I hate to destroy an illusion," Phil said gently, "but Soon Yi Sonji makes Lucretia Borgia look like Orphan Annie."

"I find that difficult to believe."

"What you believe is unfortunately irrelevant. Now, I ask you again, did you arrange a meeting between Sonji and Nick Carelli?"

She looked off beyond the terrace and murmured, "Yes."

"Why?"

"She asked me to. She said it was official state business."

"Did she define the nature of that business?"

"She said her government wanted to consult with Nick Carelli about servicing the gambling casinos in Seoul."

"Did Sonji ever mention the Reverend Rhee?"

"No."

"Did she ever tell you the results of her meeting with Nick?"

"No."

Phil rose and walked up to the open terrace. He disliked interrogating Joyce Raymond. The girl had enough of a cross to carry.

"Miss Raymond, have you spoken to Nick Carelli subsequent to Sonji's meeting with him?"

She had another cigarette going and brushed some ash from her white silk jacket. "I don't see where that's any of your business."

"That question directly involves your own safety."

Joyce's hands trembled, and she suddenly burst into tears.

Phil winked at Sid Greene. "Sid, would you leave us alone for a minute?"

"Sure." Sid nodded. "I'll be in the lobby." The FBI man softly closed the door behind him.

Phil crossed to the wet bar, poured a brandy and carried the drink to the sobbing girl.

She removed a tissue from a large leather handbag and swallowed some brandy. After a moment she said, "Nicky phoned me."

"When was this?"

"Just after he met with Sonji."

"What did he want?"

Joyce shrugged. "Who Sonji was. What I knew about her. That kind of thing."

"What was his reaction?"

"He threatened me."

"How?"

"I can't repeat it."

"Miss Raymond, I've heard everything there is to hear. What did he say?"

She took a deep breath. "He said, 'If you've given me a wrong steer, I'll cut your tongue out.' Then he laughed and said, 'What would a dyke do without her tongue?' "

"Nice," Phil murmured. "Did you tell this to Sonji?"

"No."

"All right, Miss Raymond. I'm sorry we had to put you through this."

She rose and walked him to the door.

"I can provide federal marshals to protect you," Phil offered.

She shook her head. "I don't want people following me." She stood very close to him, her green eyes reflecting fear and conflicting emotions. Joyce Raymond was beautiful and vulnerable, and he felt like putting his arms around her.

"It's only fair for me to tell you," Phil said. "Sonji is an agent working for Korean Central Intelligence. She is a soldier following the orders of a despotic dictator. She would use you, make love to you or have you killed to fulfill her mission."

Joyce stared blankly at him, and he handed her his card. "You can reach me at this number day or night."

"Thank you. And, Mr. Ricker—"

"Yes?"

"Would you see that the tap on my phone is removed?"

"We never tapped your phone. It's an illegal act."

Chapter Eighteen

Matt Crowley lay naked on the bed of his Georgetown apartment. His hands were clasped to his ears, but he could not stop the noise. The hideous whooshing sound was accompanied by the images—the bodies of his patrol, their naked flesh turned gray by swarming maggots. The sound of them eating his comrades filled the small wooden blockhouse. Although their position was hopeless, Crowley had ordered his men to hold against an entire Chinese brigade. The blockhouse near the Yalu River was a piece of America. And Americans did not surrender.

One by one the men were killed, defending the strongpoint.

Outside the blockhouse the Chinese yelled at him. Jeering. Taunting him. Crowley could see their cooking fires in the dip of a snowbank, and now and then he would fire a burst. But laughter and verbal abuse were their only response. For three weeks they kept him there. Alone in the blockhouse, listening and watching the maggots feasting on the flesh of his comrades. When they finally took him, he stumbled out, his eyes streaming from the tear gas.

The Chinese captain did not want the American colonel killed. He regarded Crowley as a curiosity. They force-fed him rice and gruel, stripped him and raped him repeatedly. They questioned him ceaselessly, but he would mumble only his name, rank and serial number. They locked him back up in the blockhouse with the rotting corpses of his patrol, and still he did not crack. A Chinese major finally ended his torment, and after the truce Crowley was repatriated.

He spent two years on and off at Walter Reed Hospital. His case had won him wide notoriety. He was personally decorated by the secretary of the army, and Dr. Belgrave

131

saw to it that Matt Crowley had the finest medical attention available.

Crowley joined the CIA in 1958 and served in Covert Operations. He left the agency in 1967, becoming chief aide to Dr. Eric Belgrave.

His loyalty to the Doctor and the fulfillment of his assignments were the essence of Crowley's life. But the mental scars of his Korean experience had damaged him permanently. The agony of his comrades' death throes and the noise of the maggots haunted his nights with increasing frequency.

Crowley rose from the bed and walked to the bureau. He quickly and expertly snorted six lines of ninety percent pure cocaine. The icy jolt of the drug cleared the terrifying sounds and images. He wished the tall, muscular black girl would come out of the bathroom. She was oiling her body. He demanded that of her. He wanted her to be greased and glistening. The combination of pain and pleasure she would bestow on him was long overdue. His flaccid penis grew hard at the thought.

Crowley went over to the full-length mirror. His body was strong and supple. He thrust two rigid fingers at his own image. The thrust directed at the Adam's apple could choke a man to death. He knew the lightning judo moves that could kill instantly: the heel of the hand on the collarbone; the hammerlock that cracked the spine; the reverse pressure of two hands that broke the neck. He had in his time personally killed eight men and three women, all enemies of the state. He grabbed his erect penis with his left hand and squeezed it gently, recalling with pleasure the murder of Mrs. Hwan. She was a member of the yellow race. He had chained her on all fours while the Korean sodomized her. And at the very moment the KCIA assassin orgasmed, Crowley had fired the slug just behind her ear.

He resented having been denied the supervision of the attack on Ricker. The man from Burgess's clandestine operations section had botched the job and deserved the shattered jaw he received. But Crowley took heart in the fact that Belgrave had charged him with the task of approaching the Reverend Rhee's attorney and convincing him to relinquish the Reverend's documentation of that secret meeting in the Glass Room. Once that matter was resolved, Rhee was a dead man. Crowley relished the thought of wasting the fat Korean preacher.

His euphoria vanished suddenly as he recalled Dr. Belgrave's words "There is no America." He hoped it was merely a metaphoric accident, spoken for effect to the overlords of organized crime.

Crowley turned from the mirror as the bathroom door opened, and in the spill of light he saw the six-foot-tall gleaming black body. She carried a jar of oil and silently walked up to the foot of the bed and picked up the whip. She placed the whip and oil on the night table. Crowley went to her, and she curled her hand around his stiff penis and draped her arm around his neck, pulling him to her. She kissed him hard, her tongue probing his mouth. She moved him onto the bed and whispered, "Turn over."

He lay belly down. The black girl poured the warm oil over his neck, shoulders and slowly down his back over his buttocks, legs and feet. She then rubbed the oil vigorously into his flesh.

The black girl rose and picked up the whip. She shook it, and the leather thong uncoiled to its six-foot length. She raised the whip high over her head and with expert leverage cracked it down across his shoulders.

The flesh split on contact, and a stream of blood poured from the wound. Crowley moaned in ecstasy. The cocaine had heightened his senses, and he whispered hoarsely, "Harder!"

She raised herself onto her toes, and the whip cracked loudly as the lash bit across his buttocks. The pain and pleasure surged again. The whip came up and down with increasing force and rhythmic tempo.

She cracked it across his naked flesh until she could no longer raise her right arm. Her sweat-soaked skin glistened like black satin. She stared at his back with professional pride. The flayed skin was a maze of bleeding welts.

The black girl knelt over him and began to suck the bloody wounds. Her lips moved from place to place. The sweating girl was caught up in the sensual frenzy of her own artistry. She grabbed his waist and roughly turned him over. She straddled him and eased herself down onto the swollen erect penis. She rocked frantically and hissed insults at him. Her words were degrading, humiliating. His inflamed back burned, and the hot sensation mingled with the moist warmth of his penetration deep inside her gleaming body.

Crowley murmured, "Now—now." She eased off his penis and expertly massaged his testicles while he masturbated himself to climax.

Matt Crowley could reach orgasm only by his own hand.

The girl applied a soothing cream to his tortured flesh, then went into the bathroom and showered.

Crowley lay naked and spent on the bed. He waited for her to come out before rising. As the girl slipped into her clothes, he went over to the bureau and took three $100 bills from his wallet and handed them to her.

She touched his cheek affectionately, smiled and said, "Call me."

Chapter Nineteen

The thirty-six-foot cabin cruiser knifed through the shimmering Gulf Stream swells. A Cuban youth wearing reflective sunglasses manned the helm on the flying bridge. The boat was headed toward an inland channel at eighteen knots and running less than half a mile off Miami's Gold Coast.

Nick Carelli and Leo Meyers were seated in bolted swivel chairs on the aft deck. Nick wore white ducks and a blue Italian polo shirt that matched the color of his eyes. His feet rested on the mahogany gunwale. His dark glasses rested atop his wavy dark hair. He looked off at the great veins of crimson painted into the horizon by the setting sun.

"I don't remember when I relaxed as much, Leo."

"I'm pleased you found time to make the trip, Nicky."

The Cuban helmsman slowed to five knots as the sleek cruiser entered the narrow channel. An angry sea gull screamed at the boat, demanding a piece of bait. But the two men had not fished. They had taken a brief cruise and spoken about things past. The time had now come to discuss current events.

The old man touched Nicky's arm. "Tell me, why have you leaned on this Korean preacher?"

"The West Coast and Vegas are my territories."

"Absolutely. But no one approved muscling this Reverend's action."

Nick removed his Gucci loafers from the gunwale. "No. That's wrong, Leo. I had the okay."

"From who?"

"The Korean government."

Leo was surprised, and for a moment his mind whirled.

Nick's answer defied logic. The Koreans were locked to Belgrave's people. "Who gave you the okay?" Leo asked.

"A girl from the Korean Embassy. She was a knock-out," Nicky continued. "Her name was Soon Yi Sonji. She had the credentials. She said her government wanted Rhee bothered. She told me where they kept their take and how much they collected."

"Why did she come to you?"

"Because Rhee operated in my territory."

"Why didn't you call a meeting of the National Council to deliberate this matter?"

Nick rose and paced nervously for a moment. He could not disguise the rising anger in his voice. "This Korean preacher has mind-fucked thousands of American kids. He's swimming in hard cash. Why shouldn't I get a piece of his action?"

"This man Rhee has strong juice with D.C. people," Leo said.

"The girl told me that the Korean president, Chung, wanted Rhee to have a partner in California."

"Maybe so. But Chung doesn't speak for Washington." Leo rose. "We met with the top guy. He wants the heat off Rhee. That's the way it has to be, Nicky."

The cruiser moved slowly up the narrow channel, pass-ing Spanish-style villas with private docks. Nick's face was drained of color, and his blue eyes were icy. "Leo, all my life I've had respect for you. But this time I gotta go against you. Fuck this goddamn preacher. I'll hit this chink bastard so long as he operates in my territory!"

Leo shook his head sadly. "You can't go against the council."

Nick stopped pacing. "All right. They want a cut of the Korean action, they got it. Let's call a meet and you slice it up."

"That's no good, Nicky."

The engines throbbed and whined as they were thrown into reverse. The Cuban helmsman expertly guided the boat into Leo Meyers's private dock. Bumpers were placed over the side, and the boat was berthed.

Leo spoke solemnly. "For the sake of your family, for your father's sake, listen to me and drop this."

"Tell Victor to drop it."

"No one can go against the council."

"I'm not taking on the council. I'm going against Maldonado. He's a *stronzo*, an *infamia*." Nick's words came with machine-gun rapidity. "He's using this Korean thing to nail me. When my father was deported, the Carelli family was number one. I should have taken over the organization."

"It's true," Leo agreed. "The son replaces the father. But the council said no."

"The council, my ass," Nicky snapped. "It was Victor! He hated my father. Okay, I didn't say anything. I stayed on the Coast. I run Vegas and everyone gets their slice. But Victor complains. He wants more. Two months ago I told him to go fuck himself. And I say the same now."

Carelli's two bodyguards waited on the dock.

"This is your final word?"

"I respect you, Leo. But I have to do what's right for the California family."

The old man nodded and with resignation said, "Give my best to Cristina."

Nick Carelli followed his bodyguards up the wooden pier toward a waiting Mercedes.

Leo Meyers entered his modestly furnished living room. His wife, Sarah, came out of the kitchen, wiping her hands on a towel. Her short hair was snow white; but her figure was trim, and her fine features had resisted the ravages of time.

"How was the ride?"

"Pleasant."

"It's time for your medicine."

He nodded, and she said, "He's a handsome man, Nicky. He could be a movie star."

"Sarah, leave me for a minute."

"What's wrong?"

"Nothing. I need to think for a minute."

She knew this was a time of trouble and went through the alcove back into the kitchen.

The old man sat by the large window that overlooked the waterway. He remained motionless for ten minutes, sifting through a variety of ideas, searching for a resolution that would permit Nick Carelli to live. But no alternative action surfaced. The organization could not afford a war. Business was business.

He picked up the receiver and dialed 1-516-555-0808. The number connected to Victor Maldonado's estate in Amagansett, Long Island. On the third ring an antiseptic voice that betrayed no regional accent answered. The voice belonged to Maldonado's *consigliere*, Martin Bender.

"Yes?"

"Leo."

"A minute."

Only in moments like this did Leo Meyers taste failure. He could not abide the fact that business disputes could be resolved only by the logic of a bullet.

"Hello, Leo." Maldonado's greeting was warm and friendly.

"How is the weather in New York?" Leo asked.

"Ah, it's a beautiful summer day. A painting; a Monet."

Leo was amused by Victor's recent allusions to the arts. "Miami is cloudy," he said.

"Well," Maldonado suggested, "maybe you should move to Los Angeles."

"Los Angeles is a place of death."

"I'm sorry you feel that way."

"So am I."

There was a slight pause, and Victor said, "Will you get a weather report from Palermo?"

"No. Palermo will recognize that no one can control Los Angeles."

"When will I see you?"

"Soon."

"You enjoy my ranch in Virginia, right?"

"Very much."

"Why don't you and Sarah visit me there next month?"

"I would like that. Health permitting."

"Ah, you'll bury us all. *Ciao*, Leo."

"Good-bye, Victor."

Leo walked wearily into the kitchen. Sarah glanced up from a pot of stew.

"When do you want to eat?"

"Anytime."

"You look like death, Leo."

"I am death."

Chapter Twenty

They were seated at a window table upstairs at Chadwick's, overlooking the Potomac. The running lights of small boats twinkled as they cruised slowly across the moonlit black water. They had eaten crab cakes, baked clams, a heaping plate of french-fried onions and consumed the better part of two bottles of white wine.

Phil always felt relaxed with Gloria. Tneirs was a casual relationship born out of mutual loneliness. Gloria Robbins was the California girl who worked for the national gun lobby. She was a cute girl who just missed being pretty. Her long red hair gave her a flashy look. Her eyes were large and blue but slightly crossed. Her nose was bent at the bridge, and her soft, full lips seemed too large for her small, oval face. But her figure was a centerfold. She had firm, thrusting breasts, a narrow waist, a flat belly and long, pretty legs.

Gloria Robbins earned her living in a political atmosphere that was totally alien to everything she believed in. She was a child of the sixties. She had attended the University of California at Berkeley and been in the forefront of all the movements. Gloria had marched through clouds of eye-searing tear gas more than once.

But the suicide of her lover, induced by a bad acid trip, had devastated her. She had severed all her youthful connections, left California for Washington and through a series of misadventures found her way into an affair with Karl Reinhardt, chairman of the national gun lobby. Reinhardt started her at a salary of $50,000 a year and expenses. The money assured him of a continuing sexual liaison and gave Gloria economic security. She had explained to Phil that being a single girl in Washington dictated a certain amount of pragmatic prostitution.

They were feeling heady from the wine, and the waiter had just placed two creamy Amarettos in front of them.

"You won't believe this meeting I went to today," she said, sipping the liqueur. "Listen to the cast."

"I'm listening." Phil smiled.

"Senator Westlake of North Carolina, his male secretary, my boss and yours truly. The senator wanted to enlist our national membership behind his anti-abortion bill."

"Nothing remarkable about that."

"Wait." Gloria lit a cigarette. "The senator gets through this whole moral speech about killing fetuses—right?"

Phil nodded.

"Well, Karl, my boss, says, 'You know, Senator, that black reverend Leroy Johnson agrees with you, and that disturbs me.'" She swallowed some Amaretto and licked her lips. "The senator looks a little puzzled, and Karl says the Reverend Johnson claims free abortion is a white upper-class genocidal act."

"I've never heard that one," Phil mused.

"Then the senator's aide drawls"—Gloria affected a southern accent—"'Well, the Reverend Johnson ain't so far wrong. Most of those abortions are performed on nigger women.' Then Karl says, 'You put through this anti-abortion bill, Senator, and the country will be drowning in pickaninnies.'"

"Christ . . ." Phil murmured.

"Now, the senator," Gloria continued, "the senator's eyes get cloudy, and he says, 'Well, perhaps this entire issue requires further study. I'll get back to you, Karl, and I appreciate your input.'" Gloria laughed. "I tripped, Phil. I really tripped. I thought if only Lenny Bruce was still around, what fucking delicious material."

Phil shook his head. "Almost the twenty-first century, and they're still knocking abortion around. There are times when I think the whole world is a Woody Allen outtake." He signaled for the check and smiled at her. "You feel sexy?"

"Like a cocked forty-five."

Gloria lay naked atop the sheets, smoking a joint. They each had a glass of wine beside them on end tables. Stan Getz's mello sax painted "Quiet Nights."

She handed the joint to Phil. He took a deep drag, and the grass hit him hard. A sudden feeling of helplessness overwhelmed him.

He had left numerous messages at the Korean Embassy for Sonji, but they remained unanswered. He had attempted to obtain a court order authorizing a tap on Nick Carelli's Beverly Hills phone, but the request had been rejected on insufficient grounds. The only positive step he had taken was to have Sid Greene assign a team of FBI men to watch over Joyce Raymond. But the maddening question of why Chung had set Nick Carelli onto Rhee remained unanswered.

Gloria whispered, "A thousand shares of ITT for your thoughts."

"I was just thinking that Jesse Helms and Percy would make a hell of a presidential ticket."

Gloria smiled. "When that happens, I'll migrate to Bogotá and stay ripped forever."

She took a deep drag of the joint and leaned over him. She kissed him deeply, letting the smoke drift into his mouth. She kissed the scar line on his jaw and moved down to suck his nipples and kiss his belly and his thighs. He felt her mouth close over him.

He moaned softly as she nursed him, but distant ghosts and demons had begun to stir behind the sensual rush.

She moved up and slipped his erect penis inside her. Holding him there, she rolled them over and draped her ankles over his shoulders.

"Like that," she whispered. "Just like that."

He pressed against her with all his strength, and she dug her nails into his back. Her stomach muscles convulsed, and her ass pumped wildly.

"Christ!" she gasped.

They were like a single throbbing column of flesh welded together, fueled by dope and demons, both seeking their own release. Their mouths pressed together, their minds racing along disparate sensual trials, connected only by the mutual demands of their flesh.

She pulled her mouth away and gasped, "Come, oh, Christ, come now!"

Phil looked down at her and blinked in horror.

Gloria's eyes were the cold, milky, staring dead eyes of

Mrs. Hwan. He saw ski masks. And Sonji's wide, curvy eyes. And Chung's cruel, flat features. He saw a ditchful of violated Vietnamese bodies. He saw his wife smiling curiously at him as if he were a stranger. He saw Sid Greene mysteriously appearing at the Reflecting Pool. And Arthur Browning's eyes glinting when he mentioned Gemstone. And Burgess peering through cigarette smoke. And Joe Barnes stuffing pieces of shrimp in his mouth.

Phil tried to keep going, thrusting himself up into Gloria's belly. Beads of sweat fell from his face onto the pillow. He summoned an almost maniacal concentration, trying to reach orgasm, as if climaxing into Gloria's sweating body would grant him absolution from the demons. But he grew soft and slipped out. He fell back onto the bed and stared up at the ceiling.

"What's wrong?" she asked.

He touched her hair. "It has nothing to do with you."

"Why don't you give it up, Phil? You've turned old on this case. Walk away."

The phone rang. Phil picked up the receiver and recognized Sonji's voice instantly.

"I can see you Thursday. Ten o'clock. Your place."

"Wait!"

"Thursday. Ten P.M."

The connection clicked off.

Chapter Twenty-one

The eye-searing pus-colored smog oozed into the white skyline like the residue of an infected wound.

Angelo Vizzoni stood on the fifteenth-floor terrace of the Century West Hotel, inhaling the poisoned air and wishing he were someplace else. Los Angeles had the "evil eye." It was a place of bad luck. His brother had been killed in this city many years ago. Vizzoni believed sinister forces lurked in its tired palms and serpentine freeways. Even the earth beneath the city moved, rattling windows like a malevolent warning of approaching doom. Vizzoni clenched his fist and extended his index finger and pinkie, forming the ancient Sicilian sign against evil spirits.

. He glanced at the $3,000 wafer-thin gold Patek Philippe watch attached to his wrist. It was 5:47 P.M. Vizzoni went back inside the bedroom and stretched out on the king-size bed. He stared up at the ceiling, thinking only a contract issued by the godfather, Victor Maldonado, could bring him to this city.

He had reviewed every detail endlessly. Still, an ominous pervading fear gnawed at his consciousness. The fear was amorphous, undefined and had to do with the city itself. Vizzoni crossed himself and got to his feet. He paced the rug for a moment, then went quickly into the bathroom, washed his hands and peered at his reflected image in the mirror. His soft brown melancholy eyes, flat nose and bow-shaped mouth coalesced into a curious attractive harmony. He touched the gold cross at his throat, then held up his wrist before him and spread his fingers. They were long and slender like those of a concert pianist.

Vizzoni returned to the bedroom and opened his large attaché case. He studied the gleaming parts of the M-14 rifle. His fingers traced the folding V stock and the blue-

144

steel barrel and the solid oblong clip box containing twenty 3-inch brass, hollow-head 7.62-millimeter bullets. The M-14 had been designed by the United States Army, and its accuracy at 300 yards was unparalleled. He lifted the Starlightscope out of its container and pulled the drapes, darkening the room. He then sighted through the small eyepiece, depressed the red button, and the darkened bedroom was suddenly bathed in a pale green light. The Starlightscope required a minimum amount of moonlight and was capable of illuminating a human figure at 1,200 yards. He snapped on the lamp and placed the scope back in the case. He stretched out on the bed once again, thinking of the $50,000 deposited in the Marine Midland Bank of New York. It was the top fee for contract killing.

Angelo Vizzoni had no feelings one way or the other about Nick Carelli. It was a job, a hit, like the other fifteen contracts he had fulfilled during the past four years. He was an ace contractor, an outside man belonging to no family. He killed for the council when circumstances precluded the employment of regular family soldiers.

Vizzoni had been one of three outside trigger men who dispatched Giancana and Roselli after they had botched the CIA-ordered hit on Castro.

The bedside phone sounded suddenly. He lifted the receiver on the third ring. "Yes?"

"Angelo?"

"Speaking."

"It's me." The gruff voice belonged to Tommy Moro, one of Nick Carelli's trusted capos. This was the final inside word Vizzoni required. "It's a go," Moro said.

"When?"

"Eight, eight-fifteen."

"Which is it?"

"Between them. You gotta be in the air between that time."

"Okay."

"Now, for chrissake, wait for the fucking lights to go out."

"What else?"

"Nothin', that's it."

Vizzoni placed the receiver back on the cradle and sat

up, his head resting against the backboard. The night hit by helicopter was exotic, but it was the only way. Nick Carelli was protected by a host of bodyguards day and night. He did not operate his own car. He used taxis, changing the call and company from day to day. He wore a bulletproof vest and employed doubles who preceded him at meetings.

Nick may have been flamboyant, a showboat, a tennis-playing pal of movie stars, but when it came to his own security, he was brilliantly cautious.

The helicopter pilot, Gabriel Torres, had been person-ally selected by Vizzoni. Torres was a cocaine runner and had made countless flights from Tijuana to a small drop area in the hills above San Diego. He was a man of iron nerves and had a drawerful of medals to prove it. Torres had flown more than 150 combat missions in Vietnam.

The twin condominiums towered over Century City Plaza, their flatiron shapes ablaze with lights. The only significant difference in the buildings was the design of their rooftops: One was used as a heliport while the other served as a tennis complex.

The four tennis courts were floodlit and busy. Men and women playing singles and doubles pressed their limited skills with a furious nocturnal energy, releasing the day's tensions. Spectators sat on green benches some fifty feet behind the chalked baselines.

In the far court Nick Carelli, wearing white shorts, white polo shirt and white Adidas, played opposite an ag-ing movie star. They were good friends off the court, but their tennis was played with a vicious intensity.

Carelli's wife, Cristina, was seated on a bench, wearing a loose smock that draped easily over her swollen belly. She was in the seventh month of her pregnancy. A honey-colored nineteen-year-old girl sat next to her, cheer-ing her movie star boyfriend on every winning point.

The sound of popping tennis balls mixed with sudden bursts of applause. Players in one court paid no attention to those in adjacent courts. The intensity of the action was profound. For most of the players, tennis had replaced the psychiatrist's couch.

Carelli and the movie star were in their third set, engaged in a long, furious volley. They played with brooding concentration, using a wide variety of shots—lobs, slams and slices—darting into the net and racing back to the baseline. Carelli's eight bodyguards were scattered at strategic places throughout the complex. His chief capo, Tommy Moro, was positioned behind the baseline on Nick's side of the court.

Carelli assumed his service position. He needed this point badly. He was behind love-30. He tossed the ball up and brought the racket down in a perfect arc, getting his shoulder, arm and wrist into the serve.

The ball moved like a blur, just clearing the net and bouncing up with great velocity and top spin. The movie star stuck his backhand out defensively, and the ball wafted lazily back over the net. Nick moved in, waiting for the ball to reach the apex of its arc. He went up on his toes and smashed it back into the far corner. The ball whizzed past the movie star, who did not bother to chase the shot. He shook his head and went back to his defensive position to receive Nick's next serve.

None of the players or spectators paid particular attention to the throbbing sound of rotor blades coming from the adjacent rooftop.

Angelo Vizzoni cradled the M-14 and watched Gabriel Torres as he went through the final flight checkoff. The instrument panel on the Bell-Jet Ranger was illuminated by soft red lights. Torres's eyes roved slowly across each indicator: the fuel gauge, the engine warning light, oil pressure and transmissions. He pushed the throttle full open and brought the compressor up to fifteen percent. He held the N-1 starter at sixty percent and refined the mix of fuel and air. Vizzoni glanced at his watch: it was 8:08 P.M.

"Come on, for chrissake, Gabby."

"*Calma, calma . . .*" Torres replied, his eyes fixed on the complex panel. He waited another minute until the generator light came on line. He rolled the throttle up to

483 rpm and fiddled with the N-2 air-gas feed until the two arrows were in balance. He flicked the radio switch on. Strobes on. Anticollision lights on. He pulled the collective lever slowly and pressed gently on the floor pedals, checking the tail rotor's steering pitch. He brought the stick up to full power, and the helicopter rose three feet and hovered. Torres made one final check: All systems were in the green. He retracted the collective and pushed the stick forward. The rotors beat the air furiously, and the helicopter climbed majestically at the rate of 1,000 feet a minute.

Torres depressed a floor pedal, and the helicopter veered sharply off in a westerly direction. The digital clock over the instrument panel displayed 8:12 P.M. They would circle in a wide 360-degree arc for three minutes before homing in on the tennis court. Vizzoni checked the M-14: The folding stock was in place; the clip locked; safety off; semiautomatic on; the sights calibrated for a 45-degree trajectory; the Starlightscope set; the battery light on.

Tommy Moro looked up at the night sky at the sound of the approaching helicopter. Vizzoni was right on schedule. The roar of the rotor blades became more ominous with each passing second. Moro could now see the dark silhouette of the helicopter and its blinking red lights. The tennis players and spectators glanced up at the helicopter as it hovered a hundred yards above the floodlit courts.

In the small Plexiglas cockpit Torres held the approach attitude at a synchronous rate of sixty knots. He moved the cyclic aft slightly, easing the nose up and changing the thrust of the blades. He pulled the collective stick for more power and maintained zero airspeed. They were in a perfectly balanced hover position, but the southwest air current forced Torres to adjust the power constantly. Beads of sweat had begun to pop out of his forehead.

"Go ahead," Torres growled.

"We wait for the lights," Vizzoni replied calmly.

"There are police choppers. We can't hover too fucking long."

Torres's complaint was valid. Police helicopters routinely patrolled the skies above Century City and the adjacent golden triangle of Beverly Hills.

Vizzoni held the M-14 at ready and said, "Just hold your position."

The tennis players still concentrated on their games, but the spectators had focused their attention on the helicopter and had begun to question one another about its presence. Tommy Moro watched Carelli and the movie star dueling over a match point, then glanced at his watch and looked up at the helicopter. It was time. He shouted at the bodyguards, "Hey, Pete! Vito! I don't like that chopper!" The warning was part of a game plan to disguise his own role in the killing. He yelled again. "Kill the fucking lights!"

One hundred yards above the court Torres's eyes were tense and lines of sweat streaked down his face. "What the fuck is going on?" he growled.

Vizzoni touched the pilot's arm. "Calm, Gabby, calm."

Cristina Carelli noticed her husband's bodyguards scurrying toward a distant fuse box. She asked the movie star's girl friend about the presence of the hovering helicopter.

"Oh, they're probably shooting a cover photograph for L.A. magazine," the girl answered.

"I've never seen one that low," Cristina said nervously.

The court lights went out. People gasped; players cursed. Epithets were hurled at the management.

In the right seat of the Plexiglas ball, high above the dark courts, Angelo Vizzoni pressed the red button on the Starlightscope. The dark rooftop was illuminated in a pale green light. The chopper tilted slightly, and Vizzoni shouted, "Hold it steady!"

Torres cursed Vizzoni in Spanish and eased the pressure on the cyclic throttle. The helicopter maintained its level attitude. Vizzoni swung the M-14 slowly, his eye fastened to the scope as the cross hairs moved over green faces and figures. The scope zeroed in on the far court, and Vizzoni found Nick Carelli. He was standing near the bench, a towel draped around his neck. He seemed to be speaking to his wife and the blond girl. Vizzoni's index finger curled around the trigger. The scope's cross hairs steadied on Carelli's handsome face, bisecting at the bridge of his nose.

Gabriel Torres wiped the sweat from his face. His eyes darted from the instrument panel to the horizon line. He fully expected a police helicopter to come skimming out from the west.

"Hold it steady!" Vizzoni shouted over the rotor blades. The cross hairs now centered at a point just above Carelli's right eye. Vizzoni squeezed his trigger finger, and Nick's face disappeared.

The helicopter peeled off sharply and climbed, its red lights blinking their way toward the Pacific.

The tennis courts' twenty-five floodlights came on, and the players assumed their positions on the court.

Nick Carelli lay in a pool of blood at his wife's feet. But Cristina had issued no cry of alarm. She was unable to. The 7.62-millimeter 3-inch hollow-head slug had passed through her husband's eye, bounced off the hard red clay and angled up, penetrating her swollen belly and exploding inside. The force of the impact had thrust her back against the wall. Her legs were spread apart. Her insulted eyes stared sightlessly. A stream of blood poured from her belly and ran down her legs, mixing with the gray fluid leaking out of her husband's head.

The movie star's girl friend stared in horror at the grisly sight alongside her. She desperately pumped air into her lungs, trying to scream, feeling as though she were trapped in a childhood nightmare. No matter how hard she tried she could not issue a scream. But suddenly a series of shrieks and cries surrounded her as others became aware of the killings. The blond girl finally emitted a low groan, then a chilling scream. The aging movie star jumped the net and ran toward the crowd milling around his teenaged girl friend.

At the precise moment of the Carelli murders it was 12:26 P.M. the following day in Seoul, Korea.

Chapter Twenty-two

President Yi Chung sat behind his desk in the Blue House, studying a series of reports. In the provincial capital of Kwangju a nine-day student uprising had been crushed, leaving 189 dead. In Seoul 300 students at Korea University had clashed with club-wielding riot police. A hunger strike of 30 Roman Catholic priests marked the anniversary of the bloody insurrection of July.

Chung leaned back and rubbed his hand wearily over his eyes. He had spent the previous evening with the cultural chairman of the People's Republic of China. The evening had been highlighted by a special dance performance conducted by the National Classical Music Institute. Chung feigned interest throughout most of the program, but his attention perked up with the concluding number: a Buddhist ritual dance using opulently costumed dancers who swayed rhythmically like sunflowers in the wind. The choreography was arresting and beautifully executed.

Chung leaned forward and scribbled a note reminding himself to dispatch the dance group on a tour of Japan. The cultural chairman of the People's Republic had agreed to an exchange of the performing arts between Korea and China. It was, Chung thought, a small mosaic in a colossal tableau embracing the Dragon, the Tiger and the Rising Sun: an omnipotent twenty-first-century dynasty unifying China, Korea and Japan into an Asian Goliath. It was his sacred mission. There would be many difficulties, but Buddha taught that a journey of great distance begins with a single step.

Chung was pleased with his progress, but the student riots and national discontent had left him edgy and restless. He desperately needed to liberate his mind and release his sensual cravings. He had ordered his executive

151

secretary to arrange a party for this evening with kisaeng girls. There would be ginseng root, yakju wine, marijuana and opium. He would have preferred one single hour of sexual abandonment with Soon Yi Sonji to all the skills of available kisaeng girls, but Sonji had become a warrior, a soldier, the true daughter of Vishnu. She was the spider's messenger. She had lit the fuse in the highest councils of the American intelligence agencies that would eventually explode, bringing down those forces opposing his dream of a great Asian industrial and military monolith.

In the exterior office Chung's executive secretary waited patiently for the president to conclude his meditations. Won held a bulletin in his hand. Sonji's father, Professor Kim, had been quoted in the press as stating: "Who can believe politics exist in Korea? Who can believe there is democracy? There is no justice in Korea. We have returned to the repressive days of Park."

Chung's five black-suited bodyguards watched impassively as the diminutive former paratroop captain paced the Oriental carpet. But if those burly silent men had had the power to read Won's mind, their expressions would not have remained passive. After two years of service Won believed a coup was necessary for the survival of the nation. The rate of inflation had climbed. Exports were down. Tourism had fallen. American aid was based solely on military considerations. Students, workers and farmers were in a constant state of unrest. The capital sweltered under a brutal heat wave; garbage had piled up in the choked streets. Peasants from the countryside streamed into Seoul, seeking employment and finding only desolation. The elders squatted in the back alleys of the Chong-Ro District, cooking their kimchi cabbage in the streets while their daughters sold themselves to Japanese tourists. Were it not for the 400,000 Koreans working in Japan and Saudi Arabia, all semblance of order would have been lost. Their foreign earnings would not have been included in the gross national product, and 400,000 jobs for highly skilled men did not exist in Korea. The president had inexorably withdrawn from realpolitik into the esoteric teachings of Buddha. He was driven by plots and counterplots, seeking some mythic dream that would unify all of Buddha's children. It was the same dream that had infected the Iron Man, Park.

Won could not fathom Chung's motives for manipulating the American power structure. On those rare occasions when he dared seek answers, the president would only smile and say, "Buddha whispers. I obey."

The doors to the outer office opened and a communications officer handed Won a cable from the Korean Embassy in Washington. He opened the sealed red envelope and read the message: "N. Carelli and wife shot to death in Los Angeles 8:26 PST."

He absorbed the words but could not evaluate their importance. A buzzer sounded loudly, and he entered the presidential office.

The president stood at the open French windows, admiring the floral displays bathed in the late July sun. The presidential garden was now called the Garden of Five Seasons. The unlucky number 4 had been removed.

"Excellency." Won spoke.

"Yes?"

"I have several reports."

"Sit down, Captain."

"The riots at Kwangju, at Pusan and here in the capital have been crushed," Won continued, "but the Catholic priests persist in their hunger strike."

"What more do you have to tell me that I already know?" Chung answered derisively.

Won shifted in the chair. "Soon Yi Sonji's father, Professor Kim, has again issued inflammatory statements."

Chung lit an American cigarette. "Go on, Captain."

"Here is a cable from our embassy in Washington."

Chung sat behind his desk, and Won slid the red envelope across its gleaming surface.

"When was this received?"

"Considering time for decoding, I would imagine forty minutes ago."

"You imagine?"

"I'm sorry, sir."

"You must not imagine. You must know. Buddha teaches only that which is complete is right. Without total knowledge one becomes trapped in the samsara."

"I do not know the meaning of samsara."

"The whirlpool," Chung explained. "To avoid the samsara, you must sit very still for a long time. Only then will you see things truly. All of life's puzzles can be solved through meditation."

The powerful shoulders hunched forward, and Chung crushed the cigarette out. "You will keep the Garrison Command at Korea University and the Tiger Division in Kwangju. The White Horse Fifth Armored Division will remain on alert in Pusan. As for the Catholic emissaries of Rome, let them starve to death. It is of no consequence. And take care, Captain, that no harm comes to Professor Kim."

"But, Excellency, he inflames the students."

"Perhaps. But I have a covenant with Soon Yi Sonji that I am not prepared to break." He then picked up the cable and smiled. "These killings in Los Angeles are geometric truths, a direct result of placing the Reverend Rhee in opposition to the American underworld."

"Forgive me, sir, but I cannot understand how the murder of this man Carelli benefits the Korean nation."

"Well then, Captain, I shall have to enlighten you."

Won watched mystified as the muscular former general moved to the fireplace and lifted a white ceramic bowl emblazoned with blue dragons. Chung carried the bowl back to the desk, placed it down and poured some water into it from a silver carafe. "Stand up, Captain," he ordered. "Watch carefully." The president took a small coin and dropped it into the water. A series of concentric circles formed and moved out to the edges of the dish. They watched in silence until all movement of water had ceased. "What did you see, Captain?"

"The water moved."

"What caused it to move?"

"The force of the coin falling into the water."

"Producing what?"

"Circles."

Chung nodded. "Yes. One circle produced another, and if not for the dish, they would have continued for an eternity, causing certain actions as they moved. The circle contains man's infinite power."

The president lit another cigarette. His fingertips had turned orange from the five packs a day he consumed.

"When Sonji informed Ricker of the meeting in the Glass Room where Park's fate was sealed, she created a circle. Ricker then knew exactly what Rhee held over the American power structure. Ricker then ·acts, sowing distrust and fear among the American intelligence troika."

"Forgive me, sir, but what do you mean by troika?"

"The chairman of the National Security Council, Dr. Belgrave; the chief of Defense Intelligence, Charles Gruenwald; and Director of CIA Covert Operations Robert Burgess." Chung sat down and leaned back. "A nerve is exposed. It triggers an irrational act." His hard black eyes glittered with a dangerous merriment.

"The circle moves, creating relentless pressure," he continued. "They murder Mrs. Hwan. The circle widens. The men who killed Mrs. Hwan now have a certain power over the troika. By setting Carelli on Rhee, Belgrave is forced into a meeting with the leaders of the American underworld. Now they, too, possess a measure of power over the Doctor. The nerve is further exposed. All of which is achieved from within. None of the events connect to this office. You are witnessing the wisdom and inevitability of the samsara."

Won felt goose bumps forming on his arms. He was chilled by the depraved cunning of the fanatical Buddhist leader. The more Won perceived, the stronger became his conviction that Chung had to be destroyed.

The president inhaled and blew the smoke up toward the high-domed ceiling.

"Now they assassinate Carelli and mangle the operation. His pregnant wife is also murdered."

Won cleared his throat and asked, "But what is the gain derived from these killings?"

The president stared at his aide, wondering whether the diminutive young man was playing a crafty game. He answered Won in the simplistic tone of a teacher addressing a bewildered pupil. "How do you think the father of Carelli will react to these killings?"

"Rage, vengeance."

"Correct. The circle moves. Dr. Belgrave and his associates will have still another force to deal with."

"But how will the father know it was Belgrave who ordered the killings?"

"It is inevitable that he will find out. The Doctor cannot long hide from view."

Won rose and stared at the autographed photo of Lyndon Johnson on the far wall. "There is a flaw, Mr. President. The father of Carelli is in exile. He is not permitted to reenter America. How will he exact his vengeance?"

"Gemstone," Chung replied.

Won was startled at the mention of the secret Hoover file. "But, sir, the Gemstone file is in the possession of Kimsan. He refuses to release it."

"Kimsan will be swept up in the samsára. The circle will move him." The president's black eyes gleamed with a canny light. "Gemstone will be Carlo Carelli's visa back to America."

Chapter Twenty-three

Low, gray, roiling clouds scudded across the Miami skyline, promising a violent summer storm. The air was heavy and carried with it a curious sensual warmth. The young Cuban who had manned the helm on the cabin cruiser drove the black '77 Buick. Leo Meyers sat alongside the Cuban youth. Two other armed Cubans were in the back seat. The car radio played an old Perez Prado mambo. The air in the Buick was stale and muggy. Leo reached down and fiddled with the air conditioner's buttons.

"*No funciona, señor,*" the driver explained.

"*Por favor,*" Leo said gently. "*Repararlo.*"

"*Sí, señor. En segida. Mañana temprano.*" The young Cuban agreed to have the air conditioning fixed first thing in the morning.

Leo mused that he could trace the course of events in this century by his own shifting use of languages. From his village of birth in Russia, Hebrew; then Yiddish; then English; now Spanish. And if Israel permitted him to return, his life would end with Hebrew.

The Buick rolled slowly through the lower reaches of Collins Avenue, passing rows of decrepit stucco apartments. The signs on the three-story pastel-colored relics advertised Jewish nursing homes for the aged. The benches and small terraces were populated by old people, staring blankly at the passing traffic. They were the human residue of lost relationships, cast off by children who could no longer bear their company and refused to deal with their infirmities, senility and complaints. The old people were victims of a sophisticated society that had prolonged their lives but could not tolerate their presence.

Leo Meyers shook his head and wondered what munificent god had permitted him to escape a similar fate.

The Buick turned right at Twelfth Street and parked thirty feet from the corner. Leo glanced at his watch. It was 10:44 A.M. The Cuban rolled the windows down. The Spanish radio station played a lively meringue. A bolt of yellow lightning snaked down from the dark clouds, followed by a rumble of distant thunder.

At 10:47 Leo Meyers got out of the car and walked across the street to a public phone booth. The Buick slid away from the curb.

Leo dropped a dime in the slot and placed a long-distance call, using the name and credit-card number of a young man who had died four years ago. The number connected to a public telephone booth outside a small restaurant in the village of Amagansett, Long Island.

Victor Maldonado's bodyguards sat on the restaurant terrace overlooking the phone booth, ogling bikini-clad teenage girls having their breakfasts of Cokes and chili-burgers.

Inside the phone booth a sweating Victor Maldonado grabbed the receiver on the first ring.

"Go ahead," Victor said.

"Where is Vizzoni?" Leo asked.

"Tijuana."

"Get him," Leo said.

"He's on the way," Maldonado replied.

"Why was this thing done from the air?"

"It was necessary. Nicky was protected like the President."

"Which one?" Leo answered sarcastically, then paused and continued. "Nick had an okay to muscle that Korean Reverend. Someone positioned him."

"Well, what the fuck could we do?" Maldonado asked. "The Doctor is the government."

"They may be moving Belgrave around, too," Leo cautioned. "Just make sure he comes through with his part of the deal. We need those teamster files."

"I'll take care of it."

"Call me after you see Vizzoni."

"Will you speak with Don Carlo?" Victor asked.

"Yes."

"I hope to Christ he understands." The line went dead in Maldonado's hand.

Leo Meyers came out of the booth and strolled slowly up toward Collins Avenue. He passed the doorway of a crumbling synagogue and was startled by a ghost sitting on the steps, a phantom out of Auschwitz. The frail woman's eyes were older than time. She held her small palms up to Leo and pleaded, *"Bitte, bitte . . ."*

Leo dropped three $20 bills in her lap. The ancient Jewish woman thanked him in Yiddish. The black Buick pulled up at the corner, and Leo got in.

They drove north on Collins, and Leo thought about the old woman's words: "A blessing will come to you in the next world."

The tropical storm broke, sending thick sheets of rain pouring down over the decaying city.

Chapter Twenty-four

"Why did you keep the liaison going with Joyce Raymond?" Phil asked.

Sonji, looking exquisite in a white Cardin suit, shrugged her shoulders, and the light rippled along her silky black hair. "I had to be certain she would remain loyal to me. That she would not have second thoughts and phone Nicky."

They were in the second-floor study of Phil's town house. The overhead lights were dimmed down, bathing the room in a soft glow. Sonji's sweet, heavy perfume permeated the air. Phil and Sid Greene had spent the last two days with FBI investigators of the organized crime squad. The special section fed details of the Carelli killings into high-speed computers, but the readouts displayed no similar *modus operandi*. The FBI experts did agree on one point: Don Carlo Carelli would seek vengeance. The murder of Nick Carelli and his wife had made coast-to-coast headlines, and the L.A. police had come under heavy criticism for the helicopter's easy access to the skies above Century City.

Sonji's laissez-faire attitude toward the killings increased Phil's sense of rage and helplessness. He walked up to her and with undisguised anger said, "How does it feel to know you caused the death of three people?"

"Three?" she asked, puzzled.

"The autopsy showed the unborn child was a perfect boy."

"I followed orders."

"You also placed Joyce Raymond's life in jeopardy. If the hit on Nicky had failed, he would've come after her."

"I followed orders," she repeated, and poured a glass of cold white wine.

Phil suddenly swung his open right hand across her cheek. The sound of the slap cracked loudly. But Sonji never moved. He grabbed her arms and shook her violently. "Don't you for chrissake feel anything?" She did not respond, and Phil shoved her against the bar. "Maybe I'm living in the wrong century. I don't understand. You speak four or five languages; you're cultured, well educated. You look like a goddamn painting, and you play with people's lives as if they were toys. And you give me the old Nazi line, 'I followed orders.' What the hell are you made out of?"

"I am made out of Tantra and *Tao* and Kali. I am a servant of the state." She walked slowly up to him. "I was fourteen when Commander Kyu placed me in an Angel Cloud house. Every act of sexual degradation, every use of mouth, body and hands, and mind were practiced upon me. I am ice. I am fire." Her words and speech had become mechanical. "I am semen. I am blood. I am the true daughter of the goddess Vishnu. I am practiced in all the Eastern arts of sensuality. I have made love to hundreds of men—and many women. Young, old, all races, all kinds. I have power, but I feel nothing. I am empty. But a day will come when I will be a person. A person of great importance. It is written in the sacred texts that giants will walk in the shadow of Vishnu's daughter. One day that prophecy will be fulfilled. And my life will have meaning. So I cannot be hurt by emptiness. The cup is emptied, and the cup is refilled. The circle will be closed."

Phil stared at her, trying to discern some expression of sorrow or anguish at her bizarre confession, but her face was like a magnificent Oriental mask. He went past her to the bar and poured three fingers of vodka over ice. He swirled the ice and glanced at her. "What the hell do you want with me?" he asked with resignation.

She rubbed her cheek where he had slapped her. "I have reason to believe Kimsan may be in peril."

Phil grew interested at the mention of the central figure in the Koreagate scandal. "Why do you come to me?"

"Because I've spoken to him and he approved this meeting," Sonji said.

"Where is he?"

"What does it matter?"

"It matters to me," Phil replied.

"He is at the moment · in Palermo. But he moves through certain cities in Italy."

"Peddling heroin," Phil snapped.

"He works at the direction of President Chung."

"As do we all," Phil said sarcastically.

"I fear for his life. Kimsan was a friend." Sonji's voice mellowed, and the rhythm of her words became singsong. "There is a Korean poem: 'How many friends have I? Count them: water and stone, pine and bamboo. The rising moon on the east mountain, welcome it, too. It is my friend. What need is there, I say, to have more friends than five?' " There was an imperceptible mist in her oval eyes. "Kimsan is the east mountain in my life."

For the first time Phil felt as if her words had come out of her soul.

"He knew my history," she said. "He understands what I became. He loved me." She leaned across the bar. "Should it ever become necessary, would you be willing to place him under United States federal protection?"

"I'll do what I can."

"He offers nothing in return."

"I understand." Phil glanced at the perfect ruby on her left index finger. "But I want a favor from you."

"Yes?"

"Why did Chung position Carelli against the Reverend Rhee? What did he gain by causing Nick's death?"

"I have no idea."

"Give me a wild guess."

Sonji moved to the window. "Chung believes in the infinite power of the circle. You drop a pebble in a pond and the circles move, creating a samsara, a whirlpool of motion."

"That's philosophy, not motive."

"There are times when they mean the same thing." She walked slowly back to him. "Chung knew that once Rhee's California temples were hit, he would complain to someone high up in your intelligence community, forcing them to act."

"Still no motive."

"It's an Asian theory of unrelenting pressure. Buddha

says the mind has the power to crumble a wall. I know it's a difficult concept for Western people to perceive."

"Not this Western person. I understand it. We had the war in Vietnam won half a dozen times, but they kept coming on. We could have bombed them into the Stone Age, and they'd have come at us with bows and arrows. I understand the philosophy, but I still don't see a motive."

"I'm sorry. I can't help you."

Phil studied her a moment. "You once told me that you played a part in the assassination of President Park."

"Yes."

"What happened that night? Exactly how did Chung pull the rug out from under everyone?"

"Perhaps the day will come when I can tell you." She paused. "There is something I can tell you. The Reverend Rhee still reports to Chung."

"I figured that one out all by myself."

She looked at him and nodded. "You will keep your word regarding Kimsan?"

"Yes." He walked up to her and touched the red spot on her cheek where he'd slapped her. "I'm sorry. I was out of line."

Sonji leaned into him and kissed him softly, then withdrew.

"When will I see you?" Phil asked.

"I don't know. I've been ordered back to Seoul." She paused. "My father has been placed under house arrest."

"Why?"

"He is a Professor at Pusan University. He makes inflammatory speeches against the state. My father is a hero to the students. But so far no harm has come to him. President Chung has kept his word to me."

"I didn't know your father was being held hostage."

"Hostage may be the wrong word." She smiled a small sad smile. "Perhaps my father is simply another ripple in the circle."

Chapter Twenty-five

The Mustang entered Sheridan Circle and pulled into the circular driveway in front of the squat gray Korean Embassy. Sid Greene cut the ignition and asked, "You believe Sonji?"

"I think she told me what she knew," Phil replied.

"So Chung's motive in the Carelli killings was simply to increase pressure on Belgrave?"

"Sonji never mentioned the good Doctor. And she never suggested a motive—only an Asian philosophy of unrelenting pressure."

"Pressure on whom?"

"Some clandestine master spook who controls policy affecting Korea."

"Logic would dictate," Sid said persuasively, "that Rhee went to Belgrave, forcing him to call the mob off."

"That's a reach," Phil replied. "The Reverend has his own hit men. Remember his bodyguards are KCIA. Professional assassins. Burgess is chief of Covert Operations. He has an array of hit men. Gruenwald in Defense Intelligence has the services of good old boy killers. And then there's Sharkey in State Intelligence. Or maybe the godfather, Victor Maldonado, had a simple business grudge against Carelli. We can't assume it's Belgrave."

They got out of the car and walked toward the embassy building. "It all comes down to Chung's motives," Phil said. "If we knew what those motives were, we could crack this thing."

The huge blowup of President Yi Chung stared benignly down at the men gathered in the ornate sitting room. Reverend Rhee was seated in a blue velvet gold-trimmed chair. His attorney, Stanford Harwick, stood beside him.

Phil spoke to the silver-haired attorney with courteous authority. "Mr. Harwick, I'm going to pose a series of questions to your client. None of this is on the record. You requested we go off the record to avoid a subpoena, with its attendant national publicity. But I reserve the right to subpoena at a later date."

"That is our understanding, Mr. Ricker."

Phil said, "Frankly the government's case against your client has been damaged by a series of violent events that I'm certain you're familiar with."

The tall, fastidiously tailored attorney said, "My presence here is merely to insure the rights of my client. I believe we agreed to that stipulation."

"That was our agreement, Counselor," Phil acknowledged.

"Proceed with your questions, Mr. Ricker."

Phil paced the Oriental carpet for a moment, then turned to the Reverend. "Mr. Rhee, are you presently an agent of the Korean Central Intelligence Agency?"

"I am Buddha's messenger in America."

"Do you know—scratch that—do you enjoy a personal relationship with President Yi Chung?"

"We have spoken privately on occasion."

"When was the last occasion?"

"Back in January, when President Chung visited Washington."

"Do you know a young Korean woman named Soon Yi Sonji?"

"I am aware that she is a cultural attaché here in the embassy."

"Reverend, did you attend a meeting in the Glass Room at CIA headquarters on July fifth, 1979?"

"I was never in any Glass Room. I have never had any contact with American Intelligence agencies."

"Reverend, were you present at any meeting where the assassination of President Park was discussed?"

"Never."

"Reverend, do you know Dr. Eric Belgrave?"

A single drop of perspiration appeared on Rhee's forehead. He was astonished at the accuracy of information inherent in the deputy attorney general's questions. "I know Dr. Belgrave by reputation."

"Do you know Dr. Belgrave personally?"

"I do not."

"Do you know Robert Burgess?"

Rhee wiped the spot of perspiration on his forehead. "No."

"Reverend, do you mean to say you've never heard that name?"

"I've heard the name."

Phil stopped pacing and faced the sweating preacher. "I imagine you have, Reverend." His repetition of the word *"Reverend"* lent it a malevolent connotation. "Do you know Charles Gruenwald?"

"I've heard the name."

"Reverend, were you not in the Glass Room with those men and others in the summer of 1979 when the decision to murder President Park was taken?"

"I am Buddha's messenger. I know nothing of these matters."

Phil stared at the black almond eyes in the jowly pasty face. "Reverend, does the name Nick Carelli have any special meaning for you?"

"I believe he is an American gangster who was recently shot to death."

"Did you have any personal contact with him?"

"No."

Phil nodded, and the tone of his voice became dramatically gentle. "Now, Reverend, you obviously are well connected with the present Korean government."

"I maintain certain ties to my native country."

"Your very presence here at the. embassy indicates a close liaison."

Rhee glanced at Harwick; but the handsome attorney said nothing, and Phil continued. "We have established that Soon Yi Sonji is in fact a cultural attaché with this embassy. Isn't that correct?"

"Yes."

"Now, Reverend"—Phil's voice grew harsh once again—"are you aware that Soon Yi Sonji had a meeting with the late Mr. Carelli just prior to the attacks on your temples?"

Rhee's slit eyes lost their assurance and were clouded

by a shadow of fear. He took a platinum case out of his jacket and extracted a small brown cigarette. "I know nothing of—"

Phil shouted, "You mean to tell me you were not aware that Soon Yi Sonji, acting on President Chung's orders, convinced Mr. Carelli to go after your temples?"

Rhee sputtered, "I know—a—an emissary approached—" Rhee suddenly fell silent.

Phil went after the sweating preacher with a vengeance. "An emissary of Nick Carelli approached you with a warning that you had a new partner. Isn't that right, Reverend?"

"I am Buddha's messenger."

"And you went to someone high up in American Intelligence and complained. And that someone ordered the murder of Nick Carelli!"

"Now just a minute, Counselor," Harwick interjected. "You're leading my client into areas of sheer speculation."

"You're quite right, Mr. Harwick," Phil said apologetically. "Forgive me." He paced the carpet for a moment in a tight circle, then asked, "Reverend, did you know a Korean woman named Mrs. Hwan?"

"Yes, she was my executive secretary some years ago."

"Did you conduct a sexual liaison with Mrs. Hwan?"

"That is absurd."

"And," Harwick interrupted, "defamatory and insulting."

Sid Greene said, "It's only fair, Mr. Harwick, to advise you that your client maintained an apartment at One fifty-eight South Maple Drive in Beverly Hills. We have the sworn testimony of neighbors placing your client and Mrs. Hwan in that apartment on a fairly regular basis during her five years of employment."

"None of which has any relevance to your current investigation," Harwick replied.

"It certainly does," Phil snapped, "when you consider Mrs. Hwan was our key witness—and wound up with a bullet in her ear."

"Bring it to court, Counselor."

"You can count on it," Phil snapped, and leaned toward Rhee. "You're a KCIA agent, Reverend. You were in on the Park assassination. You still report to Chung. But you have no idea why he set you up with Carelli. That worries you, doesn't it, Reverend? You caused the theft of my files. You caused the torture and killing of Mrs. Hwan. You caused the contract to be placed on Nick Carelli. You are a common street hustler preying on the minds and fears of children. You're a killer by collusion. Before and after the fact. And I'll be goddamned if you're going to get away with it!" Phil turned and said, "Let's go, Sid. Thanks for the meeting, Mr. Harwick."

Phil drove the Mustang carefully through the heavy traffic on Massachusetts Avenue. Sid Greene lit a cigarette and said, "You must be a tiger in court."

"None of it's admissible," Phil replied. "But I got what I wanted."

"What's that?"

"Rhee didn't know that Sonji set him up with Nick, which means he had no idea that Chung was using him as a pawn to pressure our intelligence agencies."

"Which also means Sonji's been telling you the truth," Sid added.

They drove past the Romanian Embassy, and Phil suddenly exclaimed, "Goddammit!"

"What's wrong?" Sid asked.

"I forgot to question Rhee about the missing man."

"What missing man?"

"Kimsan."

Chapter Twenty-six

The five-story brick warehouse was located on the Via della Cala where the Palermo waterfront bends into an almost perfect loop.

In the clandestine laboratory on the fifth floor Dr. Hans Kleiser was about to begin the second phase in the complicated and dangerous process of reducing the solid bricks of morphine into the white powder known as Number 4 Heroin. The sixty-seven-year-old German chemist was a graduate of the sinister I.G. Farben chemical cartel.

Kleiser lived in comfortable retirement in his villa on Lake Wannsee in West Berlin. Once a month he made the trip to Palermo to supervise the morphine refinement process. The doctor received 50,000 American dollars for three days of his expertise.

Kimsan nervously watched Kleiser and his two assistants going about their preparations. It was the fifth and final stage of the operation that Kimsan feared—the moment when the highly volatile ether gas was introduced. Dr. Kleiser had already achieved the initial phase of heating ten kilos of morphine brick and ten kilos of acetic anhydride at 185 degrees Fahrenheit. The morphine and acid had become bonded, creating an impure form of heroin.

The tall, thin master chemist was preparing the second stage, the removal of impurities by use of water and chloroform. The sharp odor of the chloroform amplified the throbbing headache lodged over Kimsan's eyes. He'd managed only five hours' sleep in the last forty-eight hours.

Kimsan had personally supervised the transfer of sixty kilos of morphine bricks from a Turkish freighter to the warehouse laboratory—the bricks having been secreted in bales of tobacco leaves.

The chief customs inspector, Luigi Marzarino, worked for Don Carlo Carelli, so that the actual transfer of the tobacco bales involved little risk, requiring only silence, efficiency and correct documentation.

The fifth-floor lab was ingeniously concealed by false walls lined with bales of tobacco. It was, for all practical purposes, a sealed chamber.

Once the pure heroin was refined, it was packaged in plastic envelopes for shipment to Marseilles, Amsterdam and New York. Kimsan employed an ingenious and incongruous network of smugglers: African diplomats, French businessmen, East European diplomats, airline stewardesses, Italian seamen and NATO military officers.

The network and distribution were financed and organized by the twenty-four international Mafia families. The Sicilian operation was entrusted to Don Carlo Carelli.

Kimsan brushed some lint from his beige linen suit and stared out of the dust-flaked window. On the horizon a dark smudge marked the path of a tanker moving its precious cargo from Dubai to the refineries of Naples. But Kimsan was not thinking about oil. His thoughts were focused on Don Carlo Carelli. He respected and admired the old man. And in return he enjoyed Don Carlo's trust and protection.

The news from America regarding the California killings had sent Don Carlo into seclusion at Lercara, the mountain village of his birth.

Kimsan glanced at his watch and walked over to Kleiser. The balding, bespectacled chemist smelled of chloroform.

"I am late for a luncheon appointment, Doctor."

"Please go," Kleiser replied. "We will not reach the final step until late this evening. Take your time. Enjoy your lunch."

●

The blue and white striped awning cast some shade over the small trattoria on the sun-drenched Corse

Emanuele. The wide, palm-lined boulevard was lightly trafficked at midday. Kimsan sat at a sidewalk table, admiring the trees across the street in the Garibaldi Garden. The splash of green transmitted a feeling of tranquillity in a city where sudden death shadowed the normal course of life.

Kimsan's luncheon partner was a homely Korean woman, a KCIA agent stationed in the Korean Embassy in Rome. She had a firm, tough jawline and small slits of black eyes. She was a veteran of numerous clandestine operations and had come down from Rome for the meeting.

They were eating linguine and clams and drinking cold white Corvo wine. The woman, whose operative name was Yan Si, spoke between mouthfuls of pasta. "It is official. Don Carlo Carelli sent word through the Ministero dell' Interno. He intends to return to America."

Kimsan pushed the half-eaten plate of pasta away and lit a Rothman cigarette. "What is it that Chung wishes of me in this matter?"

She wiped her oily lips and said, "It is our president's view that Carelli will require the Gemstone file to gain entry to America."

Kimsan took a long moment before he replied, "President Chung is aware of my historic position regarding Gemstone. I cannot permit that file to leave my possession."

"You need not produce the file, only promise it to Carelli. He, in turn, can advise the Americans that he will bring Gemstone with him."

"They aren't fools, Yan Si. The Don will at some point have to produce the file."

"Not if someone the Americans trust guarantees Gemstone. Our president suggested you mention the name of Philip Ricker to Don Carlo."

"In what way?"

"The Don does not trust government officials in Italy. They have harassed him for years. And once the American underworld knows of his offer to return and testify, he will be a hunted man. He will seek a guarantee of safety from the American Justice officials. There is no better guarantee than a personal escort." She drank some wine and belched softly. "A man who is willing to place his life in jeopardy side by side with Don Carlo."

Kimsan shook his head. "Doesn't our president know that it was Ricker who forced Don Carlo into exile?"

Yan Si leaned close to him. Her breath smelled of garlic, and the tone of her voice was conspiratorial. "This is precisely why Don Carlo will accept Ricker as his escort. During the deportàtion proceedings attempts were made to bribe Ricker. He refused. Ricker has many flaws, but he is a man of honor. Don Carlo will accept him."

A long, piercing whistle issued from a freighter moving slowly out to sea; its mournful wail reverberated in the piazza, amplifying the torpor of the city. Kimsan's handsome features were drawn by fatigue and concentration.

"Tell me, Yan Si, why is President Chung interested in Don Carlo's welfare? Why does he want him to return to America?"

Her almond eyes narrowed and glinted dangerously. But the tone of her voice was warm and persuasive. "Why do you question our leader's motives? In the past he has asked you to surrender the Gemstone file. You refused. Were you harmed in any way?"

"No," Kimsan admitted.

"At any time in any place," she continued, "you could have been tortured or killed. Here in Palermo, or Rome, or Milan. Anywhere. You can be assassinated at any moment. Is that not true?"

"Yes, yes, it's true," he nervously agreed.

"But you have not been harmed. On the contrary, you are permitted to keep huge profits from our drug operations. Why, then, do you mistrust our president?"

"Perhaps for what he has done to Sonji."

"Sonji was used when she was a child by Commander Kyu. President Chung was an obscure colonel in those days. Please do not confuse this issue with misguided sentiment. Our president has acted honorably with you. He asks you now to perform a small service: to promise Don Carlo you will give him Gemstone should he require it and to suggest Ricker as an official American escort to see him home safely."

Kimsan sipped his espresso. He turned her words over to determine if his compliance would in any way betray the Don. But in truth, his cooperation could only help the old man achieve vengeance.

"All right, Yan Si. I will mention these matters to Don Carlo."

Chapter Twenty-seven

Lercara was a small white stone village carved out of the mountain escarpment. In summer it baked under the merciless Sicilian sun, and in winter it froze under numbing, relentless rains. The cultivated hills surrounding the village undulated and rolled like a windblown green carpet.

The dark, foreboding Monte Cammarata loomed up in the north, and to the south the ice blue Mediterranean sparkled into infinity.

Lercara's graceful arches and blue window frames bore witness to its history of Moorish occupation. But a brooding sinister atmosphere hung over the ancient village. Silent groups of old men moved sluggishly down the cobblestoned main street. There was a startling absence of young men. The young men were in the cemetery, their photographs embedded in headstones. They were victims of endless Mafia blood feuds. The survivors had migrated to Switzerland, Germany and America, far away from this place of hopelessness and sorrow.

The women of Lercara remained hidden behind shuttered windows, gripping their wooden crosses and whispering secret messages to the dead. There was no cinema, no playground, no soccer field, only the puritanical presence of the church with its incongruous gold Moorish dome. The harsh, invisible black hand of the Honored Society gripped the desultory streets.

On a hill rise above Lercara columned ruins of ancient Athenian gratitude stood like silent sentinels bearing witness to the unchanging Sicilian despair. The Doric columns marked the place where Greek invaders had erected a temple to the god Apollo. Below the ruins, nestled into the jutting promontory was the Villa Carelli.

* * *

Cherubs framed in swirls of Florentine gold smiled down from their oval frescoes. The ornate ceiling of the banquet hall was supported by ten marble columns. Antique chairs and sofas that smelled of disuse were scattered about the great marble hall. Heavy fuchsia-colored velvet drapes were drawn over terrace windows, blocking the sunlight. Alongside the windows an angel on a white fluted pedestal peered into the gloom out of sightless marble eyes.

Don Carlo Carelli brushed his thinning, gray hair and stared at the photograph. It was a family portrait of another time: A pretty woman holding a small boy stood alongside a youthful Carlo Carelli. The stocky man watching the Don was his bodyguard, Luigi Ruffino, who had voluntarily followed his boss into exile ten years ago.

The Don spoke in a hushed voice. "Who would have imagined that I would suffer the torment of surviving my wife, my son . . . and my unborn grandchild?"

He turned away from the photograph. His face was aged and etched by a network of fine lines. But his powder blue eyes and handsome features bore a striking resemblance to the face of his murdered son. "Nicky was always wild," Don Carlo reflected. "Headstrong. I warned him to obey the organization. Years ago I warned him. But he went his own way. All right, I accept Nicky's death as business. But his wife and my grandson, that's not business." Don Carlo turned to Ruffino. "In America we were many things." His voice echoed faintly in the marble hall. "But here—where it all began—there was an iron morality. We were truly the Honored Society, and even in America our protection was granted to all those immigrants of Sicilian birth."

Don Carlo walked up to the marble angel and traced its cool features with his finger. "Victor Maldonado came to me in the summer of 1948. He was a kid. A zero. An ice-pick man. I gave him my blessing. I sent him to Genovese. I gave him a piece of the Brooklyn waterfront. He became important. *Un pezzo da novanta.* But Leo Meyers warned me. Leo never trusted him. I disagreed. I said, 'Victor is Sicilian—a man from my own village. We are like tribesmen. We are brothers.'" Don Carlo sighed. "But Leo was right. They took Nicky, they took his wife and they took the unborn child." He paused. "Now the price must be paid. '*Il prezzo deve essere pagato.*'"

Ruffino had listened to the same litany for the past ten days. He cleared his throat and said, "The girl is outside."

The Don nodded and gestured with his hand. Ruffino walked quickly across the room, his leather heels clicking against the polished marble. He opened the massive doors, and the girl entered.

Claudia Cassini came into the darkened hall, carrying with her the scent of life. The aroma of sweet perfume drifted into the musty room. Her dark eyes were set wide apart, mysterious and lively. She had graceful cheekbones, a small, wide nose and a full mouth. Her black hair parted in the center, and soft waves fell across her cheeks. She was tall and held her shoulders erect. She wore a blue silk dress that made a case for simplicity. Coral beads hung loosely from her neck. She wore no other jewelry.

"Sit down, please," the Don said.

She sat in a salmon-colored French chair. Ruffino stood just behind Don Carlo.

"The American officials have agreed to your return." Her voice was haunted by remnants of an English accent.

"Who gave you this information?" Don Carlo asked.

"The attorney general, Arthur Browning. I presented your conditions to him personally."

"How?"

"By phone from the ministry."

"Browning knows you work with the Ministero dell' Interno?" The Don asked.

"Yes, of course. But he insists you produce the Gemstone file on entry. They want you to come into Dulles Airport in Washington."

"When?"

"There is no specific time. They know there will be"—she paused—"difficulties."

The Don walked past Ruffino to the terrace windows. He parted the velvet drapes and looked out at the garden for a moment. "Has Ricker agreed to accompany me?"

"Not yet."

The Don turned to her. "When will we know?"

"I'll phone Browning the moment I return to Palermo."

"Ricker is the key to my safe return. They will not kill their own emissary."

"What happens if he refuses?" she asked.

Don Carlo shrugged. "I don't know."

"Perhaps you can place yourself under the protection of Italian authority," she said.

The Don smiled. "The Italian authorities . . . there is no Italian authority. There is only Italian intrigue. They have pursued me for ten years. They take enormous bribes from me. They are people without honor. The government has just fallen because of this secret Masonic society. Your own chief of the *ministero* was part of this nest of thieves and killers."

"There is a possibility that the American military authorities in Naples will assist your return," she replied.

"The American military is controlled by American intelligence agencies." The Don shook his head. "I wouldn't trust them with the life of my cat." He paused and added. "We need Ricker."

"The problem is getting him to agree," she said.

"He will not refuse me."

"Why not?"

"It's in his government's interest for me to get safely back to Washington. Browning wants the Gemstone file. Ricker is a true public servant. He won't refuse."

Claudia Cassini rose. "I will be with you as well, Don Carlo. The *ministero* will prepare an escape route."

The Don nodded. "Please call me after you've spoken with Browning."

"Of course."

As she started for the door, the Don called, "*Signorina.*"

"Yes?"

"I don't want you to undertake any personal risk on my behalf."

Her arcane eyes sparkled with old secrets. "I'm used to risks, Don Carlo."

Chapter Twenty-eight

The green radial dials glowed 3:22 A.M., and the bedroom's chilled air caused him to shiver. Phil reached over and killed the blower switch on the air-conditioning unit. The silence was ominous.

He slipped into his bathrobe and walked to the big bay window. Dumbarton Street had the look of abandonment. Its dark clapboard town houses seemed uninhabited, as if a neutron bomb had fallen, obliterating all signs of human activity while preserving the 200-year-old dwellings.

Phil's eyes narrowed as he noticed a bright red Porsche parked in front of his house. It was a startling coincidence. His own Porsche speedster had been stored in the FBI garage for the past eight weeks. He had not driven the car since the assault at the Reflecting Pool. He thought about going down and checking the license plate of the red car when he heard a muffled noise from the floor below. The sound was amorphous and difficult to define. It's tonality varied; at times it sounded like shuffling feet or someone moving a chair.

He slid open the third drawer of his bureau, shoved aside some underwear and took out a 7.62-millimeter Chinese automatic. The gun was a souvenir of Vietnam. He checked the clip; the full load of nine bullets was in place. He pulled the trigger, testing the firing mechanism, then locked the clip into the steel butt. The gun had not been fired in years, but the Chinese automatic seemed to be in good working order. He retracted the top sleeve, charging the weapon, and locked the hammer, leaving the thumb safety on.

From the floor below, the rustling, scraping noise sounded again. He gripped the automatic firmly in his

right hand and started down to the second-floor study, his
bare feet moving soundlessly on the carpeted stairway.

He entered the study and snapped on the lights. The
room was undisturbed. He was about to switch the lights
off when he heard the low, muffled noise coming from the
ground floor. The nature of the sound remained indistinct.
But something or someone was in motion in the living
room just below the study.

He removed a four-battery flashlight from the cabinet
behind the wet bar. Taking a deep breath, he wiped some
sweat from his forehead and went down to the first floor.

Phil stood just inside the living room and played the
flashlight over the bookcases and framed prints. The cone
of light moved slowly across the floor, furniture and fix-
tures. He directed the light beam cautiously across the
leather easy chairs and up onto the sofa. What he saw
stood his hair up on end. He froze and tried to scream,
but terror consumed all his oxygen. *Resting on the sofa
was the bloody grinning head of Mrs. Hwan.*

He groped his way toward the light switch and
stumbled over a hassock. The flashlight fell, and its beam
played off the sofa at a crazy angle. He grabbed the flashlight and centered it on Mrs. Hwan. But the grinning
head was gone. He panted, trying to catch his breath. A
deathly quiet descended over the room.

The steel gun butt was wet against his palm, and cold
beads of sweat oozed out of his armpits. He stood motionless, listening to the throb of his heartbeat and trying to
come to terms with the hideous hallucination. Once again
the faint, amorphous, rustling sound drifted up from below—something or someone was directing him to the basement.

He wiped his clammy palm dry, gripped the butt of the
automatic firmly, switched the safety off, and walked
down the long hallway.

Phil placed his ear to the cellar door. The sound was
sporadic. He opened the door and stepped inside.

A cold chill gripped his arms and chest, but he managed to steady the light. He played the beam off the brick
walls, across an old pool table and some broken chairs. He
took a few steps into the dank-smelling cellar and heard

the rustling sound. It seemed to be coming from a cluster of cartons at the far side of the room. He directed the light at the cartons. The sound of movement increased, but he saw nothing. Suddenly, with a resounding crack, the basement door slammed shut.

Phil whirled around, tucked the flashlight under his arm and pulled at the door handle, but the cellar door had been bolted from the outside. Beads of sweat came out of his forehead and burned their way into his eyes. He heard the sound again. This time it was defined. It was a slithering sound. He centered the light on the cartons and noticed a slight movement. *He saw the eyes first.* They shone like a set of perfect blood red rubies. Then it moved, gliding over the edge of the carton. Its fifteen-foot length unfolded as it slid across the floor. It stopped suddenly, rising up on its coils, and the monstrous head fanned out. It was a white cobra.

The snake swayed back and forth, then dropped and slithered toward him. He clutched the gun in a death grasp, his knuckles turning white. The cobra slid across the stone floor and drew close. Then it stopped. Coiled. And rose on a level with Phil's eyes. Its triangular head was fully fanned as it rocked back and forth, measuring him. He smelled a foul, fetid stench that reminded him of the Vietnamese jungles. The hideous head swayed from side to side like death on a slow metronome.

Phil summoned all his remaining faculties and extended his right arm. The gun tracked the moving head of the reptile, while the flashlight shone in the cobra's beady red eyes. He took a deep breath and squeezed the trigger. The hammer clicked, but the weapon did not fire. He squeezed the trigger again, producing another click. The weaving fanned head accelerated, shortening its swaying arc.

He pulled the trigger over and over but heard only clicks. The serpent's head and curved neck swayed backward for leverage, then struck with blurring speed. The inverted hollow fangs sank into his cheek, penetrating the skin like hypodermic needles. The sickening jungle smell filled his nostrils, and the slimy venom trickled down to his neck.

* * *

Phil bolted upright in bed. He screamed for a full minute before he realized the white cobra and the grinning head of Mrs. Hwan belonged to a nightmare. He sat up, resting against the headboard, and touched the side of his neck where the cobra's fangs had punctured the skin—but there was no wound and no venom. He caught his breath and reached across the night table for a cigarillo. He inhaled deeply, got up and went quickly into the bathroom. He placed the cigarillo in an ashtray and splashed cold water over his face. He toweled off and stared at his reflected image in the mirror. Dark circles rimmed the soft brown eyes, and his skin tone was pasty. The scar line at his jaw was purple. Phil closed his eyes and saw the fanned white head and the monstrous unblinking red eyes.

He went down to the second-floor study, snapped on the lights, crossed to the wet bar, poured a snifter of brandy and gulped the drink down. The strong cognac burned his throat and warmed the lining of his stomach.

He walked to the bureau, pulled the drawer open, shoved some papers aside and picked up the Chinese automatic. The barrel had been filled with lead, rendering the weapon useless. It was simply an old souvenir of a forgotten war. He dropped the gun back in the drawer and slammed it shut.

Phil lit a fresh cigarillo and thought about the snake. He had seen an albino cobra once before in the high jungle close to Cambodia. Fire Team Alpha had come down from the jungle canopy at daybreak, and embedded on a bayonet was the splattered head with fifteen feet of white coil trailing after it.

The men had encountered the serpent on patrol and brought it back to the base camp as a trophy. But the sight of its limp, blood-streaked white body had sickened Phil. The image of the soldiers and the snake had become an indelible subconscious symbol of that tragic conflict.

And the head of Mrs. Hwan resting on the sofa, grinning out of a bloody skull, was somehow part of the Vietnam connection.

Phil drew hard on the cigarillo and swallowed some brandy. He thought of the Reverend Rhee's piglike face sweating under interrogation and the graphic news wire photos of Nick Carelli and his pregnant wife, blood-spattered, open eyes staring. He thought of Dr. Belgrave's austere good looks and accusatory blue eyes and the arrogance of Burgess and Gruenwald. And the ski-masked spooks who had mugged him. And his vague suspicions of Sid Greene. And Soon Yi Sonji's robotlike confession of abuse and treachery. And behind it all, President Yi Chung, whose motives remained shrouded in the mystical Buddhist philosophy of the circle.

Chapter Twenty-nine

The big blue Lincoln moved slowly past the massive wrought-iron gates. Angelo Vizzoni sat in the front passenger seat, his arm resting on the open window, the gold Patek Philippe wristwatch gleaming in the late sun. The driver had the squashed features of a boxer who had taken a lot of punishment. His big hands held the wheel, and a cigar stub was clenched between his yellow teeth. Vizzoni was tired and tense. He had flown from Mexico City to New York and switched at La Guardia to the small private plane for the trip to Amagansett.

Vizzoni understood his predicament but believed the godfather would grant him forgiveness. It was, after all, an accident. He had tipped the bullet with fulminate of mercury. It should have exploded on contact. Instead, the live slug tore through Nick Carelli's eye, bounced and blew up in the belly of his wife. It was bad luck. It was the goddamn city. He should not have agreed to a contract in Los Angeles. It was the place of *malocchio*, "the evil eye."

The huge gates of the estate swung open, and the Lincoln started up the long circular driveway.

Victor Maldonado's study was a high-ceilinged room furnished with soft leather chairs and sofas. The walls were decorated by a collection of Impressionist paintings, reflecting Maldonado's recently acquired taste for the arts.

Victor stood at the foot of a Degas alongside Martin Bender. "Can you imagine creating this light with oils, with a fucking brush?" he asked his adviser.

Bender did not respond.

The paneled doors opened and the slim, ascetic killer with the melancholy eyes entered.

Angelo Vizzoni glanced at Bender, who slumped into a

leather chair. Vizzoni jerked his head around as the doors closed behind him.

Maldonado sat in a high-backed chair at his desk.

Vizzoni stood in the center of the big study like a jungle cat caught in an unfamiliar setting. No one spoke. The ominous silence was underscored by the ticking of a clock over the fireplace.

Maldonado relit his cigar and picked at an ancient hole in his pitted skin. "You asked to see me," he said through a cloud of gray smoke.

"Yes. I want to explain, Don Vittorio." The soft-voiced killer used the formal Italian title of respect.

"Explain what?" Victor asked with feigned innocence.

"About the woman in Los Angeles."

"You insult me, Angelo."

Vizzoni seemed puzzled. "How do I insult you?"

"You call Nick Carelli's wife the woman. She carried the Carelli seed. The autopsy showed it was a boy. A grandson for Don Carlo. You killed the bloodline. The contract was on Nick, not his wife." Victor rose. "Since when do we hit wives?"

"It was a thousand to one," Vizzoni explained. "The bullet was supposed to explode on contact. It was bad luck."

Victor came around the desk. "Why from the helicopter? Why so—complicated?"

"There was no other choice," Vizzoni pleaded. "You couldn't get near him. Even with inside information you couldn't get near him. The tennis thing was perfect."

"With his wife sitting two feet away?"

"I had Nick's eyes in the center of the cross hairs."

"Do you know the father of Nick Carelli?" Victor asked.

Vizzoni wiped beads of perspiration from his upper lip. "Don Carlo? He's in exile in Palermo for ten years. He can't move. What can he do?"

"What can he do?" Victor repeated derisively. "If you fulfill the contract on Nick, Don Carlo does nothing. That's business. But you wipe out the pregnant daughter-in-law, and that's not business."

He took a few steps closer to Vizzoni. "I have problems now. I look lousy with all the families. You were sloppy."

The professional killer opened his palms in supplication.

"Don Vittorio, eleven contracts in three years. Never a question. Never a whisper." He switched to Italian *"Io sono buon soldato."*

Vizzoni then shoved the sleeve of his jacket up, exposing the glittering Patek Philippe. "You gave me this in '75, after Giancana. I never took it off. When I eat, sleep, kill, make love. Never has this watch been off my wrist. Out of respect for you."

He moved quickly and knelt down at Victor's gleaming Gucci loafers. He seized the capo's bony wrist and kissed his hand. "I beg forgiveness, Don Vittorio."

Victor patted the killer's dark, curly hair. "Get up, Angelo," he said gently.

The contract killer rose slowly to his feet.

"There is some justice in what you say," Victor acknowledged. "The history of a man's service must be remembered. Accidents happen." He glanced at Bender. "Isn't that right, Martin?"

"No one's perfect," Bender agreed.

"Sure," Victor said. "Last night at Lincoln Center I heard Isaac Stern play a Vivaldi concerto, *La Caccia*, opus eight."

Vizzoni seemed to relax.

"In the middle of a glissando," Victor continued, "a string on the violin snapped in front of two thousand people. Stern had to stop and wait for a new violin. Accidents happen."

Victor smiled. "Ah, what the hell are we talking about? You're a good soldier, Angelo."

Victor put his hand on Vizzoni's slim shoulder. "All right. We put this behind us. If I have trouble from Palermo, I'll deal with it. You go back to Mexico for three, four months. *Perdonerò e dimenticherò.* I'll forgive and forget, Angelo."

"Grazie, grazie, per tutti, Don Vittorio."

Victor indicated the gold watch. "Is it true? Six years you never took my gift from your wrist?"

"Never." Tears welled up in the killer's sad eyes. "God bless you, Don Vittorio."

"Ciao, Angelo."

Bender rose and opened the study doors. As Vizzoni started to leave, Victor called, "Angelo!"

"Yes?"

"Be careful with the water in Mexico. I got sick from the ice cubes in Acapulco. Those fucking spics shit in the water they drink. Be careful."

"I will. I will be careful."

"Good." Victor smiled. "Vito will take you to Manhattan. One night in a hotel, then tomorrow Mexico."

"*Che Dio, ti benedica,* Don Vittorio." Vizzoni blessed him once more.

The doors closed, and Maldonado went up to the Degas painting. "Fantastic," he said to Martin Bender. "Look at the light on the jockey's face. Look at the light on the grass. What incredible gifts God gives to some people. I would sell my soul to have such a gift."

"You have your own gifts, Victor," the *consigliere* advised.

●

A few miles south of Amagansett a country road was under repair. The massive yellow road-paving vehicle shot its blue exhaust skyward as it chugged across the broken asphalt. The tanklike vehicle was a marvel of efficiency. Its spiked front roller crushed the old asphalt, then retracted while the rear roller laid down a thick steaming carpet of tar. The rollers' weight flattened the tar into a smooth surface. The new paved road was achieved in one simultaneous operation.

The operator of the huge Caterpillar earned his $47.50 an hour due to the largess of Vincent Andolini, the teamster boss in New York. Andolini in turn owed his exalted position to the largess of Victor Maldonado. The operator therefore concerned himself only with the complicated gearshifts and took no interest in the two men watching him work.

They lounged against a big blue Lincoln. One of them had the broken, puffed features of a fighter. He was the same man who had driven Angelo Vizzoni to the meeting with Maldonado.

The yellow fire-breathing machine retracted its front claws and moved forward, its massive rear roller laying the hot tar over the broken asphalt. The operator could not see the sun gleaming off an expensive gold watch that protruded slightly from under the chunks of broken asphalt. The roller moved over the spot of gold, and the hot tar smoked as it covered the asphalt and flattened the surface. The two men got back in the Lincoln, satisfied that Angelo Vizzoni was now permanently pasted into the country lane.

Chapter Thirty

General Ulysses S. Grant wore his campaign hat slouched low over his brow, and the collar of his tunic was turned up against the cold. His magnificent steed surveyed the lunching secretaries and frolicking tourists with majestic equine disdain. Grant and his horse were locked forever in green bronze atop their ten-foot marble platform. There were four regal lions poised on either side of the general, and charging Union cavalrymen guarded both flanks. The general, the troopers, the lions and horses had spilled their green oxidized blood onto the white marble pedestals.

Phil admired the statuary and thought it was one of the great overlooked national treasures. The artist had sculpted an incredible lifelike frieze that fused the frenzy of man and beast as they charged toward that final noble destiny waiting in the Confederate cannon.

But in the summer of 1981 on the great Mall, there were no Confederate troops, no Lee, no Pickett, no Jackson, only hot dog vendors, ice cream salesmen, Japanese tourists, and secretaries seated around the Reflecting Pool, feeding crumbs of tuna sandwiches to the gulls and pigeons.

Phil listened to the Marine Band playing, "Hello, Dolly!" from the lawn of the Capitol building.

He spotted Arthur Browning crossing Constitution Avenue. The diminutive, dapper attorney general looked like a mannequin that had escaped the window of an expensive men's clothing store.

The two Justice officials did not greet one another but fell into step and strolled leisurely toward the distant pristine needle of the Washington Memorial.

"You look tired, Phil."

"Nightmares."

"What?"

"I'm having trouble sleeping."

"Join the club. This air controllers' strike is crippling the entire department."

"Jail the bastards."

"Ah, Phil, you don't think I enjoy this. The President went absolutely berserk, called them a bunch of ingrates."

They dodged some children chasing a Frisbee. Browning cleared his throat and said, "Don Carlo Carelli has requested a temporary visa of return. He's agreed to go before a grand jury or special congressional committee and testify under oath."

"Testify to what?"

"He has agreed to tell everything he knows about organized crime from 1936 to the present," Browning answered. "Dates, names, killings, bribes, conspiracy, the works."

Sea gulls, seduced by a southerly breeze, had come in from Chesapeake Bay and flew lazily over the Mall. Phil looked up at them and said, "You're not going to fall for that, are you?"

"What do you mean by 'fall'?"

"The Don has nothing to tell us that we don't already know."

Browning lit a small cigar. "He's the ringmaster. The boss of bosses."

Phil shook his head. "Fratianno talked, and Valachi talked, along with twenty-five other Mafia songbirds we have under protective custody. They all sing the same song. They never, *never* name any important political figures."

Browning waved the cigar. "Don Carlo is no ordinary mobster. He's the cofounder of organized crime in this country."

"Don't kid yourself, Arthur. I know Don Carlo. All he's interested in is having his day in court with the current godfather, Victor Maldonado, or whoever it was that placed the contract on his son and botched the job."

Browning stopped and touched Phil's sleeve. "Think for a minute. If your theory is accurate, if the Reverend Rhee complained to someone highly placed in the intelligence community, forcing the hit on Nick Carelli, we may be able to break this case wide open."

"How?"

"When Don Carlo has his day in court with Victor Maldonado, it's a certainty Maldonado will name the man who forced the hit, if only to get himself off the hook."

"How do we know Maldonado placed the contract?"

"He's the current godfather. It's got to be him."

Phil nodded imperceptibly. There was indisputable logic in Browning's analysis.

"In other words," Browning continued, "if you're present at the meeting between Don Carlo and Maldonado, there's a good chance the name of the man at the top of the intelligence pyramid will surface."

"How do we insure my presence?"

"We'll make that part of the agreement guaranteeing Don Carlo's return."

They strolled across the sweet-smelling grass, each man lost in his own thoughts for a moment. Then Phil asked, "What is it you want with me, Arthur?"

"Don Carlo has requested that you personally escort him back to Washington."

Phil studied the dapper attorney general. He trusted Browning, but was nevertheless wary of still another ruse. His doubts belonged to the cycle of intrigue that had tormented him since the start of the Rhee case. The tangents of suspicion had spilled off onto Sid Greene and even to casual relationships like Gloria Robbins. Phil had begun to believe that agents of the secret government, the clandestine officialdom of Washington, were everywhere.

"When and how did you receive this request?" he asked.

Browning examined his polished fingernails. "Last night. It was transmitted by an agent of Italian Intelligence: the Ministero dell' Interno. Don Carlo will return only if you agree to accompany him."

"And what about my case against Rhee?"

"Frankly, Phil, we have no case. Oh, perhaps in the end we can achieve an indictment on tax evasion, but you're looking at a series of appeals that can take five years. In my reckoning, Don Carlo's safe return represents a unique opportunity for an immediate breakthrough, implicating not only Rhee but his highly placed confederates."

Browning paused. "It's a chance to bring them all down."

Phil looked off at the Washington Monument and sighed. "Christ, I despise everything the Don stands for."

"You've got to divorce your personal feelings about Don Carlo. You've got to regard him as an instrument, a tool to achieve justice—to atone for the murder of Mrs. Hwan, for the beating you suffered and for the killing of Nick Carelli and his wife. And, more important, to expose and destroy the self-serving cabal that has its hands at the throat of this nation." Browning sucked on the moist end of his cigar. "Besides, Phil, the Don claims he can produce the Gemstone file."

Phil watched a group of Japanese tourists kneeling down, composing low-angle shots of the Grant Memorial. "How the hell would Don Carlo turn up Gemstone?"

"That's irrelevant. He says he's got it, and I've made Gemstone the principal condition of his return. Without it, I will refuse him entry. That file can lift the dome off the Capitol building. Hoover had a line on everyone. There is material in Gemstone that can bring Belgrave and others to their knees."

"What do you want me to do, Arthur?"

"I want you to bring Don Carlo back."

"Is that an order?"

Browning's penetrating gray eyes seemed offended. "I don't deserve that. I've backed you one hundred percent in a case involving forces that can ruin me. Three previous attorneys general resigned under clouds, victims of misinformation fed to the White House by the very people you've gone after. My support for you has never wavered."

"You're right." Phil sighed. "I'm sorry."

They started back toward the Reflecting Pool, once again skirting children tossing orange-colored Frisbees.

"The thing is, Arthur, if the Italian Ministero dell' Interno knows the Don is coming back, our own intelligence agencies know, and that means the mob knows. How the hell do you expect me to get him home in one piece?"

"The Don has his own network of protection, and you

will have the assistance of our embassies in Europe. You'll be armed. You will be totally self-reliant, your movements secret. You'll have an open-end supply of currency and safe numbers to call. You're no good to me dead." Browning smiled. "Besides, you were once a pretty good cowboy."

"Vietnam was a long time ago, Arthur. I'm a middle-aged, out-of-shape lawyer, with a shattered jaw, a fucked-up case and nightmares."

They circled the secretaries seated around the Reflecting Pool.

"Look, Phil, I've been assured by Carelli's emissary that Italian Intelligence will protect you and provide backup all the way."

"The *ministero* is riddled with double agents," Phil said. "They can't even protect the Pope."

"Do you for one minute think Don Carlo would jeopardize his life?" Browning pressed. "If so, he denies himself vengeance."

Phil shook his head. "The Don is seventy, seventy-two. He's on borrowed time. He's got nothing to lose."

They reached the corner of Constitution Avenue.

"All right." Browning sighed. "Let's put it where it's at. You're the one who claims that the democratic process is in jeopardy—that our citizens are being manipulated by unseen, unelected forces. You're the one who says when America plays Empire, kids die, and I happen to agree with you. And I ask you, what's the next intrigue that robs the citizens of their freedom and murders their children?" Browning paused. "Of course, there are risks, but it seems to me everything you stand for dictates accepting this assignment."

"Arthur, you could sell life insurance to the Holy Ghost."

"Just laying out the facts, Phil."

The Marine Band played "The Stars and Stripes Forever." General Grant's stern countenance was not distressed by the sea gull perched atop his campaign hat. The black water in the pool shimmered under the hot August sun. The white Capitol dome gleamed with architectural nobility. The relaxed atmosphere and the patriotic music lent the great Mall a feeling of tranquillity and permanence, far removed from the treachery and intrigue being discussed by the two Justice Department officials.

"When would I have to go?" Phil asked.

Browning took out a sealed manila envelope and handed it to Phil. "The Concorde to London, Tuesday, and an open ticket from London to Palermo."

Phil took the envelope. "Pretty sure of yourself."

Browning smiled. "You may have doubted me, Phil, but I never had any doubts about you."

BOOK TWO

Gemstone

Chapter Thirty-one

The Concorde check-in and security clearance had been accomplished with professional dispatch, but the attitude of the British ticket agents was one of awesome disdain for the passengers. Phil guessed the employees could not handle the disparity between their salaries and the jet set wealth they serviced.

The supersonic aircraft accommodated 100 passengers, but there were less than half that number in the lounge. Phil sat on the blue plastic sofa, sipping his brew of Taittinger and orange juice. He scanned the faces and dress of the other passengers, trying to spot a spook who might be performing a tail job.

A noisy group of Japanese businessmen chatted and bowed occasionally to the waiter serving canapés. There was an infamous Saudi bagman named Adam Kalaadi. Any American firm wanting to do business in Saudi Arabia had to grease Kalaadi, who in turn deposited the bribe into a Swiss account code-named Rosemark. The dapper Saudi was traveling with a six-foot-tall German girl, who laughed lasciviously at the bagman's every word.

Phil noticed the handsome woman who had written a best seller by describing her sexual adventures with unsuspecting congressmen. She was on her way to London to publicize the British edition of her book, entitled *D.C. Tricks.* There was a Colonel Rollins, military adviser to the Senate Armed Forces Committee, who owed his position to the influence of a West Coast aerospace firm.

There were two UN diplomats, one from Sweden and one from Oman. The latter was famous for his incredible collection of pornography, which was purported to contain the only actual "snuff" film ever made: death throes and shuddering orgasm caught in the same frame.

A famous English rock group was heatedly discussing
the faulty report on the gross box-office take of their
Washington concert. Phil could hear their American agent
assuaging them with typical professional reassurance: "I'll
nail that motherfucker with ASCAP. He won't be able to
book his own ass on a toilet seat."

The other passengers were a mix of businessmen and
bureaucrats. There were no visible spooks.

Phil felt a sharp twinge of a nerve in an upper molar
and pressed the tip of his tongue against the offending
tooth. He had spent four hours at his dentist's the previous day. The thought of a toothache erupting in Palermo
was enough to warrant the long, painful session.

Finally, the attendant called for immediate embarkation
and the melange of supersonic travelers trooped out of the
lounge.

Phil spotted the spook on the self-propelled shuttle that
transported passengers from the terminal to the waiting
aircraft. The man had obviously boarded the vehicle while
the other passengers were in the lounge. Among the fash-
ionably dressed jet-setters, the spook stood out like silver
plate at Tiffany's. Phil never ceased to wonder at the
CIA's conformity of dress. The agent had the usual short
haircut, flushed alcoholic pallor, plaid suit with pants legs
two inches too short and wing-tipped shoes with a ribbed
border. But Phil's amusement vanished with the awareness
that the spook's presence meant a leak had already occurred.

The Concorde screamed through the stratosphere at
60,000 feet, its four Rolls-Royce engines producing 38,000
pounds of thrust. The green digital machometer attached
to the forward bulkhead displayed the airspeed at 1,340
mph. From his aisle seat Phil glanced out the small oval
windows.

The sky was deep purple, just foreshadowing the midnight black of outer space. The beefy man seated next to
him perused State Department bulletins concerning the
gross national product of the African republic of Upper
Volta. The seats were smaller and more confined than
those on regular commercial aircraft, but the Iranian
caviar and cold Polish vodka were pure Concorde.

A pretty stewardess came down the aisle and stopped in front of Phil. She went up on her toes, stretched her arms up and rummaged for something in the overhead compartment. She curved her body, thrusting her pelvis into his face. Her hands came out of the overhead empty, and she smiled down at him. "Would you care for some more vodka?"

"No, but I wouldn't mind another jar of caviar."

"Certainly, sir."

Phil picked up the Washington Post. U.S. Navy Jets had downed two Libyan jets over the Mediterranean. The American President agreed to resume shipments of F-15's and F-16's to Israel if the Israelis promised not to use them. Dr. Eric Belgrave, chairman of the National Security Council, had appeared before the Senate Foreign Relations Committee, urging approval of the AWACS sale to the kingdom of Saudi Arabia. Soviet authorities had recommitted a noted poet to an insane asylum in Leningrad. A student uprising in Seoul was crushed by tanks of the Regular Army. Five mullahs were blown to pieces in their office in downtown Teheran. The baseball strike was over, and the professional football teams had started their exhibition games.

Phil slipped the paper back into the sleeve of the forward chair, tilted his seat back, closed his eyes and thought about his phone call to his former wife. Audrey had listened for a minute and then laconically said, "Take care, Phil." The brevity of the call suggested she had someone in bed with her and brought with it the startling realization that if he were killed in the course of this mission, there was no one to bury him.

He'd paid a visit to his attorney and made the necessary arrangements to have his body interred in the family plot at St. Alban's Cemetery in Westchester County. His stock certificates, bankbooks, and 100 Krugerrands stored in his vault would be left to New York University's Law School. It was a lousy time to be thinking about wills, but they had him positioned in the cross hairs. The underworld would be gunning for Don Carlo, and the overworld spooks would be after him. He was counting on the Don to provide some network of protection in Italy. If they managed to reach Switzerland, he could use the services of Franz Kohler, chief of Swiss Internal Security. Phil had worked with Kohler years ago on the Cornfeld-Vesco IOS stock swindle. He had provided Kohler with invaluable data, and the Swiss police chief owed him one.

Still, it was a tight spot, and while he could have refused, Browning was right: It was a last chance to crack the case. When and if Don Carlo faced Maldonado, Phil would finally know who ordered the hit on Nick Carelli. As for Gemstone, only God and Hoover knew what political dynamite that mythical document contained. Browning had practically drooled at the mention of the secret file.

Phil's thoughts turned to Sonji and the robotlike recital of her brainwashed life and the mystical hope that her salvation was contained in some obscure Buddhist text. But she retained enough humanity to care still about Kimsan's welfare. And despite himself, Phil had a soft spot for the beautiful kisaeng girl.

"Coffee and dessert?" The stewardess interrupted his reverie.

"No, thank you."

The heavyset State Department man seated next to him put his Upper Volta documents in his attaché case, locked it and said, "Excuse me."

Phil stood up to permit the diplomat passage and remained on his feet, deciding the time had come to deal with the spook.

He walked through the rear compartment and spotted the man sitting in the last row before the aft toilets, reading *Penthouse* magazine.

Phil leaned over the agent and smiled. "Hard to believe we're traveling at twenty-three miles a minute." The spook glanced up and nodded. "First time on the Concorde?" Phil asked.

"No. I've been on it before."

"Same run?"

The man knew his cover had been blown. Someone in the agency had dumped him. He could not conceive that he'd been betrayed by nothing more complicated than his own attire, and the glaring mistake of not having waited in the regular lounge with the other passengers before boarding. "No," the spook answered. "I flew from Bahrain to London on the Concorde."

"You in the oil business?" Phil asked.

"Drilling equipment."

"I got drilled yesterday," Phil said. "My dentist, Dr. Robert Burgess—you know him?" The spook shook his head. "Well, enjoy the centerfold. Christ, I don't know where they find them. Makes your mouth water, don't you think?"

"Yeah . . ." The man hesitated. "I guess so."

"Nice talking to you. Drilling business, huh? Must be exciting. Desert. Arabs. Oil. Lots of traveling. Gets you away from the little lady at home."

Phil entered the tiny bathroom and urinated. He had blown the spook's cover, but the problem wasn't over, just temporarily contained.

The captain's voice sounded on the toilet speaker: "The deceleration you feel has reduced our airspeed to subsonic levels. We are presently approaching Harland Point and are cleared to land on runway twenty-eight. At this time all passengers are required to return to their seats. Thank you."

Phil belted himself in and placed his seat in the upright position. The no smoking sign came on, and through the windows he noticed the flashing red wing lights.

They reminded him of the blood red eyes of the albino cobra.

Chapter Thirty-two

Walton's was an L-shaped room with white damask walls. A single stem rose in a cut-glass container decorated each linen-covered table. Dappled sunlight filtered through heavy iron grillwork protecting the windows. The waiter explained the presence of the grillwork: Several months ago an IRA terrorist had lobbed a grenade through the windows, killing five patrons.

Phil nodded, wishing he hadn't asked the question. He swallowed the chilled vodka and thought about the CIA spook he had flushed on the Concorde. The agent was probably on his way back to Washington, replaced by someone in British Intelligence. Its MI 5 section worked closely with Burgess's Covert Operations.

Phil studied the customers in the small, elegant restaurant. They were a mixture of staid English businessmen and striking girls who had the appearance of high-fashion models. The room seemed to be free of professional agents.

A whispering couple at an adjacent table stared into each other's eyes with that unmistakable longing peculiar to afternoon lovers. Their presence triggered a profound wave of loneliness in Phil. He shook his head, realizing there was no one with whom he shared a meaningful relationship. It almost defied credibility that a man could live more than four decades, fight wars, grow accustomed to death and pain, practice a profession that demanded compassion, yet not feel any love or be loved by a single soul.

He sighed, wondering whether the windmills were worth the fight. Sancho Panza would have counseled against it. But the legendary Spanish valet had not lived in a thermonuclear world. Someone had to care. If not, everyone was going to wind up missing. Victims of doomsday devices set off by self-appointed demigods. And in the radioactive ruins a single surviving intelligent creature would be crawling around, wondering how it happened. Who was accountable? The Americans? The Russians? The Africans? The Asians? Who did this? Who was responsible? The overlords of secrecy and manipulation would not be around to answer. There had to be an unmasking. Halloween had to end before Armageddon began.

Glancing out the window, Phil saw a Silver Shadow Rolls with smoky windows pull up to the entrance. A tall girl in a beige coat got out and entered the restaurant. The maître d' took her coat, and she followed him into the room.

Phil stood up as she said, "I'm Claudia Cassini. Sorry I'm late."

He smiled. "I'm Phil Ricker, and it's no problem."

They sat down, and she ordered a Kir. She had those fine features that gave her a leg up on intelligence. Her hair was parted in the center, the dark waves framed her oval face and her black eyes were mysterious and intense. She took a blue pack of Gauloises out of her handbag.

"I've been trying to stop this dreadful habit for years." Her voice, low and fragile, carried a trace of an English accent. The waiter placed the Kir in front of her, and she raised the glass. "Cheers."

"Good health."

She stared at him for a moment, thinking the file photograph did not reflect the sadness in his eyes and the severe scar on the jaw. There was a sense of fatigue about him, yet a curious underlying strength. They were the in-person life signs that photographs seldom caught.

"Would you care to order, sir?" the waiter asked.

Phil looked at her. "Hungry?"

"Yes. But I'd like to finish my drink."

"We'll wait."

"Very good, sir."

As she leaned forward, the scent of a subtly provocative perfume drifted across the table. "I'm with the Ministero dell' Interno," she said conspiratorially. "I was selected by Don Carlo Carelli to negotiate the conditions of his return with the American authorities."

"American authorities means my boss, Arthur Browning."

"Yes. I know who you work for." She smiled. "As a matter of fact, I know everything about you. Back to the day you were born."

"Really?"

"Well, that may be an overstatement. Your mother's maiden name was Rachel Dean. Your father was William Ricker. They were killed in a plane crash in Florida, June 1977. You graduated New York University. You served in Vietnam. You—"

"Enough," Phil interrupted. "You did your homework."

"Just an exercise in memory."

He signaled the waiter for a refill.

She said, "There is a seat reserved for you on tomorrow's Alitalia flight to Palermo."

"What time?"

"Leaving London at three-fifteen P.M., arriving Palermo at 6:05 local time. There is a room reserved in your name at the Villa Igiea Hotel." She crushed out the cigarette, took a slip of paper from her bag and pressed it into his palm. "Phone this number on arrival."

Phil pocketed the slip. "Who does it connect with?"

"Luigi Ruffino. I believe you know him."

"Yeah, I know Luigi. He tried to bribe me back in the good old days."

"When you caused the deportation of Don Carlo."

Phil wondered about her use of the word "caused." It seemed to have been spoken with a trace of personal resentment. But the girl was simply a courier; why would she resent his past legal actions against Carelli? He decided to let it go. "May I have one of those?"

She handed him a Gauloise, and he lit it, inhaling the strong Algerian tobacco. "Tell me something," she said. "Why did you refuse the bribes?"

"Nothing complicated." He smiled. "They just didn't meet my price."

Claudia had met men like Phil before—men who were not for sale. In her world they had become a curiosity. She stared at him over the rim of her glass and, despite herself and contrary to her orders, felt a growing attraction for him.

"What happens when I contact Ruffino?" Phil asked.

"He'll take you to Don Carlo."

"You're aware that our agreement requires him to produce the Gemstone file."

"Yes, but I have no information regarding Gemstone." Claudia Cassini smiled a small, sudden smile. "Can we order? I'm starved."

"Sure. I'm an old hand at feeding hungry girls. Had my own food stamp program for a while."

"Really?"

Phil nodded and signaled the waiter. "Yeah. I was a well-known mark for a free dinner. It sort of comes with divorce."

They exchanged small talk during lunch. She revealed very little about herself but seemed interested in his comments. After espresso and brandy she offered him a lift back to his hotel.

The limousine rolled through the quiet dignity of Eaton Square on its way to Hyde Park.

"Pretty fancy way to travel," Phil said.

"In this business, being conspicuous is sometimes the best of covers," Claudia replied.

The gray Rolls entered Hyde Park, picking up speed, traveling parallel to Park Lane.

"How much help can your agency provide?" Phil asked.

"That's a problem," she said. "Don Carlo does not trust the *ministero*. Nor does he trust the American agencies. It seems he's placed all his chips on you."

The Silver Shadow Rolls came out of the park and waited for the light. She glanced out the window, and he thought her profile could break some hearts.

"Don Carlo is not the same man you knew ten years ago," she said almost to herself. "Only one emotion keeps him going." She turned to Phil. "Vengeance."

The limousine pulled into the semicircular drive at the entrance to the Dorchester.

"When will I see you?" he asked.

"I don't know."

Phil stared at her for a moment and was struck by the thought that she reminded him of someone—someone out of the past. He smiled and said. "Take care, Claudia."

Chapter Thirty-three

Claudia Cassini got out of the Rolls-Royce at Berkeley Square and walked slowly around the small park immortalized in the World War II song. The tall, stately plane trees were thick with bright green leaves. The old square reminded her of a long-ago summer evening and an after-dinner stroll she'd shared with the only man she'd ever loved—a man she had unknowingly set up for murder. The fallen leaves caught the breeze and played across her beige coat as she rounded the park. She crossed the cobblestones, still gleaming in the late sun, and entered Curzon Street.

She walked toward the three-story red-brick building with the gabled octagonal roof. Iron grillwork surrounded its thirty-three windows, and a permanent sign hung from the top floor: MUROD ESTATES—TO LET. The rooftop electronic dish was hidden from public view by a false chimney, and there was no number on the polished brass door plate. But almost everyone in British political life knew the building was headquarters of Section MI 5. Claudia rang the bell.

A voice came out of a speaker. "Yes?"

"Cassini."

The door lock clicked, and she entered the building.

The third floor of MI 5 was a warren of quiet cubicles. Cipher rooms, computers and translation machines were located in the basement. Claudia was escorted down the hall by an armed guard, and monitored every step of the way by miniature TV cameras hidden behind prints of the English hunt.

Bill Edwards's office was a boxlike room with several green file cabinets, a battered desk, harsh overhead lighting and a wall calendar with the month printed between the thighs of a naked girl.

Edwards was a well-built man with small, regular features whose sandy hair had begun to recede. He was on the phone and did not rise to greet her but waved his free hand to indicate the wooden chair in front of his desk. "Yes. Perfectly," he said into the phone. "The information will be given to Andropov. The Soviets expect no less. In my opinion we cannot throw Adams to the bear." There was a pause, and he concluded, "Thank you, sir." He hung up and leaned back in the swivel chair.

She thought his alcoholic flush was more pronounced, and the once-steady hazel eyes seemed furtive and menacing.

"You're looking marvelous, Claudia." He paused as if concentrating. "It's been what—a year and a half?"

"Sixteen months."

"Yes. That's right. March fourteenth. You spent the night with Freddie Sill."

"As a favor to you."

"Not me, sweetheart. Your own MDI was suspicious of Freddie. I acted as your pimp that evening to accommodate your Italian masters."

She crossed her legs and said, "I heard you had married."

"Briefly. The young lady was killed in a crash on the M-four Expressway."

"God, I'm sorry to hear that Bill. I . . ."

Edwards waved his hand. "Nothing to be said." He leaned forward. "Cigarette?" She shook her head. Edwards lit the Player cigarette, clasped his hands behind his neck and leaned back. "How did lunch go?"

"Fine."

"Where is Ricker staying?"

"The Dorchester."

Edwards felt relieved. She was telling the truth. MI 5 had followed Phil from the airport to his hotel. The fact of the American spook's blowing his cover was irrelevant. MI 5 had been on the case from the time the Concorde had departed Dulles International Airport. "Old Burgess and the good Doctor, Belgrave, are certainly angry with this fellow Ricker. Want him removed with extreme prejudice."

"They also want Gemstone," she replied.

"Yes. I know. We simply have to keep Ricker in the cross hairs until that mythic document shows up, although that could change at any moment." He unclasped his hands, stood up and peered out the grimy window. "I would guess the American underworld have their own ideas about the disposition of Mr. Ricker and Don Carlo Carelli." He turned to her and noticed a cloud pass across her dark eyes.

"Victor Maldonado has agreed to permit them safe return," she said.

"Yes . . . well, I wouldn't care to have my safety depend on the word of Mr. Maldonado." He glanced at the wall calendar with the month of August imprinted between the pinup's creamy thighs. "Where does our quarry go from here?"

"Palermo, on tomorrow's Alitalia flight at three-fifteen P.M."

"What hotel?"

"Villa Igiea."

Once again Edwards felt relieved. Claudia was being truthful. He had checked all direct flights from London to Palermo. There was only one a day, and a seat on tomorrow's flight had been reserved for Ricker. "How did he strike you?"

"Bruised, haunted. Attractive in a sympathetic way."

"His file is interesting," Edwards said. "Not much sympathy there. Tough. Obsessed. War veteran. Went right at Belgrave's people and the Reverend Rhee. Aquitted himself well when assaulted by CIA professionals. Pity you left him so quickly."

"I was not instructed to sleep with him," Claudia replied.

"Remarkable control you're exercising these days, love—considering your past promiscuity."

"If your intention is to hurt me, forget it, Bill. You're five years too late."

"Right," Edwards said, and picked up a photograph of Phil Ricker. "How close is this to the real man?"

"Close enough."

"Where is Don Carlo Carelli at the moment?"

Edwards had no way of knowing, but if he did, it was a risk she had to take. "I have no idea," she lied.

"Where do you go from here?"

"I've got to check with Rome."

"You still enjoy working for those spaghetti benders?"

"It's a job."

"Have you been to Geneva lately?"

"That's none of your goddamned business."

He sat on the edge of his desk. "You're absolutely right. Two million in Swiss francs deserves proper privacy."

"I've never seen that money."

"Yes, I know." He nodded. "How about dinner at the White Elephant? Food's improved since they took the gambling out."

"I'm busy tonight."

"Pity." He touched her cheek. "What is your impression of Don Carlo?"

"I rather liked him."

"Do you remember Freddie Sill?"

"We just covered that, Bill."

"Oh, I'm not referring to your bacchanalian night. This is a recent event. It seems Freddie was waiting for his usual number six bus when a nice-looking young man pricked his leg with the tip of an umbrella. Freddie ran a slight fever for a few days before dying slowly and painfully. His case at the time seemed relatively harmless—the protection of a Bulgarian defector. Are you certain about the White Elephant, love?"

"Good-bye, Bill."

"I'll need a number, old girl."

"You have it. MDI. Rome."

"It isn't often I have a free night."

"What's the point?" Claudia shrugged.

"None. Just that of late, when I occasionally make love, I feel I'm cheating death. But then Jung said that death and sex are administered by the same lady. Take care, Claudia."

"You, too."

Edwards went back to his desk, glanced at the spread-legged girl with the August cunt, circled the day and picked up the phone. "Maxine, try the concierge at the Dorchester."

*   *   *

Claudia Cassini walked toward the waiting limousine. She was playing the treacherous game of double agent and if she stayed alive, she would betray them all: MI 5, and MDI and the American CIA. Her true allegiance was to Don Carlo. The old man was Christ on her personal cross. As for Ricker, well, perhaps she could save him, but as a practical matter he was expendable.

Chapter Thirty-four

The Pusan National University was ten miles from the downtown section of the Korean seaport city. Its fifteen buildings, dormitories and 14,000 students spread over a thirty-two-acre site at the foot of Mount Kumjung. The pine-covered mountain and modern beige-colored buildings lent a surface tranquillity to the university, but underneath the placid exterior the campus seethed with tension. The Student Union Building had been converted to a penal punishment center, and special green-fatigued troops patrolled the grounds.

The July student riots had been ruthlessly crushed, and the university was infested with black-suited thugs of President Chung's Social Purification Committee. The dormitories' phones were bugged, and miniature cameras photographed classroom activities and monitored the corridors of the principal study centers.

Soon Yi Sonji got out of the military sedan at the Humanities Institute, and two KCIA men escorted her to the low red-brick dormitory immediately behind it. She looked up at the puffy white clouds floating over the pine-covered forest; it was a perfect early fall day—the cruel bite of winter had not yet arrived.

Professor Kim was a tall frail man with large, tragic eyes and fine features like those of his daughter. She threw her arms around his bony shoulders and embraced him. He kissed her cheek, stared at her for a moment, and said, "Come, have some tea." He indicated the low table with traditional hassocks. "Are you well, Daughter?"

"Yes. I am well."

"You saw those vermin at my door?"

She nodded. "They have devices to record our conversation," she warned. "It is better not to speak of politics, Father."

"I say what I wish."

"You are already under house arrest," she replied, and placed the porcelain teacup down. "You cannot speak out against the regime, Father. I have managed to protect you, but there are limits to my power."

His tired, intelligent eyes brightened as he spoke. "No, Daughter. There are limits only to your perception of power. You are in a unique position to help the nation. It is your generation that will perish in the next war. You must not remain neutral in this struggle. Years ago my activities caused you to lose your natural name and life. But do not hold yourself hostage to my welfare any longer. I am old. My friends are dead. I have nothing more to fear."

He rose wearily and moved slowly to a small radio. He turned up the volume and motioned her to the window. Professor Kim whispered, "Chung wants you to believe that my situation gives him power over you. This is false. They will not harm me. They will not make a martyr out of me. Besides, I have lived long enough. There is a time when one is no longer afraid. But you must make a choice. The nation cries for freedom. You are close to the president. Things can be done."

"There is nothing I can do."

"There is much you can do. Books have been burned; professors jailed; student leaders tortured. President Chung is exactly like Park. Our people are dying." His voice grew louder. "You must care. You must act!"

Sonji embraced the tragic, frail figure. "Contain your thoughts, Father," she whispered. "Trust me."

●

A blackout drill had been added to the midnight curfew, and from Namsan Hill across to the huge high-rise districts of Chamsil and Youido all the way to the Han River, Seoul was dark. No cars moved on the elevated expressways; no civilians or tourists walked the alleys of the Chung-Do District. The tearooms, casinos and kisaeng houses were shuttered. Only in the bars and rooftop clubs of elegant hotels did the English, American and Japanese tourists continue to pursue their varying amusements.

In the tunnels bisecting the city, armored cars, M-60 tanks, missile launchers and self-propelled howitzers were manned, fueled and ready. The capital Garrison Command patrolled the streets, and veteran troops of the elite White Horse Division guarded the Coast, coordinating with swift-moving naval patrol craft. Surface-to-ground missiles rose up out of their silos, and from the Yellow Sea to the Sea of Japan, an awesome, doomsday force of half a million men and women above and below the earth were poised to repel an attack that everyone hoped would never come.

The president of the republic was naked in his sumptuous bedroom in the south wing of the Blue House. Sonji sat on her haunches, leaning over the scarred muscular leader. She had made love to him voluntarily, displaying a hungry passion that required total concentration as prescribed in the Vishnu. They had smoked three cigarettes containing ginseng root and marijuana, and during their lovemaking she had whispered the pornographic delights of *Tao* in his ear. Her performance convinced him that he had finally caused her to feel a sensual connection.

He leaned against the headboard. "Light a cigarette for me, Daughter."

Sonji rose and walked across the room. She lit two cigarettes and handed him one. She slipped on her robe and poured two glasses of Bell's scotch, the same brand favored by former President Park. She sat on a divan and intentionally spread her legs so he could see her bare thighs.

"For many days and nights I wished for this moment," he said.

"Distance and time make for need."

"You felt a need for me, Daughter?"

"Must I say?"

"No." He smiled. "I need no words."

The command shouts of the presidential security police could be heard from below as the guard changed.

The president's forehead creased into fluted lines, and he spoke softly. "You found your father well?"

"Yes. I thank you for that."

"We must give gratitude to Buddha."

"I pray to him always."

"You are the true daughter of the goddess Vishnu, and you have done many good things for me." He swallowed half the scotch. "But I have still another task for you."

"You need only to ask."

"My secretary, Won. You know him?"

"Yes, but not well."

Chung nodded, inhaled deeply, and twirled the ice in his drink. "Find out what crawls through his mind. I suspect he is a Christian. I suspect he funnels currency coming into my private account from Kimsan and uses that currency to support Christian causes. Won refused to permit the Social Purification Committee to enter the Christian college."

"Perhaps he believed it was proper politics not to upset the Christians," Sonji suggested. "The Americans could take offense."

Chung shook his head. "The Americans are preoccupied with Poland and the Middle East. They will do nothing, and Won knows that. Find out what you can about his political beliefs."

"I will. You need not be concerned."

"Good, Daughter." He paused. "The other task I mentioned will be pleasant for you. I want you to go to Rome, to meet with your former colleague Kimsan."

She tried to maintain a mask of indifference at the mention of her former lover's name. "I did not know he was in Rome," she said innocently.

"He will be when you arrive."

"What is the purpose of this mission?"

"We will discuss that after your meeting with Won. After you have penetrated his thoughts."

She rose and walked provocatively to the bed. She slipped off her robe, revealing her lithe, naked body still glistening with oil of jasmine. She saw the hungry look in his black eyes and thought her father was right: She possessed a unique and very great power.

Chapter Thirty-five

The grazing cows did not bother to look up as the Alitalia
jet screamed over their heads on its final approach to
Punta Raisi Airport.

Phil's suitcase came off the baggage carousel between
wooden crates jammed with chirping yellow chicks.

He stepped out of the small terminal into the blinding
Sicilian sunlight and cursed himself for not having picked
up a pair of sunglasses at the Rome airport.

Four men surrounded him, pitching the individual vir-
tues of their Fiat taxis. He selected the first in line and
departed for Palermo amid a chorus of contemptuous epithets from the other drivers.

During the long drive into the city the driver explained
that Sicily had endured invasions by Phoenicians, Greeks,
Romans, Saracens, Normans, Spanish and in World War
II the Germans and finally the English and Americans.

"The blood in our veins is a whirlpool." He said it without pride, as if it were simply an accident of history.

Palermo was a bizarre architectural blend of graceful
pink-domed Moorish palaces, stark Gothic churches and
drab gray-cement apartment buildings. The taxi circled a
palm-lined piazza with sparkling fountains before turning
into the dark, narrow streets of the old quarter. The pungent aroma of roasted coffee mixed with the acrid fumes
of orange buses and swarms of noisy motorscooters.

They followed the single-lane waterfront road as it
curved up a slight rise to the Villa Igiea. The six-story hotel was a converted Saracen fortress complete with rooftop
archers' positions.

The room was small, clean and starkly furnished: a

chair, a bureau, and a narrow bed with a large crucifix above, complete with a bleeding Christ. Phil tipped the bellboy and went directly to the phone. He flashed the cradle bar, and the operator's voice came on: *"Pronto?"*

"Do you speak English?" he asked.

"Yes."

"Would you please call 58-65-33?"

"Hang up," she said. "I call you back."

Phil opened the wooden shutters, flooding the room with sunlight. He looked out over the gardens and dining terrace. There was a palm-lined walk leading down to a kidney-shaped swimming pool, where a group of tourists sunbathed on lounges and small children splashed in the water. A cluster of Roman ruins faced the sea, their pitted marble columns guarding the hotel from still another invasion. Off to the right a huge dry-dock facility ministered to three freighters.

The phone rang sharply with no breaks between rings.

"Hello?" Phil said.

"Your party is on the line."

"Hello . . ."

"How the hell are you, Phil?" Ruffino's voice was warm and familiar.

"I'm good, Luigi."

"You're in early."

"Yeah. I switched planes—went from London to Rome."

There was a pause and Ruffino said, "Meet me at five P.M. in the Capuchine convent."

"Where is it?"

"Just outside the city. Take a taxi to the Piazza Santa Cappucine. Its catacombs are a famous tourist place. The driver will know. I'll meet you at the entrance."

"Isn't there a nice cool café somewhere?" Phil asked.

"It's cool where we're going—and safe. Five o'clock."

Phil crossed the ancient cobblestoned square. The heat of the day had subsided, and the sky showed traces of crimson. He saw Luigi Ruffino lounging at the busy entrance of the foreboding medieval convent. A noisy group

of Japanese tourists were lined up, waiting to descend into
the catacombs while a party of grim-faced Spanish-speak-
ing pilgrims emerged.

"Long time." Ruffino smiled.

"Yeah, long time."

In the ten years since Phil had last seen him, Ruffino
had aged considerably. The once-powerful shoulders were
stooped, the black hair had turned yellow-gray and heavy
lines crisscrossed the clownish face.

"Let those Japs go in," Ruffino said. "We'll tag behind
them."

"Whatever you say."

"Were you followed?"

"I don't know." Phil sighed. "I'm so fucking tired I
can't see straight."

Ruffino looked past Phil and studied the faces of the
customers seated in a nearby outdoor café. The monk
leading the Japanese tourists down the steps turned to
them. "*Signori, volete venire?*"

The light grew faint as they followed the tour group
down a steep spiral staircase, and a dank, musky odor rose
from below. They reached an earthen floor and entered a
limestone tunnel illuminated by dim incandescent bulbs.
Ruffino touched Phil's sleeve, and they stopped until the
tour group moved out of sight.

"This way," he said.

The long corridor was quiet except for the faint echoes
of the tour guide's voice coming from the adjacent chamber. They moved down the tunnel for a few hundred feet
before entering an illuminated cave. Phil stood stock-still,
and goose bumps pimpled their way up his arms.

Standing erect, lining both sides of the wall, were the
mummified bodies of dead humans, their parched, claylike
skins drawn taut against grinning skulls. Some still wore
their funeral raiments of tails and top hats; others wore
trench coats and suits. The corpses of women were
dressed in skirts and bonnets. There was a row of em-
balmed doctors in dusty white coats and a line of small children, still clutching smiling dolls in their skeletal fingers.

It was a cold tomb of petrified bone and flesh.

Phil noticed a woman visitor conversing with the bent skeleton of a man in a tuxedo.

"The relatives still come and talk to the dead," Ruffino explained. "They discuss important matters. To be buried here is a sign of respect. But the monks have no money. The dead suffer from neglect."

They walked past the mumbling woman. "You have to understand," Ruffino said. "Death and Sicily are lovers."

At the end of the tunnel in a special glass-topped coffin an infant seemed to be sleeping. "This child is the embalming monk's masterpiece," Ruffino continued. "She died a century ago, but she will be two years old forever."

The next chamber was lined with skeletons in black robes. "The monks' tomb," Ruffino said.

"Where's the room with your colleagues of the Honored Society?" Phil asked, "or do shotgun blasts mess up the embalming process?"

"There's not much honor left in the society. But this *infamia*, Maldonado, will see justice."

"Where is Don Carlo?" Phil asked.

"Tomorrow afternoon go to a mountain village called Lercara. It's less than an hour from Palermo."

"Then what?"

"Tell the driver to take you to the Villa Carelli, just above the village."

They passed the hooded figures of the dead monks. The only sound was the crunch of their own footsteps.

"Tell me, Luigi, who is this girl Claudia Cassini?"

"An agent of the MDI."

"Yeah, I know. But who is she?"

"Someone Don Carlo trusts. Now follow my instructions. You leave first. I'll wait ten minutes."

"How the hell do I get out of here?"

"Go back to the small child in the glass case, and follow that chamber to the end. You'll see the tunnel that leads to the staircase." He put his big hand on Phil's shoulder. "You're a stubborn son of a bitch. You caused the Don a lot of grief. But he considers you a man of honor." Ruffino stared at Phil for a few seconds, then turned abruptly and disappeared around the corner of the chamber.

Phil walked back through the tunnel of the hooded monks. He tried to keep his head down, averting the grinning skulls, but the supernatural fear that one of the cadavers might move forced him to keep his eyes up, checking each skull as he passed.

Ruffino took the passageway leading to the Chamber of Doctors. The tunnel was darker than he remembered. Only a single, flickering light bulb at the far end still burned, and as he approached the last of the white-robed cadavers, the light went out. He took out a cigarette lighter and snapped it on. The yellow flame danced off the bleached skulls.

He began to move slowly, shielding the flame against the cold, damp drafts of air. He heard a sudden whooshing noise, and the lighter went out. A powerful forearm slammed into his neck from behind, applying pressure against his windpipe, and the razor-sharp point of a stiletto broke the skin of his throat.

A faceless figure in front of him held the knife and rasped, *"Dov'è Don Carlo?"*

Ruffino knew it was over. If he answered the question and revealed the Don's location, they would kill him, and if he remained silent, they would kill him.

The voice snarled at him again, *"Dov'è Don Carlo?"*

The point of the knife cut a little deeper, and he felt the warm trickle of blood running out of his throat down his collar and wetting his chest. Ruffino suddenly jammed his right elbow back into the ribs of the man holding him from behind and simultaneously aimed a kick at the groin of the figure in front of him. The pressure on his neck eased, and the knife man dropped to his knees.

Ruffino broke into a run but tripped over the fallen man and sprawled headfirst into the dirt.

Phil missed the turn at the place of the "sleeping" child and moved directionless through a series of limestone chambers.

He felt as though he were permanently trapped in the maze of half-finished clay figures with their cavernous eyes, emaciated cheeks, bleached limbs and fingers outstretched, trying to gesture, their teeth and jaws set in a smile or a shriek, anger or peace—emotions stilled, petrified into permanent grotesque masks.

Phil heard voices coming from an adjacent chamber and picked up his stride.

He came into a long tunnel and slowed down. The chamber seemed vaguely familiar. It was poorly lit by a single flickering light bulb. Phil walked slowly past white-robed cadavers. Then he heard the sound: It was liquid dripping on stone.

He passed two skeletons holding flowers. The dripping sound grew louder. Phil looked up at the ledge.

Luigi Ruffino was propped up between the cadavers.

His dead eyes open. His throat cut from ear to ear. Blood dripped from his soaked jacket, staining the limestone shelf.

Phil bolted and ran full out down the passageway. He turned at the fork in the tunnels and saw a chalky light up ahead. He bumped into a monk entering the main corridor, knocked over a Japanese woman and did not slow down until he reached the base of the wooden steps.

Phil stepped out of the subterranean horror into the balmy night air of the Piazza Santa Cappucine. Lights twinkled over the sidewalk cafés, and people were dining in the trattorias. The horror of the caverns below did not affect the surface life of the ancient piazza. Phil trembled as he walked slowly across the cobblestones toward a line of waiting taxis.

The night was warm, and the Mediterranean surf, just in from Africa, lapped gently against the seawall. Phil sat alone at a corner table. The hotel's elegant terrace restaurant was crowded with its well-dressed clientele. There were couples speaking French and large tables of boisterous German tourists. Two handsome Swedish girls sat together staring into each other's eyes. A long table in the center of the room was occupied by Sicilian businessmen. A young man wearing a white dinner jacket sat at a white piano playing "Moonlight Serenade."

It had taken Phil three straight vodkas to blur the

image of Ruffino's blood-soaked body. He had a pretty good idea of how Ruffino had gained his place of honor on the wall of the dead. Someone, probably Maldonado's hit men, wanted to know where Don Carlo Carelli was, and had Ruffino talked, their problems would have been instantly solved. The killers had nothing to lose if Ruffino remained silent. They could always follow Phil—either way Ruffino was expendable. His body would be on display until some monk noticed his bloody remains in the morning. They would then summon the *carabinieri*. There would be headlines and promises of investigation, but all too late to help Ruffino.

Phil sipped his drink, and his thoughts shifted to the dark beauty and mystery of Claudia Cassini. Her conection with Italian Intelligence was dangerous: The MDI worked with the CIA, and both intelligence services were wired to British MI 5. The Cassini girl could be a plant. But then again, Don Carlo trusted her. He sighed and thought Sonji had been right: They were all ripples in Chung's circle.

Chapter Thirty-six

The ancient truck belched black clouds of choking exhaust. Its sulfurous fumes were sucked back into the open windows of the following taxi. Phil asked the cabdriver if he could pass the offending vehicle, but the man shook his head and muttered, *"Pericoloso."*

The taxi was trapped on the winding mountain road behind the dilapidated open truck, carrying a group of laborers whose faces were darkened by the harsh Sicilian sun. The men neither spoke nor displayed any interest in one another. Their glassy eyes seemed mesmerized, as if the passing scenery were a mirage. They reminded Phil of combat-weary infantrymen who had experienced the kind of horror that precluded speech or physical motion.

Although it was late afternoon, the usual cooling mountain breeze had not yet risen, and a searing, unforgiving wind whispered through the open windows of the taxi. A cluster of buzzing green flies crawled up the inside pane of the windshield, and the cab's radio played a sad song, whose soulful lyric was interrupted by intermittent static.

Phil's eyes narrowed against the glare of the sun, and his arm felt heavy as he adjusted the visor. He was gripped by an overwhelming fatigue aggravated by another sleepless night. The real and surreal coalesced in his consciousness, and the only relief was the temporary lift induced by alcohol. He had finished almost a fifth of vodka during the night. The morning edition of the Palermo newspaper had carried a photograph of Ruffino's body being wheeled out of the Capuchine convent. The hotel concierge had translated the caption: "Luigi Ruffino, a longtime associate of Mafia Capo Carlo Carelli, was discovered in the Hall of the Dead with his throat cut. Carelli is being sought for questioning by the police."

They reached a fork at the summit and passed the farm truck. A sign read *Lercara 2 km.* The taxi continued to climb, circling slowly up the mountain road. As they came around a severe S curve, Phil caught a glimpse of the dark blue Mediterranean off to the south; its surface sparkled like chips of diamonds.

The yellow and black taxi entered the village of Lercara and rolled slowly through the main street. The cobblestones were spotted with the dried droppings of tired burros and mangy dogs. No women or children could be seen. Old men sitting in the shade playing cards stole surreptitious glances at the taxi and its foreign passenger. The cobblestoned road slowly disappeared, dissolving into a primitive path of hard-baked red clay. They curled around serpentine curves for another mile until the road stopped abruptly at the gates of the Villa Carelli.

Phil felt slightly dizzy as he got out and paid the driver. He draped his jacket over his arm, went up to the gate and pulled a bellcord. He wiped the sweat off his face and waited for a moment, listening to the high, buzzing sound of cicadas. As he reached for the bellcord again, the huge wrought-iron gates creaked slowly open.

Two men cradling sawed-off Lupara shotguns appeared. The older one came up to Phil, eyed him for a beat and said, "Passport." It was not a request. It was an order. Phil handed him the small blue book. The man examined the photograph, then glanced at Phil, repeating the same sequence several times.

"That picture is four years old," Phil explained.

The man's wrinkled sunburned face stared uncomprehendingly.

Phil tried some pidgin Italian. *"Questa photo sono quarto anni velo."*

Some of it got through, and the bodyguard returned the passport and said, *"Andiamo."*

As they walked up the pathway, Phil shook his head, thinking he must have aged a hell of a lot in the last four years.

Tall Italian cypress trees and floral gardens bordered the walkway from the gates all the way up to the villa's massive front door.

A middle-aged woman, wearing a black dress and white

apron, greeted them under the portico. "Don Carlo no here," she said.

"Did someone leave a message for me?"

"Signora Cassini here."

"Where?"

"She go up to the ruins. You like cold drink?"

"I'd like to see Miss Cassini."

The woman turned to the gun-toting men and spoke to them in rapid Italian.

Phil walked between the two bodyguards as they climbed the steep path single file. After twenty hard minutes they reached the flat bluff of the mountain escarpment and stood before the great marble pillars of Apollo's temple. The bodyguards motioned for him to wait while they left to find Claudia Cassini.

Phil stared in awe at the Hellenic ruins. The tall Doric columns were silhouetted in a crimson halo cast by a dying sun. He walked up a few crumbling marble steps and entered a large courtyard dotted by fallen capitals and remnants of mosaic designs depicting Greek warriors. Phil stood silently listening to the wind moaning eerily through the pitted columns. He sensed the presence of pagan gods and timeless mystery.

Shivering slightly as the rising wind caught his sweat-soaked shirt, he sat down on a fallen capital and draped his jacket around his shoulders. He felt light-headed, stoned on fatigue, floating in time.

It was a dreamlike sensation, as if he had wandered onto a Fellini set and at any moment Mastroianni, wearing a white suit and huge sunglasses, would step out from behind a column and glance over at a pretty Italian actress squatting behind blocks of fallen ruins relieving herself. And the trail of her amber stream darkening the Greek marble would carry with it the tinkling sound of mankind's history ending in the holy water of an actress's piss.

Phil shook off the end-of-the-world vision as Claudia Cassini slipped between the columns. She came toward him like Aphrodite in a black linen dress. The bodyguards trailed behind her, cradling their shotguns. She came slowly up to Phil, the heels of her shoes clicking against the ruined mosaic tile. "I'm sorry," she apologized. "I didn't realize how late it was."

"Ruffino's dead," he said.

"Yes," she whispered, "I know." The wind pressed her dark hair against her cheeks, and she turned to him. "Ruffino thought the Capuchine convent would be safe."

"Well, he was wrong." Phil sighed. "Dead wrong."

"You have to understand," she said. "In Sicily death is more respected than feared. There is a day that celebrates death called Giorno dei Morti. People receive gifts in the name of the dead. The Capuchine convent is a place of death, therefore a place of respect. It was inconceivable to Ruffino that an act of murder could be committed there."

"Well," Phil said, "we can send Ruffino a train set or a Santa Claus outfit on the next Giorno dei Morti."

She stared at him coldly and contemptuously said, "There's nothing amusing about having your throat cut."

"You're absolutely right. I was with him. I saw him up there on that sacred wall—and it wasn't pretty. Now I've flown five thousand miles, lost a case I worked on for two years. My name is at the top of a spook hit list, and the only reason I accepted this assignment is that Don Carlo may help blow the whistle on those bastards."

"But let me tell you something, sweetheart," he said caustically, "I don't intend to play hide-and-seek waiting for him to show up while I'm in the center of those cross hairs. Now you produce the old man or I'm gone."

"Don Carlo is on the island of Ischia," she replied.

They dined on a terrace overlooking the villa's lush semitropical gardens. Crickets chattered in the tall acacia trees, and the night breeze had turned warm and sensual. High above them the ghostly columns of Apollo's temple were illuminated by a full moon. The cold pasta caprese was perfect, and the local white Corvo was strong and dry.

They sipped after-dinner Sambucas and smoked Claudia's Gauloise cigarettes.

"I suppose you're entitled to a case of raw nerves," she said. "You were very lucky."

"They weren't interested in me."

"How do you know that?"

"Ruffino knew the Don's whereabouts, not me. His killers had no reason to take me out. All they had to do was follow me. If Ruffino had talked, they would've saved time."

Claudia thought the blue circles under his soft brown eyes gave him a haunted look. She knew the cruel scar line at his jaw was the residue of a wound he'd received in Vietnam. She felt a twinge of guilt about betraying his movements to Bill Edwards in MI 5, but it was necessary to follow orders, at least for the moment. The American and British covert sections were not concerned with stopping Don Carlo; their quarry was seated opposite her, and despite herself, she empathized with Phil.

"Why so quiet?" he asked.

"Just thinking."

"About what?"

"Nothing really."

"You know something?" He leaned toward her. "It would be nice if you leveled with me. As a matter of fact, it might keep us alive."

"I'm simply a courier. Why do you persist in making a mystery out of me?"

Phil sipped the sweet liqueur. "You are a mystery. But I have a few clues. Want to hear them?"

"Why not?"

"Your mother's name was Sandra Cassini. She was born in Agrigento, Sicily, February 1925, and entered the United States in March of 1948. She was killed in a car explosion on a summer day in 1973. The car was driven by Aldo Gilante, a known Mafia hit man."

"Go on," she said coldly.

"You were born in Chicago, and after high school you attended a private Swiss college in Lucerne for two years. You returned to New York in '74, got a job as a stewardess with Pan Am. You had an affair with a British citizen named Michael Weaver."

"Not bad." She sighed.

"It gets better." He paused and lit another cigarette. "Your boyfriend, Mr. Weaver, was a bagman for Onassis. In 1978 Mr. Weaver suffered a fatal fall from a rooftop of the Villa d'Este Hotel at Lake Como. You were sharing a suite with him at the time."

"We shared a lot of things," she said.

"Mr. Weaver's English wife requested an investigation, and British MI 5 got involved, along with Italian intelligence authorities. It seems two million of Onassis's Swiss francs were missing. Weaver was to have delivered those francs to a Saudi official for an oil deal utilizing Mr. Onassis's tankers. After Weaver's death you were questioned by an agent of British MI 5 named Bill Edwards." He paused. "How'm I doing?"

"Fine," she said curtly.

"Edwards got nowhere," Phil continued. "Neither did the Italian agents of the MDI, who later recruited you, and the two million in Swiss francs was never recovered." He refilled their wineglasses.

"Where did you get all this history?" she asked.

"A cable this morning from my colleague Sid Greene. You just tickle those FBI computers, and they sing like Caruso."

Claudia was beginning to feel the wine and the Sambuca. "So the mystery is solved." She sighed.

"Not really." He crushed out the cigarette. "Your mother had Mafia connections. You had no father, at least according to your birth certificate."

"My father died just before I was born."

"Okay. But there's no name on the document. You're probably involved up to your beautiful neck in a bundle of missing Swiss francs and your lover's sudden demise. You work for an Italian Intelligence agency." Phil paused. "Now Don Carlo is a man famous for his suspicion, yet he trusts you. Why?"

Claudia shrugged her shoulders and rubbed the glowing end of her cigarette back and forth across the surface of the ashtry. "You'll have to ask him."

She seemed vulnerable and innocent, and there was a trace of hopelessness that reminded him of Sonji. He had obviously hurt her, and it bothered him. He covered her hand with his and leaned forward. "Listen, for chrissake, I'm sorry. You have a line on me. I had to get one on you. I don't enjoy it. But that's the business we're in. Believe me, if I could do it all over, I'd be Mario Andretti and die a noble death fighting a tachometer."

She studied him with a mysterious passivity, then suddenly smiled and said, "Let's walk."

The sweet scent of jasmine caressed the sultry night wind as they strolled past sculpted fountains and marble lions with angel's wings. Phil stopped, leaned against a lion and gazed up at the moonlit pillars of Apollo's temple.

"Talk about secrets," he said. "Imagine what they know."

"Yes, it's fascinating," she replied. "I went up there and just got lost. Time, place, everything forgotten."

She studied his morose eyes and scarred jaw and felt a compelling attraction for him. Perhaps it was a sense of common peril, but none of it mattered—they were on borrowed time.

"What dark secrets are turning over in that pretty head?"

Claudia moved into him. Her arms circled his neck, and she whispered, "I was thinking of making love to you."

She pulled him close and pressed her lips against his, softly at first, moving, brushing. Then his arms went around her. Their lips burned against each other's, and they clung together in the moonlit jasmine gardens while the gods looked down and the monsters of betrayal and intrigue slipped away.

Chapter Thirty-seven

Soon Yi Sonji drove her red Pony Sedan through the narrow streets of the Mukyong District. She was leery of this rendezvous with the president's executive secretary. She was following Chung's orders but had no way of knowing whether Won had been given a similar directive: to effect a liaison with her and determine *her* true political beliefs. Sonji remembered Won as the young captain who had escorted her home the night they assassinated Park, but since he had assumed the role of presidential secretary, she had spoken to him only briefly and on rare occasions.

She parked the Pony on the rooftop lot of a department store and walked two blocks to the Chensi Café. The smoke-filled restaurant was crowded with noontime secretaries, off-duty soldiers, students and omnipresent Japanese businessmen. She noticed the handsome, wiry presidential secretary sitting at a street-side window table.

Won rose and pulled the table toward him, permitting her to be seated. Sonji ordered a glass of cold California rosé and advised the waiter she wanted a bottle of the same wine opened and recorked.

"I'm sorry I was so direct with you," Sonji said. "But it was a matter of some urgency."

"I understand," he replied. "I have reserved a room for us at the Shilla Hotel."

She swallowed the chilled wine and shook her head. "The Shilla will not do."

"Why?"

"Let's be frank. President Chung may have ordered you to meet with me, and that hotel room may be wired or bugged."

"I can assure you, no one ordered me to meet with

you," Won replied. "For all I know you may be wired right now, at this moment."

"As you may be," Sonji replied. "We must strip naked and inspect each other's clothing."

"As I said, there is a room reserved at the Shilla."

"No." Sonji shook her head. "I will suggest a group of tourist hotels. You select one."

"Fine."

She ticked them off: "The Chosun, the Seoul Garden, the Lotte, the President, the Sheraton."

"Five is better than four." He smiled. "I am very superstitious."

"Well, which will it be?"

"The Lotte."

●

They entered the spacious room, and Sonji placed the bottle of wine on the bureau.

Won said, "Your handbag and wristwatch, please." He examined the watch carefully and turned her handbag upside down, spilling the contents on the bureau. Swiftly and expertly he tested the keys, coins, lipstick holder and perfume atomizer for a possible bug. He then ran his fingers over the lining of the handbag and turned to her. "Your clothes."

She took off her shirt and tossed it to him. He caught it and for a fleeting moment stared at her jutting breasts. She removed her jeans, and he carefully went through the pockets. She pulled off her boots, and he turned them over gripping the heels. They did not move or slide under the pressure of his hand.

Sonji poured a glass of wine and drank it slowly as she watched him strip. When he stood before her naked, she put down the glass and went through his jacket, pants, shoes and shirt, then said, "Turn on the shower, tub and sink faucets."

She wondered how they had arrived at this fearful place where they could not even speak without undertaking this bizarre ritual. But the reality of their situation dictated their caution.

She walked over to the radio-TV console and snapped both switches on. A movie appeared on the color television screen, and rock music played on the radio. She turned the volume up on both.

Won came out of the bathroom, leaving the door open, permitting the sound of running water to mix with the voices coming from the radio and television.

Sonji carried the wineglass and bottle to the king-size bed and sat down with her back resting against the headboard.

"Now we can speak freely," she said. "We are not bugged, and no one will ever know what was said in this room. And should one of us attempt to betray the other, it will be totally unsupported by any documentation."

"Agreed," Won said, and poured a glass of wine. "You were ordered to meet with me, correct?"

"Yes, but I have my own reasons."

"As I do," he said. "The obsession of our leader with creating circles of action may be our good fortune. I will speak openly with you, Sonji."

"Please do."

"You have been abroad for a long time. You do not understand how the nation suffers."

"My father spoke of the repression to me." She felt a sexual arousal by virtue of their nakedness and the clandestine nature of their discussion.

"I will tell you some things about myself and our government." Won kept his voice low, despite the dissonant sounds of the radio, television and running water. "I served with Chung in Vietnam and later in the Garrison Command. I supported the removal of Park and Kyu, as you did. My reasons were clear: Park's regime was brutal and corrupt. I trusted Chung. I was wrong. The government of law he promised was a lie."

Won moved his chair closer to the bed. "The Committee for Social Purification has jailed thousands of innocent people. Student leaders are arrested and tortured. I've seen the methods of torture." He poured another glass of wine and refilled hers. "A man is strapped to a table. A rat is placed on his belly. A Plexiglas cover is heated over the rat, and it claws and chews its way into the intestines—"

"Please, I cannot listen to that—"

"You must hear it. I've seen a drill go through the kneecaps. I've seen legs and arms nailed to the floor. I've seen wires attached to the genitals, men and women. I've heard their screams. General Ro, a noble soldier, has been reduced to a vegetable by electric shocks. Student leader Kwai Lee has been castrated. Han Sun, our most distinguished journalist, has had his fingers broken, and once they came out of the cast, they were broken again. Six hundred students and workers were gassed in Kwangju, all under the direction of President Chung. We have even been denied the right of silence. He keeps the nation under surveillance while he schemes to unify China, Korea and Japan. He plots against Dr. Belgrave and the American intelligence community. He feeds information to the Soviets to gain favor with Kim Il Sung in the North."

Won leaned forward. "Sonji, you are in a unique position to help our nation."

They were the same words her father had spoken. "How can I help you?" she asked.

"By employing the methods we used to assassinate Park."

She rose and stared at him. It was a moment that required no words. Sonji walked to the bureau and rummaged through the spilled contents of her bag. She found a marijuana cigarette, lit it and inhaled deeply, holding the smoke in her lungs for a long time. She felt a rush of relief, of euphoria as the tension slipped away.

She walked slowly, provocatively back to him.

"I must tell you, Sonji," he said. "I was ordered to meet with you."

"I am grateful for your honesty," she replied.

"Will you help the nation?" he asked.

"My sympathies are with you and with our generation, but I cannot sacrifice my father and Kimsan. I cannot place them in jeopardy."

"Every day Chung lives both Kimsan and your father are on borrowed time. Our president plans to send you to Rome. It is part of his plot against Belgrave and the Americans. But upon your return we must act. Chung has orgies with kisaengs. He has even taken to drinking Park's favorite scotch. He speaks to Buddha. It's as if he has been possessed by the ghost of Park. We can assassinate him in the same manner. You can arrange the evening. You are his one weakness."

"And the Army?"

"General Kim awaits my word."

"And what of me?"

He seemed puzzled. "I don't understand."

"If we succeed, what will my position be?"

"You will have the highest position in the Supreme Presidium. Our generation will at last be in a position of authority."

"And the Americans?"

He shrugged. "They will do nothing. We are their Cubans. We hold the frontier for them in Asia."

There was a pause as they listened to the cacophony of movie and the Bruce Springsteen lyric coming from the radio and the rushing sound of the water.

Sonji got off the bed and knelt down in front of him.

His hands gripped her shoulders. "I am homosexual."

"I can still give you pleasure."

"You have already."

●

President Yi Chung sat behind his desk, smoking the first cigarette of his second pack, and it was not yet noon. The lines crisscrossing his face were deeper, and a nervous tic had developed under his right eye. He had just received distressing news. His request for five billion in economic aid had been rejected. The American secretary of state had used the diplomatic idiom "still under study," which was synonymous for refusal. Dr. Belgrave's view had prevailed—an industrial Goliath in Korea was incompatible with American corporate interests.

Chung inhaled and coughed violently for a full minute. He took out a quart of Bell's scotch and drank from the bottle. The scotch gave him a feeling of well-being, and he thought all matters would be properly resolved; Ricker and the Italian Don would inevitably cause Belgrave's demise. The fall of the Doctor and his associates would bring about a vacuum of power. All things would then be possible. He pressed the button under the top of the desk, and the huge carved doors opened.

Sonji wore a traditional blue silk Korean dress slit up to her calf. She had drenched herself in an obscure French perfume exuding a heavy, sweet scent that pleased Chung.

"You look well this morning, Daughter."

"I am well."

They sat on deep plush velvet sofas facing each other. He puffed the American cigarette and studied the lines of her perfect figure, the luminous quality of her large oval eyes and her wide, soft mouth. Time had not diminished his unquenchable thirst for this girl-child. She was a true daughter of the goddess Vishnu and therefore dangerous. The meeting he had ordered her to undertake with his executive secretary was twofold in purpose: He was testing not only Won's loyalty but hers as well.

"Tell me of your meeting."

"We spent the afternoon together."

"Where?"

"The Lotte."

"And what were his thoughts?"

A warning tumbler clicked in her head. There were certain facts she would have to relate, like Won's homosexuality. Chung would certainly be aware of that aberration. She had to be careful. "It was difficult for me," she said softly. "Won is a homosexual."

Chung felt relieved. The stunning imperial kisaeng was telling the truth. "I had suspicions of that. But he was a courageous soldier and is a meticulous administrator. I suppose I have ignored his sexual problems, but then again he partakes in certain entertainments I arrange."

"It is a façade," she said with the finality of an expert. "He is homosexual. Nevertheless, I met the challenge."

"How?"

"We smoked marijuana and drank wine. It was difficult and required great patience, but finally he relaxed and we spoke."

She tossed her long hair. "He admires you but fears you. He believes you do not appreciate his efforts?"

"And what of his Christian beliefs? His politics?"

"He believes only in the Army. In my opinion, Won is still a simple soldier."

"It's true enough," Chung agreed. "Perhaps I raised him too high and did not sufficiently praise him. But I am relieved to hear of his continuing loyalty." He rose and walked to the window. It was the time of day when the presidential guard detachments changed.

Sonji lit a cigarette and relaxed in the knowledge that a wide choice of options had opened to her. She could eventually betray Won and gain extraordinary favor with Chung; or at the appropriate moment she could press the button that would trigger his assassination; or she could betray them both to a third force of her selection. All that would depend on Chung's continued protection of her father and Kimsan.

The president turned from the window and came slowly up to her. "You will proceed to Rome in one week. Kimsan has requested that you act as a courier for him."

"For what purpose?"

"He will give you a file code named Gemstone. You will deliver the document to Philip Ricker."

"In Washington?"

"No, no . . . Ricker is in Italy. He is escorting Don Carlo Carelli. At some point Kimsan will locate Ricker. You will then deliver Gemstone to him."

"What if something happens to Ricker?"

"In that case you will bring the Gemstone file to me."

She nodded, but her oval eyes betrayed doubt.

"What troubles you, Daughter?"

"I have heard past rumors of this file. It contains many things of great political importance."

"Gemstone is not a rumor. It was given to Kimsan by J. Edgar Hoover in the early spring of 1972."

"Perhaps Kimsan will refuse to part with the file."

"He has given me his word," Chung said emphatically. "He has given Carelli his word. He personally requested your appointment as the courier. But should he have second thoughts, you will tell him he is forfeiting his own life and the life of your father and yours as well." The president then smiled, his eyes softened and he touched the silky strands of her hair. "Of course, this is a ruse, a game of persuasion. You understand?"

"Perfectly. But there is a question I should like to ask you."

"Anything you wish, Daughter."

"When Kimsan surrenders this document, will he be in jeopardy."

Chung registered no surprise at the question and replied matter-of-factly. "He is in no danger from me. He never has been."

Sonji rose and lied magnificently. "The last time you and I were together, I felt my mind and body possessed by Buddha."

He traced the curve of her cheekbone. "It does not surprise me, Daughter. You see, Buddha is with me always."

Chapter Thirty-eight

The brilliant morning sun turned the Ionian Sea into swells of iridescent blue glass. The Messina—Calabria car ferry plowed through the shimmering water, escorted by a swarm of silver gulls. A slight breeze was up, and in the distance puffy white clouds climbed the dark slopes of Mount Etna.

Claudia's sunglasses were pushed up on her head, and the wind played with her hair. She stood alongside Phil at the prow with other passengers who had left their cars to enjoy the sea air. The 8:00 A.M. ferry was not crowded. There were a few produce trucks and the usual summer tourists in their rented Fiats and Alfas.

Phil noticed a blue 450 SEL Mercedes with two men seated inside behind closed windows, its engine turned on to power the air conditioner. It was impossible to discern the nationalities of the men except for the fact they did not have the dark Sicilian complexions.

A car ferry coming the other way passed and sounded its whistle in greeting.

"Lovely, isn't it?" she said.

"Didn't Homer sail around here looking for the Golden Fleece?"

She shook her head. "Homer never stuck his toe in the water. He just wrote about the sailors, and—"

Phil cut her off. "Of course, it was Ulysses."

"Wrong. Jason sailed around looking for the Golden Fleece."

"You're right again. Ulysses was seeking a Club Med with sirens and monsters."

"More or less." She smiled.

"One day I'll go back to NYU and major in history."

"You'll never go back."

"Why not?"

"Because men like you never change," she said pensively. "And they never go back."

"How do you know that?"

"Because I've lived with them. And I've buried them." She stared at him briefly, then looked off at the approaching Calabrian coastline. The ship's whistle blasted shrilly, sending the passengers back to their cars.

Phil maneuvered the Fiat carefully off the steel ramp onto the dock, and after a short drive through the port section of Reggio di Calabria they picked up the A3 *autostrada* north to Naples. He had familiarized himself with the Fiat's five-gear stick shift on the drive down from Lercara to Messina.

At Vibo Valentia the superhighway curved inland away from the sea. Phil brought the Fiat's speed up to 100 kilometers and cruised in fifth gear. "With any luck, we should make the Naples dock by ten-thirty."

"It's an easy drive," she said and turned on the radio.

The highway was shrouded by mountains with stone villages clinging to the slopes. Claudia fiddled with the radio dial and found an Italian vocalist singing a romantically sad song.

"What's she saying?" Phil asked.

"The words are the same in all popular Italian songs: how things were, how they might have been if only someone wasn't married. The themes never change."

"There's something to be said for tradition," Phil said, and glanced at the rearview mirror. The big blue Mercedes that had crossed the Strait of Messina with them was only three cars back, following an oil truck. The presence of the Mercedes was not remarkable—Route A3 was the principal highway from Reggio di Calabria to the north. But the placement of the German car was suspicious. It made little sense to be trailing the heavy exhaust of the petrol truck when passing was easily accomplished by switching to the fast, left lane.

"Put your shoulder belt on," Phil said.

"Why?"

"I'm not sure."

He swung out into the fast lane, gearing down and accelerating simultaneously. The Fiat shot forward, the speedometer needle entering the red zone and hovering at 140 kilometers per hour. The wind whistled through the air vents as they passed the line of cars in the right lane. The Mercedes was far back, still following the petrol truck.

"Looks like I was wrong," Phil said, and, noticing a break in the slow lane, veered back in between a Fiat and a produce truck. He adjusted the side-view mirror, extending his line of sight, and cruised at traffic speed for half a mile.

As they passed Cosenza, Phil saw the Mercedes pull out into the fast lane and pass a long line of cars before it ducked back into the right lane, positioning itself three vehicles behind them.

"Looks like I was right," he said, feeling a surge of excitement. "Hang on."

She watched the perfect coordination of his hands, feet and darting eyes as he swung into the fast land and tailgated a stubborn tour bus that would not move aside. He flicked his lights and sounded his horn, but the bus doggedly maintained its position. Phil dropped back into the slow lane behind a white Ferrari, then crept up even with the bus in the parallel lane. He pushed the Fiat up to the very bumper of the Ferrari, measuring the distance between it and the front bumper of the bus to his left. He geared down, floored the gas pedal, swung the wheel and geared up. The Fiat catapulted into the fast lane, its tail fender clearing the front bumper of the bus by inches.

Claudia felt frightened and helpless. Her safety was totally dependent on Phil's skill. He glanced at the rear-view mirror and saw the blue Mercedes passing the tour bus some 300 yards back and closing fast.

"What's the next cutoff to the coast road?" he asked.

"Castrovillari," she replied.

"How far?"

"Fifteen kilometers."

Phil poured on the speed, moving in the fast lane, flashing his lights as he loomed up behind cars. The Mercedes was less than 200 yards back. He caught a glimpse of the sign: CASTROVILLARI—3 KM. He had less than two minutes to gain the right lane in order to exit. But the lane was blocked by a solid wall of trucks and trailing passenger cars. The Mercedes was omnipresent, looming up only fifty yards back. Phil noticed a small space to his right between two huge trucks.

Claudia understood at once what he was thinking. "You'll never make it! There's a grade coming up; those trucks will slow down!"

He geared down, double-clutched and spun the wheel. The Fiat changed lanes, darting between the trucks. Phil eased off the gas pedal, pumped the brakes twice and at the last moment swung the wheel right and shot onto the exit ramp.

He glanced back at the *autostrada* in time to see the speeding Mercedes still trapped in the fast lane.

"Don't ever do that again," Claudia sighed.

"I was in perfect control every second."

"What about the car? Suppose a tire or a part went?"

"Moments like that require a certain amount of trust."

"Who said so?"

"I think it was Mario Andretti." Phil smiled. "They were wheeling him into intensive care at the time."

They stopped at a seaside café in Salerno. The coffee was strong and the bread was hot. The café overlooked a sandy beach dotted with sunbathing Nordic girls. And way out on the Mediterranean, red, green and yellow sails wheeled back and forth in a ballet orchestrated by the wind. Phil noticed a rusted steel turret protruding just above the waterline, and up on the seawall a remarkably well-preserved German pillbox was still standing.

He wondered what this tranquil beach must have been like in September 1943, when the British and Americans stormed ashore in the face of entrenched panzer divisions. He knew it had been a bloodbath, one of General Mark Clark's blunders that would continue throughout the ill-conceived Italian campaign. Phil shook his head, thinking how men had died in this place and now there were sun-worshipers in bikinis on the same beach. "Curious," he murmured.

"What?" she asked.

"How battlefields turn into resorts."

She studied him for a moment but did not respond. They sat quietly drinking their coffee and listening to the surf and the cry of gulls and the laughter of the Swedish girls on the beach. "Who do you suppose was in the Mercedes?" she asked.

"MI 5 or your guys from the MDI or Mafia hoods. Take your pick." He glanced at his watch. "We might just make the eleven-thirty hydrofoil."

"I don't know," she said, flicking her sunglasses down. "The Amalfi drive is one long hairpin curve, and the boats leave for Ischia every half hour. Why don't we just relax and enjoy the drive?"

"I have a feeling you don't trust my driving."

"With good cause." She smiled. "Something happens to you behind the wheel."

"Okay, you drive and I'll listen to the sad Italian songs."

"I don't think your ego can take that."

He kissed her softly. "You're right."

The hydrofoil crossed the eighteen miles of blue water from Naples to Ischia in twenty-eight minutes.

The drive from the small harbor to the interior of the island was a spectacular trip through tunnels of sun-drenched purple bougainvillaea shading red-tiled white stucco villas.

The estate was on a mountain top overlooking the small cove and marina of Lacco Ameno. Two armed men escorted them to the entrance. The huge rosewood doors were opened by a big man with spread features as if his face consisted of reworked clay. He greeted Claudia. "Buon giorno."

"Buon giorno, Gino. Come sta?"

"Bene, grazie."

Claudia introduced Gino to Phil; the big man looked at Phil and grumbled, "Andiamo."

The study was a cool, dark, high-domed room. Heavy

medieval tapestries hung on the walls and the furniture was Renaissance. Don Carlo Carelli, silhouetted in the backlight coming through the windows, turned as he heard them enter.

His handsome patrician face was etched by fine lines, and the color of his powder blue eyes seemed to have faded. Carelli walked up to Phil, and they shook hands.

"Long time," Phil said.

"A lifetime," the Don replied. "How about a drink?"

"I'd like an iced tea," Claudia said.

"And you, Phil?"

"Vodka on the rocks."

The Don nodded to the burly bodyguard, and Gino left. "How was the trip?"

"We were tailed from the Messina ferry, but I think we shook it."

"He drove like a madman." Claudia smiled.

"Well, you're here," Don Carlo said. "And I can assure you this place is secure."

They sat down in plush velvet gold-leafed chairs.

"You live well, Carlo."

The Don crossed to a rosewood desk and took a cigar from a humidor. "This villa belongs to the Conte Bellini, a Sicilian nobleman." He bit off the top of the cigar. "Some years ago we shared the dream of an independent Sicily, free of Roman corruption."

"You're one hell of an advocate for morality," Phil said curtly.

The Don lit the cigar and blew a cloud of gray smoke up at the frescoed ceiling. "You never really understood our organization. We were born out of centuries of rape. Sicily was Europe's whore. Our identity was taken from us, along with our work and our hope. The Mafia was not a criminal organization. It was a people's revolution against a feudal system. We were truly the Honored Society. We extended our protection to the poor, and in return for loyalty we defended our people against all outside enemies."

"Then you exported your revolution to America and corrupted its political institutions."

Claudia watched them, wondering if they could overcome their historic disdain.

The Don paced the priceless Persian rug. "We corrupted nothing," he said. "In 1930 America was a monarchy run by maybe twenty elite families." He pointed at Phil. "Listen, my sanctimonious friend, if Leo Meyers had been a WASP, if I had been born on Beacon Hill with a good Anglo name like Cabot or Lodge, we'd have run Union Oil instead of the Union Siciliana."

A butler came in with a tray of drinks, served them and left.

"What about all the kids strung out on heroin?" Phil persisted. "Permanently consigned to the junk pile?"

"What about them?" the Don asked quizzically.

"That's something you have to answer for, or am I wrong?"

"The American Congress can stop drug traffic in two minutes—all they've got to do is legalize it, control it, dole it out in hospitals, like they do in England. It's that bullshit WASP morality that keeps the mob in business. Just like Prohibition. In 1933 I had a summer place out in Great Neck, Long Island. The Four Hundred—the bluebloods—would come every Sunday. Hitting little wooden balls through hoops on the lawn. Eating my food and drinking good Prohibition scotch and sniffing pure cocaine. They swarmed over me like I was Gatsby. Their blood was so blue you could fill your pool with it. They never invited me to their homes or private clubs, but when they got jammed up with broads or swindles, they came to me. We were nothing compared to them. We didn't make wars; we didn't control the banks or steel or shipping or oil. We gave Americans their candy: booze, gambling and broads. We were small potatoes."

"The mob takes in fifty billion a year," Phil said. "You call that small potatoes?"

"Look, I'm not going to argue with you. I need you and you need me."

"Yeah—so did Ruffino."

The Don's eyes clouded. "He's part of my vengeance now. Like Nicky, like my dead grandson."

Phil sensed a compelling need somehow to beat the old man into submission, and he hit him where he lived: "Did you ever think if you had been legitimate, Nicky might be alive?"

Claudia said, "Why rake up those coals?"

"No, no, he's right," the Don admitted. "That's a burden I must carry."

"Like the heroin operation in Palermo," Phil added.

"I never promoted drugs. When you forced me into exile, the council directed me to organize operations in Sicily."

"With Kimsan?"

"Right. And if you want Gemstone, you better pray for his continued good health."

Phil was startled by the Don's remark. "What the hell has Kimsan got to do with Gemstone?"

"He was the courier in 1972, from Hoover to Park. Only he never gave it up."

"What was the connection between Park and Hoover?"

"How would I know?"

"When do we get the file?"

"It depends."

"On what?"

"Kimsan requested a certain courier from the Korean president, someone he trusts. If that request is granted, we'll get the file."

"When do we know?"

"Today . . . tomorrow."

"I'm not going to wait around here forever."

"I had to wait for you," the Don replied. "Without Gemstone you have nothing. And without me you have nothing."

"I want you to know my feelings about you haven't changed," Phil said. "I want to clear the air on that score."

"Okay," the old man said. "Just remember you caused me plenty of grief. You know what exile is like for me? I lived for thirty-five years in that greatest of all cities. I was a king in New York. That city was my world. And because of you, I'm forced to spend the last years of my life in that Sicilian hellhole, harassed by police and politicians."

"You're lucky you didn't get life in some federal pen."

"Yeah, I'm a lucky man." The Don sighed. "A dead son, a dead daughter-in-law, a dead grandchild."

"You created Maldonado."

"You're right. I did create Victor. Now I must destroy him. And if you wanted a surrender from me, you have it. I'll do anything you ask. I'll testify when we get back. I'll produce the Gemstone file. But you must guarantee my meeting with Maldonado."

"You've got it," Phil said. "But I can't guarantee your people. Ruffino was a mob hit."

"Not possible," the Don replied. "Leo Meyers gave me the council's word. My meeting with Maldonado is agreed by all parties."

"Leo can't control everything."

"What about your people?" Don Carlo asked. "The American secret society?"

Phil shook his head. "They hit me now and they don't get Gemstone."

"Don't count on that. Those people have survived for years without that file."

Claudia rose and said, "All of which means we should be thinking of a way out instead of raking up the past."

"Got any ideas?" Phil asked.

"The *ministero* does," she replied. "We go by private boat to the Naples dock. A car will be waiting with MDI agents to take us to Naples Airport for a connecting flight to Rome, then a direct flight to JFK. The American security will be operative on arrival at Kennedy and all the way to Washington."

"Forgive me, Miss Cassini," the Don said. "But first, I regard those arrangements in the same way I would regard my funeral arrangements. Naples is full of Maldonado's soldiers, and if Phil is right, if Victor has betrayed his agreement, we would not live five minutes in Naples. Second, I don't trust strangers to escort me to and from three different airports. Your *ministero* is like all the other secret agencies. I won't place my life in their hands."

"Well," Phil said, "at least we agree on something. I'll move us, at the right time. And in my way. But we don't leave Italy without Gemstone."

Chapter Thirty-nine

Security men with guard dogs patrolled the floodlit grounds of Dr. Belgrave's estate. All alarm systems and sensory night-seeing devices were armed and operative. Lights blazed in all eighteen rooms of the Tudor estate.

Napoleon brandy had just been served, and the smoke of Cuban cigars drifted up to the ceiling of the drawing room.

Dr. Belgrave, Matt Crowley, Robert Burgess, Charles Gruenwald and the Reverend Rhee's attorney, Stanford Harwick, were seated in the study. Belgrave had just concluded a persuasive argument for Harwick's surrender of the Reverend Rhee's papers documenting the secret conclave in the Glass Room on July 5, 1979, the fateful meeting that had sealed Park's fate. Belgrave's plea had been made in the name of national security.

The tall, distinguished attorney uncrossed his long legs. "Doctor, as you well know, I have always maintained that the security of the nation is directly related to the strength of our intelligence services. My every inclination is to help you. But you are asking me to reveal documents placed in my trust by my client. As Rhee's advocate I cannot betray that relationship without violating privileged communications. Every attorney is an officer of the court and sworn to uphold its legal tenets."

"Your attitude is perfectly proper," the Doctor agreed. "This is a most distasteful task for me. But let me be frank with you, Stanford. Your client, the Reverend Rhee, is blackmailing certain agencies of this government. Rhee is and was a KCIA operative. He therefore was trusted with certain sensitive data. Now, if the documents Rhee has placed in your hands are made public, the security of this nation will have been gravely compromised." Belgrave paused. "It's entirely up to you, Stanford."

Harwick studied the Doctor for a moment and said, "You realize, of course, these documents will be made public only should the Reverend meet a violent end."

"I understand," Belgrave replied. "But this is a fragile life we lead: my wife and son met violent ends; our presidents have met violent ends. None of us has any guarantees, Stanford."

"Believe me, gentlemen," Harwick said, "I would like nothing more than to be of service. But professional allegiance to my client precludes my involvement in this matter."

Belgrave rose and shook Harwick's hand. "I appreciate your position, Stanford."

There was an exchange of pleasantries and a promise by Harwick to keep the matter confidential. The attorney complimented the others for their patriotic service to the nation, shook hands with Belgrave and departed.

The Doctor waited for the sound of the front door closing before speaking. "Well, gentlemen?"

"Break in," Burgess said.

"We have no choice," Gruenwald agreed.

"Matt?" Belgrave addressed his aide.

"Steve Bechtel of Intersel handles security for the Magno-Tel Corporation, a major client of Harwick's. Bechtel can get us a floor plan of the law office."

There was a momentary pause as they waited final approval from Belgrave. "Harwick is an honorable man—" the Doctor said thoughtfully "—and it was worth a try. But I'm convinced this is one of those occasions where no action is the best action. Without Harwick's cooperation there are too many imponderables." The patriarch brushed his fine snowy hair. "Besides, I have learned that Rhee may soon be facing charges of tax fraud, a residual fallout of Ricker's case against the Reverend."

Defense Intelligence Chief Gruenwald said, "A federal indictment would cause the Reverend's deportation."

"In any event," Belgrave said, "if pressed, we can gain control of the Rhee documents. Let us turn our attention to Ricker and Gemstone." He glanced at the director of

Covert Operations. "Robert, have you heard from Edwards in MI 5?"

"Yes," Burgess replied. "The Cassini girl contacted him. She'll keep Edwards posted on Ricker's movements."

"What do you make of the killing of the Don's man Ruffino?" Belgrave inquired.

"That was mob," Burgess answered. "One of Maldonado's Calabrian soldiers."

Gruenwald said, "I take it we will not wait for Ricker to acquire Gemstone. Edwards will terminate him at an opportune moment."

"That's correct," Belgrave said. "If Ricker is eliminated, Don Carlo is frozen in Italy with the Gemstone file."

"I would like to volunteer for that one," Crowley offered.

"No, Matt, we cannot afford to risk any personal involvement. Edwards is a professional."

"A top-drawer man," Burgess concurred. "Our British colleagues are quite capable."

"In the pig's ass!" Crowley snapped. "What about Philby and MacLean? And Blunt, and Burgess—those goddamn Cambridge-Soviet moles?"

"Well, Matt, it is unfortunately true British Intelligence was severely compromised by those gentlemen. Those treacherous few exist in all nations, and all intelligence agencies are vulnerable to deep-cover moles. But the British Assassination Bureau of MI 5 is unassailable."

"And," Burgess added, "I assure you, Edwards is one of their best."

"Fine." Belgrave rose. "Now, assuming Ricker is removed and Gemstone wanders into the Don's hands, how do we retrieve it?"

"Only one way," Burgess said. "By introducing someone who is trusted by Carelli. Gemstone can be acquired only from the inside."

There was a moment of silence before Defense Intelligence Chief Gruenwald said, "Curious how it all interlocks: Ricker, Don Carlo, Gemstone, Rhee."

"There's nothing curious about it," the Doctor replied. "It all springs out of Ricker's investigation of that bogus Korean preacher."

"Still, it worries me. I have this nagging sensation."

"What sensation?" Belgrave asked testily.

Gruenwald shrugged. "I can't define it. But I have this feeling that we're part of someone else's architecture."

The chairman of the National Security Council leaned across the table. His penetrating blue eyes blazed at Gruenwald. "I will not tolerate superstition, supposition or doomsayers. You've theorized in the past that President Chung is the source of Ricker's information. And I maintain it is of no consequence. If that Buddhist despot plays poker with me, I will bring him to his knees. I can handle his Greater Asian Co-Prosperity dreams in exactly the same fashion as I did his predecessor's." Belgrave's voice trembled with anger. "We are not being positioned. We are not being manipulated. *We* are the manipulators. Our *modus operandi* has succeeded because it is not based on vengeance, or profit, or personal fame, but pragmatism. And pragmatism transcends all of man's philosophies. It is the wellspring of mankind's survival."

There was a moment of silence in the study. A sharp pain centered in Crowley's stomach. It was the ulcer of doubt. Pragmatism was not patriotism.

Chapter Forty

Twinkling lights of hillside villas tumbled down from their lofty perches, and the Lacco Ameno cove shimmered in a pale light cast by a full moon.

There was a small seaside café nestled in the cove whose terrace extended above the water and overlooked the marina.

The Don's back was to the sea; Claudia sat to his right and Phil to his left. Their table was crowded with an array of wine bottles and mineral water.

Sleek cabin cruisers bobbed gently at their moorings, and far out at sea the lights of the shrimp boats sparkled like dancing fireflies.

Gino and two other bodyguards were seated close by, their eyes constantly in motion, watching the marina and the interior of the restaurant. There were no other customers on the terrace.

Phil twirled the linguine on his fork, and washed the pasta down with cold white wine. Claudia picked at her food and stared wistfully out at the sea.

Don Carlo seemed tranquil, the obsessions of death and vengeance softened by the wine and romantic setting.

A tape amplified by hidden speakers played the old Sinatra recording of "Laura."

"Sinatra . . ." Phil murmured.

"What about him?" the Don asked.

"I hear Sinatra and I get homesick."

"Homesick for Washington? It's a city of thieves, pimps and killers."

"That's why I miss it."

A pretty girl in a bikini came up on the deck of one of the moored cabin cruisers. She carried a bottle of champagne and waved to them as she went aft.

The Sinatra tune changed to a lively rendition of "New York, New York."

"Now that's my town," the Don said, touching a napkin to his lips. "There's no action, no excitement, no city in the world with the magic of New York. And because of you, my friend, I've been stuck in exile for ten years."

"Please," Claudia said, "let's not get into that again."

"Right," Phil agreed. "Besides, I probably saved you from doing life in some federal pen. They were preparing a major narcotics case against you about the same time you were deported."

"Well, Christ, the goddamn government owed me," the Don replied indignantly. "In '42 the U.S. Navy Intelligence came to me and Leo Meyers to spring Luciano."

"I always thought they pardoned him because he helped with the Sicilian invasion."

"That's horseshit. Fairy tales. Luciano planned nothing. It was Leo's idea to burn the *Normandie* at its pier in New York."

"Why?" Claudia asked.

"To get the Navy Department nervous. Leo made a deal with the feds. In return for security on the waterfront, they would pardon Luciano when the war was over. That Sicily invasion business was nonsense. The Chief of Staff of the Italian Army gave the Americans and British all the key German defense points."

The waiters came and went. Gino and the bodyguards ordered more pasta but drank little wine.

"You can't imagine, Phil, how I miss New York."

"Well, Italy's better than Sing Sing."

"This country is a toilet. Terrorism. Corruption. Strikes. Nothing works."

"Not like the good old blackshirt days," Phil said.

"Ah, Mussolini was a horse's ass. He confused Italians with Romans. He drove by the Colosseum too many times. But this system—Christ, they shoot the Pope, kidnap businessmen."

"Democracy has its price."

"Listen." The Don swallowed more wine, his face slightly flushed. "Democracy in Italy only means the people share in the intrigue. Now Sicily is something else. We had our own thing. We could have gained independence, but we were sold out by the Communists. My allegiance with the Sicilian nobility would have brought prosperity to the island. We almost made it."

"You probably required the wizardry of Leo Meyers to figure that one out."

The Don smiled and lit a small cigar. "Great man, Leo. A true genius." He leaned forward, the tired blue eyes stirred to life by old memories. "You know how the numbers game started in America?"

"Not a clue."

"It was the summer of '32. We were in Atlantic City. I was there with a dancer." The Don sipped some wine.

Claudia rose. "Excuse me."

Don Carlo watched her leave, and Phil sensed some personal tension pass between them.

The old man waved his cigar. "Anyway, the girl's name was Kitty. A mick. She danced in a gin joint on the Boardwalk. She had the face of a madonna and the soul of a vampire." The waiters cleared the dishes. "She had a smile—a small, wicked smile that could melt an ice cube across the room." His eyes were full of yesterdays.

"You were telling me how Leo Meyers invented the numbers racket."

"Yeah, well . . . it was at the height of the Depression. Leo and me were in this suite in the hotel. 'Brother, Can You Spare a Dime?' was playing on the radio, and suddenly Leo jumps up and says, 'Nickels!'"

"Nickels?"

"Nickels." The Don nodded. "He says, 'Carlo, we take the last three mutuel numbers from the last race at Belmont, and we make the odds four hundred to one. Someone plays a combination for five cents and they win twenty bucks.'" The Don puffed the cigar. "Twenty dollars in 1932 was a fucking fortune. Leo says we go into the ghetto, the streets. We get runners to sell the numbers. If they want to bet a buck they win four hundred; five bucks, two thousand, and so on. Well, by 1936 the organization grossed thirty-five million on nickels."

Claudia came back, and they rose while she took her seat.

The Don said, "That Leo is an Einstein. A genuine mind, a man who never knew the word 'betrayal.'"

"Well, he must have changed."

"Why?"

"He had to know about the hit on Nicky."

"Nick played into Maldonado's hands."

"Nick played into more hands than Maldonado's."

"What do you mean?" Claudia asked.

"Nicky hit the Reverend Rhee's temples. Rhee's been blackmailing the American Intelligence community. Someone high up ordered Maldonado to hit Nicky."

"Who's the finger man?" the Don asked.

"That's a question for Maldonado. I want that answer as much as you do."

The distant sound of powerful boat engines drifted in from the open sea.

Phil peered into the darkness. No running lights were visible, but a powerful cabin cruiser was unmistakably coming in toward the cove.

Gino stirred at the adjacent table and rasped something in Italian to the two bodyguards, who stared out at the sea.

After a moment the engine sound subsided, and their attention shifted back to the terrace.

The waiters served cups of espresso and snifters of brandy.

"Did Kimsan mention the name of the courier?" Phil asked.

"He may have. I can't be sure."

"Was it Sonji?"

The Don paused, then shook his head. "I don't remember. He said it was a girl—or a woman—and he expected her in Rome."

"When?"

The Don never answered.

They were blinded by a sudden cone of brilliant hot light, accompanied by a thunderous throbbing of revved-up high-powered marine engines.

The blacked-out cruiser swept into the marina like a shark homing in on a kill. It swerved parallel to the café. Its engines died, and the explosive chatter of automatic weapons shattered the night.

Phil threw Claudia to the floor and covered her body with his own. Gino was on his feet and shoved their table over, toppling Don Carlo. A spurt of blood shot out of the Don's cheek as he hit the floor. Slivers of glass whistled across the patio. A hail of bullets ricocheted off the stucco walls.

Gino fired a .45 automatic at the beam of light coming from the flying bridge of the cruiser.

Phil held Claudia and out of the corner of his eye saw one of the Don's bodyguards slumped against the wall, a gaping hole in his belly. The other bodyguard lay prone across a fallen table, the top of his head gone.

Screams from the customers inside the café could barely be heard over the metallic rat-tat-tat of the automatic weapons. Tracers bracketed the exterior patio in a slow crossing pattern. A waiter was down, bleeding from a neck wound. Bottles and glasses burst, and pieces of tables and chairs tumbled in the air, dancing on a constant rain of lead.

Phil felt a sudden searing pain in his right shoulder. His full weight was pressed down over Claudia, and the warm flow of blood seeped through his jacket down onto her white blouse. He knew the wound was not from a bullet; a slug from a heavy-caliber automatic weapon would have torn his arm off. A line of bullet hits stitched their way across the stone floor, coming straight at them. At the last moment the trajectory rose and split the wooden railing.

Then suddenly the terrace went dark. Gino had scored a direct hit on the cruiser's searchlight. The blacked-out cruiser's engines thundered and revved up. It wheeled sharply and roared out of the marina toward the open sea.

Phil glanced at the Don, lying under the wrecked table. His cheek had been cut by flying glass, and his color was ashen. Phil then examined the source of pain radiating from his right arm. A piece of glass protruded from the hole in his jacket, the sliver embedded in the fleshy part of his bicep.

They remained prone: shocked, chilled and soaked by a syrupy mixture of blood and wine. The plaintive haunting sound of an Italian ballad drifted across the terrace from a still-functioning speaker.

Chapter Forty-one

They were gathered in Don Carlo's sumptuous bedroom; a doctor had cauterized and stitched the wound in the Don's cheek and performed a similar treatment on the punctured bicep in Phil's right arm. Both men were then given an injection of ampicillin as a precaution against infection. Only Gino and Claudia had emerged from the attack unscathed.

The police had found dozens of spent bullets bearing the rosette type of crimp peculiar to the AK-47 Soviet-made assault rifles. The captain of the *carabinieri* was a stern-faced man with a clipped manner of speech that seemed more suited to German than Italian. He had assumed total control of the chaotic scene on arrival. The wounded were placed in ambulances and rushed to the local hospital. Witnesses were subjected to thorough questioning. The dead were photographed, fingerprinted and taken to the morgue.

Phil glanced at Gino, thinking he would never forget the sight of the big man standing in the cone of light, firing the .45 automatic, oblivious to the hail of incoming fire.

After delivering a final speech to Don Carlo, the *carabinieri* captain left with his two lieutenants.

Phil lit a fresh cigarette. He had been chain-smoking since the assault—the fear of tobacco diminished by the more immediate lethality of hot lead.

Don Carlo sat up in the huge bed, resting against a set of pillows. His eyes seemed to be in another place, as if he were examining a complex equation on some distant chalkboard.

"You were lucky," Phil said.

"We all were," the Don replied.

"Yeah, but your back was dead center in that cone of light."

The Don forced a slight smile and shrugged. "I've been shot at before."

Phil indicated Gino. "That's some man you got there."

"He and Ruffino were with me for a long time. They are people whose loyalty you can't buy. They stay with you out of love. Nothing else."

"That may be true," Phil said, "but someone betrayed us tonight."

"Maybe someone traced you. But I was not betrayed."

For the first time Phil felt an affinity for the old man. The Don's unshakable faith in honor and loyalty was reminiscent of infantrymen who displayed an almost grotesque heroism in the face of betrayal and incompetence.

"I think you'd better phone Leo Meyers," Phil said.

"Why?"

"Because that was a mob hit."

Before the Don could respond, Claudia said, "They could have been CIA hit men working for Burgess."

Phil shook his head. "Not their style." He crushed out the cigarette and poured a generous drink of cognac. "The agency hit men operate one on one: a sniper shot; a remote button attached to a car's ignition system; exotic poison; a bullet behind the ear. They don't use machine guns from a cabin cruiser. This was a mob hit."

"Mafia soldiers don't hit public places," the Don disagreed.

The wound in Phil's arm began to throb, and the cognac had not relieved the insistent pain. "We weren't so goddamn public," he snapped. "Your *paisan* at the restaurant had us isolated on the terrace. That beam of light was directed at our table."

"I know the owner of that restaurant since I was a kid," the Don replied stubbornly. "He's from my own village."

"So is Victor Maldonado."

Claudia rose and addressed the Don. "Phil's right. Neither the Italian MDI nor British MI 5 is concerned with you."

"Leo gave his word," Don Carlo replied. "An agreement was made by the National Council. And their judgments are respected."

The ache in Phil's arm and the aftershock of the near brush with death triggered a burst of anger. "Respect! What respect? I don't want to hear that fucking word! Now, goddammit, get that Jewish Pope on the phone and tell him to put the fear of God into Maldonado."

"All right," the Don said with resignation. "By the way, the *carabinieri* captain wants us off the island."

"That makes two of us. Now pick up the phone and call the Pope."

Phil left and Claudia went to the phone.

Leo Meyers sat in the afternoon sun; a warm breeze off the Gulf rattled the pages of his *Wall Street Journal*. His Cuban bodyguards stood at the rail of the sun deck, looking out over the channel and speaking softly in Spanish. Leo heard the phone ring from inside the living room, and a moment later Sarah appeared.

"It's Italy."

Leaning heavily on his cane, Leo got to his feet and went into the living room.

He lifted the receiver with trepidation and said, "Hello?"

The international operator's English was heavily accented. "Is this Leo Meyers?"

"Speaking."

There were some clicks, then an exchange of *prontos*, followed by the familiar voice of Don Carlo.

"Hello, Leo."

"How are you, Carlo?"

"All right. Can we speak?"

"The phone is clean."

"The Cassini girl, myself and Ricker were machine-gunned in a seaside café. We came out of it all right, but two of my people were killed. And you know about Ruffino?"

"I heard about Ruffino this morning," Leo replied.

"Victor has Calabrian soldiers gunning for me."

The words of his lifelong friend sank in, and Leo knew it was a difficult call for Don Carlo to make. The Don was in effect questioning the trust not only of Maldonado but of the National Council itself.

"I gave you the council's word." Leo reminded him. "No violence. You return and you have a one-on-one meet with Victor."

"Still, I make this call, Leo," the Don persisted. "Ruffino was a mob hit. This was mob. Speak with Victor. He's using the government threat to Ricker as a screen to hit me."

"I'll take care of it, Carlo."

Leo Meyers hung up, then lifted the receiver and punched eleven buttons. The phone rang twice before the word spit itself out of the receiver: "Bender."

"This is Miami."

"One minute."

Leo glanced through the living room window and saw the crimson sun sliding down into the distant palm groves.

"Hello." Maldonado's raspy voice reached for warmth but missed.

"I just spoke with Italy," Leo said. "The man in exile believes Calabrian soldiers hit Ruffino—and made an attempt on him and his people."

"When?"

"A few hours ago."

"Where?"

"A café in Ischia—on the water."

"He's all right?"

"Yes." Leo paused. His next words would be critical. The nature of Victor's response would reveal Maldonado's culpability or innocence. "The man in exile believes you hired the Calabrians and you ordered a contract on his life."

"What! That fucking dago cocksucker! That—"

Bender shook his head, cautioning Maldonado. But it was too late.

"I'm sorry for the language," Victor said, controlling his feigned fury. "But our friend in Italy insults me. I gave my word to the council. I gave my word to you."

"He doesn't trust your word," Leo Meyers replied.

"Maybe he's too old to trust anything."

"I'm older than he is. What's age got to do with trust?"

"Ah, shit," Maldonado blurted. "Look, I didn't put a

contract on Ruffino. I didn't contract anyone in Italy. My honor is not gonna be questioned by anybody."

Bender stared across the room at Maldonado. He knew the old Jew in Miami had tripped his boss, and whatever Victor said now was irrelevant. It was at that moment that Bender began to reassess his own position.

"I'm sorry to get tough," Maldonado continued, "but my word is at stake here—and I'm not picking up the marbles for something going down five thousand miles from here. Besides, we *never* machine-gun a public place."

The trap had closed and Leo gently said, "I didn't say how the hit was made."

Victor coughed and cleared his throat. "You said they were hit at a café. I just assumed—"

"The National Council is everything," Leo cut in harshly. "Be careful you don't break the council's word."

"I'm clean," Victor rasped nervously. "My hands are clean."

"Keep them that way."

Leo hung up and sat quietly for a moment, wondering whether to notify the Gasparis in Chicago, but thought better of it. He was convinced Victor would call off the Calabrian hoods; besides, this was not the time to summon a meeting of the council. There was sixteen million in cash on Leo's bed, three days' worth of cocaine proceeds—and the boat from Bermuda was due within the hour.

Maldonado snapped at his tall, austere *consigliere*. "Those Calabrian assholes shot up a restaurant, fucked everything up!"

"Difficult to control, Victor."

"You should have advised me against this."

"You're playing results," Bender said. "It looked like a perfect cover. It's probably a miracle that the Don is still alive."

"Yeah, well, he was always lucky. I swear to Christ, he's bulletproof. Just call it off."

"Okay," Bender replied, and started for the door.

"Martin!"

"Yes?"

"Speak with Matt Crowley. Make sure those teamster documents are ready for return when we get to the Virginia ranch."

"I talked to Crowley—the documents are all set."

"And, Martin . . ."

"Yes?"

"Get that cunt Cindy."

"All right."

"And tell her to bring those other two cunts. Those dancers."

"Sure, Victor."

The tall, phlegmatic counselor departed, thinking the day of reckoning was not far off. Scales would be balanced. Humiliation would end. His proper position in the organization would be realized. But patience was the soul of ambition.

Phil walked down the long tapestried hallway. He had placed a call to Sid Greene, but the circuits to Washington were busy. Gino was still positioned at the bedroom door. His heavy features remained impassive as Phil went by him into the room.

The Don was propped up in bed. Claudia stood at the open French windows, looking out at the moonlit sea.

"Get away from the window!" Phil snapped. "And pull those drapes."

She stared at him briefly, then followed his orders.

"I spoke with Leo," the Don said. "The matter is closed."

"Let's hope so. You said Kimsan expected the courier in a couple of days."

The Don nodded. "We're talking about forty-eight, seventy-two hours."

Phil crossed the ornate room and poured some brandy. His arm still burned, and a headache throbbed over his left eye. He swirled the gold-colored cognac for a moment, then said, "You're sure the name Sonji doesn't ring a bell?"

The Don shook his head.

Claudia asked, "Why is the name of the girl important?"

"Because Kimsan and Sonji were once a team. He trusts her. Sonji is KCIA. She takes orders from President Chung. If Chung agreed to send her to Rome, Kimsan will deliver."

The Don waved his hand. "The girl is not important. Take my word. He'll deliver."

"What makes you so sure?"

"Because it was Kimsan's idea. And so were you."

Phil was startled. "What do you mean?"

"Kimsan came to me. He suggested I promise the Gemstone file to Browning and that I request you escort me back to Washington; if this was done, the federal people would permit me entry."

"It wasn't Kimsan's idea," Phil said. "He takes orders from Chung. That son of a bitch is using us to bring down someone high up in government."

"To hell with Chung," Don Carlo said. "All that counts is the delivery of Gemstone."

Phil nodded. "We have to assume Kimsan will produce Gemstone in seventy-two hours or thereabouts. Now, the *carabinieri* want us off this island. Besides, the mob has our location—and probably agents of MI 5. So it makes good sense to get the hell out of here and hole up somewhere."

"Got any ideas?" the Don inquired.

"Venice," Phil replied.

"Why Venice?" Claudia asked.

"Because it's one of the few cities in the world where you can get in and out by plane, train, car or boat," Phil said. "It's always full of tourists. And probably the best-policed city in Italy."

"He's right. It's perfect," the Don agreed. "I can use the private *palazzo* of Dottore Montaldi. He's a Sicilian nobleman—and an old friend."

"So is Maldonado," Phil said sarcastically.

"Trust me, Phil. The house of Montaldi will be secure. The question is, how do we get there in one piece?"

"We go public. Covert agents of MI 5 or the CIA won't try anything with tourists around us. 'Covert' means what it says."

He then turned to Claudia. "Call the MDI; ask someone in the *ministero* to arrange train connections for us from Naples to Venice. I want to get out of here first thing in the morning."

Phil walked past the protective gaze of Gino, down the dimly lit carpeted hallway into his room. He entered the bedroom, picked up the phone receiver and dialed the operator.

"*Pronto?*"

"I want to place an international call."

"To what country?"

"United States."

"To what city?"

"Washington, D.C."

"One moment."

There were clicks and rings. After a moment of confusion the operator came back on the line. "I'm sorry, but the circuits to Washington are still occupied. I suggest you try in one hour."

"Thanks." Phil hung up, snapped the light out and stretched out on the bed. The stabbing pain in his right arm had subsided.

His mind whirred like a computer, adding, subtracting, sifting and feeding names: Park; Rhee; Belgrave; Mrs. Hwan; Browning; Burgess; Gruenwald; Joyce Raymond; Nick Carelli; Leo Meyers; Maldonado; Kimsan; Sonji.

And finally, Chung—it all came down to the Man of Circles.

The door opened and Claudia came in. She stood in the darkness for a moment, then crossed to the bed and sat down.

"We must make the seven-thirty A.M. hydrofoil to Naples in order to reach Rome in time for the Freccia della Laguna."

"What the hell is that?"

"Literally it means 'Arrow of the Lagoon.' It's a crack train that leaves Rome at eleven forty-seven A.M. and arrives in Venice at seven-sixteen P.M. We have a first-class compartment reserved."

He studied her for a moment then said, "When are you going to level with me?"

"You know all about me."

"From a computer."

She rose and walked up to the window. "The computer should be enough. After all, it can't reason. It simply conveys facts."

The pale moonlight painted shadows on her face, and once again he was struck by the thought that she reminded him of someone—someone out of his past.

Claudia watched the moonlight being swallowed by the dark Mediterranean. "The sea is magnificent at night," she said softly.

"Only on the surface," Phil replied. "Underneath, all hell is breaking loose. Just like you, sweetheart."

She came slowly back to the bed and stood over him for a moment. She then knelt at the bedside and brushed her lips slowly across his. She kissed the scar at his jawline while her hands caressed his body.

He pulled her to him, and their mouths burned into one another's, fused by a lethal bond belonging exclusively to survivors of sudden death.

They made love in that special place where there is no past, no future, only the moment.

Chapter Forty-two

The huge clock in the Rome Stazione Centrale read 11:32 A.M. as they boarded the gleaming green Freccia della Laguna. The porter showed them to their compartment, and Gino hefted their bags up onto the overhead rack. The compartment was glassed-in, with two settees facing each other. The train ride from Naples had been uneventful, and during the forty-minute wait in Rome Claudia bought a *Corriere della Sera*, the *International Herald Tribune* and an Italian fashion magazine.

Phil's right arm still ached, but he felt emotionally renewed. The last twenty-four hours of blood, terror and sensuality had been like a rush of speed.

He glanced at Claudia, absorbed in her magazine. Her skin was radiant, and for the first time she seemed relaxed. The subsurface tension in her dark eyes had disappeared.

The Don sat beside Phil, reading the front page of the Italian newspaper. The bandage on his cheek had been removed, revealing a scarlet welt of stitches. Gino stood outside in the narrow windowed aisle.

"What time does the club car open?" Phil asked.

Claudia looked up from her magazine. "The bar opens as soon as we clear the station."

Phil scanned the front page of the *Tribune:* Anthony Blunt, the fourth member of British Intelligence to be exposed as a Soviet agent in the ring that included the former Cambridge alumni Philby, Burgess and Maclean, indicated there was a fifth man—a deep-cover Soviet mole operating in the highest echelons of American Intelligence.

The President had signed a bill permitting the CIA to engage in domestic intelligence.

265

Idi Amin, former dictator of Uganda, had surfaced in Riyadh as an honored guest of the Saudi royal family.

Phil turned to the sports section. The aborted baseball season was nearing the play-offs. Pro football was under way, and a courageous thoroughbred named John Henry had won the Jockey Club Gold Cup at Belmont Park.

The car stirred slightly, and the Don said, "You see, thanks to Mussolini the trains run on time."

"Shame he's not available," Phil said. "Think of what he could do with Amtrak."

"What the hell is Amtrak?"

"Forget it, Carlo."

The train stirred again, moving now, gliding through the station and plunging into the darkness of a tunnel before emerging into stuttered flashes of sunlight coming through a line of telephone poles. It picked up speed and wound around a severe curve before straightening out and running parallel to the *autostrada*.

The sun hid behind a shifting blanket of gray clouds, casting a dark and light patchwork across the cultivated terraces.

Phil looked at Claudia. "How about a drink?"

"Sure."

Gino blocked the compartment door and glanced at the Don for approval.

"It's come to this." Phil smiled. "I've got to get permission from you to leave the room."

"Gino is Gino," the Don said.

"He sure as hell is."

They moved down the glassed-in corridor, swaying with the motion of the train, passing compartments occupied by German tourists and priests wearing robes and wide-brimmed black hats.

The club car was spacious and elegantly appointed. Its oak panels glowed under soft lights, and the tables were covered with expensive white linen. The car was not crowded. A few businessmen, attaché cases open, were doing their homework. Two stunning girls, a blonde and a brunette, sat opposite a slim young man.

Phil stared out the window as the train knifed its way through rolling farmland.

Claudia noticed the melancholy look in his eyes. "What's wrong?"

"I wish I hadn't thrown that stuff at Don Carlo. About his being responsible for Nicky's death."

"You weren't wrong," she said. "If he had been legitimate, chances are Nicky and his wife would still be alive."

"No . . . Everyone has a choice. And Nicky made his. I hit the old man below the belt."

The blonde across the aisle burst into laughter and hugged the brunette. The slim man snapped a Polaroid of them.

"Fashion models on their way to Florence," Claudia explained.

"Looks like they're having fun."

"Most of them are gay."

"How would you know?"

"I lived with a famous model for three months."

"Why?"

"Orders. She was suspected of membership in the Red Brigades." Claudia suddenly looked past him, to the far end of the car.

"What is it?" Phil asked.

"Nothing."

"Any idea where the bathroom is?"

"One car up ahead," Claudia replied.

Phil rose and smiled. "If you can find the waiter, order a beer for me."

The bathroom was occupied and Phil went out into the open space coupling the cars. The angry clatter of steel on steel was jarring, but the rush of fresh air was bracing.

A wiry man wearing a houndstooth jacket and fedora exited the forward car and came out onto the open platform. He had small, regular features and a receding hairline. "Looks like the loo is popular." His English accent was pleasant and friendly. "Spent half my life waiting for my wife to come out of bathrooms." He took out a pack of Player cigarettes. "Care for one?"

"No, thanks."

"Headed for Venice?"

"Yeah . . ."

"American?"

"Right."

"Been there before?"

"Long time ago."

"Wet and foggy in the fall. But a jewel." He inhaled deeply. "I'm getting off at Padua. Marvelous Roman ruins. Twenty B.C. They say it was a temple to Juno. You interested in archaeology?"

"No more than the next guy."

"Americans don't have much truck with the past." He stepped on the cigarette. "Pity. A lot to be learned from our predecessors."

The bathroom door opened, and an elderly nun came out and entered the forward car.

"If you're in dire need, I'll wait," Phil offered.

"No, no, old chap, go ahead. I'm enjoying the breeze."

A sudden vicious, searing pain exploded in the back of Phil's neck. The force of the karate chop dropped him to his knees. A pair of hands gripped his shoulders, and the Englishman dragged him toward the open steps. Phil saw the tracks whizzing by and felt his legs being raised. The Englishman was moving him head down toward the top step leading to the railbed.

Phil's left hand shot out and grabbed an iron handle on the side of the stairwell. The pebbles along the roadbed blurred into a gray mass.

The Englishman decided to turn Phil completely over, forcing him to let go of the handle or break his wrist. The blood rushed to Phil's head, and the vertical position made the pain in his left hand unbearable. He let go of the iron bar.

"That's it, old boy," the Englishman grunted. "Now out you go!"

Phil's body swung out over the steps, head down, a few feet from the flashing tracks. He reached out with his right hand and grabbed the iron rail on the opposite side of the stairwell.

"Back to that, are we?" the Englishman said, and brought the heel of his shoe down across Phil's fingers.

Phil screamed but held on.

"Stubborn bastard. Well, all right, let's play this game." Again he smashed his heel into Phil's bleeding fingers.

Phil's hand went numb, and his fingers uncurled, slipping one by one off the iron bar.

Two deafening reports exploded in the stairwell. The Englishman's head bounced off the steel deck. His right eye was a blood-filled socket.

Phil eased himself away from the stairwell, turned over and saw Gino tucking a .38 revolver into his shoulder holster. The big man with the permanent scowl knelt down and removed the Englishman's wallet, along with a small, wicked-looking automatic. Gino straightened up and kicked the Englishman's body off the platform onto the tracks.

Claudia entered the open enclosure. She stared at Phil's soot-covered clothes, his pallor and the bleeding, raw fingers of his right hand. She then noticed the thick pool of bright red blood running down the steel stairwell to the tracks.

"Let's get out of here." Phil sighed.

The compartment lights played against the gathering exterior gloom.

Don Carlo held the .25-caliber Walther PPK automatic taken from the Englishman. "Why didn't he use it?"

"It was supposed to look like an accident. The karate chop should have broken my neck." Phil paused. "Let me see that."

The Don handed the German gun to him. There were nine bullets in the clip. Phil checked the safety and tucked the small automatic into his belt. "You wanted to go public," Don Carlo said.

"I wasn't with the public when it happened," Phil replied and glanced at Gino and motioned for the Englishman's wallet.

Phil stared at the name on the blue MI 5 identification card, and a distant tumbler clicked into place.

"Carlo, tell Gino I owe him. And I can never repay him."

The Don spoke in Italian to the big man, who nodded and muttered a brief response.

Phil took his right hand out of an ice bucket, flexed his fingers and said, "Someone ought to tell the Pentagon about Gino. Come on, let's get a drink."

⚹ ⚹ ⚹

Phil drank two quick shots of brandy and asked Claudia for a cigarette. He lit the Gauloise, inhaled deeply and opened and closed his injured hand.

"What do you make of it?" the Don asked.

"I don't know," Phil said. "There's only one thing I'm sure of: this wasn't a mob hit."

Claudia toyed with the ice in her vermouth cassis and dreaded the inevitable confrontation with Phil. She did not need to see the name in the wallet. She knew who the assailant was. She sighed and thought perhaps it was for the best. She had long ago learned that nothing was permanent, nothing was absolute. If Don Carlo evened the score for Nicky, all the debts would be paid—all the ghosts would finally be laid to rest.

Chapter Forty-three

The Freccia della Laguna slowed and glided across the causeway over the ancient Austrian bridge into the sheds of Santa Lucia Station. It was 7:12 P.M. The train was four minutes early and minus one passenger.

Two men in gray uniforms, porters of the house of Montaldi, met them at the siding. They exchanged a few words with Don Carlo and took their bags. The Don turned to Phil. "Everything is prepared. The *dottore* is in Milano, but the staff is expecting us."

Ornate gondolas bobbed at their peppermint stick moorings alongside waterbus-*vaporetti*, private launches and sleek motorboats. A confused racket rose from the bizarre assemblage on the busy quay. Black-market moneychangers shouted their exchange rates; male and female prostitutes solicited sailors and tourists. Vendors sold fake artifacts, and small children begged for coins on the steps outside the railroad station.

They followed the porters through the crowd to a large motor launch that bobbed with the swelling tide. The Don entered the enclosed cabin with Gino. Phil stood on the fantail next to the flapping red, white and green Italian flag. Claudia went up to the prow, the wind playing soft games with her dark hair. The engines throbbed into life. The launch eased away from the noisy quay, picked up speed and swung toward the broad expanse of the Grand Canal.

Venice loomed up out of the Adriatic mist in dream-like splendor. Its arabesque domes, Gothic spires and marble palaces glowed through shifting cobwebs of fog.

They slid under the Rialto Bridge and passed the flood-lit Piazza San Marco and Doges' Palace with its spectacu-

271

lar architectural blend of Byzantine and Venetian Renaissance. The launch struggled against the tide as it turned toward the billowing white domes of the Church of Santa Maria della Salute.

"Have you been here before?" Don Carlo asked.

Phil nodded. "Years ago."

"You must take care here," the Don cautioned. "Venice is small, but it's a maze. No map can help you. Bridges lead nowhere, and streets end in cul-de-sacs. There are alleys and canals that have no air, no light. They twist and turn without reason. There are slums and old quarters where even the *caribinieri* cannot find their way out."

"It's still one hell of a city," Phil replied.

"Don't be fooled by its beauty. The city is dying. It's sinking into the sea. Every winter more and more is lost to the Adriatic."

The sound of engines died as they glided toward the mooring poles. The Montaldi crest was mounted over the huge oak doors: two elaborate bronze horses holding a gold crown between their front hooves. The rose-colored palace was three stories tall with lacy balconies facing the Grand Canal.

Following the porters, they entered a frescoed marble hall bisected by a great spiral staircase leading to the upper floors. The stained glass dome of the ceiling three floors above was a mosaic of gold, red and green. They walked up to the second floor and passed a huge, remarkably sensual Titian painting of a pregnant Venus coyly covering one breast. Her exposed nipple was erect, pink, with a small drop of white milk at its tip.

The Don and Gino were shown into one bedroom, while Phil and Claudia were ushered into another suite some fifty feet down the brocaded hall.

Claudia opened the window shutters, and a breeze off the canal floated in, stirring the stale air in the unused bedroom. The walls displayed a bizarre collection of large paintings vividly depicting a variety of female bestiality. Phil glanced from one to another. A naked Amazon had a sword raised above her head, about to decapitate a kneeling man. A second giantess drove a spike through a boy's skull. Another group of huge-breasted naked women clustered over a prone man, their gleaming daggers performing an act of castration.

"My God," Claudia said. "These paintings must have been commissioned by Lucrezia Borgia." She shook her head and walked to the open shutters and looked out over the canal.

Phil moved alongside her and said, "The man on the train who tried to take me out was Bill Edwards—the MI 5 agent who questioned you some years ago, when your former lover took his last tumble."

She chewed the inside of her lip, walked past him, took a cigarette out of her bag and lit it. She stared at him for a moment, then crossed to the bed and sat down.

"Bill Edwards was my husband." She sighed. "And when Michael died at the hotel in Como—"

"Who's Michael?"

"Michael Weaver, the man I had the affair with."

"Right. Onassis's bagman. The man with the missing two million in Swiss francs."

"Michael was a British citizen. When he died, Edwards was sent to Italy from MI 5 to question me. Bill was convinced I had the key to the Swiss francs. He hammered at me for days."

"Why did you marry him?"

"I was ordered to by the Italian MDI. They gave me a position, money and cleared me of any involvement in Michael's death."

"And gained penetration of a sister intelligence agency by virtue of your marriage," Phil added.

The smoke curled out of her lips, and in a resigned voice she said, "I left Bill after two years. I couldn't get over Michael. I never have."

"How did your divorce sit with the MDI?"

"They were upset. But nothing more."

"Why did you tell Edwards we were on that train?"

"My orders were to keep MI 5 aware of our movements. They were on to you from the time you left Dulles."

Claudia rose and walked to the open window. "I met with Edwards in London after you and I had lunched. I wanted to be certain it was you they were after—not Don

Carlo." She paused and turned. "You see, Don Carlo is my father."

And everything fell into place.

Phil paced for a moment, then said, "Of course, blood and family had to be the only reason Don Carlo trusted you. When we first met in London, you reminded me of someone. I couldn't put it together. It was Nick you reminded me of."

"Nicky and I were close." She sighed. "He was much more than a half brother to me."

"What about your mother?"

"She was Don Carlo's mistress for years, but he would never leave his sainted Rosa. Out of spite, I suppose, my mother moved in with Gilante—a family capo in Chicago."

"The man she was killed with?"

Claudia nodded, and her eyes grew misty. "I hadn't seen Don Carlo in years, but after my mother's death Nicky called me. He said her death devastated our father, and he urged me to see him. I knew Don Carlo was in exile in Lercara. I agonized over it, but finally I went to see him. I remembered him from his occasional visits when I was very young—a handsome, smiling man, full of life. The man I found in Lercara was a wasted old man. He cried when he saw me. We spoke for a long time, and I promised to visit him again. Then, when Nicky was killed, I felt the same need for vengeance that my father did."

Phil went up to the window and stared at the glowing white domes of the Church of Salute. "Quite a story."

"It's the truth."

"What about your former lover, Mr. Weaver?"

"I assume he was killed because he skimmed Onassis's money."

"You're not certain?"

"No. I never asked Michael any questions about his business." She paused. "I just loved him. And I've paid the price ever since. I was forced to marry Edwards—and forced to join the MDI. I've lost my brother and my mother. All I have left is that vengeance-ridden old man. And because of Nicky, I'll see him through this."

Phil stared at Claudia and thought of the striking similarity between her background and Sonji's. Two women from totally different cultures, manipulated by systems that had robbed them of their lives.

"What about the Swiss money?" he asked.

"That secret died with Michael. I never saw a trace of it. I never wanted any of it. I wanted him."

There was a momentary silence, punctuated by the angry claxon of a passing *vaporetto*. "Why did you make love to me that night in Lercara?" Phil asked.

She shrugged. "It was one of those beautifully irrelevant moments. You. Me. Those pagan ruins. I was empty. I haven't been touched emotionally by a man in a long time. Not since Michael. I'm frightened of involvements. Everyone I ever cared about is dead. All that matters now is that my father has his day in court. . . ."

Chapter Forty-four

Soon Yi Sonji got out of the taxi at the top of Trinità dei Monti. She fastened the belt on her beige cashmere coat, turned the collar up and walked to the marble balustrade overlooking the Spanish Steps. The domes and spires of the Eternal City were suffused in a magenta light. She was both tense and excited over the impending meeting with Kimsan. They had not seen or spoken to each other in three years.

She had been in Rome once before during the summer of 1976 with a United States congressman. It was the time when she and Kimsan had begun to weave their Koreagate web around the American lawmakers. She had tolerated the congressman—but found the city fascinating. Most of all she remembered the ruins: the Roman Forum, the Colosseum, the Quirinale and the Baths of Caracalla. And the cats—the legions of cats prowling the crumbling marble relics of imperial Rome.

It was a city where the present and future were overwhelmed by the past. Rome was a place for memories.

Sonji took a final look, turned and walked directly across the small cobblestoned piazza into the Hassler Hotel.

A group of white-robed Libyans stared at the Oriental beauty as she strode past them toward the polished brass elevator.

She moved quickly down the carpeted hallway and stopped at the suite numbered 608-609. She took a deep breath and pressed the pearl button.

The door opened, and she saw the handsome, intelligent face and the soft brown eyes.

Kimsan closed the door.

Sonji moved into him.

His arms closed around her.

They made love wordlessly, their bodies almost motionless, permitting the reflexive throbs and pulses to swell their erotic pleasure, bringing them to a climax that transcended sensuality. It was an affirmation of life.

Finally spent, they fell back, her head cradled against his shoulder. They slept for a while, then showered and dressed.

Sonji and Kimsan stood on the small terrace and looked out at a distant hill dotted with umbrella pines and crowded by the glowing ruins of a forgotten pagan temple. His arm circled her waist, the taste of her perfume still in his mouth.

They had suffered the damage of servitude and prostitution, but were grateful to be alive.

They toasted each other and ate with the hungry appetite that follows lovemaking. Kimsan spoke about Rome, Palermo, the Mafia and being under the constant eye of KCIA agents. He then asked about her father.

"He is well," Sonji said, "but as always he cries for the nation."

"Professor Kim is right. If America does not support political freedom in Korea, there will be civil war. The Army of the North will invade and American boys will again die alongside our boys, and their fight will be for nothing. Your father is correct in what he says."

"I know nothing of politics."

"You know Chung."

"He assured me of your safety," she replied.

"Well, for three years he has not harmed me." Kimsan lit a cigarette and added, "My activities provide him with great sums of money."

"I want you to understand," Sonji said gravely, "that if the surrender of Gemstone endangers your life, I will not take it. I spoke with Ricker before I left Washington. He promised to place you under protective custody should you require it. He gave me his word, knowing there would be nothing in return."

Kimsan kissed her softly and said, "Listen to me carefully. The Gemstone file can destroy certain elements in the American hierarchy—elements that stand for everything I despise. I've been their pimp, bagman and briber. I've bowed at their feet on orders, but I detest them. The risk of giving up Gemstone is well taken. A man comes to a place in life when a price must be paid. There is a Confucian saying: 'If you cross the path of the dragon and he does not breathe his fire upon you, a day will come when you will be required to protect the dragon from his slayer.'" He crushed the cigarette out and sighed. "I've had a better life than my parents. I fought no wars. I lost no limbs. I joined the KCIA to promote myself into a sphere of influence and wealth. I paid a price. But I made the choice."

"As did I," she whispered.

"No. You were blackmailed. You had no choice. Your life was stolen."

She rose, paced for a moment, rubbed her wrists, then turned to him. "We must find a way to free ourselves."

"There is a way," he said. "When you return home, ask Chung if you can be assigned to our embassy in Rome. Tell him Buddha spoke to you in a dream, that a plotter exists in our Rome embassy staff. Once you are here, we can manage something. But for the moment we must follow his orders."

Kimsan took a small spool of pink thread out of his pocket and handed it to her. "This is Gemstone. Under that thread, wrapped around the core, are fifteen frames of sixteen-millimeter film. Each page has been reduced to a single frame. The frame can be either projected or read through a magnifying glass."

Sonji stared at the small spindle of thread, astonished by the thought that the fate of the American power structure resided at its core.

Kimsan took an envelope out of his jacket and handed it to her. "Your plane ticket for tomorrow. You leave Rome at ten in the morning and arrive in Venice one hour later. I think you will be able to return on the two o'clock."

"That would permit us the entire weekend," she said hopefully.

"No . . . I must leave for Palermo tomorrow morning. There is a possibility that I can get back late Saturday night." He poured some champagne into her glass and

said, "I'll phone Don Carlo to advise him of your arrival."
He kissed her cheek, turned and went into the bedroom.

Sonji stepped out onto the terrace and sipped the dry
champagne. She wished they had more time, but she was
grateful for the moment. The cool night air and the shimmering lights of the ancient city added to her feeling of
well-being. It was a revelation to her that despite the
years of intrigue and degradation, she still had the capacity to feel. Their lovemaking had imparted a sense of
spiritual liberation. She would summon all her powers to
convince Chung to assign her to the Rome embassy.

Chapter Forty-five

The Montaldi dining hall was surrounded by huge murals depicting the surrender of the Venetian Republic to Napoleon. Phil and Claudia were being served dessert when Don Carlo entered. "The Gemstone courier arrives from Rome at 11:05 tomorrow morning." He sat down, looking proud and satisfied. His part of the bargain had been fulfilled.

"You're positive?" Phil asked.

"Kimsan just spoke with me. The courier's name is Sonji."

"Which means I've got a call to make," Phil said, and walked quickly out of the room.

The Don sipped his espresso and glanced at Claudia. He thought she had her mother's beauty. "You like him?"

"Yes."

She lit a cigarette and glanced up at Napoleon accepting the doge's sword.

"You seem sad," he said.

"I'm all right. I'm fine."

Claudia stirred her coffee and stared into the cup as if it contained some elusive eternal truth.

Phil was on the phone. "Give me what you have, Sid; then I'll talk."

"Okay. Hoover-Park connection: J. Edgar made six trips to Seoul from 1963 to early '72. Shortly after his '63 visit Park dispatched two crack Korean divisions to Vietnam. Hoover died May second, 1972. The Koreans pulled out of Vietnam three weeks later. Hoover's assistant, Foley, testified that Kimsan met with Hoover in March of '72. Gemstone is authentic. It all goes together."

"Anything else?" Phil asked.

"That's it. Where are you?" Sid inquired.

"Venice. I'll give you a phone number when we're through. Gemstone will be in my hands tomorrow. I want you to arrange a military jet at Geneva International Airport for the following day. The plane will take us directly to Andrews Air Force Base. It's only half an hour from there to the Madison. I want the presidential suite. Got it?"

"Got it," Sid replied.

"The plane should be ready to take off from Geneva at, say, ten A.M. Sunday," Phil paused. "I want to hear from you no later than two P.M., my time, tomorrow afternoon."

"Give me the number," Sid said.

"040 is the area code; the number is 70-70-22."

"Got it," Greene replied. "I'll be back to you, maybe not two P.M. on the nose, but close to it."

"Thanks, Sid."

Phil came into the hall. Don Carlo sat alone at the long banquet table puffing on one of his infrequent cigars. Gino was seated at the marble entryway. "Why didn't you tell me Claudia was your daughter?" Phil asked.

"First place, it's none of your business. Second place, she's a half daughter."

"Half daughter," Phil repeated sarcastically, and glared at the old man. "Which half is yours? You're the man concerned with family, bloodline, seed. That's what this whole thing is about, isn't it? They killed your unborn grandson, and now you're going to avenge that bloodspill. Only it's bullshit. Your vengeance is based on your own ego. They hit your son and fucked it up. And now they're gonna pay. You didn't give a damn about Nicky. You used him, the same way you used Claudia and her mother."

The Don's blue eyes smoldered, but he remained silent as Phil continued.

"You sat at the top of a violent, corrupt world and your flesh and blood were victims of your own greed and ego. And you have the fucking gall to refer to Claudia as a half daughter. And it is my goddamn business because she was forced to play a game that almost cost me my life!"

"Don't talk black and white to me," the Don replied angrily. "You want to know about Claudia. All right. Her mother was a woman I loved with all my heart. But she was afflicted by certain problems that no man could deal with. I tried to shield Claudia, but I failed. Her mother broke my heart." He rose and walked up to the mural, puffed the cigar, then turned to Phil.

"You speak about my violent, corrupt world." The old man's cheeks were flushed, and his eyes blazed. "Take a look at *your* world: the political world of professional assassins and power brokers who send kids off to die in bullshit wars; international bankers hustling blood money. Our world's peanuts compared to yours."

He walked up to Phil. "Look at yourself. On the run from your own people. Why? Because you're disturbing their action. Like Nicky. Like anyone else who bothers them. Let me tell you something, my friend"—he used his cigar like a pointer—"our words are exactly alike. Only we don't bother legitimate people. We kill our own. And we deal our own justice. Your masters kill everyone. And in the end they'll kill you, scrape your name off the door and shred your papers as if you never existed. You're a small cog in a big machine. The same machine that controls the underworld." His voice grew soft. "We work for the same company."

Claudia sat up in bed, reading a magazine. She put it aside as Phil entered. He slumped into a velvet easy chair and stared at the grotesque murals of Amazons committing their butchery on naked males.

"You look awful," she said.

"I just went toe to toe with your father."

"About what?"

"You. Nicky. Your mother. The system."

She rose and came up to him. "What did he say about my mother?"

"He suggested she had problems."

Claudia walked to the window and opened the shutters. The sound of claxons and horns from the canal traffic drifted into the room. "My mother was a heroin addict. We tried everything, but in the end Don Carlo could only finance her habit."

"Finance?" Phil said incredulously. "Christ, he was the dealer."

"I'm not defending him. But until his exile he never dealt in narcotics traffic. He was part of an organization that did." She sighed. "Anyway, you can't blame him for my mother's habit. She was hooked before they met."

After a moment of silence Phil rose, walked up to her and put his arm around her shoulder. "Let's have a drink at Harry's Bar."

"I don't know," she murmured.

"Come on. I can't look at these giant vampires anymore. Talk about women's lib—"

She smiled. "All right. Give me five minutes."

"Take your time."

Phil went to the phone and placed a call to Geneva to Franz Kohler, chief of Swiss Internal Security.

Chapter Forty-six

The glass furniture in the crystalline tomb reflected glittering highlights from overhead pinspots. There was a profound dimension of gloom in the translucent chamber. Clouds of blue cigarette smoke hovered in the air above the heads of the intelligence chiefs.

Dr. Eric Belgrave, looking tired but determined, chaired the meeting. Matt Crowley was seated at the wall behind the men lining either side of the huge glass table.

These were the moments when Crowley most admired the Doctor: times of crisis when Belgrave summoned all his powers to rally the sensitive agencies of government around the President.

They had assembled hurriedly upon Belgrave's return from the emergency meeting at the White House. President Anwar Sadat of Egypt had been assassinated at 6:05 A.M. Washington time. The twenty-eight men had been locked in the Glass Room for the past two hours. The discussion had concluded. The moment of decision was at hand. All eyes were focused on the chairman of the National Security Council.

Belgrave rose, and a hush fell over the fail-safe room. "We have heard a variety of views, but I agree with the majority opinion. We must not turn our backs on the Saudis. The instability factor inherent in Islam is a condition we simply have to live with—and I find the risks acceptable." The Doctor paused for dramatic value. "The President's prestige and the credibility of American foreign policy are at stake. We cannot permit this tragic assassination to deter the pending sale of AWACS to Saudi Arabia. I therefore ask you all to do everything in your power to assist the President in passing this arms package through the Senate."

The representatives of fifteen sections of State, CIA and Defense Intelligence gathered their files, snapped their attaché cases shut and filed out of the icy tomb.

Gruenwald, Burgess and Crowley remained. The great glass doors slid closed. Burgess rose, lit a cigarette and addressed Belgrave:

"Bill Edwards was found near the railbed outside Florence with two thirty-eight-caliber bullets in his head. The attempt on Ricker has failed."

The Doctor rubbed his hand wearily over his eyes. "Do we have a current location on Ricker and Carelli?"

"Venice," Burgess replied.

"How do we know that?" Belgrave asked.

Burgess deferred to Crowley, who said, "A one-way tap on Sid Greene's phone gave us an unlisted Venice number. My guess is they are in a protected residence somewhere in that city."

"How do we confirm that?" Gruenwald asked.

"We can't," Burgess replied. "But MI 5 agents are at the moment working with the Italian MDI to pinpoint the location of that Venice number."

"I would like to personally track Ricker," Crowley blurted. "I warned all of you that we couldn't trust those limeys to do the job."

"Now, Matt," the Doctor said. "Edwards was a capable man. There was some personal history between him and the Cassini girl. He had an inside track. It seemed perfect."

"She may have set Edwards up," Crowley said.

"Well, we can't play results," Burgess replied testily.

"In my book it's a fuck-up," Crowley snapped. He stood motionless under the pencil beams of light, a beast of prey, confused, bitter; a murderous figure molded by hate and distrust.

Belgrave recognized the malevolent signs in his longtime aide and soothingly said, "What's done is done. We'll play our trump card and exercise patience. Keep me posted. Now, gentlemen, I have work to prepare for this afternoon's meeting in the Oval Office."

As the men started to leave, Belgrave said, "Matt."

"Yes?"

"Would you kindly pick me up at seven-thirty tomorrow morning? I want to visit my son's grave at Arlington."

Crowley nodded and followed Burgess and Gruenwald out.

Belgrave sat alone in the prismatic, dada-like transparent cube. He refilled his pipe and thought of the sophisticated equipment lost to the Soviets when the shah of Iran fell: electronic listening dishes with secret radio frequency codes; the most advanced electromagnetic laser guns; the F-14 fighter; the Phoenix and Harpoon air-to-air missile systems. He lit his pipe and reflected that all the previously compromised technology would pale in significance should the AWACS share a similar fate.

The Doctor smiled a small, ironic smile.

Chapter Forty-seven

Ghostly patches of fog shrouded the surly green water of the Grand Canal; barges, gondolas and *vaporetti* stole their way slowly through the eerie mists. The sound of a pounding surf coming from the open sea echoed like the heartbeat of a distant monster stalking the doomed city.

Sonji stood at the prow of the Montaldi launch. Her camel coat was belted tightly around her waist, the collar turned up against the chill. She had left Kimsan in the Rome airport. He boarded the Palermo flight a few minutes before she departed for Venice. Despite the cheerless light and cold fog, she felt alive and purposeful. For the first time in memory the future existed. She would not have to wait for the ancient prophecy to be fulfilled. She had her own plans: assignment to the Rome embassy. She and Kimsan would finally be together.

The Montaldi library was a large room with a vaulted ceiling. The walls were lined by glassed-in bookcases filled with medical books and journals. There was an ornate painted desk with a baroque gold desk set that included an inkwell, a penholder, a letter opener and a magnifying glass.

Sonji stood in the center of the room. She wore jeans, jade earrings and ivory bracelets. Her straight black hair fell across the shoulders of a white turtleneck sweater. Phil had introduced her to Claudia and Don Carlo. Sonji had eyed both of them suspiciously, and outside of a brief exchange of pleasantries, she would not broach the matter at hand until they had left the room.

"Coffee?" Phil asked.

Sonji shook her head.

He poured a cup, and she noticed the purple bruises on his right hand. "What happened to your hand?"

"An accident on a train."

She sat on the dark brown leather sofa. "You look tired."

"Drank too much last night." Phil smiled. "We closed Harry's Bar."

"She's very pretty."

"Yes. She is."

"What is her part in this?" Sonji asked.

"A courier," he replied. "Did you tell Kimsan I offered him protection?"

"Yes. But he trusts Chung. He believes there is no reason not to."

Phil noticed a changed expression in her eyes. The usual ambivalent mask was gone, replaced by a look of vitality and expectancy. She returned his stare for a moment, then suddenly bent down and proceeded to remove her right boot. She clasped it by the heel, turned it upside down, and a tiny spool of pink thread fell silently onto the Oriental carpet.

"What the hell is that?"

"Gemstone," she replied, pulling her boot back on. Phil picked up the spool and examined it. Sonji smiled at his consternation. "Underneath that thread, curled around the wooden stem, are fifteen frames of sixteen-millimeter film." She rose and stood alongside him. "Each frame represents a page of the Gemstone file."

He unspooled the thread, pulling an arm's length at a time. She watched him repeat the action until the core was exposed and the first shiny frames of film were visible.

Phil sat down at the desk and held the ten-inch filmstrip up to the light of the lamp, and using the magnifying glass, he saw block letters of lower-case type reproduced in each frame. He placed the filmstrip down and said, "It'll take hours to go through this, and I don't want to hold you up. Did Kimsan tell you how he got this?"

"No."

"Did he mention J. Edgar Hoover?"

She shook her head.

"Did he say why Chung wanted me to have this?"

"He was simply following orders."

"As do we all." Phil sighed. "But Kimsan did request your services as the courier."

"Yes."

They stared at each other for a beat, and he asked, "What about your father?"

"He is well."

"So you go on being Chung's soldier?"

"For a while. Kimsan and I have certain plans."

"You once promised to tell me what happened the night Park was assassinated."

"Why is that important?"

"I don't know that it is. It might be."

She studied him a moment and said, "Let me have a cigarette, please."

He shook one out of a pack and lit it for her. The smoke curled from between her lips as she related in graphic detail the violent events of October 26, 1979.

As Phil listened, he realized in amazement that a world-shaking assassination had pivoted on the sensual talents of one carefully trained, brainwashed girl.

He walked her to the door, opened it and turned to her. "When do you return to Seoul?"

"Monday." She kissed him quickly on the mouth and left.

●

Phil held the frames up to the light while gripping the magnifying glass in his bruised right hand. His arms ached, and a severe pain knifed out of his neck, spreading across his shoulders, running down his back.

He had been reading and transcribing the contents of the black-and-white frames for the past two hours and had just finished the fourteenth frame.

A terrifying mosaic of global treachery spanning five decades had emerged from the frames of Gemstone. It was an incestuous amalgam of the overworld and the underworld, of foreign and domestic intelligence agents, of international bankers and multinational corporations directed by a handful of internationalists. Their tentacles

circled the globe; crisscrossing boundaries, transcending
political ideologies, snaking and intertwining, plotting and
manipulating, operating a monstrous self-serving, self-per-
petuating clandestine cartel controlling and directing the
affairs of mankind. They had the power to create war or
peace; their only allegiance was to the god of profit.

Phil rubbed his hand wearily across his eyes. The lawyer in him wondered how much of Gemstone's content
could be corroborated. Many of the rich and famous
named in the file were dead. Therefore, the practicality of
pursuing any legal action was doubtful, and whether it
was honorable or proper to bring disgrace down on surviving family members was a matter of conscience.

He crushed out the cigarette, picked up the filmstrip
and held the fifteenth frame to the light. He steadied the
magnifying glass until the name Eric Belgrave came into
sharp focus. He moved the glass slowly over the block letters. The implication of the words caused his heartbeat to
accelerate and his blood to rise.

The astonishing line-by-line revelations sent a chilling
wave of shock and trepidation through his body. But as
he continued to read, the initial shock gave way to anger
and finally to exhilaration. It was the unique and thrilling
sense of achievement that accompanies a major breakthrough in any complex case. He finished the fifteenth
frame and leaned back in the chair, his heart still
thumping with the excitement of discovery.

He now understood the source of J. Edgar Hoover's en-
during power. But more important, he knew the true identity of Dr. Eric Belgrave. The material in the fifteenth
frame could be corroborated and demanded action; the
fate of the nation hung in the balance. . . .

The phone rang sharply. It was Sid Greene. "I'm calling
you from London."

"What the hell are you doing in London?" Phil asked
incredulously.

"After we spoke, I met with Browning and told him
you wanted a government plane from Geneva to Andrews
Air Force Base. It's a goddamn big deal. Complicated.
Pentagon's involved with Air Force ATC. We've got to
get a seven-forty-seven out of West Germany. There are

manifests to sign and a ton of red tape to work through. Browning told me to take care of it personally."

"Fine with me," Phil said.

"Don't sound so enthusiastic, old pal."

"I've been submerged in Gemstone for almost three hours."

There was a pause.

"What the hell is in it?" Sid asked.

"Tell you when I see you."

"Okay. I'm taking Alitalia, leaving London five twenty-five, arriving Venice eight-forty P.M."

"Where are you booked?"

"The Gritti."

"Check in; then meet me at Harry's Bar at ten."

"Good enough. See you then. And, Phil—"

"Yeah?"

"Congratulations."

Phil hung up and slowly wound the pink thread over the curled frames of film.

Chapter Forty-eight

The lights of Palermo Harbor blazed under the brilliant yellow glare of a full moon, and the sweet, pungent aroma from a spice-laden ship drifted across the busy waterfront. The port was crowded with freighters, tankers, cruiseliners and warships of the American Sixth Fleet.

Almost unnoticed, a battered oil-smeared freighter, flying the Panamanian flag, was getting up steam. The ship rode high in the greasy black water, having unloaded 5,000 drums of Libyan oil.

The Turkish captain stood on the bridge, feeling relieved as he listened to the throb of turbines beginning to stir. His role in the clandestine enterprise was over. The first seven oil drums unloaded that afternoon contained a precious cargo that did not appear on the manifest. Secreted in a specially designed waterproof chamber at the base of each oil drum were bricks of morphine. The captain could see clearly the outline of the warehouse on the Via della Cala, where the morphine was at this moment being refined. He sighed heavily and wondered why he took the risk. The answer was simple: money.

Naked bulbs suspended from cords slung over ceiling beams threw phantom shadows across the brick walls of the warehouse laboratory. Kimsan stood near the blacked-out windows, watching Dr. Hans Kleiser and his assistant preparing for the fifth and final stage of refinement; they reminded him of surgeons in an operating room with their white smocks, rubber gloves and white gauze masks.

The tall, stooped German chemist worked at a long

metal table. Chemicals, vials, strainers and instruments were lined up in order of use. A huge glass vat containing granules of impure heroin sat in the center of the table. The doctor peered at the jar intently, watching the white particles dissolving in the warm alcohol. Kleiser calculated it would take three more minutes before he could introduce the volatile ether gas.

Kimsan was tired, and this last lethal step in the process added to his tension. He craved a cigarette, but with the highly flammable ether liquid present, lighting a match would be suicidal. The silence in the room was broken by the occasional rumble of heavy-duty trucks, whose movements rattled the building's frame.

Kimsan began to pace in a small circle, his thoughts centering on Sonji. The events of the past twenty-four hours had taken him back to a distressing emotional place. Sonji had made him feel hopeful, and that was dangerous.

He had experienced enough intrigue and danger for three lifetimes. He had served many masters and had been the catalyst in plots and counterplots. He took the fall for Koreagate, then served as Park's bagman, before being pressed into the drug operation by Chung. He moved between Chinese warlords who ruled the opium fields and Mafia dons who controlled the refinement and distribution. He walked a treacherous tightrope through a maze of smugglers, assassins, dealers, pimps and junkies—always under the surveillance of KCIA agents.

Kimsan trusted no one. He had surrendered the Gemstone file because he owed Don Carlo more favors than he could ever repay. And if the loss of Gemstone cost him his life, so be it. He had long ago made peace with himself. But now the emotional need for Sonji, the chance of a future brought with it the fear of death. He wanted to live and spend the money locked in his Swiss bank account. There was enough for them to live luxuriously for the rest of their lives. Well, it was up to Sonji. She alone had the power to convince Chung to let them go.

The sudden sharp, acrid odor of ether snapped him out of his reverie. He moved to the back wall and watched the aged German begin the last stage of refinement.

Kleiser placed a siphon dish in the mouth of the glass

vat while his assistant pulled a large cork from a jug of
hydrochloric acid.

The master chemist snapped on a button just under the
tabletop and checked to be certain the exhaust fan was
activated. The fan was critical; it sucked the ether fumes
into its ducts, clearing the air of the lethal gas. Kleiser
poured the hydrochloric acid into the vial. The solution
cleared, and the granules of impure heroin were trans-
formed into floating white flakes.

The silence in the room was painful. Kleiser reached for
the tin of ether. He raised it over the siphon and with exquisite care controlled the flow, drop by drop.

*The sharp stench of ether covered the smell of burning
wires.*

Drops fell into the vat's solution one by one.

Flakes of heroin swam to the bottom of the jar.

The shadows of Kleiser and his assistant played off the
stark brick wall. Kimsan's face was covered with beads of
perspiration.

*Beneath the table, a blue arc of flame jumped between
two worn wires and shorted the exhaust fan; the last revolution drew the volatile ether fumes into the duct.*

There was an earsplitting explosion, accompanied by a
searing flash of purple-red flame. The roof went skyward.
The walls buckled under the pressure of concussion rings.
Fragments of metal and shards of glass screamed across
the room. Kleiser's legs were ripped from his body and
hurled against the windows. A great rush of blood
pumped out of the neck of his assistant. A sheet of glass
sliced through Kimsan, severing his body just below the
shoulders. The concussion rings traveled up and out,
bursting all four walls. The entire five-story warehouse
trembled, and from its shattered center a brilliant fireball
rose up, illuminating the Palermo waterfront.

Chapter Forty-nine

Harry's Bar on the Grand Canal was a legend, not for its food but for its easy camaraderie and the haunting presence of Ernest Hemingway. The sedate second floor belonged to romantics who wished to dine with a view of the canal. But the ground floor caught the action. It was a long, narrow room with small tables jammed against a wall running parallel to the marble-topped bar.

The space between the bar and the tables was four-deep with Venetian royalty, international film people, expensive English call girls, Saudi princes, Nazi war criminals, MDI agents and wealthy tourists.

Waiters, carrying trays of food, moved expertly through the Saturday night frenzy. The babble of languages mixed with shrill bursts of laughter and rattling dishes. Harry's Bar was a classic study in beautifully organized confusion.

Claudia and Phil were seated at a corner table in the rear, near the open kitchen. The choice table was offered to them by the maître d', who remembered them from the previous evening.

They studied the people at the bar with detached amusement. A Spaniard in a black velvet tuxedo was talking excitedly on the public phone near the kitchen. Sitting on a barstool close to the phone, a stunning blond woman spoon-fed caviar to a toy poodle. Alongside the blonde a famous Italian film director kissed the ear of a teenage German prostitute.

Phil's face was flushed and the food and wine caused him to perspire. His topcoat was hung on a rack behind him, the .25-caliber automatic nestled in its deep slash pocket. He wiped his forehead and drank some iced mineral water.

Claudia sipped a pony of Sambuca and said, "Tell me about Sonji."

"Her story is not much different from yours. She's been manipulated by a different system."

Claudia crisscrossed her cigarette along the surface of the ashtray. "Is her father still being held as a hostage?"

"I suppose so."

"You think she and Kimsan have a chance?"

"They're both survivors. I guess there's always a chance."

The Spaniard hung up the phone in disgust and returned to the bar just in time for the blonde to hand him her caviar-eating poodle, which promptly urinated on his ruffled shirt.

"Did you see that?" Phil asked.

"The price of romance." Claudia smiled.

They sat in silence for a moment; then Claudia wistfully said, "I hope Sonji makes it."

"So do I."

Phil glanced at his watch. "I wonder where Sid Greene is?"

"He's only a few minutes late," Claudia said. "What's the difference?"

"We've got one hell of a day tomorrow."

"How did you manage official Swiss help?" she asked.

Phil flagged a waiter and ordered two espressos. "Some years ago the Vesco-Cornfeld IOS stock swindle almost wrecked the Swiss banking system. And to the Swiss nothing is more important than preserving the integrity of their banking institutions. Franz Kohler is chief of Swiss Internal Security. He was on the griddle, and I provided him with some critical data. Cornfeld went to jail and Vesco into exile. Kohler was indebted to me, and one thing about the Swiss, they never forget a connection."

The waiter served the coffee and asked if they wanted to see the dessert tray. "Not for me," Phil said. Claudia shook her head.

"You know, Don Carlo admires you," she said.

"Well, half of me admires him."

"Which half?"

"The part that isn't the lawyer."

The stunning blonde at the bar threw her peach vodka

into the tuxedoed man's face, grabbed the toy poodle and fought her way up to the other end, bumping hard into Sid Greene, whom she cursed in Swedish.

Sid's almost handsome face looked drawn and haggard. "Hello, Phil."

They shook hands, and Phil introduced him to Claudia.

"Sorry I'm late," Sid said. "Plane circled for twenty minutes—goddamn fog."

"Sit down. Have a drink."

"No, thanks. I did enough drinking on the plane. Besides, I'm running out of time." Sid seemed tense, and his fingers trembled slightly as he lit a cigarette. "There's a mountain of red tape connected with this Air Force jet you wanted. We've got to talk."

"Give me a minute."

"Sure. I'll be outside."

Phil leaned toward Claudia. "If I'm not back in, say, thirty minutes, go over to that phone and call Gino. Wait for him. Don't leave without him. Thirty minutes," Phil repeated, then slipped on his topcoat, gripped the small automatic in the slash pocket and made his way through the four-deep bar.

The air was cold and damp. Thick rolling fog had reduced visibility to less than fifty feet.

Phil and Sid walked in silence for a moment past couples whose shapes loomed up ominously in the chalky mist.

At the Piazza San Giuliano they turned left into a maze of narrow streets. The crumbling buildings on each side were decorated with stone gargoyles.

"I have good news, Phil. Levy succeeded in getting a federal tax fraud indictment on Rhee."

"Christ . . . that's great."

"They nailed him for moving illicit funds through his foundation into a Panamanian bank."

"So the religious foundation was a laundry."

"Right."

"Has he been arraigned?" Phil asked.

"Next week. About fourteen counts in all. He could do five to ten years."

"Where is the good Reverend?"

"Presumably back in Seoul."

They walked over a humpbacked bridge into an ancient quarter with dark, twisting streets that led to sudden dead ends. The fog obscured the shuttered houses, and the only light came from wooden poles with lanterns suspended over small canals.

"I wonder if Chung will let him take the fall?" Phil asked.

"Why not? Rhee was Park's man."

"I wish we had nailed him as a KCIA operative."

"Well"—Sid sighed—"that went down the drain with Mrs. Hwan."

They crossed a stone bridge over a canal and found themselves in a circular cul-de-sac.

"Where the hell are we?" Sid asked.

"Beats me." Phil shrugged. "We're only a few minutes from where we started. Let's get back to the bridge."

Silky wisps of fog rose up from the canal, spreading into amorphous shapes, enveloping them in a damp, transparent cocoon. On each side of the bridge curving streets meshed and disappeared as if designed with artful secrecy.

"Got a cigarette?" Phil asked.

"Don't you ever buy a pack?"

"Not if I can help it."

Sid Greene took out a pack of English cigarettes and struck a match. Phil cupped it with his right hand, and Sid noticed the swollen purple fingers.

"What the hell happened to your hand?"

"A hit man out of MI 5 named Edwards."

The foul smell of raw sewage rose from the small canal, and a burst of raucous feminine laughter came out of a nearby window.

"I have a ticket for you, Phil. Paris to Miami. A week of rest at the Doral Hotel, then home to Washington." Sid paused. "Browning wants me to take it from here."

Phil slipped his right hand back into the coat pocket and gripped the butt of the automatic. "What about the girl?"

"She'll be fine."

"And the Don?"

"Under control. Three federal marshals will meet the

Air Force transport in Geneva. Browning feels you've done the job. All that's required now is Gemstone."

Phil took a final drag of the cigarette and flicked it into the canal. "You're a little late, Sidney."

Sid shook his head. "There's no way you can come out of this thing alive unless you do what I tell you. Now give me the file. Take the tickets and forget the case. It's over."

Phil stared at him for a long moment. "So long, kid." He took a few steps down the near side of the bridge.

"Hold it!" Sid commanded.

Phil turned and saw a .38 revolver in Sid's right hand. There was a moment of silence as the fog swirled around them. Phil slipped the safety off the automatic in his pocket. Technically he could now raise the coat and fire through it, but it was chancy. Greene took regular FBI small-arms practice. He had to keep Sid talking. "Do you actually think I'm walking around with a fifteen-page file?" Phil asked.

"No. But the Don doesn't return without it. You take the Miami tickets, go back and tell Claudia I'm going the distance—and have her give me the file. If you don't agree, everyone's going to be hit. There are people from MI 5 with me. I'm sorry, Phil."

"No, I'm the one who's sorry. I picked you out of a big field, for a lot of reasons, but I guess I confused ambition with brains. Not to mention loyalty."

"I don't enjoy this," Sid replied. "And believe it or not, I'm convinced it's for your own good."

A gondola passed below them, riding the swift current.

"What did they promise you?" Phil asked. "Don't tell me, let me play it back for you. Belgrave said they're kicking Burgess upstairs because the director of the CIA is in legal trouble, and with your background you can assume Burgess's old spot as director of Covert Operations. 'Just do this one small job. Phil trusts you. Go over there, get him off the case. We have no desire to damage Mr. Ricker. On the contrary, he deserves a vacation.' How'm I doing, Sid?" Greene just stared at him, and Phil continued. " 'Get that Hoover file, son, and you're sitting in the big chair at Langley.' "

Phil took a few steps toward him, and Sid snapped, "Hold it!" and cocked the hammer on the snub-nosed .38.

Phil held his ground and said, "Maybe I'm giving Belgrave too much credit for subtlety. Once you threw in with him he wouldn't have to fuck around with salesmanship. Your orders were simple 'Hit him, Mr. Greene. He's a threat to the security of the nation.' Sure. That's exactly what went down. You're the ideal hit man. After all, we worked together for two years. We trust each other. Once you take me out, it's all over. Gemstone's a dead issue. The Don is frozen in Italy. Belgrave's happy. Maldonado's happy."

Phil's hand was clammy against the concealed gun butt. "Well, here I am, sweetheart. In the middle of nowhere, with ceiling zero. You couldn't ask for a better setup. How can you miss?"

Sid's finger gripped the trigger. Phil raised his concealed automatic slightly. They stood on the humpbacked bridge like surreal figures sculpted in the shifting patches of chalky fog.

Phil shook his head. "Christ, don't you understand the frame you're in? Once you hit me, the MI 5 guys who came with you from London will take you out. They have the perfect cover. You were sent to arrange my return, but acting out of greed and against orders, you decided to grab Gemstone for yourself. And you were nailed by one of Don Carlo's men. You're in a frame designed by experts."

Sid shivered and his gun hand trembled. He steadied the cocked weapon with his left hand.

Phil took a deep breath, exhaled and said, "They made one serious miscalculation—you may be a fool, but you're not a killer."

There was a moment of silence.

Sid Greene's shoulders convulsed, and his left hand fell away from the .38. The gun shook visibly as he slowly lowered it and said, "You'll never make it, Phil."

He turned abruptly, walked down the far side of the bridge and disappeared into the swirling mists.

Chapter Fifty

The Montaldi launch struggled against the strong Adriatic tide. Don Carlo and Gino were seated in the cabin. Phil and Claudia stood at the prow.

The canal traffic was heavy; garbage scows, produce barges, *vaporetti*, gondolas and private launches threaded their way through the rising fog. The air was cold and salty, and the spray off the dipping prow turned into golden beads as it caught the sunlight. Stone palaces and ornate churches seemed to be soaking up the warmth of the sun in preparation for the oncoming winter. The bells of St. Mark's began to toll and were joined by a chorus of chimes from the surrounding churches.

Phil stared down into the murky waters. The passing Renaissance beauty no longer interested him. He felt like a racehorse turning for home, trying to summon all his energy and concentration for the last few furlongs. He had phoned Franz Kohler and requested he purchase three first-class tickets on Swissair's flight 110, leaving Geneva at 2:30 P.M., arriving at JFK at 6:05 P.M.

He wanted no part of the Air Force jet arranged for by Sid Greene. Kohler phoned back, confirming the booking, and said he would be waiting at the Venice airport with a Swiss police jet for the direct flight to Geneva.

Don Carlo, followed by Gino, came up on deck as they cruised past the Oriental lace arches of the Doges' Palace. The old man looked rested and refreshed. The shiny red scar on his face was less pronounced, and his eyes seemed vibrant and alive.

"I'm glad to see the last of this city," he said. "They ought to put it all in a frame, hang it in a museum, and let the Adriatic swallow it."

"Well," Phil said, "in six, seven hours you'll be in New York."

Gino suddenly moved past them going up to the nose of the prow. He shouted in rapid Italian to the Don.

"Something wrong up ahead," the Don explained. "Police boats at the Rialto."

At the cry of a siren the helmsman throttled down, and through the clearing mist they could see a cordon of highly lacquered mahogany speedboats with large spotlights and the word *Polizia* on their sides. Pulleys and block-and-tackle posts were fixed atop the humpbacked Rialto Bridge, and throngs of people were gazing down into the water below.

The canal traffic had backed up, and the boats circled, waiting for passage through a narrow channel between police cruisers.

As they drew near the bridge, Don Carlo said, "They're fishing a body out of the canal. It happens this time of year. Fall is the suicide season in Venice."

There was a babble of shouts as orders passed from uniformed police on the bridge to the men below. Phil saw two frogmen bob to the surface. One of them held the collar of a coat; the other snaked a line under the submerged shoulders of the body. The frogman signaled to the police on the bridge, and the hum of a generator started up. The block-and-tackle line grew taut.

The body rose out of the canal, trailing streams of water. It revolved slowly, and Phil suddenly found himself staring into the open milky eyes of Sid Greene. His face was purple, and there was a dark red congealed spot in his belly.

"Christ Almighty," Phil whispered.

"Did you know him?" Don Carlo asked.

"Yeah, I knew him."

"He was an FBI man," Claudia explained. "He worked with Phil."

"I'm sorry," the Don said.

The *carabinieri* officer shouted at them to move. The engines throbbed, and the launch threaded its way into the line of boats cleared to pass under the Rialto.

The launch picked up speed and moved out into the open lagoon. Phil moved to the stern and stood alone watching the disappearing spires and domes of Venice. He thought of the irony of Sid Greene's death occurring in this voluptuous, doomed city.

Inspector Franz Kohler, dressed in gray topcoat and black homburg, waited on the quay at Marco Polo Airport. His regular features were set off by kind blue eyes. He seemed more the Swiss banker than the chief on Internal Security.

Phil introduced the others to Kohler, who said, "We can go directly to the autobus and board the plane."

The captain released the Learjet's brakes, pressed the throttles forward and sent the sleek plane hurtling down the runway.

They climbed steeply for fifteen minutes before leveling off at 22,000 feet.

Phil went to the bar and poured a stiff vodka over ice. Kohler joined him and said, "We'll be in Geneva in forty-seven minutes."

Phil sat on the arm of a small circular leather settee and glanced at the cabin's rich interior. "You sure live well, Franz."

"A small convenience," Kohler said. "Tell me, Phil—what happened to Cornfeld and Vesco?"

"Well, Bernie's living the good life in Beverly Hills—and I don't begrudge him that. He got a royal screwing from Vesco."

"That's the man I would like to get my hands on."

"You're not alone. But Vesco has classier protection than the President."

The seat belt sign lit up, and through the oval windows they could see the snow-covered Alps.

"We'd better take our seats," Kohler advised. "By the way, have you read today's *International Tribune*?"

"No."

Kohler pulled a folded newspaper from an overhead rack and handed it to him. "Finish your drink and get your seat belt on."

"Franz."

"Yes?"

Phil handed Kohler the German automatic. "I can't take this into America."

He returned to his seat and glanced at the front page. The headline story announced the passage of the AWACS sale to Saudi Arabia. There was a photograph of the President smiling in triumph, and standing behind him were Senator Percy and a somber-faced Dr. Belgrave. Phil felt a tingling pervasive fear, knowing that the sophisticated equipment going to the feudal Moslem kingdom was certain to be compromised. The fifteenth frame of Gemstone bore confirmation of that inevitability.

The other news was the usual mix: IRA bombs in London, PLO bombs in Brussels and Soviet Army maneuvers along the Polish border. Down at the lower right corner of the page was a Reuters item about an explosion on the Palermo waterfront. Three unidentified bodies had been found in the wreckage of a warehouse. The Italian police speculated that a bomb had been planted by terrorists of the Brigate Rosse.

They landed at Geneva International Airport, transferred to a police sedan and drove directly to the waiting Swissair 747. Kohler boarded with them and spoke with the chief steward, who was aware of the special circumstances surrounding the three early arrivals. The steward showed Don Carlo and Claudia to their seats, and Phil shook hands with Inspector Kohler.

"You're one up on me now."

"Good luck." Kohler smiled, then waved good-bye to the Don and Claudia.

The steward handed Phil a glass of champagne. "You couldn't change this for a vodka on the rocks?"

"Certainly, sir."

"You drink too much, Phil," Don Carlo said.

"Some people jog—I drink."

"How do we get from New York to Washington?" the Don asked.

"Hire a limo."

"Where do we stay?"

"We've got the top floor of the presidential suite at the Madison."

"You think we should stay with those hotel reservations?"

"Why not?"

"They were made by Sid Greene."

"We're okay as long as we have Gemstone," Phil replied.

They arrived at JFK twenty minutes late—it was 6:25 P.M. New York time. The chief immigration officer hustled them through customs and personally initialed Don Carlo's temporary visa.

Phil phoned Browning's office and advised his secretary they would be arriving at the Madison Hotel close to 11:00 P.M.

They followed the skycap through the milling crowds out to a private VIP circular parking lot. The cold night air smelled of jet-fuel exhaust, and their eardrums throbbed with the continuous scream of planes landing and taking off.

The big white limousine with the smoky windows moved out of the lot and threaded its way through a maze of turns before entering the expressway to Manhattan.

They passed the ruins of the 1939 and 1964 world's fairs and an illuminated sign appeared: TRIBORO BRIDGE.

The Don suddenly leaned forward and tapped on the glass partition.

"How are you going into the city?" Don Carlo asked the driver.

"Well, sir, I plan to take the Triboro Bridge, then cross a Hundred Twenty-fifth Street to the West Side Drive, down to Forty-second Street and into the Lincoln Tunnel."

"That's no good. The Triboro is for Japanese tourists and Arabs. Take the Fifty-ninth Street Bridge, then—"

Claudia interrupted. "Why are you disturbing him?"

"I want to see the city."

Phil was amused by the old man's nostalgia.

"Go ahead, Carlo—tell him how you want to go."

"I don't mind," the driver said. "It's just faster this way."

"I waited ten years for this ride," the Don said. "I'm in no hurry."

"Whatever you say, sir."

The Don nodded. "Take the Fifty-ninth Street Bridge, then go west to Park Avenue, turn left and slow down when you get to Fiftieth Street. That's the Waldorf Hotel. I want to see it, Okay?"

"Yes, sir."

The limousine exited the expressway at Queens Boulevard. The Don leaned back and studied the brick apartment buildings lining the broad street. After a few minutes he suddenly exclaimed, "Did you see that?"

"What?" Claudia asked.

"That Chinese restaurant with the neon dragon."

"What about it?" Phil asked.

"I swear to God that was Frankie Copolla's place. The Napoli. It was our joint. Great clams casino. I remember a particular meeting. It was summer. There was a small garden in the back. Someone played 'Amapola' on an accordion. It was '36 or '37—maybe '38 . . . we were trying to decide what to do about the Dutchman."

"The Dutchman?" Phil asked.

"Dutch Schultz. He was nuts. Wanted to kill Tom Dewey. It was a hell of a night. The Brooklyn mob was there: Kid Twist, Pittsburgh Phil, Happy Maoine, Louie Capone and Bugsy Goldstein. We couldn't agree. Leo Meyers was in Havana. But we ate like kings." He shook his head. "Now it's a goddamn neon dragon."

They drove past the drab, hopeless apartment buildings for fifteen minutes before coming to the long onramp of the Fifty-ninth Street Bridge.

The New York skyline appeared magically, like a dazzling, glass-steel mirage of a futuristic city.

"Manhattan . . ." the Don whispered with reverence.

The big car came off the bridge and traveled west toward Park Avenue. The streets were jammed. Subway entrances coughed people up and swallowed others. Clouds of steam rose from manhole covers. Jackhammers screamed at the asphalt. Sirens wailed. Horns blared. Neon blazed. Taxi drivers and pedestrians cursed each other.

At Park Avenue and Fiftieth Street the limousine slowed and Don Carlo lowered his window and stared at the Waldorf-Astoria Hotel.

"Christ," he whispered. "Thirty years I lived in those towers . . ."

The limousine followed the heavy traffic and entered the Times Square area. Don Carlo saw the pimps, pushers, addicts and hookers lounging in front of pornographic theaters and sex shops. "What the hell happened?" he asked. "It wasn't pretty when I left, but Jesus . . ."

"Pornographic center of the Big Apple," Phil said.

"You mean to tell me they show hard-core stuff?"

"It doesn't get any harder."

Phil turned on the radio and tuned to the all-news station. The announcer was concluding the world news. There was a brief commercial break, and he came back on. "Here's an item just in from Rome, a follow-up on the warehouse explosion in Palermo, Sicily."

Phil turned the volume up. "The incident, first thought to be an act of terrorism, is now considered to be the result of a Mafia narcotics feud. Italian police have determined the warehouse contained the largest heroin-refining factory in Europe. Three bodies found in the wreckage have been identified: Kimsan the mysterious Korean who figured prominently in the Koreagate scandal of 1977, a German chemist named Hans Kleiser and another West German citizen named Karl Bleucher. It is thought that—"

Phil snapped the radio off. "Well, there goes Sonji's second chance."

"It had to be an accident," Don Carlo said.

"What about Chung?" Claudia asked.

Phil shook his head. "No motive. Kimsan made money for him."

"I'm sorry about Kimsan," the Don said pensively. "He was a man of honor."

Chapter Fifty-one

Three hours later they arrived at Fifteenth and M streets and pulled up at the canopied front of the Madison Hotel. The porters came out of the lobby, followed by Arthur Browning and three federal marshals.

After the greetings and introductions Browning, in an expansive mood, said, "You're all checked in. You must be exhausted. Let's go up to the suite."

The presidential suite was spacious; but the furniture was worn, and the air smelled of stale cigar smoke. Claudia directed the placement of their bags and trailed after the porters into the bedrooms. The federal marshals huddled at the doorway. Arthur Browning motioned to them to wait outside.

"It's good to see you, Phil." The dapper attorney general seemed pleased with himself. "I knew you could handle it."

"You certainly did, Arthur."

The Don watched Browning but remained silent.

"What happened to that plane we sent for you?" Browning asked. "At great cost, I might add."

"Sid Greene changed my mind."

Browning's eyes clouded with consternation. "I don't understand. I asked him to meet you and handle the red tape."

"They fished Mr. Greene out of the Grand Canal this morning. He tried to play ball on two courts at the same time."

"My God, I had no idea."

"Neither did I. Now here's the drill, Arthur. Tomorrow night my friend Don Carlo meets with Victor Maldonado at his Middleburg ranch."

"That's all set."

308

"No," the Don cut in. "Not until Leo Meyers gets here. When he tells me it's all okay, we move."

"Mr. Meyers arrives in Washington at five tomorrow afternoon," Browning replied.

"I'll have to speak to him first," Don Carlo said.

"Suit yourself," Browning answered, then turned to Phil. "What about Gemstone?"

"After tomorrow night's meeting."

"That's going to be difficult. I have to attend a charity event at the Smithsonian tomorrow night. The cream of Washington will be there: congressmen, senators, diplomatic officers, the Vice President, Cabinet officers and, of course, old money and high society. It's for the National Endowment for the Arts."

"Well, we should be back from Middleburg by eleven," Phil said.

"I don't understand," Browning said. "Why can't you simply hand me the file now?"

"After Don Carlo has his meeting," Phil replied.

There was a moment of silence as Browning chewed on an unlit cigar.

"All right, Phil."

"One other thing," the Don said. "When Leo Meyers gets here, we go to Middleburg without marshals."

"Any way you like it, Mr. Carelli," Browning said. "As long as your security is protected."

"Don't worry about my protection. I used to sell protection."

"Fine. I'm looking forward to your testimony."

"You'll have it."

Browning placed his scotch on the bar.

"Get some sleep, Phil. I'll be at my office all day tomorrow. You have my numbers. The marshals will remain on duty here in the hotel."

The little man turned abruptly and left.

The Don walked over to Phil. His skin was pasty, but his eyes seemed strangely bright.

"I appreciate what you did. You stuck by the arrangements."

"A deal's a deal, Carlo."

The old man nodded and went into his bedroom. Phil

double-bolted the front door and snapped off the living room lights.

In the bedroom Claudia rubbed her arms nervously.

"What's wrong?" Phil asked.

"I was thinking of Sonji—of how she must have felt when she heard about Kimsan." Claudia paused. "I've been in that place."

Chapter Fifty-two

The leading edge of a frigid Siberian air mass moved down the Korean peninsula, carrying with it a swirling snowstorm. A fragile sheet of ice covered the surface of the Han River, and a lacy white mantle draped itself across the mountains ringing the city. The towers of Seoul's skyscrapers were screened by snowflakes and shrouded in a gray, metallic light.

Soon Yi Sonji maneuvered her car carefully along the slippery sixteen-lane Sejong Avenue. The heater was on, and the windshield wipers beat a steady tattoo, clearing the snowflakes.

She glanced at the rear- and side-view mirrors, but the storm made it virtually impossible to detect a following car. She had taken a long, circuitous route from her apartment, passing through the maze of glass and brick towers in the Chamsil District, then circling back into the twisting alleys of the old city and finally heading south on Sejong. Sonji doubted she was under surveillance, but she was taking no chances. She had to maintain her freedom and security for another seventy-two hours—until Monday evening, the night they would assassinate President Chung.

From the moment she had learned of Kimsan's death the need for vengeance became an obsession. The possibility that it was an accident had never occurred to her. She knew nothing of the inherent dangers in refining morphine into heroin. Chung had alluded to Kimsan's demise with innocence and dismay. But in her mind the explosion coming on the heels of Gemstone's delivery to Ricker was conclusive proof Chung had deceived her. And now murder and vengeance were the only seasons of her life.

311

*   *   *

Sonji parked between two military sedans on busy Chong-Ro Street. The arctic air stung her face and she wrapped her scarf tightly around her throat and made her way through the swirling gusts of snow.

She paused just inside the door and removed her coat, shaking off the melting snowflakes. The warm, smoke-filled café was crowded with noontime customers, and Pat Benatar on tape sang "Fire and Ice." Sonji scanned the room slowly. The perennial Japanese businessmen sat at low tables, eating strips of meat grilled over charcoal burners. At the bar students from nearby Seoul National University mingled with office workers and off-duty American fliers. Two Chinese prostitutes negotiated with a dark-skinned Saudi labor recruiter. She finally spotted Won at a window table.

The presidential secretary stood up, took her coat and hung it on a wall peg. They ordered two mugs of hot rice wine and remained silent until the waiter served them. She swallowed the strong yakju wine and felt it burn its way down her throat.

Sonji had spoken twice to Won since her return, and a bond of mutual trust had been born out of their conspiratorial union. Won noticed a brutal, cold reflection in her oval eyes; they were like pieces of black glass devoid of life. Yet her astonishing beauty and inherent sensuality remained undiminished. And it was on those extraordinary physical attributes that the success of their plot pivoted.

Sonji noticed an American flier at the bar staring at her. She encouraged the long-distance flirtation, exchanging surreptitious glances with the blond officer. The flier's interest was a good cover, enhancing the impression that she was a prostitute meeting with her pimp.

Won drank some of the steaming wine. "Have you confirmed the arrangements?"

She nodded. "I have chosen the kisaeng girls. The president's favorite food will be provided, and his scotch will be laced with Seconal. His chief bodyguard, Kwan Yee, will be selected first to go into the bedroom with two girls. The others will remain in the kitchen. Your men will await the signal in the corridor."

"Who will give the sign that the bodyguard is murdered?"

"Chang Min will slit the bodyguard's throat the moment of his climax. She will then come into the living room, pass the sign to me and continue out into the corridor and alert your men."

"Why did you chose this particular kisaeng?"

"We have worked together in the past. Her cousin, a student, was tortured to death by Chung's Purification Committee. Her motives are as strong as ours. The moment she leaves for the corridor I will kill Chung." Sonji paused. "Everything will be done in the same manner and with the same precision used to assassinate President Park."

Won had begun to perspire. He had never heard an act of murder recited with such tranquillity. He was fascinated by the brutal transformation in her character. The once-placid robotlike beauty was now a dangerous predator, totally consumed by hatred and a visceral need for vengeance.

They ordered more wine, and Sonji smiled again at the American pilot. After the waiter placed their drinks, she said, "Now, what of your part?"

"At precisely eleven-fifteen P.M. the radio and television station, all key highways, military installations and munitions depots will be secured by units of General Kim's Garrison Command. The Second Battalion of the White Horse Division will seize the presidential compound. I have, of course, no choice but to place my trust in General Kim."

"It is not misplaced," she said. "I spent an afternoon with him. His hatred of the president matches our own."

Won nodded. "We have agreed on all political points as well. A new government will be formed with an elected Parliament reporting to a thirteen-member Supreme Presidium."

Her tongue slid across her lower lip. "And what of me?"

"You will be the first woman to serve on the presidium. Your father will be speaker of the Parliament."

"I see."

"Are you displeased?"

"No, it is all as we agreed." She sipped her wine and thought she would not for long remain one of thirteen. The prophecy of Vishnu was at hand: *Giants would walk in her shadow.*

Won glanced out at the whirling snowfall and thought the time would inevitably arrive when Soon Yi Sonji would have to be terminated. They would be in a contest for survival, but history had mandated that inevitable fate to all conspirators.

"What of the Americans?" she asked.

"To hell with them," he replied. "The commander of I Corps will have no choice but to accept the new regime. They will acquiesce, as they did with Park."

A nerve in Won's cheek twitched. He sipped the wine and for the first time displayed a feminine gesture in the movement of his wrist. "I must confess to you, Sonji, there are times when I am fearful."

"That is only natural. But you are capable of great bravery. You displayed extraordinary courage in Vietnam."

"Combat is different from assassination."

She stared into his eyes and touched his hand. "Our actions will be recorded as supreme patriotism, and if we are killed, our sacrifice will not be in vain. The people will rise up in the wake of our blood."

"I am prepared," Won said. He squeezed her hand, got to his feet and made his way unobtrusively through the noisy noontime crowd.

Sonji smoothed her long hair, took out a tortoiseshell compact and checked the hint of rouge on her high cheekbones. She called the waiter over and told him to ask the American flier to join her.

She glanced out the window. A ray of sunlight had pierced the gray, metallic skies, and the falling snowflakes shone like golden crsytals.

"Hi, there." She looked up and saw the American flier. "Do you speak English?" he asked.

"A little." She smiled.

Chapter Fifty-three

The two old men sitting opposite each other in the Madison's presidential suite had authored the history of organized crime in America for half a century. Leo Meyers's cane rested against the sofa, and he held the scotch in his bony hand. The strong Miami sun had painted an even tan on his surprisingly unlined face. The Don was several years younger than Leo, but his pale, drawn features made him appear much older.

Phil was amazed that the two men had managed to maintain a lifelong allegiance despite the countless intrigues that had shaped their lives.

"I spoke with Maldonado after you called," Leo said to Don Carlo. "I trust there were no more incidents in Italy."

"There was a move on Phil, but Gino took care of it."

"Hell of a man, Gino," Leo said.

"He and Ruffino were aces." They sipped their drinks, and Don Carlo said, "You look well, Leo."

"It's the tan."

"No, you seem younger to me."

"I've been blessed with a good woman." Leo paused, then reflectively said, "I've been blessed in many ways."

"I can't say the same." The Don sighed.

"With children you need luck," Leo said. "Nicky was headstrong. I tried to talk to him, Carlo. I advised him not to go against the council, to lay off that Korean preacher, but—" Leo Meyers shrugged.

"I know. Nicky would never listen. But his wife and the baby, that I can never accept."

"Well, the council has made the rules for tonight's meeting—no violence."

"The man is an *infamia*," the Don replied with controlled anger.

"I said no violence tonight," Leo smiled, "not forever. You make your case. He'll make his. And I'll make my recommendation to the council. I have my own score to settle with Victor, but the rules for tonight are written in stone."

"What time is the meeting?" Don Carlo asked.

"Seven-thirty at the ranch. The drive to Middleburg is more or less one hour. I have a limousine downstairs." Leo glanced over at Phil. "I saw federal people all over the lobby."

"That's right," Phil replied. "But they won't accompany us. Browning has agreed no federal marshals. We go alone."

"What do you mean by 'we'?"

"Phil goes with us, Leo," the Don answered. "I made that deal with him."

"This is family business," Leo said warily.

"He goes with us," Don Carlo repeated stubbornly. "A deal is a deal."

Leo Meyers studied the Don for a moment, then nodded.

Phil walked across the spacious suite and sat on the arm of a chair facing Leo Meyers. "I'd like to ask you something, Leo."

"Go ahead."

"You were involved in the decision to hit Nicky, right?"

"Yes."

"Where did that meeting take place?"

"Acapulco."

"Who was at that meeting?"

"Maldonado, myself and certain other parties."

"What parties?" Phil pressed.

Leo ran his hand over the smooth wood of the cane. "Mr. Ricker, I've made it a lifelong practice never to disclose anything that involves business. The people who requested the hit on Nicky had business with our organization. Personally I detest them. But I never break business rules."

"I have a few rules, too," Phil replied forcefully. "And let me tell you something: Unless I get the names of those who attended the Acapulco meeting, Don Carlo isn't going anywhere, except maybe back to Sicily."

"Phil," Don Carlo said soothingly, "let's talk privately for a minute." He rose. "Excuse us, Leo."

They went into a study off the living room.

"I understand your position," Don Carlo said. "The name of the man at the Acapulco meeting nails your case. I promise you that Leo will give you that name. He's a man who lives by ancient codes. He has to be handled in a certain way. But you have my word. I'll get that name for you."

"How can you promise that?"

"No one in the National Council wants me talking to the feds. No one in the organization wants me upset. Leo will come to understand that it's good business for him to give me that name. Now we've been through hell together. Trust me."

Phil stared at the faded blue eyes and nodded. "Okay, Carlo."

Phil went into the adjoining bedroom, and the Don returned to the living room.

"He's a stubborn fellow," Leo Meyers said to Don Carlo.

"Maybe so, but I owe that man. Without him I wouldn't be here. He needs that information, Leo."

"Let's see what happens at the meeting."

Phil and Claudia stood on the terrace, staring off at the quiet beauty of the glowing presidential monuments.

"It's quite a sight," she said. "From here at night, it all seems so eternal, so indestructible."

"I'd lay the price that someone said the same thing about Sparta." Phil sighed. "We're spying on ourselves, and any nation that distrusts its own citizens is in trouble." He turned from the view and leaned against the terrace wall. "Those two old bastards in that living room may have more honor between them than the whole alphabet soup of federal spooks."

Chapter Fifty-four

Victor Maldonado sat at his desk in the large, comfortable study. Behind him, the floodlit grounds of the ranch were clearly visible through a huge picture window. The study's oak-paneled walls were decorated with brass horseshoes and framed photographs of great thoroughbreds.

Martin Bender stood behind the wet bar, sipping a scotch and looking like the ambassador to the Court of St. James's. He wore a black mohair tuxedo with a pleated white silk dress shirt and a black silk bow tie.

Maldonado took a Havana out of a humidor, bit the end off and spit the shred of leaf on the Navajo rug. "That blueblood Reynolds is not gonna nickel and dime us."

"He'll pay the price, Victor. He wants a foal out of Snowball."

"Goddamn right. They all want Snowball. She has more heart than their stallions. She beat the boys in five stake races. If Reynolds wants to breed his stallion to Snowball, he'll pay the price. I don't give a shit if he was born on Plymouth Rock." He rose and paced, chewing on the unlit cigar. "These bastards think they got special privileges because their great-grandfathers murdered the Indians." He stopped and used the cigar as a pointer. "They want to do business with me, but always on the phone. They never set foot on the ranch. Who the hell are they? They make millions and never pay a quarter in tax. They look down on us. Well, I got the mare, and without Snowball, Mr. Reynolds is holding his cock."

"He'll come around, Victor."

"Pour me a beer."

Bender opened a bottle of Beck's beer and carefully

318

poured the liquid, tilting the glass. Victor walked up to his *consigliere*, took the glass, swallowed some, belched and said, "You look like a movie star, Martin."

"Well, it was thoughtful of Belgrave to invite me."

"Why not? We do business with him. What the hell is the occasion?"

"A charity ball at the Smithsonian for the National Endowment for the Arts."

"When are you going?"

"As soon as we conclude our meeting with Don Carlo."

Maldonado lit the cigar and blew some smoke at his adviser. "Unbelievable, that old dago bastard made it back with Ricker."

"Not so unbelievable. Our people screwed up, and Belgrave's people missed. But what does it matter?" The tall, austere Bender continued. "Leo set the rules. You'll say the killing was an accident. The Don will display some anger and go back to Sicily."

"Yeah, but after the meeting Leo Meyers is gonna talk to the National Council."

"Pro forma. Eyewash. You're not responsible. An ace hit man was employed and failed. The council will not rule against you."

The study door opened, and a swarthy man with a drooping enormous belly blocked the doorway.

"What is it, Vito?"

"Crowley's here."

"The teamster files," Bender said.

"Take care of it, Martin. I'm gonna wait for Reynolds's call."

"I think you ought to personally inspect these documents."

"What have I got you for?" Maldonado growled. "Leo Meyers and Don Carlo will be here in maybe twenty-five minutes. Check the goddamn files and get rid of that lunatic Crowley."

Martin Bender's hand trembled imperceptibly as he adjusted his bow tie and said, "I'll take care of it, Victor."

The bodyguard with the enormous girth stood aside as Bender left.

Maldonado walked up to a framed picture of a thoroughbred with intelligent eyes and a gleaming white coat.

The name Snowball was fixed to a brass plate beneath the photograph.

Bender watched as Matt Crowley snapped the attaché case open. There were two piles of documents bearing the teamster seal on the letterheads. Crowley emptied the case, removing the documents and placing them on the table. He then pressed two brass buttons at either side of the case, and the bottom lid sprang open. He lifted the false bottom out, exposing a blue-steel MARK-A nine-millimeter Uzi submachine gun.

Crowley put a pair of black leather gloves on and gently lifted the legendary weapon out of its configurated holder. The Israeli-made submachine gun was only eighteen inches long with its stock folded, and it weighed less than ten pounds. It accommodated a forty-round clip, and its muzzle velocity was 1,300 feet per second. Crowley inserted the clip into the magazine, bolted the cocking handle, set the change lever on semiautomatic. He then screwed a tubular silencer onto the short muzzle and flashed his black eyes at Bender. "Where do we start?"

"The man in the foyer," the *consigliere* said.

They walked casually down the long corridor, past closed doors. Bender carried the attaché case, and Crowley held the Uzi under his topcoat in the manner used by Secret Service agents.

A short, stocky man in shirt sleeves, wearing a shoulder holster and automatic, was seated near the front door eating a hero sandwich. He looked up as they approached and took a vicious bite out of the sandwich. There was a hissing sound, and his forehead burst apart. He fell over, still clutching the sandwich.

Bender and Crowley retraced their steps back down the hallway. The obese bodyguard, Vito, stood just outside the study door, scratching his swollen belly. The Uzi hissed, and five slugs shredded his chest cavity, slamming him against the wall. Crowley kicked the dead man's feet out of the way and nodded at Bender, whose skin color had turned chalky. The tall, formally dressed *consigliere* opened the study door.

Bender held the attaché case, and Crowley concealed the Uzi under his coat. Maldonado was seated at his desk, the phone cradled to his ear, the cigar clenched between his teeth. He motioned to them to be quiet, cupped the receiver and exclaimed, "I've got that blueblood son of a bitch by the balls!" He then spoke into the phone. "Mr. Reynolds, I'm here to do business. It's not complicated. Twenty-five grand for each mating session. And I guarantee a foal from Snowball." Victor listened for a moment and smiled. "Anything's possible in this life, Mr. Reynolds, but the vet tells me Snowball's 'in season,' as you fellows say, and if your stallion doesn't shoot blanks, we should be fine."

Crowley felt the strong sexual arousal that always accompanied his murderous actions. He exercised extreme patience waiting for the pockmarked *mafioso* to conclude his call.

"Good," Victor said into the phone. "My trainer will be down from New York on Sunday, and you're welcome to bring your own vet. Fine with me." He paused. "Pleasure to do business with you, Mr. Reynolds." He hung up and smiled at the pasty-faced Bender. "You were right, Martin. That blueblood prick knuckled under."

Bender nodded.

Maldonado stared at him, noticing his color. "What's the matter with you?"

Bender did not reply.

Crowley uncovered the Uzi.

Maldonado's crafty eyes went cold. He stood up and glared at Bender. "You WASP bastard! You sold me out!"

Maldonado's head jerked back to Crowley. "Listen to me, Matt. This is a setup that's gonna backfire. You and me are in the same—"

Crowley cut him off. "You ginzo piece of shit. You and I have no similarities at all. You're not even the same species." He slipped the selector lever to single fire. There was a hiss, and Maldonado's left kneecap exploded. He screamed and fell back in the chair. There was another hiss, and Maldonado's right shoulder erupted in a burst of blood and bone. Crowley pressed the trigger again, and a red hole appeared just above Maldonado's navel.

"For chrissake, Matt," Bender pleaded, "finish him off."

"Whatever you say, Martin." He slipped the selector mechanism to full automatic and pressed the trigger. A line of blood spurts moved vertically up Maldonado's belly, chest, neck and face. The force of the slugs spun him around in the swivel chair.

The hissing stopped. The only sound in the study was the creaking of Maldonado's chair as it revolved slowly, coming to rest facing them. A single open eye was all that remained of his face. The sharp odor of gunpowder, gas and human excrement filled the room.

Crowley said, "Well, Martin, we've got a party to go to."

Bender noticed the shining madness in Crowley's black eyes. "Go ahead," he said hoarsely. "I'll follow in ten minutes."

Crowley held the Uzi with its muzzle pointed to the floor. "What did Belgrave promise you for selling out that dago?"

The grizzly mess in the chair and the rising foul stench were making Bender nauseous. "A mutuality of interest. Nothing complicated."

"Well, whatever the reason, you're my kind of guy, Martin."

Crowley raised the Uzi, and four bullets tore through Bender's heart.

Chapter Fifty-five

The Cuban bodyguard drove the Cadillac limousine. Leo Meyers sat beside him. Phil and Don Carlo were in the rear. Claudia had remained at the Madison, and at Leo's insistence, one of his Cuban bodyguards was keeping her company. Leo Meyers did not share Phil's confidence in Browning's federal marshals.

The gleaming black car sped along the country lane. Leo saw a signpost and said, "*Derecho*." The Cuban nodded and turned right. They traveled for half a mile before entering the private driveway of the floodlit ranch.

"Curious," Phil murmured.

"What?" the Don asked.

"Gate open. No one around."

They came slowly up the winding driveway and parked at the entrance of the white Colonial house. Leo Meyers, leaning heavily on his cane, led the way up the front steps. The door was ajar.

"Hold it, Leo, there's something wrong here," Phil said.

Meyers turned back to his bodyguard. "Pedro! *Ven acá y trae tu pistola.*"

The Cuban took out a snub-nosed .38 revolver, came up the steps and kicked the door full open. He stepped inside, saw something on the floor and motioned them in.

A foul odor rose to greet them as they entered the foyer. The Cuban pointed to the floor with his gun, and they saw the bodyguard's crumpled figure, the remnants of a hero sandwich still clutched in his right hand.

"Christ . . ." Don Carlo whispered.

Meyers motioned for the Cuban to lead the way. The absolute silence spoke for itself as they followed Pedro down the long corridor toward the study.

The fat man, Vito, eyes open, was slumped against the wall, a gaping raw hole in his chest cavity.

Pedro bent down and picked up some spent bullet casings. "*Es de nueve milimetros disparada de una ametralladora.*"

"He says they're nine-millimeter slugs, fired from a submachine gun," Leo translated.

Phil, Don Carlo and Leo Meyers stood back as the Cuban kicked open the study door, leaped inside, crouched and held the .38 steady with both hands. There was a momentary pause; then Pedro straightened up and nodded.

They saw Martin Bender's corpse first. His black tuxedo appeared to have been dipped in red paint. Maldonado's grotesque body sat erect in the chair, the single eye in his skull wide open.

Don Carlo crossed himself, and Leo Meyers shook his head. Phil was no stranger to the sight of violated flesh, but the overpowering smell of blood in the warm room made him feel queasy. He picked up a chair and hurled it through the picture window. A rush of cold air entered the study.

"Well"—Phil looked at Don Carlo—"so much for vengeance."

Leo said something in Spanish to the Cuban, and Pedro left.

Phil's hand trembled as he picked up a few spent shell casings. "Nine-millimeter, same as the others."

"Who did this?" Don Carlo asked Leo Meyers.

"I have no idea. But it must have been one hell of a hit man."

"You're looking at the state of the art," Phil replied.

Pedro reappeared in the doorway. "*Hay documentos oficiales en la mesa.*"

"There are official documents in the anteroom," Leo explained.

"Let's see them," Phil said.

Leo nodded to the Cuban.

"They sure unloaded on Victor." Don Carlo sighed.

"And not too gentle with the former *consigliere*," Phil added.

Pedro came back with the teamster files and placed them on the desk. Leo Meyers thumbed through them quickly, avoiding the one-eyed corpse in the chair. "These are the teamster documents we were promised."

"By whom?" Phil asked.

"Dr. Belgrave."

"Was he at the meeting in Acapulco?"

"Yes. With his man Crowley."

Phil nodded. The good Doctor had been calling the shots right from the start. But he felt no sense of triumph, the contents in the fifteenth frame of Gemstone made Belgrave's actions in the Rhee case almost irrelevant.

Phil lit a cigarillo and glanced at Martin Bender's body. "I wonder why he was wearing a tux?"

Leo spoke in Spanish to Pedro. The wiry Cuban knelt down and quickly went through Bender's pockets. He came up with a wallet and an engraved envelope.

Leo Meyers opened the cream-colored envelope, studied the enclosed card and said, "An invitation for tonight's charity function at the Smithsonian."

"Is there a name on that?" Phil asked.

"Yes. Sam Lewison."

"He's Belgrave's press secretary," Phil said.

"What do you make of it?" Don Carlo asked.

"Belgrave couldn't permit Maldonado to walk around with the knowledge of the Acapulco meeting. So he got to Bender. The same way he reached Sid Greene."

"With what?"

"The right bait: money, power, position. It doesn't take much. Once he had Bender in his pocket, he sent a professional killer out here with those files and took them all out."

Phil glanced at Leo Meyers. "I'm sure you're on Belgrave's hit list."

The tanned gray-eyed wizard sighed. "I wouldn't be surprised."

Chapter Fifty-six

Amber spotlights bathed the dome of the museum. The Stars and Stripes waved in the cold wind at the brilliantly lit entrance. Security guards in smart blue uniforms lined the steps, forming a protective cordon around the arriving dignitaries.

Phil showed his ID card to the security chief at the ground floor entrance. "Myself and my associate Mr. Carelli have urgent business with Attorney General Browning."

The security chief signaled to another guard. "Escort the deputy attorney general and his associate into the rotunda."

As the escalator rose, they heard the sounds of chatter, laughter and the music of an orchestra playing an old arrangement of "Stompin' at the Savoy."

The marble rotunda vaulted three floors, soaring 200 feet up to the great dome. The centerpiece of the rotunda was an eight-ton African bush elephant. But for the evening's festivities, a wooden bandstand draped in red velvet, enclosed the huge pachyderm. Waiters in black velvet jackets, velvet knickers, white stockings and Colonial wigs served champagne and canapés. There was a long buffet table with an ice carving of the twin theatrical masks of comedy and tragedy.

The Vice President, members of the diplomatic corps, chiefs of the judiciary branch and senators who chaired important committees mingled with a variety of hand-picked writers, painters, musicians and entertainers.

The crowd was festive, lively and elegant. The charity ball was the crowning social event marking the end of the first year of the new administration.

Arthur Browning registered surprise at the sight of Phil

nd Don Carlo. He detached himself from a group of sentors and motioned Phil to a clearing near a mean-looking arble statue of a naked Greek athlete. "What the hell re you doing here?" he asked with annoyance.

"Wait a minute, Arthur—"

"I cannot tolerate this sort of impulsive—"

"Shut up, Arthur!" Phil exclaimed.

Browning was shocked into silence.

"Just stick close to me," Phil said, "and don't ask any oddamn questions."

As they walked through the elegant crowd, Don Carlo as struck by the thought that political reunions were always performed in the grand manner, while underworld atherings were held in spaghetti joints. He smiled to imself, knowing that half the elected officials in the room ere supported by mob money.

They circled the dance floor, heading toward a cluster men that included Belgrave, Kissinger, Helms, the periatetic Vice President, Charles Gruenwald and Robert urgess. Matt Crowley stood behind them.

Phil came up to the startled group and addressed Belrave. "I require a moment with you, Doctor."

"This is hardly the time or place for business, Mr. icker."

"This business has to do with Gemstone."

For an instant Belgrave's bright blue eyes clouded. He en forced a smile, swallowed the last of his champagne d handed the empty glass to Gruenwald. "Excuse me, entlemen." He glanced at Crowley. "Come along, Matt."

Accompanied by a security guard, they moved around e dancers and walked through a Grecian alcove into the all of Fossils.

A cyan light cast an eerie glow in the exhibit chamber. everal skeletal prehistoric predators circled the principal chibit: a ninety-foot-long eighteen-foot-high dinosaur. he sign below the monster read: "Diplodocus—voracious d predatory. Habitat: Colorado-Wyoming: Mesozoic eriod, two hundred million years ago."

The men were dwarfed by the awesome dinosaur, and e blue light lent a reality to the monster as if at any moent its great head might descend and its gaping jaws vallow them whole.

Eric Belgrave, the senior adviser to five Presidents, looked like an aging, once-handsome stage actor. His silver hair turned blue under the lights and matched the color of his accusatory eyes. Crowley, wearing a shiny tuxedo, stood a few feet behind his master.

"I'm listening, Mr. Ricker," Belgrave said.

"Just for the hell of it, let's start with my case."

"You have the floor, Counselor."

"I've got more than the floor; I've got you cold, Doctor." Phil's voice echoed off the stone walls. "You, Burgess, Gruenwald and others met in the Glass Room on the night of July fifth, 1979, with KCIA agents and the Reverend Rhee. It was at that meeting the plan to assassinate Park was approved. The killing went off almost perfectly. Only one critical piece fell out of place. General Chung assumed control, rather than your handpicked man, Kyu. And to this day you don't know why."

"Enlighten us, Counselor."

"I'll do my best. All your sophisticated planning took second position to Park's weakness for a certain Korean lady and her sexual dominance of Chung. There may be a geopolitical lesson in there somewhere. I wonder how you explained it all to the President, but you managed to stay clean. When I zeroed in on Rhee, he put the heat on you. So Crowley here, tortured and killed Mrs. Hwan, stole my case files and Burgess's cowboys assaulted me at the Reflecting Pool. You with me, Doctor?"

"I'm listening, Mr. Ricker."

"When Mr. Carelli's son, Nicky, was induced into knocking off the Reverend Rhee's temples, the Reverend again exerted pressure on you. At that point you met with Maldonado and Leo Meyers in Acapulco and ordered the killing of Nicky and promised the return of certain teamster files. And you were a man of your word. Crowley, or some spook hit team, delivered those files earlier this evening and, in the doing, clipped Maldonado and his adviser, Mr. Bender, who was reached with some major promises, in much the same way you seduced the late Sid Greene."

Phil paused. "What you didn't know is that you were being manipulated from the start, as we all were, by President Chung, sitting in his office in the Blue House, twelve thousand miles away. But let's skip current events; let's go back in time."

"To what, Mr. Ricker?"

"To Gemstone. You'll have to forgive my chronology, but I think you'll recognize the facts: You advised Kennedy not to contest the construction of the Berlin Wall. You sanctioned and proposed the disaster at the Bay of Pigs. You ordered the late Victor Maldonado to assign Roselli and Giancana to assassinate Castro—a doomed enterprise which increased Castro's stature. You devised the Tonkin Gulf incident and sucked LBJ into a no-win war which cost fifty-eight thousand lives. You designed the assassination of Allende, making him a saint and at the same time elevating Castro as the true hero of the poverty-stricken masses of Central America."

Browning felt an icy circle forming in the pit of his stomach. Crowley's murderous black eyes smoldered. But Belgrave retained his outward calm.

"Is that all, Counselor?"

"No. Just bear with me, Doctor. You blessed the shipment of three sophisticated missile systems to the shah of Iran, even though you knew his regime was falling. You succeeded once more with the recent AWACS sale to the Saudis." Phil paused. "You were the architect of détente, and your actions over the last four decades have cost this nation its technological edge over the Soviets."

A deadly silence enveloped the huge room. Belgrave cleared his throat and said, "You can, of course, prove all this?"

"Gemstone can. In 1934 you attended Trinity College at Cambridge. You were part of a secret debating society called the Apostles. Your fellow members were Kim Philby, Guy Burgess, Donald Maclean and Anthony Blunt, all of whom operated British Intelligence for the KGB."

Phil paused. "You're the fifth man. You've been a deep-cover Soviet mole for fifty years."

The Don glared at Belgrave in astonishment. Browning stood stock-still, alternately glancing from Phil to Belgrave. The security guard merely stared at the gaunt chairman of the National Security Council.

Matt Crowley was sweating, and his black eyes blazed at Phil.

"Is that all, Counselor?" Belgrave asked.

"That's the essence of it, Doctor."

Belgrave took a few steps forward. "I find it extraordinary that well-educated men and women in the judiciary, in the Senate, in the intelligence agencies, and in the Oval Office are as ill-informed and unsophisticated as that prehistoric creature towering over our heads. I neither deny nor apologize for the advice and counsel you claim I have rendered the nation in my long years of service. But I do resent being described as a mole—a spy—a Soviet agent."

His voice rose and trembled. "My allegiance is to no nation. My allegiance is to *mankind*. Yes, I was an Apostle. I was indeed part of a secret circle whose numbers included Philby, Burgess, Maclean and Tony Blunt. We were all young men of great and unique vision. Long before the invention of hydrogen bombs, ballistic missiles and multiple warheads, we perceived that man could not survive his own technology."

Belgrave's piercing blue eyes shown with evangelical fervor. "We knew, beyond any shadow of doubt, that human survival depended solely on an allegiance between the Soviet Union and the United States. A partnership bereft of secrets. A union that had the vision, courage and capacity to partition the planet into logical spheres of geo-eco influence. A partnership that precluded either side from attaining a military or economic edge over the other. A union of two great powers assuming their proper responsibility to neutralize and eliminate the proliferation of doomsday devices in the hands of Latins, Asians and Moslems."

Belgrave took another step forward and pointed at Phil. "Events forged by destiny have dictated this marriage. It has fallen to the American and the Soviet people to insure the continuity of the species on this fragile planet." His voice trembled with messianic fervor. "The world is ruled by neither justice nor morality. It is governed and stabilized by productivity and profit. The industrial might of the Soviet Union and the United States must flourish in order for the world to survive. Patriotism and nationalism are pushing us toward oblivion!"

His voice dropped, and his speech pattern slowed. "I have paid a terrible personal price for my years of service, but divine guidance has kept me on the proper path. I have done everything in my power to prevent global catastrophe. And if you or anyone else labels my actions treason, then so be it!"

A deafening roar reverberated off the stone walls. Belgrave dropped to the floor, the right side of his face blown away.

Crowley held a .45 automatic, his face contorted, his lips pulled back over his teeth. He swung the automatic at Phil. The Don lunged. There was another blast, and Don Carlo fell. The security guard fired at Crowley. The slug grazed Crowley's neck, and blood spurted from the wound. He raced out of the room.

Phil leaned over the Don, cradled his head and gently closed his eyes.

In the great rotunda the orchestra continued to play, but a strange buzzing sound rose from the celebrants. A handful of revelers had heard the shots, and a fearful whispering spread through the marble hall.

The ominous chatter was suddenly pierced by screams as Crowley, holding the automatic aloft, burst into the room and bulled his way through the dancers. Secret Service men leaped on the Vice President and pulled their Uzis but could not fire in the panicky crowd.

Crowley ran up the bandstand steps and faced the crowd, his white shirt crimson with blood flowing from his neck wound. The musicians cowered behind him. He grabbed the microphone, and his amplified voice resounded off the circular marble walls as he screamed, "Betray-allll!"

He then placed the muzzle of the automatic in his mouth and pulled the trigger.

Chapter Fifty-seven

The Man of Sorrow gazed down at the open coffin from his place of nails high up on the chapel wall.

Don Carlo appeared to be at peace in repose. Phil stood at the coffin and sent up a silent prayer to his own mythical god. He had reproduced all the data contained in the fifteenth frame. It would be a vital part of his testimony in the forthcoming congressional investigation. But the rest of Gemstone's contents would remain buried with Don Carlo.

Phil reached out and opened his hand. The spool of thread fell into the crevice of the coffin. He turned and walked back up the aisle to the anteroom, where Claudia and Leo Meyers waited.

Granite angels and marble madonnas looked down on the three mourners standing silently before the open grave. White clouds raced across a dark blue sky, and on the far side of the river, the steel-glass skyline of Manhattan shimmered in a gold autumnal light.

Claudia dropped a single-stem rose into the grave, then stepped back and crossed herself.

After a moment Leo Meyers handed her a card. "This is the business address of a law firm."

She stared blankly at the three engraved names on the card.

"Your father left you a sizable trust fund," he explained. "Use it as you wish." He kissed her cheek, then turned to Phil. "Good-bye, Mr. Ricker."

"Before you go, Leo, I'd like you to clear up something for me. You don't have to admit to anything." Phil smiled. "Just tell me if I'm right or wrong."

"Go ahead."

"You sent Bender to Belgrave to arrange the hit on Maldonado, which made sense because Belgrave wanted Victor clipped. You probably offered Bender the position of *consigliere* for the National Council. He went for it and got clipped himself."

Leo Meyers glanced at his two Cuban bodyguards waiting nearby, then looked at Phil and said, "Go on."

"The attempted hit at the seaside café in Ischia could not go unpunished. Maldonado, acting on Bender's advice, went against the council. By using Belgrave's people to take them out, you avoided internal strife in the organization and gave Don Carlo his vengeance."

"I neither confirm nor deny your speculation." Leo smiled. "But how did you know?"

"Well, for a man who shunned violence all his life, you took that grisly stuff at the ranch like a combat veteran."

Leo leaned on his cane. "I'm afraid I was never much of an actor."

"On the contrary," Phil said. "I think you could play King Lear with the Royal Shakespeare Company."

"That would be bad casting since I never had any daughters. Besides, you make too much of me, Mr. Ricker. I'm a retired businessman who renders occasional fiscal advice. I have my sun deck, my fishing, my *Wall Street Journal* and the blessing of a good woman for fifty years. I'm a simple man with simple tastes."

They shook hands, and the Jewish patriarch of the Sicilian Honored Society turned and made his way slowly down the walk, followed by his Cuban bodyguards.

Phil and Claudia stood alone at the gravesite. Her cheeks were flushed, and her dark eyes misty.

"It was kind and thoughtful of you to arrange this," she said softly. "To have him buried here—in view of the city he loved."

"Your father took a bullet for me," Phil said sadly. "I wish we hadn't been adversaries years ago."

Claudia looked off at the Manhattan skyline. "I suppose when he was very young, he was simply a rebel fighting against that brutal Sicilian system. But when he came to America, he turned into something else."

"Your father had a strong sense of honor. And in a

world that operates on luck and larceny, he was no better or worse than the next man."

Phil paused. "Come on, we've got a weekend in New York."

"Then what?"

"Back to D.C."

"I'll never understand that."

"Why?"

"Because it's fighting windmills." She sighed. "They'll have a new set of players—but the game won't change."

"Well." Phil smiled. "Maybe there's something to be said for windmills."

They walked down the path. His arm circled her waist, and the last yellow leaves of autumn danced in the cold November wind.

Epilogue
Seoul, Republic of Korea

The president's birthday had been celebrated by dancing dragons, parading gymnasts, columns of armor, screaming jets and afternoon cocktails with the diplomatic corps.

Chung stood at his window, looking out over the Garden of Five Seasons and beyond to the evergreen trees snaking their way up Pugak Mountain. A white carpet of snow covered the grounds of the Blue House. The security lights in the presidential compound grew vivid in the gathering dusk. He took deep breaths of the cold Siberian air, trying to clear his mind before she came in.

Soon Yi Sonji sat in a leather chair outside the presidential office. She wore a full-length white chiffon gown with ruffled sleeves, and a pink sash circled her narrow waist. The gown was a favorite of the president's.

Chung's five bodyguards glanced occasionally in her direction but did not speak to her or in any way acknowledge her presence. Their chief, a dour-faced, muscular man, leaned against the wall. His eyes were fixed on the presidential secretary, Won, who was seated at his desk, preparing documents for the president's signature.

Sonji avoided Won's attention, and he maintained the same indifferent attitude toward her. Earlier in the day at the Lotte Hotel with General Kim, they had reviewed the timing and sequential steps designed for tonight's assassination. She had gone from the Lotte to the apartment of the kisaeng girl called Chang Min, who would slit the throat of Chung's chief bodyguard.

Sonji had honed and sharpened the stilettto that she herself would plunge into the belly of Chung.

The phone on Won's desk buzzed. He answered,

glanced at Sonji and said, "The president wishes to see you."

Chung had his omnipresent cigarette clenched between his nicotine-stained fingers. He smiled as she entered the office. He always experienced a sensual stirring at the mere sight of her. "I missed you, Daughter."

"As I missed you."

"It was a grand trip to Manila," he said expansively. "I had many meetings with the premiers of Japan and the People's Republic of China. The son of Kim Il Sung also attended."

He went to the wet bar and mixed two scotches. "There was a sight, Daughter: North Korea, South Korea, China and Japan." He brought the drinks with him, handing one to her. "In that conference room one could see the great Asian dynasty of the twenty-first century—the fulfillment of Buddha's prophecy. His children will yet rule the world."

The ice tinkled as he touched his glass to hers. "You have, of course, heard the news from Washington?"

"Yes."

"Belgrave's military-industrial conspiracy has been smashed. Those traditional American forces opposed to the great Asian alliance are in disarray." He smiled. "All of which was performed from inside their own infrastructure. They were moved by circles of the samsara, caught in the whirlpool."

"We have much to celebrate." She smiled. "The circle is closed."

He looked at her for a moment, then walked up to the French windows and gazed down at the snowy landscape.

The plotters would be executed within the hour. They all had been under constant surveillance. And the Reverend Rhee, branded as a coconspirator, would die with them.

But Sonji would be spared. He understood her motive, and it was unfortunate that he had failed to convince her Kimsan's death was an accident—an aberration of the samsara. But more important, he was forbidden to execute her. The Scriptures said: "That which Buddha creates with exquisite beauty, man must not destroy."

He turned from the window and stared at her. It was astonishing to think she had been the very pebble in the pond, and even she did not understand: The circle is never closed.

ABOUT THE AUTHOR

STEVE SHAGAN is the author of the novel and award-winning screenplay *Save the Tiger*, which won the Writers Guild of America Award as Best Original Drama of 1973. His second novel, *City of Angels*, was the basis for the Paramount movie *Hustle*. In 1976, he received his second Academy Award nomination for his screenplay and adaptation of *Voyage of the Damned*. His last novel was the smash best seller *The Formula*. Steve Shagan resides in Los Angeles.

RED DRAGON

THOMAS HARRIS

RED DRAGON
". . . is an engine designed for one purpose – to make the pulses pound, the heart palpitate, the fear glands secrete"

New York Times Book Review

RED DRAGON
". . . is an extraordinary book. A thriller in its own right, with pace, tension, and a capacity to prickle the skin with excitement, but more than this, a superb study of character, seen and understood and created in depth . . . Enthralling, frightening, totally professional. It is quite simply the best of its kind that I have read in twenty years"

Lord Ted Willis

RED DRAGON
". . . simply comes at you and comes at you, finally leaving you shaken and sober and afraid . . . the best popular novel published since THE GODFATHER"

Stephen King

0 552 12160 6

£1.95

CORGI BOOKS

OTHER THRILLERS AVAILABLE
FROM CORGI/BANTAM